Meeting Eve

Meeting Eve

a novel

JANEE PENNINGTON

Newton & Crockett Publishing, LLC
1700 7th Avenue, Suite 116-227
Seattle, Washington 98101

Published in the United States of America

ISBN 978-0-9860644-0-1

For my mother, Carol
I will always know how much she loved me and how much writing this book meant to her.

To my five beautiful nieces
May you soar through life making new discoveries and conquer whatever career choices come your way.
I love you!

And to all those facing a crisis
This book is for you.

ACKNOWLEDGMENTS

I COULD WRITE pages and pages of peoples' names here, but here are a few who actually helped bring this book to print: Judy Bishop, Gloria Campbell, Sara DeHaan, Lyzah Douglass, Josh Drechsler, Gayle Enright, Kyra Freestar, Phyllis Hatfield, Beth Jusino, Gretchen Nehrling, Stacy Stas, Andy Walker, Colin Watson, Carrie Wicks, Sharon Wilson, Frances Woods, and John Woods. Eric and Oriana Iverson—thank you for writing a special song. It captured the moment perfectly! Please visit iTunes for their song "Love on My Mind."

One special thank-you to Stacy: if it wasn't for you, Eve would be a mess! Thanks for helping to clean her up!

And a loud shout-out to my friends and family who, along this journey, have kept me enthusiastic and inspired even when I wanted to give up. You know who you are, and I love you for believing in me and Eve!

CHAPTER ONE

"**A**ND THERE'S ONE more thing…What do you think about having a high-wire act with real tigers and lions? Maybe we could even dress them up in costume with black top hats and tails…"

Did I tell my assistant to order the black napkins for the event in Newport? Which reminds me, did I pick up my black dress from the cleaners? I should call what's-his-name back. But what was his name? It was nice to have a date at least once this year, but if I can't even remember his name a day later, it's more than likely it isn't going to work out.

"Eve?"

Ugh, working out—I really need to get to the gym at least once this month. If not for the few extra pounds of cushioning I've added lately, at least it'll curb that tiny voice of guilt punishing me for buying a membership and never using it. Not to mention, it would be nice to feel hot again. Yikes! Hot acts! I need to have the staff look into which top bands we can round up for the big Microsoft event coming up.

"Earth to Eve."

The staging for the London show needs to change to an LED dance floor. Oh, and the invoice for the last Oppenheimer CEO event needs to be sent today . . .

"Eve! Come back to me!" Miles snaps his fingers in front of my face.

"Are you crazy?!"

Oh no! Did I just say that out loud?

I flash a sheepish grin at my client and force myself to refocus.

"Well, what do you think?" Miles asks—luckily, ignoring my brief outburst.

"Okay, Miles, let me get this straight. You want an innovative party during a major convention for a thousand guests, on another continent, two months from now?"

Miles stares back. "That would be correct."

And he wants real tigers and lions?! Next thing you know, he's going to ask for the Dalai Lama to make an appearance! Even without his outrageous requests, I'm sure that every half-decent place has been rented out at least ten months ago. Not to mention, my devoted staff of four is already bogged down with five other events. Am I in the twilight zone, or more to the point, is he?

There really is no formula for creating large, high-end corporate events. Organizing them for over ten years and running my own company for five, I should know. Every client is different, and there are no two events alike, which is exactly what I love about this industry. In my job, I wear many hats—sister, mother, financial advisor, chef, dog walker, and therapist, to name a few. Over the years I have become friends with many of my clients, but no matter what the dynamic between us is, it's my job to make their dreams come true.

And now, sitting in front of me on this warm July afternoon, on the patio of the Park Ranch Hotel, is Miles Emerson, one of my longest-standing clients from 1-2-1 TV. I have to admit, I do enjoy working with him, and it doesn't hurt that Miles oozes charm, his deep-set, ocean-green eyes gleaming as the sun hits his face. Most women swoon at his six foot two frame and chiseled, cocoa-brown features. I know I do. And when he smiles—well, you can just about pick me up off the floor. However, I have to remain steadfast in my convictions. I need to do an about-face and tell myself his charisma isn't working on me today. Although we have worked together on dozens of events over the years, and I think of him as one of my favorite clients, even I have limits.

"Come on Miles, two months?!" I twist my shoulder-length hair into a tiny knot. "You understand that an event like this usually takes a year to prepare and organize, right? I mean, we have the site inspection, a budget to create, hotel rooms to block for your team and ours. That is, if we can get a hotel at this late date, air travel, electronic invitations to prepare, the venue, entertainment, food and beverage, rentals, transportation"—my arms are now flailing about—"the complete design of the event, creating the hype, staff to work the program, uniforms, audio visual, etcetera, etcetera. This is why we require adequate preparation time! And unless you know a miracle worker to find a fabulous venue for the party and get a few of the A-list, on-site travel directors to work, this event is nothing short of impossible."

He shrugs. My inner Eve shudders. Are those my shoulders rising to my ears? I feel as if my entire body is turning into a tight ball of expletives. This is no time for a panic attack! Take a deep breath, Eve. Just say no.

"I guess I shouldn't ask why 1-2-1 TV didn't decide to attend this convention ten months ago. I know how your CEO thinks, but just two months' notice? Are you willing to settle for anything I find?"

What happened to "just say no"?

Putting on his soft, sexy voice, Miles leans in close. "Well, I do in fact know a miracle worker. Her name is Eve, and I happen to know she never disappoints." I melt a little and sigh as he goes on. "I know this is a lot to throw at you with such short notice, but you can always use me as part of your event staff—an extra hand or brain to help get it done."

I force my lips into a smile. "If you multiplied yourself by ten, I'd feel much better."

"Look, Eve"—he touches my hand and smiles—"the last event you did for us was more spectacular than anyone dreamed of. Everyone, and I mean everyone, is still talking about it. When you had all those giant panels open up from the side of the ballroom, illuminated, each with an electronic mini-stage holding a belly dancer in full costume, dancing on cue? It was brilliant!" He leans back in his chair, releasing my tingling hand. "I even got a promotion because of it."

Okay, maybe his charm is working on me a little...

"On the very off chance that I am able to find a venue, do you have a theme in mind? Unless you were serious about the circus act?"

Clearing his throat, he grins. "Well, not really." Something must be up because he takes an unusually long pause and I notice his eye twitching. "Since this event is part of the broadcaster's convention, we want something that will draw the audience in our direction and away from other entertainment. We're aware that we'll have a lot of competition..." I'm concentrating on taking notes as Miles carries on. He's right—arriving so late in the game, they only have a few seconds to score.

Miles hesitates, then continues. "And I don't know how to explain this to you any other way than to say that the atmosphere at these events, and especially in Amsterdam, can be rather, um...raunchy." For a guy who normally looks me straight in the eyes when he's talking, he's doing everything he can to avoid them now. "But we don't want you to cross the line. Gray area is okay—a little sexy, curious maybe. Innovative yes, but no live sex."

Live sex?!

I feel my cheeks instantly burn. Sex! Just hearing the word from Miles's lips makes my legs shake like a Southern California earthquake.

All of a sudden he's back to casually taking a sip of water, catching my eye. "So, Eve, that's the job description in a nutshell. Come up with a way to grab a crowd in a city famous for its enticement. Can you, Ms. Walker, turn up the heat without going to the dark side?" He leans in again as if to whisper in my ear. "Your mission, should you choose to accept it..."

I'm speechless.

"Well, hello, handsome. What a fabulous surprise to see you again."

Knowing Marla's brilliant timing, I should not have been shocked to see her. Marla, one of my best friends, as well as manager of the Park Ranch Hotel here in Beverly Hills, slides her hand along his broad shoulders. Typical Marla move. But because of her aggressive nature, she is a key reason why this exquisite hotel is so successful. This is the place where celebrities and dignitaries seeking to keep a low profile play and stay. Paparazzi are not allowed, and with security tight, they don't come near the place.

Marla runs a tight ship. She is also exotically gorgeous, with long, glossy black hair, sun-kissed skin, and legs from here to eternity. She lives for Chanel, Prada, and pearl necklaces. Appearance and reputation are everything to her, which is probably why she refuses to admit she was born in Mexico, claiming instead to be Italian. *"La mia famiglia viene da Cortona,"* I have overheard her say many times, including to her own family! Ay papi.

But whether she's Mexican or Italian, there are two things I'm certain of. First, her temper is hotter than a mouthful of jalapeños doused with Dave's Insanity sauce. Don't get on her bad side; it's just plain stupid. Second, she is as opinionated as a *Huffington*

Post editorialist, and when you get her started, she's apt to talk until your ears bleed.

"Do you have a minute to join us?" I ask, hoping to buy some time to either figure out a way to fit this event into my already busy calendar or tell my client thanks, but I can't jump through hoops this time. Every pun intended.

Marla's face lights up as she sits down. Of course, she has time for anything involving Miles. In her words, he is a hunk of hot meat, and she can't wait to throw him on the grill. Whatever that means. I watch as her gaze travels down Miles's leg, resting at his feet. Immediately I know where this is going. For as long as I've known Marla, she has had a foot fetish. And Miles happens to have rather large feet.

"So Miles, I don't believe you've seen the property since we renovated," she purrs, playing suggestively with the strands around her neck. "Would you like a tour after you meet with Eve?"

Miles flashes his heart-stopping smile. "The hotel is cheetah-chic, Marla. You've done a great job."

Cheetah-chic? Must be a new Miles-ism. Over the five years I've worked with Miles, I have come to know that when he gets nervous, he makes up his own words to describe something or someone.

And over these same years Marla, too, has come to appreciate Miles-isms. Every so often I will hear her use one—holding her chest, closing her eyes, and letting the words roll off her tongue as if she's quoting Jane Austen. For some women, chocolate or oysters are an aphrodisiac. For Marla, it's a Miles-ism.

"Why, thank you, Miles. What do you think of the fountains that I chose for the terrace?"

"They're great—you've really warmed it up."

Marla's in her element, selling the place as she gestures around the patio. "Yes, and it all lights up at night, very romantic. You really must come back and see it sometime."

There it is! The one thing Marla is even better at than timing is angling clients to hold events at the Park Ranch Hotel. I try not to laugh as she hikes her skirt up a little higher, almost begging Miles to take the bait.

With my head still reeling from the Amsterdam event details, I find it hard to stay involved with the small talk that Marla has brought to the table. Nonetheless, I try chiming in: "I like the new adobe fireplace with the candle sconces, and the more casual place settings."

But of course, there's no response from Marla as she sits and recrosses her legs, her full focus on Miles. Fine by me. Deciding what to do about Miles's proposal has now moved straight to the top of my to-do list.

Just as I'm about to hop aboard my own train of thought, I'm distracted by Marla launching into one of her favorite complaints: "fams" or familiarization trips. Not again! This is Marla's personal broken record. Ever since the Park Ranch began offering free trips to event planners to showcase their property, Marla has had something to whine about. And apparently today is no different.

Focus, Eve. Focus! A risqué event in Amsterdam in two months . . . yes or no, Eve. Yes? Or no?

"Can you believe it, Eve? I mean really. This guy from New Zealand who claims to be an event planner cancels because he's having problems with his sheep?! Something to do with the grass being poisoned and losing half his stock. Who has sheep? We're in Beverly Hills. I just can't relate."

I shake my head, giving her a sideways glance. "Run out of compassion this early in the day?"

"Yep!" she snaps back.

"I hate to do this," Miles interrupts, "but I've got limited time today, ladies. Shall we get back to the business at hand?"

"Absolutely," I say, game face back on.

"Anything I can help you with?" Marla asks, batting her eyes.

"As a matter fact," Miles says, facing her, a slow grin forming, "a glass of cabernet would be wonderful."

She fights hard to keep the smile on her face as she marches off to fill his order. I'm guessing here, but fetching wine was most likely not the kind of help she wanted to offer. Even still, I know Marla has been trying to get another 1-2-1 TV meeting since the last one held here three years ago. Using her charm and persuasive skills, she convinced the company to buy out the hotel for four days. The owners were so impressed that when they started the search for a new manager, she was the natural choice. The fact that she also knew the hotel inside and out, having worked her way through college from housekeeping to reservations, was voted best concierge in Los Angeles five years in a row, and increased sales by an amazing 40 percent didn't hurt. The hotel is practically her home. Her "hood." And yet, even still, fetching a drink never fails to piss her off.

With Marla gone, I let out a wary sigh. "So, a thousand guests?"

If I turn the three Mercedes events over to someone who is only working on two other programs and shuffle around the hotel and association meetings I have lined up . . . And also cancel my attendance at the SITE awards ceremony, I guess I can try to squeeze it in.

That is until he blurts, "Well, I mean it could go higher."

Do I dare ask?

"How much higher?"

Miles looks away, avoiding eye contact once again. I brace myself, knowing this isn't a good sign.

He stretches his words, "Oooh...I dunno...twooooooo, possibly threeee thousand."

My heart starts jumping around like a hyperactive child on a jungle gym. I'm afraid it might explode.

Three thousand? Three thousand? THREE THOUSAND?! I want to say something else, should say something else, but my brain is stuck on repeat.

Miles leans his head to one side with puppy-dog eyes. "Eve, normally we wouldn't even think about something like this at such a late date, but we're having a banner year and we want to make a splash. And...well...you are you, and if anyone can do it, you can."

Well, great. What do I say to that?

"You do understand we will have to work day and night to get this event prepared to meet your level of expectation."

Miles smirks. "I do. And we'll make certain we reward you handsomely."

Just then Marla saunters back carrying Miles's cab, a complimentary bottle of champagne, and a bowl of fresh strawberries. I don't normally drink in the afternoon. In fact, I don't normally drink much at all, but what the hell—I need one. Scratch that, I deserve one.

With a leap of faith and a swig of champagne, I raise my glass: "To Amsterdam, where I'll be heading tomorrow."

Toasting to a new event that I have no idea how I'll pull off, I clink glasses with Miles, who is grinning from ear to ear, and Marla, who is looking lost and confused.

"Why the hell are you going to Amsterdam?"

"I'll fill you in later," I say, waving the comment off.

I swear I hear Miles giggling softly.

CHAPTER TWO

THIRTY MINUTES LATER, the three of us elbows deep in chopped salads, I become aware of an odd feeling, that disturbing sensation you get when you realize someone at the next table is listening in on your conversation. Along with standing in lines, this is one of my few pet peeves. Maybe because I just agreed to take on an overwhelming event, my patience is all out of whack, or perhaps it's because of the champagne; whatever the case, I begin to feel irritated. Not that our dialogue is confidential, but still, listening in on another's conversation is just, well...rude. Should I make eye contact with this person to let them know I know? Should I ignore it and carry on with Miles and Marla? Or maybe, should I start spewing complete lies to throw this eavesdropper off?

Just as I decide the will-you-mind-your-own-business look is the best choice, I hear a chair sliding out from the table of per-petrators. As I glimpse over, a statuesque, graceful older woman, in a beautiful periwinkle designer suit, stands as if to be certain we catch her eye. In fact, she's caught the eye of everyone in the dining room as well. I watch as she excuses herself from her table of "suits," and heads toward us.

Following my gaze, Marla jumps up from her seat. "It's so nice to see you again, Amanda," she cries out, shaking this spy-named-Amanda's hand.

The beautiful woman smiles. "Same to you, dear. And who are these nice people you are dining with?"

I'm embarrassed. Because one, she called me nice. And two, it's clear she was probably looking at Marla and not *really* listening to our conversation. But it sure felt like it.

Miles is standing, as am I. He leans over to shake Amanda's hand while Marla conducts the introductions: "Miles Emerson is with 1-2-1 TV, and Eve Walker, in my opinion, is one of the best meeting and event planners in Los Angeles. Miles, Eve, may I have the pleasure of introducing you to Amanda Schwartz."

Aah...Well, well. *The* Amanda Schwartz herself. A true icon here in Hollywood.

"Amanda runs Imperial Studios. Her daughter was married here at the hotel last year."

Miles and I ooh and aah.

"So nice to have you dining with us again, Amanda." Marla goes on to ask about Amanda's daughter and the family.

After the small talk wanes, a moment passes, yet she stays put. Clearly there's something else on her mind.

Her eyes settle on me. I'm not sure if she thinks she knows me, knows someone I know, or just wants me to feel uncomfortable. She certainly doesn't have to work hard at it; I'm already there.

She raises a manicured finger, pointing it at me. "I've heard a lot about your parties, Eve. Funny enough, if I weren't running a studio, I think event planning would be divine."

Hmm...how interesting. If I only had a dollar for every time I've heard that line. But I'll take it as a compliment. She's certainly a strong and courageous woman and has made a name for herself in this town.

I can feel Miles fidgeting next to me. I guess I'm not the only one who feels nervous in Amanda's presence. He takes a step closer to me, placing his arm around my waist. Almost inaudibly, he whispers in my ear, "She's Coco-Vix." Just like Miles to spout another "ism" in a time of need. As if to cover his tracks he quips, "Me too," and grabs me tighter. "But at least we do the next best thing by hiring her!"

Amanda wrinkles her brow, patting her chin with her index finger as if she's conjuring up something.

Please don't tell me that she wants to quit the studio and come work with me. That would be worse than having a client ask if I can give their kid a job.

"You know," Amanda begins...

And here it comes.

"I have a friend." She pauses, placing her pointer finger on her chin, then redirecting it back at me.

I am now adding pointing fingers to my list of pet peeves.

"His name is Blaine. He's currently working as a screenwriter but hasn't had any luck lately."

Wait...why is a studio executive worried about an out-of-work screenwriter. Can't she just hire him?

"Do you remember him, Marla?"

"Umm..." Marla mumbles, furrowing her brow as if she's trying to remember. But the second Amanda looks away, she catches my eye, shaking her head, mouthing the word, "No!"

What the hell? Is he a freak? A creep? A druggie? Did he stalk her? A thousand thoughts fly through my head. This habit of dissecting things is one of my not-so-good qualities, and the tragedy is that I'm very much aware of it.

Amanda continues. "He can be a bit shy, but he is an incredible creative force. I think he would make a great asset to your company."

A bit shy but an incredible creative force—isn't that code for some kind of disorder? I'm sure of it. I'll look it up when I get home.

"How about I set up a meeting at the studio so you can meet him? I overheard you're headed to Amsterdam tomorrow. I'm guessing you're most likely on one of those early evening European flights, so perhaps you can meet him in the afternoon. How's one o'clock for lunch?"

This is obviously not a question but an offer I can't refuse. I mean, shouldn't refuse.

I knew she was listening in!

"Well... I'm not so sure..." I murmur. I want the studio business, but...

"Great," she says while extending her hand. She points at me one more time as she turns to walk away. "I'll see you tomorrow. This is fabulous. Just fabulous."

Uh-huh. For whom?

I send her a warm, seemingly sincere smile, all the while feeling Marla's eyes boring down on me. She shoots me a look, then follows Amanda out of the restaurant.

I plop back onto my chair. "What just happened?"

Miles snickers. "You are amazing, my friend. You are the only person I know with more than twenty-four hours in a day."

I lower my head toward my plate. "What did I just do?"

I can hardly bring myself to answer myself before Marla returns to the table, ready to burst. I can only guess it's about this so-called Blaine character.

Marla shrugs, then lets me have it. "He's weird, he's a loser, and has no personality. End of story."

Huh? There has to be more.

"A personality-less loser? So how do you know him?"

She gives me the what-the-hell-does-it-matter look. "We were in grade school together. He was the kid who was always tortured for being—well, a complete geek. He's all grown up, but he's still the same nerd, writing his childhood fears down for the little and big screens."

That's Blaine's story? How sad.

"I feel sorry for him. I think it's a good idea that you're meeting with him, Eve," Miles interjects. I look over at him as he folds and refolds his napkin. Miles has told me, he is one of nine children who grew up in a run-down, two-bedroom home in the projects of Philadelphia. He never had the affections of his parents or siblings, always feeling like an outsider who wanted more out of life than they did. No wonder he thinks I should meet with Blaine.

"He's a creep! If I were you, I'd cancel that meeting!" Marla shrugs.

Miles and I shoot her a scornful look, though she seems completely oblivious.

"Now," Miles says, changing the subject. "Before we call this an afternoon, I have a question for you, Eve."

"Business or personal?"

"Both."

"Oh?" Miles doesn't ask too many questions, so this is rather curious.

"So, I was lying in bed last night..."

He thinks of me when he's in bed? My legs respond with a predictable aftershock. I'm thankful for the long tablecloth.

"Thinking about you... And Eve, I just have to know." He pauses briefly. "How do you do it? How do you make each event so unique and different, and *so creative*?"

"Which event are you talking about? Paris? Dubai? Montreal?"

"No, Eve, I don't just mean our events. I mean *all* of your events. How do you conjure up these fantastic ideas one right after the next?"

"She's not going to tell you!" Marla bursts. "She won't even tell me! For God's sake, her competitors have wanted to know the answer to that question for years. She could have a reality show based on that very mystery, alone!" Marla looks around the patio even more confident than before. "You'll never get it out of her."

My face warms. I glance back and forth at my friends. Do I dare? Do I disclose my trade secret?

I have been asked this question many times in the past. In fact, a few years ago, I was even asked to be part of an industry article titled "The Secrets of My Success." I shrugged it off. The last thing I wanted to do was talk about myself, but there was another reason, too. A much bigger reason. The truth is, I have never revealed how I create the events I do.

What seems to be an awkward amount of time passes. They are both staring at me, Marla with an impatient eye.

I know I need to let it loose to someone, yet I feel myself struggling to get the words out. I must look like some kind of droid, short-circuiting.

Just do it. It's really not that big of a deal...

"Another time. It's getting late, and I have to get to work."

Miles and Marla boo, heckling me. "Come on, Eve. Do you really want to keep me up at night wondering about these kinds of things?" Miles begs.

I shake my head—it's just not the right time.

Miles pushes on: "Okay, how about this. If Amsterdam goes off successfully, will you tell me then?"

I take a moment. Amsterdam may just be the greatest endeavor yet. It's certainly by far the most challenging. It could be the perfect time to spill the beans. I extend my hand. "If we can pull this event off, I just may tell you."

"I guess that's good enough." Miles smiles as we shake hands, and I'm aware all the while of Marla's fierce jealousy at even our slightest touch.

CHAPTER THREE

LEAVING THE OFFICE well after midnight, I find myself aching for the peace and solitude of my apartment. My home, my refuge. I've always loved the beach and been drawn, by an undeniable need, to water; it makes me feel alive. I don't quite live on the beach, but knowing that it's twenty blocks away is comforting. Pulling onto my quiet street lined by coral trees, in a residential section of Santa Monica, I feel happily exhausted.

I was lucky to find my place. Peter, my best guy-friend, lives in the area, and one day, five years ago, we were walking his cairn terrier when we came across a little old lady wearing a blue hat, walking her Jack Russell. The dogs had obviously met before, wagging their tails and sniffing each other like old friends. Stopping so that they could roll around in the grass, Peter introduced me to Mildred.

"How are you, Charlie?" Mildred asked as Peter's dog jumped on her leg with an expectant look.

Grabbing a couple of dog treats from her dress pocket, Mildred gave one each to Manny and Charlie. Then, saying goodbye, she slowly made her way up the front walkway of the most beautiful, massive white adobe structure, draped in fuchsia bougainvillea, with cornflower-blue trim, Spanish roof tiles, and arched doorways.

Incredulous, Peter shouted after her, "You live here?"

"Yes," she responded, "but I'm not the only one. This is not one large house, my dear. It's a condo conversion with a main house on the side."

I remember her pointing to each of the different units on three levels, then turning to us and lowering her voice: "An insider's secret I'll let you in on. The one next to mine up there on the third floor is going to be available soon."

Peter nudged me with his elbow. "That's unheard-of in this neighborhood."

After a few probing questions, we came to find out the two-bedroom, two-bathroom, high-end-appliance unit was going to be available the following month.

"She'll take it!" Peter exclaimed, pointing at me. "I have been trying to get her to move over to the West Side forever!"

"Peter!" I said, blindsided. "Don't you think the condo's already taken?"

Mildred gave me a friendly smile. "Actually, it's not, dear. And it would be so nice to have some young, new energy about the place..."

And that was that. The month that followed was filled with two big events: a nasty breakup with my boyfriend of one year and a move into my new, wonderful home. Two years later, thanks to another "insider's tip," Marla snatched up a courtyard unit for herself.

The one and only downside to my little gem is the abhorrent parking situation—no parking except on the street. Sometimes if I practice "The Secret" hard enough, I'll find a place within a block or two, but more often than not I'm not so lucky. Tonight, however, I must've racked up some good karma, because I hit the curbside jackpot—a parking spot right in front of the building.

And thank god, because I'm ready to fall over. Eyes heavy, I open the blue-painted metal gate to find Marla's condo door wide-open and Marla, in a robe and pajamas, seated on the communal distressed-wood bench, with what looks to be a microwave in the courtyard fountain.

"Marla! What happened?"

She places her hands over her face. "It wasn't working, so I got mad at it."

Obviously, she hasn't figured out that appliances don't have feelings.

I sit down and place my arm around her. "You did the right thing, M. Definitely an appropriate punishment for a disobedient microwave. Anything else, um, bothering you?"

And cue the floodgates.

"I don't know...I'm fat. I'm old-ish. I'm still alone. Eve! What's wrong with me? Why can't I find a decent guy, settle down, and get married?"

Let's see, Señorita: (1) you lie about who you are, (2) you have a horrible temper, and (3) you have the patience of a two-year-old.

I pat her back and launch into a pep talk. "First of all, you aren't fat. You're a size six, and gorgeous. Second, I hear timing is everything. You know what they say—when the timing is right, our soulmate will find us. When it's meant to be, it will be. But M, maybe you need to make time for someone in your life instead of spending all your time at work."

She slumps over. Clearly she wants to wallow in her angst. "You're one to talk, Ms. I-don't-have-time-to-get-together." She stomps her foot. "I have nothing! And I hate it! Unlike you, I'm not okay with being alone forever."

Excuse me?

I stand, helping her up. "When have I ever said I am okay with being alone? Is that what you think? Is that how I come across? That I'm just okay with being single forever? Because I'm not."

"You could've fooled me." She breaks away, taking a few steps from the bench. Like she's done at every other breakdown, she throws her hands in the air and then shakes her body as if to rid herself of some evil demon.

I let out a sigh, knowing Marla will believe what she wants to believe.

"So what's his name?" I ask, looking into the Spanish tile fountain.

"Whose name?"

"The microwave's. I think he needs a name."

She shakes her head, giving me a small smile as she fishes the drowned appliance from the water. "How about Flash?"

"Flash it is. Sadly, Flash has lost his drive to produce hot foods and beverages for you. It may be time to let him go."

Marla nods somberly, staring at Flash. "Be honest with me, Eve. Do you think he likes me?"

I'm confused.

"Who? Flash?"

Marla crosses the walnut entryway into her condo and rests on the back of her oversized, ultramodern lavender sofa.

"Miles, Eve."

My wearied eyebrows shoot to my hairline. I knew she found Miles attractive and has always flirted with him, but I never would have guessed she was serious about dating him. I mean Marla has made it her mission to only date guys in a specific tax bracket.

"Well...has he shown some interest in you?"

"Umm. Sort of." She pauses. "Well, not yet. I thought if I turned up the heat, he might."

I place my leather satchel down and take a few steps into her place. I'm too tired to think about it since it's the middle of the night, but I'm her friend and this is what friends do. "Well, how about I ask him the next time I talk to him, and I'll let you know?"

Marla jets from the sofa over to me with renewed vigor. "Call him tomorrow and ask him! Do you think he could be the one?"

The one? I must be verging on delirious. There's no way Marla would say something so ridiculous out loud.

"I mean, he could be the one, Eve. I've always felt like there was something different about him."

Yeah, he's a working-class man.

I collect myself with a sigh. "Okay, I won't be able to call tomorrow, but as soon as I get back from my trip, I will.

"Thanks, Eve. I'll take the extra time to get in the best shape of my life."

Probably not a good time for me to suggest that she work out instead with a counselor, or hire an appliance repairman.

Climbing the three flights of stairs—or, as I not so endearingly refer to them at this hour, Mount Everest—I reflect on Marla's words. My head begins to spin, but then I remember once again that I have many other things to think about before rectifying Marla's love life.

After brushing, flossing, and throwing on a soft jersey tank and boy shorts, I'm tucked away in bed, finding myself in a familiar place—wide-awake, with hundreds of to-dos racing through my busy train station of a head!

I reach for my laptop, opening up my email. And there they are—over two hundred messages sitting in my inbox just waiting for an answer. They're staring at me like hungry, angry fish swirling around in an aquarium.

One email in particular is glaring at me. A couple weeks ago a reporter called, asking if I would participate in an article he was writing for *Corporate & Incentive Travel* magazine. I told him to go ahead and send me the questions, and I would get back to him within a couple of weeks. Needless to say, I haven't even attempted to open the message until now.

The note reads:

> Ms. Walker,
>
> I have been a big fan of yours since the "Perfectly Paired" dinner you arranged for the ISES conference there in Los Angeles a few years ago and would love to include you in our upcoming series, "Getting to Know the Pros." I understand and respect your busy schedule, and I only hope you can squeeze a little time in to answer the following questions—
>
> Who is the real Evelyn Walker?
>
> Who are you outside of the industry?
>
> That's it! If you will kindly respond no later than July 15, we will be delighted to include your answers in our September issue of the magazine.
>
> Many regards,
>
> Paolo Rodriguez

I sit up a little against the padded backboard, laughing out loud; this should take all of five minutes to write. I'll conquer it now and be asleep in a few minutes. I press the reply button and start typing:

> Paolo,
>
> Thank you for the generous offer to include my responses to your interesting editorial. Here are the answers to your questions:
>
> 1. I am a successful businesswoman who enjoys... enjoys... who enjoys...

Hmm...maybe I should make a list of WHO I am instead of trying to write a dialogue first. Okay, let's see here.

2. I am a dedicated professional.
3. I push the boundaries of creativeness for events.
4. When clients need me, I'm there for them.
5. My relationships with my clients are secure.
6. I get excited when I hear the words "you've got the job" or "we need you."
7. I mean really, is there anything else in life more thrilling than pulling off a grand event?
8. I think about events just about 24/7. I go to sleep thinking about to-dos and my brain won't turn off and...

Argh!

My breath catches in my throat as I stare at what I just wrote. Could Marla be right? Is my life all about my work?

I slam my computer shut and turn off the light. Oh my god! Is this the person I want to be? What about a relationship? Don't I want a husband, let alone a boyfriend? My last long-standing relationship was six years ago before I started my own company. All of my friends are connected to the events industry. I only socialize with people I work with in an industry that never stops. And I never seem to stop working eighteen- to twenty-hour days. Come to think of it, my itinerary isn't even complete for tomorrow. When do I have time...?

CHAPTER FOUR

WALKING INTO IMPERIAL Studio's commissary, I'm not surprised to find its décor looks like other studios I've visited. I wonder if there's some organization of studio restaurants that upholds a specific code of interior design. "Hear thee, hear thee, images of celebrities, past and present, must clutter the walls. Ordinary white cotton damask cloths will don the tables, and most importantly, a clear vase holding fresh hydrangeas or orchids must always sit atop the tables. All studio restaurants must heretofore have large windows with white painted wood blinds and leather or faux leather booths, and the perimeter shall be dressed in a nondescript color."

Beyond the décor, Imperial Studio's restaurant has three tiers for dining. The top tier, I'm told, is reserved for the executives and their guests. Here Amanda holds court. I straighten my jacket as I follow the hostess to what everyone on the studio lot must know as *Amanda's* table.

Spying me from afar, Amanda rises, and as I approach to shake her hand, she surprises me with a hug as if I am a long-lost friend.

"Hello, Eve. I'm so glad you could join us today."

Did I have a choice? What I don't do for new business!

"Now, Eve, I need to join another group for lunch, but..."

Excuse me? I thought we were having lunch.

She gives the just-a-moment finger to a table of what look to be actors across the room. Then she beckons me to the table where a lone man with a dark mop-top haircut sits. Placing her hand on my shoulder, Amanda introduces us.

"Blaine darling, this is Eve, the planner whom we discussed last night on the phone."

Great. I wonder what she said to him. And why isn't he standing up to greet me?

I smile like a robot.

"Eve, this is my friend, Blaine Stone. I think you two have a lot in common."

Did I misunderstand her? What's this "we have a lot in common" business about? Could this be worse than I thought? Is she setting us up on a blind date? I thought he was interested in event planning?

"Blaine and I go back a few years, Eve. He is the brilliance behind many of the horror pictures we have released over the last decade."

I try to get a closer look at Blaine, but I can't get past that mound of dark hair. He hasn't said a word, and this conversation is becoming quite uncomfortable.

Amanda places her hands on the outside of my arms. "I know you probably don't want me here to interrupt your little lunch, so I'm going to head off to my meeting. Blockbuster talk. I'll see you later."

The next thing I know, she's scurrying off to a table across the room.

Perfect. Just perfect.

Body stiff, Blaine sits, obviously nervous, wearing a pair of blue jeans and a long-sleeve checkered shirt. The only thing missing is the plastic protector with pens in his right breast pocket. I do, however, have a feeling they may be in the black nylon computer case he's gripping tightly to his chest.

Because he is holding his head low, I have a feeling he won't be starting the conversation; I guess I'll have to take the reins. I sit down across from him and extend my hand. "Blaine, I am thrilled to meet you. So, um, why would you like to be an event planner?"

He doesn't make eye contact. Instead, his gaze moves between the plate, napkin, and silverware. "Can we order something for lunch? I'm starving, and honestly, I can't think straight if my blood sugar is low." Judging from his high-pitched voice, I believe him.

Marla was spot-on. The red warning light inside my head goes off as I look for an exit sign. Great, the nearest one just happens to be right past the table where Amanda sits. She catches my eye, giving me a smile. I'm stuck.

"Absolutely," I smile back. "I'm famished too."

I glance down at the menu. Exactly as I thought—standard studio menu full of burgers and salads. I order an Arnold Palmer and a chopped salad. Blaine orders a large seafood cobb, the pasta special, and a piece of apple pie. He is hungry! Does he live on the streets? Is this his only meal of the day? Looking down at his slim waist, I wonder if he has a tapeworm. Well, whatever the case, I begin to feel sorry for him.

Very little is said until he starts eating his pasta. Miraculously, his voice sounds deeper than before. "You're pretty, Eve. I mean, I hope that isn't weird that I'm saying it, but it's a simple fact." He glances down at the table again.

I don't know why, but I feel myself softening a bit. Maybe it's because he's so shy.

"Um, thank you, Blaine. I appreciate the compliment."

He wipes his mouth with a napkin and looks across the room. "You know, I've always been creative," Blaine mumbles. "But the truth is, I have had writer's block for a while. I think it's time I find another outlet. Here, look. I organized this for you last night."

He reaches down to his computer bag and pulls out an iPad. Turning it on, he shows me an image of three young professional dancers dressed from head to toe in white spandex costumes.

"I'm not really following...?"

"Just wait," he says, pushing the play button.

The dancers start moving, their bodies covered with moving projections, geometric shapes in all colors. I've used projection plotting before, when we turned a museum's white walls into a video of sea life or mapped logos on all kinds of surfaces. But by multiplying compositions projected from a single video projector onto moving targets, Blaine has taken it to a whole new level. Wow.

I am awestruck! "Have you shown this to anyone?"

He finally makes eye contact. "You're the first."

I suddenly can't help seeing Blaine differently. His mop of hair is almost Beatles-like—if it weren't for the thick-rimmed eyeglasses atop his nose.

He removes his specs for a moment to wipe his brow, revealing a set of unusually striking amber-colored eyes. I don't say a thing. The depths they hold captivate me.

I want to know more about him. In fact—I can't believe I'm even thinking this—but if I'm going to hire him, I need to know more. It's time to dive in. "You don't seem very confident. Why is that, Blaine? I mean you just created something with incredible innovation in one day. That's impressive." I bring my hands together, interlocking my fingers. My eyes are smiling. "I am really impressed. I can tell you that doesn't happen very often."

He gives me a slight smile, making full eye contact with me.

"Thank you, Eve. Years ago, I was very successful. My business partner and I wrote a popular sitcom, and then I had a run with horror flicks. But after a short break, I fell into a depression and couldn't get back on track. I tried my hand at a couple of movies and corporate gigs, but nothing panned out. About a year ago I started working at a large restaurant on the West Side." He hands me a piece of paper. "You can see it listed there on my résumé. Recently, I've been working banquets, but I know I can do so much more. My boss, however, doesn't want to give me the opportunity. When Amanda contacted me yesterday, I not only wanted to prove to you I could and do want to become a planner but also needed to prove it to myself."

Back up: He works at a restaurant? So why is he so skinny?

Okay, I probably won't be able to place him in front of a client for a while, but he will be great working behind the scenes. That's what he's done as a screenwriter, after all. And I really could use someone who doesn't want the limelight—not to mention who will ingeniously create events so that I won't have to do it all myself. And from what I have seen today, he may just master our IT capabilities.

Call it woman's intuition, but I am going to take a chance on him.

"You're hired, Blaine. You...are...hired." I scoot my chair out and stand up, grabbing his hand with a strong grip. Giddy, he pumps our connecting arms up and down with excitement. After three seismic gyrations I break away.

"I have to dash now. Call my office next week and they will give you the details," I say. "We have a party to plan in Amsterdam. You may want to start thinking about how we can use some of your creative talents and tech savvy to wow the crowd."

I head down the first tier, waving good-bye to Amanda. Just as I hit the door, I glance back to see Blaine smiling from ear to ear. Welcome to the team, Mr. Stone.

CHAPTER FIVE

LOS ANGELES TRAFFIC is like one monstrous parking lot that goes on forever. Kicking myself for not leaving earlier, I doubt I'll be able to make the two stops I need to before heading to the airport. The first stop is Peter's apartment to pick up my camera he borrowed for a weekend trip and hasn't returned. The second is the salon. My hairstylist understands my erratic work schedule and fits me in when I need a little "trim-skim" at the eleventh hour. Hedging my bets, I exit the freeway toward Peter's.

Ten years ago we met while working separate events at the same hotel in Tokyo. After watching him dash around the hotel dazzling guests with his extraordinary customer-service skills, I felt the need to stop and ask about him. I'm not known for poaching other talent, but that night, I couldn't help it.

It may be cheesy to approach staff as they work on another company's program, but honestly, everyone in this industry does it at one point or another. It's how we build our freelance travel-director portfolio.

Since that fateful day, I've traveled the world with him, working events and becoming close friends. In fact, best friends. Not to mention, Peter is also an excellent chef, inviting me to all of his dinner parties so that I can be his taste tester before he serves his dishes. In all the years we have known each other, we have had only two fights. Once, because he told me that my hair was too short and I looked like a guy-friend of his. The second occurred when we went to a movie premiere together and he asked if I had gained weight. He said something to the effect of, "Are you sure you want to wear those pants? Your legs look like tubes of pork sausage." Needless to say, I don't remember anything about the movie, and I will never, ever cut my hair that short again. Or wear those pants. Or eat sausage.

It's now three o'clock, and I have a six o'clock flight. I have no time to waste.

At Peter's apartment I dash up the stairs and knock on his door. And knock. And knock.

The sound of Charlie barking his little head off is all the response I get. Where can Peter be? I texted him earlier to let him know I was coming by. And I'm sure he knows I'm in a hurry.

Trying my best not to get upset, I rush back down to my car and pull out my cell. After the third ring he answers.

"Hey, Ms. Ev-el-yn. Are you at my place already?"

"Peter, where are you?"

"I'm at the market picking us up some drinks and snacks. I thought I would serve tea...or maybe...Oh look at these"— I grit my teeth—"gorgeous European napkins they just got in. You know, I may have to pick a couple of these up because the ones I've been using really don't go with the new Italian table-cloth I snatched up in Capri last month."

"Peter, I don't have time to catch up. Remember, I'm headed to the airport and have to get a haircut before I leave?"

"Eve, I can be there in five. Let me get the drinks, and I'll dart home. I do need your opinion on the new staff uniforms before you go gallivanting around the globe, though."

How different can a polo shirt look?

Five minutes turn into ten, and I decide it's not worth another minute to stick around and wait for the ever-late Peter. I can use my phone to take the photos in Europe. I jet halfway down the stairs, ready to call to explain, when I run straight into him. I do a quick Matrix move, avoiding a collision with the two large bags of groceries he carries. No surprise, not one of his spiky, black hairs is out of place.

"I know you're going to want to come up," he says, passing me, "due to the fact that the lipstick you are wearing should be banned from any store that carries it."

Argh!

"Its fine, and I have to jet," I say, grabbing a tissue from my purse and wiping the color off my lips. "Peter, just give me the camera. I have to go."

I truly think Peter convinced himself he grew up in England or some other prestigious place in Europe. He always acts ever so proper. Case in point: the slight disapproving pout on his face telling me he is offended by my flash-and-dash appearance.

Peter doesn't budge. "Come up and take a quick look at the uniforms I've picked out for the fall events. I'll pour us each a cup of tea and then you can run."

Where is that instant awareness of another's need that a best friend should have? Camera you borrowed, I need it, give it to me, and good-bye. *Please.*

Not only is Peter a travel director for the company, I also hire him to handle a number of other responsibilities. Whether it's researching hotel properties, conducting site inspections, checking out caterers, applying for permits, or in this case, selecting new uniforms.

I feel the need to give in. Walking into the apartment, no Leica in plain sight, I can tell that I will be here for a little while.

I sigh as Charlie runs around me in circles with his half-stuffed rag-doll toy, wanting to play. Guess my dull, drab hair is just going to have to wait until I return from my trip. I had better call my hairstylist.

Following Peter into his pearly white kitchen, I lean against the counter while he sets the groceries down. "Take a seat in the nook, and noooo, you cannot help me put these away. Just sit there, hold Charlie, and tell me how much you've missed me lately," he quips with a twinkle in his eyes.

"I have missed you, Peter, and I have great news."

Peter fills the teapot under the hot-water dispenser, then hands me the cups along with a couple of coasters.

"Pray tell."

"I've hired a new creative type for the company. We'll start him off by having him coordinate the details of the 1-2-1 TV event as a service manager. His name is Blaine Stone. He'll begin next week."

Peter works as a subcontractor for my company as well as a few others. However, even so, I've come to realize he doesn't like competition.

One brow rises. "Why didn't you consider me for the job?"

I tilt my head, giving him a curious grin. "But Peter, you have always liked to have an array of companies to work with, not just one. Wouldn't you get bored with all the mundane daily tasks?"

He brings two teacups and a plate of beautifully arranged cookies over to the kitchen table. He sits, crossing one leg over the other with his arms folded across his chest—a sure signal he's upset.

"Peter, please. You know you're my favorite travel director and subcontractor, but I know well enough that you need more stimulation than being in an office all day, every day, grinding out the small details."

He lets out an uppity snoot. "So who is this guy anyway?"

I chew a chocolate-mint wafer before answering with my mouth half-stuffed. "Well, he's currently a waiter, but he used to be a screenwriter."

"So he's gay!"

I almost choke on the wafer. "Why, do you know a lot of screenwriters who are gay?"

"No," he replies, "but I'm just sayin'."

I roll my eyes as Peter, in his tight blue T-shirt, plaid shorts, and flip-flops, gets up and walks over to a large box sitting next to the 1920s Art Deco–style leather couch. He picks up the boxful of uniforms and brings it over. "Let's go through these together, shall we?"

After deciding on black slacks for both—an ebony silk sweater-set for the women and a black thin-layer crew neck for the men—it's finally time for me to go. I give Peter a quick kiss good-bye, rub Charlie's belly, make sure I have my camera and a few extra cookies for the road, and head out.

Twenty minutes after a bumper-to-bumper crawl, I walk into LAX with, surprisingly, time to spare. And for me, time to spare generally means more than ten minutes once I'm at the gate. Today, I have fourteen.

Taking my seat in business-class, I settle in, getting comfortable with my surroundings. I take my shoes off, change into my loungewear, and hang up my clothes for the trip. The rather tall, blonde flight attendant, whose head almost grazes the ceiling, brings me a menu.

After a takeoff that was bumpier than I would have liked, I am pleasantly rewarded with a delicious-looking shrimp salad. Unfortunately, that's all it was—delicious looking. I could hardly manage a few bites. I applaud myself for the foresight I had in bringing those cookies from Peter's. They aren't particularly healthy, but they will at least tide me over until breakfast. After reading up on the various venues for the 1-2-1 TV event, exhaustion sets in.

I don't travel well to Europe. I never have. I'm a ball of nerves the entire flight. Going through my relaxation routine, I adjust my seat until it's flat. I pull my eye mask down and begin to meditate. I send my mind into a tranquil state, telling each muscle to relax... calm down... unwind...

When that doesn't work, I try the "rainbow treatment," transforming each part of my skin and skeleton into colors: orange, yellow, blue, green, red. And even still my to-dos are front and center.

Why do I need to continually have a mental checklist of every person in my life as well as every event, every client, and every vendor? Geesh! Is this my subconscious distracting me from having a life, or am I simply being swallowed up by my work?

"Ladies and gentleman," the voice says over the loudspeaker, "we will be serving breakfast in a few minutes and landing in one hour. If you would like to have breakfast, please place your tray tables down. Thank you."

Um... uh... what? We're about to land? How did that happen? I grab my phone out of my purse to see the time. Four hours of sleep? Impossible! Still not nearly enough to get by for the day, but just enough to get me through passport control, out of the airport, and to the hotel.

After standing in line for longer than I expected, I finally get the good ol' stamp of passport approval and am free to gallivant into the Netherlands. I climb into a taxi with a driver who is foreign not only to me but also Holland itself. He doesn't speak much English and is taking far too long finding the hotel. My Dutch is nonexistent, so I try my high school German, which is weak at best. *"Richtige Umdrehung."* Right turn here.

"Nein, nein, nein!" he growls back, sounding like a big black bear.

I've been to Amsterdam enough times to know the canals, and we are definitely not near the right ones. After swerving through the streets as if we're in a bad action movie, we end up one hour later in front of the hotel. It's the wrong hotel, but it is a hotel, and I am not about to go any farther in this car with such an out-of-control driver who growls like an animal, reeks of curry, has a strong case of body odor, and no doubt has a fake driver's license.

As the hell-on-wheels pulls away, a nice old man directs me to the hotel where I should be snuggled up in a comfortable bed by now. Not daring to chance another taxi, I hoof it for another fifteen minutes. Thank god I travel light.

CHAPTER SIX

It takes me no time at all to check in. Because the registration desk is starting to look like a pillow, I barely manage to sign my name before heading to the elevator.

Propping myself up against the wall, I wait as the elevator makes its way down to the lobby. Ding! I'm about to let out a sigh of relief when the doors open and I come face-to-face with a disturbing sight: a man with long, straggly hair dressed in skintight, bright yellow spandex pants; a ripped T-shirt; and Vans tennis shoes. In his hand he's holding an ice cream cone, which he's licking like he's performing some kind of lewd sexual act. Not what I was expecting. Not what I was in the mood to see. As his eyes travel the length of my body—twice—he greets me with a smile and a come-hither look. "Hi there," he says, drawling the words slowly and seductively as he passes me, heading into the lobby. In Amsterdam, you're going to find all types. I guess a Zander Maine impersonator isn't all that odd. I give him an awkward smile and press the close-door button a few times in a desperate attempt to speed up the car. A weary smile spreads across my face for no apparent reason. I do love Zander Maine, even if that was just a guy dressed up like him. I could seriously listen to every album of his beginning to end, on repeat, forever.

By the time I hit the fourth floor, my luggage is just about carrying me. Dropping it on the floor, I plummet onto the bed. I move my arms and legs back and forth, making a bed angel on Egyptian cotton.

An hour later I wake up, feeling—well, horribly hungover. Jet lag is my mortal enemy, and I feel as if I've just lost the war. But there's no time for a pity party. I need to get myself in gear and find a venue for this event. I only have a few hours to scope out five locations.

Taking a peek outside the window, I notice most people are in shorts and tanks, the sun beating down on them. Warm weather, roger that. I slip on a pair of white linen slacks, a designer tank, and red blazer. My hair isn't quite long enough to sweep up, so I let my curls fall where they like.

Just before I leave my room, I go over the places my staff set up for me yesterday, in the order I am scheduled to see them:

Ajax Stadium (pronounced Ah—yahx)
The Port Terminal
The Rijksmuseum (pronounced Rye-ks museum)
The Factory
De Oude Kerk (The Old Church)

Five minutes later I'm standing in front of the elevator, ready to take on this city. Just as the doors open, I feel an unexpected and sudden ripple of panic run through my body. Please, eccentric-looking impersonator guy, don't be in there. Is he waiting for me inside? Is he dangerous? Does he still have that ice cream?

Whew! The doors open wide and I'm pleased to find no one inside. I could have hallucinated him when I arrived at the hotel.

I was extraordinarily tired. I've heard of such cases—when people get dehydrated, mixed with lack of sleep. They not only have hallucinations, but convulsions and even body tremors.

With my bag and directions in tow, I exit the elevator to find, to my surprise and may I say horror, all of the members of Trip hanging out in the reception area. All of them, including the womanizing charmer himself, *Zander Maine*! Even though the band's heyday was twenty years ago, they have kept a huge fan base. I'm guessing whenever one of them gets another divorce and needs to make alimony payments, it's a signal to hit the road. They all look a bit weathered now, but I've no doubt they still play to packed houses.

Silence falls on the foyer. I feel their eyes boring into me as they lick their lips and whisper comments under their breath to one another. Okay, now I'm uncomfortable, yet at the same time it's kind of nice to be noticed. Ah! Cheeks, stop blushing! I catch a glimpse of myself in a mirror and blush even more when I see that I'm blushing.

"Hi," I say with an embarrassed smile as I scurry past them.

In the cab I let out a loud, long-overdue breath. I'm almost sure I hadn't breathed since the elevator doors opened. That really was Zander Maine! At least it's a relief to know, when I'm exhausted and run-down, my mind doesn't hallucinate eccentric musicians.

Thirty minutes later I find myself at Ajax Stadium, home to Amsterdam's professional soccer team. Or as they call it, *futbol*. A tall woman with short, strawberry-blonde hair and a face full of freckles comes running around the building calling my name with a strong Dutch accent.

"Hallo," she says, half out of breath. "You must be Evelyn Valker?"

"Yes, I am. I'm Eve Walker," I say, emphasizing the *W*.

We both chuckle as she attempts my last name again—with no luck—then we head through the gates, up the escalator, and into the stadium. For now, I'm Eve Valker.

I take a few steps on the sea of green to feel it underfoot. She recoils. "Oh, don't do that!" she admonishes. "Here in the stadium the grass is god. You don't touch god."

I soon learn that under absolutely no circumstances is anyone to touch god. If we are to book this facility, a special walkway will be installed over the grass (I mean over god) to protect its sanctity. Already I know this place will not work. Thousands of people being told, "Please, don't touch the grass," and suddenly, everyone wants to be on the field, doing cartwheels like third graders so that they can tell everyone back home they did something in a foreign land they weren't supposed to. Although I often feel like one, I am not a babysitter. I'll need to pass on this venue.

On to the next place!

From the Port Terminal, a giant glass building resembling a wave, I look out on a magnificent view of the U-shaped harbor. The architecture alone is worth a visit. This place could easily handle our crowd, although sound may be an issue—the ceilings are very high, the floors made of hard tile, and the huge windows are, of course, glass. A challenge for sure, but still a great venue. As I rush out, I make a mental note to keep this place in mind.

On to number three.

Wow. Only twenty minutes later I am standing in one of Amsterdam's jewels, the Rijksmuseum. Designed by the famed architect Pierre Cuypers, and built in 1885, it holds an impressive collection of art from the Golden Age. The place is awe inspiring. But, sadly, it may be too elegant for this group. Plus the space is far too tight.

I could spend days here myself, but that's not why I'm here. After the event, if I have any life left in me, I'll have to return to soak in these fabulous works of art.

Three sites down and two to go. I'm a few minutes behind schedule, but the growling monster inside my stomach is begging me for a snack. Wish I had some more of those cookies I scarfed on the plane. But then again, I really need to curb my terrible habit of eating unhealthily when I'm on the road.

Walking out into the sunlight, I spot a café just outside the museum. My mouth waters at the delicious pastries inside the window. Seconds later I'm savoring a sweet Vlaii, the buttery crust and warm fruit filling quieting my now happy stomach. I can't say that it's necessarily wholesome, but oh my, is it delicious!

Forty-five minutes behind schedule, I stand before Jasper Aldenzee, a tall, fresh-faced Dutchman at The Factory. My mouth is running like a motorcycle on jet fuel. As he watches me, I'm sure that he's sure I've indulged in too many of the "substances" available here in his country. And now I'm really sure I shouldn't have had so much sugar. "What's your maximum number of people? Can we open up both studios? Which catering company do you use? Can we use your in-house lighting? Where can the stage be set?"

Even though I'm rambling and practically bouncing off the walls, I am able to catch a few interesting facts about the place. The venue actually sits on the site where Peter the Great learned how to build ships way back in 1665. A fascinating place, but again, is it too small for this group? Or is it the sugar high giving me this claustrophobic feeling?

Ruling The Factory a no-go, I make my way to de Oude Kerk, the oldest church in the city, built in 1306.

From outside the enormous stone structure, I can already see that this will be a great place for music yet a challenging one due to its size. Once inside, I'm amazed to discover that not only did the painter Rembrandt frequent the church but also his wife is buried underneath. In fact, the entire floor of the church consists of none other than...gravestones!

Fascinating and creepy.

As I walk across the concrete slabs where the names of Jan, Jacob, Cornelius, Frans, and Willem are engraved, I sense that I'm not alone. I also sense—or rather experience—it's hard to walk from one end of the church to the other due to these uneven gravestones.

If de Oude Kerk is the place, high heels cannot be allowed or there will be a lawsuit ready to happen. I think this over as I glance around, overwhelmed. This place is incredible. It has weathered massive fires, the Reformation, numerous additions, and competition from other churches. And funny enough, it sits next to the red-light district. Are they hoping to receive some lost souls wandering in the wrong direction?

Wait a minute...sits next to the red-light district? We are competing with other company parties offering sexual entertainment, so by designing a party next to the place where, well, let's say, the oldest profession in the world is conducted...I'm onto something here...CREATION!

Ideas swarm inside my head. This church represents how things are created and how they come to be. And it will accommodate more than two thousand people. Do I dare say I may have found the perfect place for this event? Yes, yes, I believe we have a winner!

With the venue selected, I head back to the hotel to meet with two different caterers—one that I have worked with in the past and another that was recommended by a friend.

I'm just sitting down when a short, robust woman and an equally stout man walk into the hotel lobby with white dust trailing from their aprons. "Hallo!" They burst out laughing together. "We are Adrianus and Agneese." I can only assume they are from the newly recommended company.

We take a seat in a nearby meeting room to discuss their qualifications. After giving them the details, I begin the interrogation.

"So," I ask, smiling back at their rosy cheeks and overextended smiles, "please tell me about your company."

They both exchange confused looks.

I try again. "How large is your company?"

"Large?" Adrianus asks puzzled.

"Yes." I pause, raising my voice as I gesture to the two of them. "How... many... people... work... for... you?"

That should work.

No such luck. They mumble in Dutch to one another and then shove their portfolio across the table toward me.

I turn the pages of food photos. Half of the items I'm unfamiliar with, but they look delicious and well made. They point to the photos explaining veal croquettes, smoked mackerel on crackers, Gouda cookies and witloof, bacon and goat cheese bites.

Okay, their food looks great, better than great, but I still have to know whether they have enough staff on hand to handle a group this large. I find myself talking to them even louder than before. "DO... YOU... THINK... YOU... CAN... HANDLE ... A... PARTY... FOR... ONE... OR... TWO ... THOUSAND?"

"THOUSAND?" Adrianus and Agneese stand up simultaneously and shake their heads in unison. "Hundred, yes. Thousand, no."

All three of us agree that they aren't equipped for this particular party. I say good-bye to the jolly couple, pocketing their business card for future events.

"Well, there's a familiar face," I say to the striking, profession-ally dressed woman who walks into the room moments later. "How are you, Saartje?"

Saartje has worked with me before on a few events in the Netherlands. She knows how we operate. Unfortunately, dur-ing the last event, her people ran out of food, and we ended up ordering Chinese takeout from a nearby restaurant. To be fair, one of my staff dropped the ball, forgetting to tell her of the increase in numbers. Needless to say, we both learned a lesson from the incident.

Her eyes bulge. "Two thousand guests?!"

After the shock, I hesitate and then nod, asking for ideas.

"Okay," she says, pondering. "With this many people, you may want to consider passing some canapés and having a few buffet stations."

"I agree."

She hands me a list of hors d'oeuvres to choose from. My eyes lock on the smoked salmon, capers, and dill on a cracker, then travel to the Brie cheese with onion compote on sourdough.

Now we're making progress!

I lay out a blueprint of the church, and we begin pinpointing sites for the buffets and bars. Feeling a sense of relief wash over me, I can't help but smile. Things are coming together nicely.

CHAPTER SEVEN

ALL THIS TALK about food has awakened the monster within once again. This time there's no denying it: I need to eat a real meal. I run up the four flights of stairs to my hotel room—my way of getting exercise while on the road—change into an appropriate little black dress, flatiron my hair, splash on a hint of makeup, and head off to the Supper Club. Before I left L.A., Peter told me that it's one of the hottest restaurants in town. Insisting that I go, he made me a VIP reservation for this evening. I'm guessing he has some sort of in with the owner.

The taxi driver seems to know exactly where it is, and I'm thankful he does. If I didn't know better, I would think that I was back in 1920s Chicago, sneaking down a dim alleyway toward the speakeasy door where I have to give the secret knock to gain entry.

Outside the Supper Club I'm greeted by a six-foot-tall specimen of a woman. No, wait, she has an Adam's apple. The statuesque figure is wearing a body-hugging, white sequined minidress; fishnet stockings; and more makeup than I wear in a year. Bunny, as I am instructed to call her, trills, "Hi, Doll, let me take that gorgeous wrap of yours. I understand that you're here alone, so Bunny wants to show you a good time."

I wasn't quite picturing someone like her when I thought of having a "good time" tonight, but...okay.

Heading inside, Bunny by my side, I'm impressed. This place has a wonderful underground-nightclub feel. Consisting of one big square room, its shiny white walls are washed with an array of rotating colored lights. Large white floral displays are strung about the place. In the distance I can see a large mirrored bar with Goth-looking characters mingling about. The only person missing in the room is Peter. I can imagine him here in his tight leather pants, all painted up in bright colors, donning an elephant mask or something equally bizarre.

Bunny walks me up the staircase in her five-inch-heeled red leather lace-up boots. "Now, Doll, don't be shy while you're dining. I have a great bed with a few scrumptious morsels of male flesh just for you."

Bed?! Male morsels? Oh god, what have I gotten myself into?

At the top of the staircase, I follow behind her swaying derrière, clutching the railing in hopes that I don't fall and smash into the tables below. My fear of heights is making it difficult for me to place one foot in front of the other. We pass by one white linen-clad bed after the next filled with gorgeous people lounging about, dressed to the nines in trendy designer duds. Bunny finally screeches to a halt in the center of the mezzanine, which overlooks the stage below. "Here we are," she says waving her hand down as if she were a model on some cheesy game show.

"Thanks, Bunny," I say. Then I notice the four rather gorgeous European men with their shirts wide-open, sitting and lying down just a step away.

Her voice drops a register as she whispers in my ear over the soft techno background music: "I don't think they're all tinkers and tailors, honey. Have a good time."

Huh? What are tinkers and tailors? Did she mean sailors?

"Bunny?" I ask with a scorched throat. "Will you bring me a glass of water?"

She places her hand firmly on her hip. "Sorrrreeeee," she says, pivoting the other way. "Homey don't do that. I'll send your waiter up to bring you one, Doll."

She sends me an air kiss and a wink, and walks away. "Enjoy, Precious."

I slip off my pumps and cautiously take a seat on the corner of the bed, tucking my dress between my legs. Still wondering what the hell tinkers and tailors are, I open my menu and dive in.

Hours later, I notice one of the guys checking his phone and get a glance at the time. No surprise—after sharing three bottles of champagne, a decadent five-course meal, one tarot-card reading, a drag-queen fashion show that resulted in the best knock-down, drag-out cat fight I have ever seen (not that I have actually seen one before), and an hour of dancing on the bed with four of the most fun, exotic, and unpretentious men I have ever met—it's well after 2:00 a.m. I excuse myself from my new smoking-hot friends and head toward the restroom.

Bunny pulls me aside as I enter the ladies' room.

Wait a minute . . . should you be in here?

By the way she's looking at me, I have a feeling she's going to dis my once nicely straightened hair that has since transformed into a rather unattractive bird's nest. Instead, she pulls out a glowing green bottle and pours me a shot right there on the counter.

"What is this?" I ask as she shoves it into my hand.

"We're celebrating, darling. Cheers!"

Opting to clink glasses with her, I swallow the sweet burning liquid. And gag.

Bunny laughs. "Don't tell me this is your first time indulging in absinthe, honey?"

I guess I left my inhibitions at the table, because I find myself giggling as I accept another shot. When in Rome or in my case, Amsterdam...

Downing it and smiling broadly, Bunny surprises me with something else completely.

"Eve, if you need any help with entertainment for your upcoming party, I'm your gal."

Ah, good ol' Peter. He must have dished the dirt on our event.

"Thanks for the offer, Bunny—I may take you up on it," I reply, as I try to make sense of my do, which is starting to take on Medusa-like life right before my eyes.

What did I just drink?

She slips me her number as she reapplies her gold lipstick. Taking a sideways glance as if seeing me for the first time, she cringes and points at my head, "Ohhhhhh, my sweet raven, girl! Take care of that thing. Something may try to land in it."

Half an hour later, I stumble into my hotel room. A beautiful red light is dancing in the corner. Walking is too difficult, so I crawl over to check it out, only to discover it's the light on the phone alerting me of a message. Dare I pick it up? Dare I wait till morning?

I decide to decide after I take a shower.

I awake to a steady dripping sound and the keen awareness that whatever it is, is landing on my head. I open my eyes to find I'm fully clothed, kneeling in the shower, my hair wet from the leaking showerhead above.

Confused and sore, I climb out of the shower, scaring myself half to death when I catch my own vision in the mirror. A long, deep red groove travels the length of my mascara-stained cheek where I had apparently rested my head against the shower-door handle all night.

Dear god!

Groaning and mentally kicking myself for letting far too loose last night, I head back into the bedroom where I once again see the blinking red light on the phone and this time don't wait to pick it up. I am a professional working woman after all . . . or so I thought. The voice on the message is none other than Miles. Weird that he didn't just call my cell.

"Eve," he starts, sounding hesitant, "you are so incredibly amazing. You must be exhausted, and if we haven't placed too much pressure on you already . . . well . . ."

Hang up the phone now. Just hang it up. Oh please, not now. Not when I have what feels like a woodpecker knocking away at my head!

His voice turns softer. "Um . . . will you make a tiny little stop-over in Berlin before you head back to L.A. so that you can scout another location for, um, another party? Craddledimpsum." He clears his throat. "I mean, this event is one week prior to Amsterdam but much smaller, about four hundred. We figure that since we'll already be over in Europe, why not attend this symposium as well?"

Sure. Why not? Let's just add a few other parties, too, while we're at it.

Couldn't they have thought about these events a year ago, like most normal companies?!

"Eve, I'm so stressed out about this new event, I just finished off two baskets of hush puppies and they're bringing me a third. Shanger-barn." He clears his throat again. "I don't know how you girls survive PMS every month. I'm gaining weight by the second. Anyway, I've emailed all of the details to you, but basically we need a fun party with an edge. You don't have to put so much creativity into it as the other."

Is that line supposed to make me feel better? Because there's a whole different word that describes exactly how I feel right now and "better" is far from it.

His message continues: "Eve, you are invincible, and there is nothing you can't handle! I know it and so do you. Make me look good. No—make me look cheetah-chic."

What a lame attempt to keep me working twenty-hour days on his behalf. I half-expect a message to follow that says, "Gotcha...just kidding," but "you have no more messages" is all I hear. I hang up with a sinking feeling, knowing I have a major change of plans.

I look in the mirror at the deep groove that has taken temporary refuge on my cheek. Letting out an exasperated sigh, I start searching for flights. I originally thought I would be able to sleep in and take the nonstop home from here. But that's someone else's life, not mine.

Three hours later and not even two minutes before boarding, I arrive at the gate, promising myself to discuss this timing issue with my therapist during my next session. Of course, I should start seeing a therapist first. Yet another mental note.

CHAPTER EIGHT

THE FLIGHT FROM Amsterdam to Berlin takes only an hour and fifteen minutes. With no time to waste, I force myself to carefully check the taxis in the queue before dashing to my hotel.

The first driver has an attitude. And simply put, I have no time for a driver who criticizes the heavy bags under my eyes and the lingering smells of last night's debauchery. Ugh. Still kicking myself!

The second driver smokes. Yuck.

The third driver has a jalopy of a car, but at least he's nice and looks respectable, and the car doesn't smell like an ashtray. With the line long and only a few choices, I opt for his beat-up old taxi. Besides a few clanking and grinding sounds and his apologies for them along the way, the ride is uneventful. I thank him with a nice tip and suggest that he have someone look into the belly of the car. My guess? A broken exhaust pipe. But who am I to say?

"Is there something wrong, Ms. Walker?" asks the graceful woman, who resembles a beauty queen, on the other side of the front desk.

I'm suddenly hit with a flashback of my terrifying hair from last night. "No, should there be?" I ask, messing with my hair, trying to straighten it.

I watch astonished as her eyes check me out from head to toe.

"I'm sorry," she says with a plastic smile, "I just expected you to be...well...somehow different."

Different? Really? How so? Like a model or a princess? Did she expect me to walk in toting an expensive dog dressed to match my equally expensive outfit? Come on, lady! In case you forgot, you're not here to judge me, but to make sure my reservation is intact and get me to my room. So get to it!

Setting down my bag, I lean over the counter. "You know what, I have a lot of work to do, so if I could get my key and directions to my room, I would appreciate it."

Just then, a man in a business suit walks up beside me to the "platinum member lane." The beauty queen holds up a finger, sashays over to him, then glancing back my way quips, "I appreciate your patience, Ms. Walker."

I hope she's aware it's wearing a bit thin.

Ten minutes later, she's still flirting with him. In my most threatening voice I level with her. "You have exactly three seconds before I ask for your manager to come and help me."

The guest, obviously European from his accent and impeccably tailored suit, walks away looking disturbed. The beauty queen whips her hair back and flings me my room key, which was prepared before my arrival. I snap turn and walk away. What exactly does she have against me? Maybe I remind her of her ex-boyfriend's new girlfriend. I'd like to think so.

My tension increases when I receive a text from my office. The convention service manager in charge of working the

Amsterdam program must have received my message before she left work yesterday. Poor girl, it's now the middle of the night for her, and she's still working on hotel rooms. *Working with the CVB, no rooms in sight 1 hr. from city. Will try other avenues. Back w/u shortly.*

Hating to do this, I emergency text Marla in hopes she may have a connection in Amsterdam. If she can help, I have a feeling it will come with Miles as the price tag.

I drop my things off, freshen up, walk by the runway model at the front desk, shoot her a very deliberate glare, and decide to head over to the Ritz-Carlton Hotel to speak with their concierge.

Walking through the sea of buildings, I'm feeling more alive. The day is beautiful and warm. A few puffy clouds swept along by a summer breeze. I love discovering cities, trying to blend in with the locals. A block from the Ritz-Carlton, a couple with a large city map that covers most of their jeans-clad bodies stop me and shout, "DO YA'LL SPEAK ANG-LISH?"

Normally I would oblige, but today I'm in a hurry, so I shrug my shoulders and say, *"Nein."*

When I enter the Ritz-Carlton, the concierge is occupied with a man sporting a long black ponytail speaking American English. He sounds upset. "I have a sick child upstairs and I need to find a store where I can pick up this medicine." He shows her the bottle. "Where can I find this?"

The concierge is doing her best to understand, but the ingredients are in English, and she's getting no help from her malfunctioning computer. She excuses herself to find a colleague who can read the container's ingredients.

"May I help?" I ask, feeling guilty that I just blew off the Texans.

When he turns around, I immediately recognize his overly tanned face. He is one of the members of Trip. "It's you!" he says with a stunned grin. "The chick from the Amsterdam hotel!"

"And it's you! How did your concert go last night?"

"We killed it. But now I have a kid upstairs with the flu. You don't happen to speak German, do you?"

He hands me the bottle, and I read the label. "I can try my best." When the concierge returns I say in my rusty German, *"Wo gibt es Health Lebensmittelgeschäft?"* praying I didn't just ask where the men's toilet is located.

She gives me a relieved smile, draws directions on a map, and sends him on his way.

Just before he leaves, he turns back toward me. "Hey, out of curiosity, you aren't following us, are you? I mean, are you a groupie or a stalker or something?"

I glance down to review my wardrobe. "I'm a thirty-five-year-old in a business suit with a computer bag. Do I *really* look like a groupie?" I raise my brow. "You know, I could ask you the same question."

Hands tucked in his torn skinny-jeans pockets, he pauses for a brief moment, then replies, "Touché. Regardless of who is stalking whom, how about being my guest at our concert tonight?"

I flash back to last night's wild Supper Club and my stomach begins to turn. A concert tonight is probably not in my best interest.

He clocks my hesitation.

"Really. I'm serious. Come tonight. We'll take good care of you."

I visualize myself in ripped jeans and a halter top rockin' out to the beat, holding a lighter in the air.

"Well, I was going to go to bed early tonight, but what fun is that?" I flash him a big smile.

He looks pleased. "I'll leave you credentials at will-call. What name should I use?"

"Walker. Evelyn Walker."

"Okay, Walker, we'll see you later." He struts out the front door just as my inner teenager lets out a tiny squeal. Composing myself, I return to the concierge. Over the years I have learned that next to the Internet and my employees, the concierge can be my most valuable resource. The best ones have an internal Rolodex that makes it all look effortless. Others can be rude, overworked and underpaid, but I never underestimate the abilities of a good concierge.

I stand in front of the woman in her hotel uniform with the shiny gold nameplate that reads "Birgit." Her welcoming smile gives me the green light. I tell her what I need, and with German efficiency she gives me a short list of the hottest clubs on both the east and west sides of Berlin, then offers me a car and driver.

"Thank you, but I'm not staying at your hotel on this visit."

"But you have utilized Ritz-Carlton hotels before, yes?"

With that, I now have a car and driver for the day.

Like yesterday in Amsterdam, I arrive at the first venue on my list—a large dance hall with worn-out hardwood floors and hideous eggshell-colored walls—and immediately say, "No, thank you." On my way out I call, *"Auf wiedersehen"* to the woman who let me in.

Next I arrive at an old, abandoned-looking building in what seems to be an industrial part of town. Most of the windows above the first floor have been shattered or are cracked beyond repair. Not normally a venue I would consider, but I'm here, so I decide to take a look anyway.

I press the call button on a panel at the front of the old building.

"Hallo. Wer ist es?" A young man's voice comes over the speaker.

I explain in English who I am and why I'm here. The young man changes languages to accommodate me.

"Hello, Ms. Walker, please come in."

Looking at the solid steel door, I'm wondering how to open it when it automatically retracts. Have I just landed on a Star Trek spaceship? Is Captain Kirk inside? I walk through a steel-lined corridor and into the club, where a twenty-something hipster-type is waiting for me.

"Nice to meet you, Eve. I'm Wolf." I notice his T-shirt, which reads, in bold type, "Don't be lookin' at my bad self," and his gold corduroy jeans that leave the top of his boxers exposed.

"I'm sorry I didn't give you any warning I was coming by, Wolf. This is a very last-minute event."

He smiles. "I'm happy to show you around. Follow me. We have three rooms here."

The first two are filthy, but the third room is workable, with its charming, large, freestanding go-go boxes around the perimeter, wood veneer walls, and the saffron sofas and tables, which give it a living-room atmosphere I could use to develop my color palette.

"Do you think you can clean this place up in a few weeks and get new carpet installed?"

Wolf answers without hesitation, "Oh yes, that's easy. I can make it ready for your event."

Relieved I have found a place so quickly and easily, I head for the car, asking the driver to take me to a nearby mall. I need something to wear tonight, since last night's black evening dress shall never be resurrected again.

As the driver pulls away, I gaze up, fascinated, at the large glass cone-like structure of the Galeries Lafayette. I have never been a big shopper. I like to have a list, find what I need, and get out as fast as I can. Maybe that's why I like the movie *Mission Impossible* so much. But here, there are floors and floors of clothing, perfumes, accessories, and French, Italian and German delicacies giving me every reason to stay for a while.

Taking a deep breath, I get my bearings straight. Now, what should I wear to a rock concert? You'd think this would be easy, since I spent most of my youth pining after the newest, hottest rock stars. I sift through shorts, leather pants, ripped T-shirts, and torn skirts; finally, on the back of the rack, I luck out. Holding them up, I inspect a pair of Italian jeans with just enough stretch to hug me from my hips to my ankles. Okay, so they are a little hard to pull on, but I must say, they do fit me perfectly. In fact, they make me look like a size two. I punch the air, letting out a mini war cry. Turning around in the communal dressing room, I find a multicolor, backless halter-top staring back at me. Did someone leave it hanging there? Is this divine intervention? I wait a few minutes to see if anyone is going to claim it and then I pounce. As I look at myself in the mirror, I actually like what I see. I can show off my arms and not show off too much cleavage. I'm not heavily endowed, but still, showing off the goods to a bunch of rock stars could give the wrong impression. I mean, they're rock stars. Enough said.

New outfit in hand, I head downstairs to grab a pair of stilettos and earrings. I'll be out of here in no time at all.

Walking back to the hotel, happy with my purchases, I find myself excited about the evening. As I'm about to enter the lobby, my phone chirps. I have a text from Marla: *A grp cxld. U're in @ De L'Europe. Get me Miles.*

Oh, thank you, Marla! My thumbs click fast. *Wow! 5 stars in Amsterdam during the International Broadcasting Convention. You're a lifesaver! Thanks! I'll work on Miles.*

It's the favor I was afraid of.

CHAPTER NINE

AFTER SENDING THE good news to the office, I start to check my email and notice it's nine o'clock! Where did the time go?

After a quick fluff, brush, and curl, a taxi ride that included scoring every raised pavement marker on the road to the stadium, and a badge mix-up at will-call, I'm standing on the side of the stage, in my new outfit, watching Trip rock the house.

The music is so loud, it's almost deafening. Feeling old and incredibly uncool, I shove my fingers in my ears, praying I'll be able to hear tomorrow. Just then, the guy with the ponytail jumps in my direction, strumming his guitar. He yells, with a wink, "There's wax on the table behind you. Grab some."

Turning around, I come face-to-face with a handsome man, with soft, sandy blond curls, holding out a handful of wrapped earplugs. Our eyes connect, and he gives me a warm grin. I'm completely mesmerized—until two young, gorgeous, giggling blondes come up and steal him away.

Men: they're all so predictable.

I refocus my attention on the band, who happens to be playing my favorite song, "Weathering Without You." It's a slow, romantic song about a young man who loses his soulmate and must face life without her. I melt as Zander Maine's voice brings back deep emotions from my high school years.

Suddenly I feel a hand touch my shoulder. I turn to find the handsome man, minus the giggling girls, smiling at me. He's so close to me, I can't help noticing the tiny gray hairs taking root at his temples. In a German accent, he shouts in my ear, "You like this song?"

Maybe it's the magic of the moment or simply the music, but my shyness is nowhere to be found.

"Yes," I shout back. "It's beautiful that a man can love a woman so deeply and be so profoundly moved by her even after she's gone. This song touches me to my core."

Um, I hadn't expected to yell something so personal.

When the song ends, he turns me around and softly wipes the tears from my cheeks. In that unexpected gesture, he disarms me completely. I smile, savoring the moment. I half-expect him to kiss my hand when he asks, "Will you join me in the VIP room?"

Backstage we pass the extra lighting trusses, ropes, and speakers, then walk behind the large screen into a hallway. Everyone along the way acknowledges him with a nod or a wave.

Who is this guy?

Under harsh fluorescent lights, we approach a door labeled VIP ACCESS ONLY. My mysterious companion waves at the giant bouncer, who ushers us in, directing us to the bar.

"What may I get you to drink?" he asks.

I smile, feeling the flutter of butterflies in my stomach. "A glass of chardonnay would be nice, thank you."

He gathers the glasses, signaling me to take a seat on the comfy, chocolate-colored sofa. As he sits down at the other end facing me, something changes. I grab one of the throw pillows, placing it on my lap. Normally I can manage to have a somewhat intelligent conversation with just about anyone. Interacting with people is what I do on a daily basis, but now I can't seem to say anything at all. My feet and hands are numb. And I've lost all consciousness of where I am. I think I'm blushing and I'm sure I'm perspiring. Who is this guy? And what has he done to me? Sipping the wine, I steal a moment to shake off my nerves.

"What is your name?" he asks, staring into my eyes.

What is my name? What IS my name? I know this answer. It's not a difficult question. Don't panic. You've got this. Take another sip.

"Eve! Yes. My name is Eve. Eve Walker." I smile proudly for answering, and then, realizing how I must look, I pray he doesn't think I'm mentally challenged.

"I am Sebastian," he says, looking amused—I'm guessing at my expense.

Just then, all of the band members file in, their female entourage in tow. The leather-faced guy with the black ponytail who invited me flops onto the couch, his sweat flying between us.

"Hey, guys," he says as his excited, intoxicated eyes pop wide open. "I don't want to pollute your space, but what did you think of the show?"

"Incredible!" we both say.

"So, you don't waste any time at all, Eve, do you?" He grins, playfully punching Sebastian.

Huh?

"You go straight for the money man, don't ya?"

Before I can raise an eyebrow, he continues, "He owns this arena, you know. And a beautiful arena it is."

Sebastian stiffens.

I glance over at him, uncomfortable and surprised. With his denim jeans and worn blazer, he looks more like a professor than a businessman. Money or no money, his charm and good looks are what caught my eye.

But does he really own this place?

Sebastian finishes his drink. Setting it down, he smiles. "Thanks, Hash, for announcing my résumé."

Hash winks, rolls off the couch, and lies on the floor.

I look back at Sebastian, who is now staring at me. "I like your arena..." I stammer, saying the only thing that comes to mind.

Sebastian sighs, then stands, reaching for my hand. "I know an excellent place where they serve a dessert to die for. Would you like to go?"

"At this hour? It's almost midnight."

His eyes alive, he shrugs. "Trust me on this one."

Something about him feels so familiar, like the home where I was raised.

But dessert to *die* for? I hope that isn't in the literal sense. I did *just* meet the guy.

"Okay." I blush, and when I stand, I feel the familiar tremor in my legs.

Outside, he touches the small of my back, guiding me toward his chauffeured Bentley. I shiver from pleasure. The sensation runs down my body.

Hmm, that's new...

We are driven to the central borough of Berlin. An area called the Mitte. My body tenses as we make our way around the dark streets and abandoned manufacturing plants, coming to rest in front of an old brick building. To say it looks sketchy would be the understatement of the year.

Visions of bodies lying in dumpsters fill my head. Oh god, and all I wanted was a piece of cake.

"We're here," he says as the driver opens the door.

My body now shaking for a completely different reason, I follow Sebastian as we make our way through a graffiti-clad door, walking over scaffolding to the back of the café. All of a sudden, I'm hit with an explosion of senses. In the room in which we now stand are dozens of artists busy covering the walls with beautiful illustrations in bold and vibrant colors. Even in the dimly lit room, the chalk drawings seem to pop off the walls. I gaze around, beside myself with wonder. The spell is broken when a young sketcher approaches us. He greets Sebastian as an old friend would and asks if we would like to take part.

Sebastian fixes his emerald eyes on me. "Well?"

I flash back to my hopscotch days, a tidal wave of giddiness coursing over me. We each pick up a stick of chalk; he smiles, tapping his to mine. "Cheers. Thank you for trusting me." Together we color between the lines, filling in the gaps, the young artist showing us different strokes to use.

"This is the Loft Café," Sebastian tells me as people pass by patting him on the shoulder. "It's my little secret. I hope you can keep it for me."

Speechless and honored, I can only nod.

Turning toward me, he takes the chalk from my hand, setting it down. "But this isn't where we are going to have dessert."

He heads across the room, signaling to a young woman as we make our way toward a wooden staircase. Climbing to the top of the building, we arrive at an incredible view of the sparkling city beyond. It seems as if the entire city has been illuminated just for us. Sebastian places his arm around me, taking in the moment until the young woman arrives to direct us along a gravel path, passing large pots of small trees intertwined with Tivoli lights, to a private cabana. The rooftop is a garden oasis.

Settling in around a bistro table, Sebastian speaks to the waitress in his native tongue. She nods, folding the cabana entrance closed. As soft shadows dance around us, I feel like we are the only two people left in this world.

"Are you cold?" Sebastian asks, eyeing a blanket on top a small table in the corner.

"No, I'm fine," I say, gazing back at him.

The waitress returns with two crystal dessert wineglasses and a small bottle.

"I hope you like Muscat?" Sebastian asks, pouring.

"Yes, as long as it isn't absinthe."

He shoots me a curious look.

"Don't ask," I respond with a cringe.

As the server relights one of the candles, Sebastian breaks our gaze to order: *"Boskop Äpfel."*

Again she nods and leaves.

I take a sip of the sweet wine. "So, what I know about you so far is one, you have an arena; two, you are quite a gentleman; and three, you are an excellent chalks-man." I lean in with glass in hand. "You must love the art of creating."

Sebastian leans in, too, so we are face-to-face above the glow of the candles. "Well, thank you very much. I do love art. Not just chalk, all art. Art was a sort of refuge when I was a child. Things weren't always so good." He looks away for a moment. "I think my mother is still disappointed I didn't become an art-ist." He chuckles. "What about you? You seemed like a natural downstairs."

"Well," I say, feeling my body temperature rise, "I feel like the entire world is one giant canvas just waiting for us to paint and make it come alive." Okay, that was a bit more poetic than I intended.

Sebastian gently tucks a stray hair behind my ear. "That's beautiful, Eve." A heart-pounding chemistry erupts between us. It's so tangible, I feel as if I could touch it if I tried.

"Darf ich reinkommen?" rings out from the other side of the tented gazebo, and the moment slips away. Sebastain responds, "Yes, please come in."

The server sets down a colorful plate that resembles a fine piece of art made of apples, jelly, champagne foam, and other delicacies.

"Are we going to eat this?" I ask, astonished. It's stunning. "It's art."

Sebastian laughs. "Art comes in many different forms. In this case, I don't think we should offend the chef."

Sebastian takes a fork, holding a morsel up to my lips.

Our eyes lock as I take the bite... It truly is a gastronomical masterpiece, and yet I find it hard to focus my attention anywhere else but on him. "Tell me more about you."

"What do you want to know?" he teases, feeding me another bite.

Will you sleep with me? Wait, Eve, lock it up.

"So, um, what do you do for a living, Sebastian?"

"Well, Eve, I run a news organization."

"And have an arena?" I goad.

"Doesn't everyone these days?" He chuckles. "But do you really want to talk about work?"

I blush, knowing how exhausted I feel after a long day at the office. He's right, people who work lots of hours rarely like to talk about it.

"Ich habe einen wunderbaren Abend. Danke schön," I say with a sincere smile, trying to impress him with my high school German. *"Ich glaube, sie reichen schrecklich."*

Why is he laughing?

"I'm glad you're having a wonderful evening, Eve, but do I really smell bad?"

Oh no, another mental note—RIP high school German.

"What? No! You smell so good. I mean—" I say, fumbling over my words. I giggle and grab his wrist. "You smell really nice. You smell like something...familiar."

"Familiar?" He leans in closer, touching my face with the soft side of his hand, sending bolts of electricity right through my core. We look at each other. The air is still so alive. This is the moment. He moves closer, closing the gap between us. I close my eyes, when—"Is that your phone ringing?" he asks, wearing that only-a-boyfriend-would-be-calling-you-at-this-hour look.

Flushed, I break away, reaching for my phone. "I'm sorry, Sebastian," I say as I rummage around to find it in the giant black hole it calls home. Pulling the ringing buzzkill out of my bag, I see that it's work.

And "Work Eve" wins again.

While I discuss details of an upcoming event in Aspen, I can't help but shiver. Without Sebastian's warmth, the air has gotten crisp. I watch Sebastian make his way over to the blanket on the table. Removing the raffia from around the soft cashmere, he covers my shoulders without a sound.

"Yes, no, and three. Thanks, I need to run." I hang up with an apologetic smile.

"Business is business. I understand. How about some fresh air?"

Twisting the piece of ribbon between his fingers, he leads me outside the tent.

Together we stand looking over rooftops as I snuggle deeper into the blanket. "What a beautiful city you live in, Sebastian."

He wraps his arms around me. "I'd like to see you again, Eve. May I take you on a proper date tomorrow night?"

I gaze up at him, lost in the moment. No wonder those two girls at the concert wanted to drape themselves all over him.

"Well?" he asks, his request sounding more like a plea.

"As much as I'd like to, Sebastian, I take off in the morning for home..."

"Then stay so I can get to know you better. I want to know who you really are."

There's that dreaded question again. Who am I?

"I need to get back. My work awaits me. I have two large events to organize, and my client will be incredibly disappointed if I don't follow through. I'm sorry."

He smiles, disappointment in his eyes. "A respectable woman you are, Eve." I watch as he takes the intertwined ribbon, wrapping it around my wrist. Another ripple of excitement runs through me as, together, we look up at the most captivating work of all, the stars glimmering overhead.

CHAPTER TEN

It's four o'clock in the afternoon in Los Angeles. I have already completed eight phone calls, locked down a few on-site staff for Berlin, and received acceptance from the nuns at the Oude Kerk to serve alcohol at the Amsterdam event. I'm on fire, and even though it feels like it's been a month since I left, it's only been three days. I'm used to working long hours, dealing with jet lag, and running around feeling like a zombie. It's just the way of life. Jetting from the parking structure at LAX, I need to get to the office, check in with my team, and see where we are with the events. My car screeches into our small office building's parking lot on Wilshire. After pulling into my spot, I reach down to grab my bag when the bracelet that Sebastian tied around my wrist so delicately peeks out from beneath my sleeve, catching my breath and reminding me of our date. But I can't go there right now. There's too much work to get done.

In my office I find a list of 101 things to do at my desk. Most of the staff has gone to a cocktail party hosted by the Beverly

Hills Chamber of Commerce, so disruption should be minimal, as long as I can keep my mind from wandering back to Berlin. I start with Marla's message asking me to call her ASAP.

Marla answers on the first ring, sounding out of breath. "Eve, thank god you're home! Something terrible has happened. I've got the curse!"

"Calm down, M. It's just one week out of the month."

I can hear the frantic click of her heels as she paces. "NO! Not that curse! Jesus, Eve. Listen—while you were away, Gabriel Santiago was staying here at the hotel. When he departed, I escorted him to the valet and out of nowhere, *he kissed me*."

Ah, here we go again.

"So who is Gabriel Santiago, and why on earth does it matter that he kissed you on the cheek?"

"For Christ's sake, Eve!"

I can almost hear her pulling her hair out. "You need to get out more! Gabriel Santiago is the world's sexiest soccer player. You know the one who dates all the young female starlets…"

Name still doesn't ring a bell.

"Well, they're starlets until they're seen with him, then their careers tank. The poor girls are rarely heard of again…Eve, it's the Santiago curse."

"Come on, Marla, is this a joke? I have so much work to do."

"Eve! He's even being sued by one of them for destroying her career. What am I going to do? I can't hide. The tabloids have a photo of us!"

"Did it make the cover?"

I hear her exasperated intake of breath. "Almost! It's on page twelve. The caption under the picture reads, 'Santiago's New Mistress.' Mistress! How do you think Corporate is going to take it when they hear this? I have worked so hard to get to where I am, and this whole stupid, exaggerated story can ruin it in one day—one day, Eve!"

I'm trying hard to understand her angst. "M, just a thought—have you tried explaining to your GM that it's all a misunderstanding?"

I don't give her a chance to answer, just continue spouting common sense. "Consider the hotel's position. The owners have to know that you deal with an array of eccentric guests. If you tell them about the situation before someone else does, won't you be much better off than if they hear it from another source?"

There's a long pause.

"You're right, Eve, I'll call them now. Oh, before I go, how was your trip?"

"My trip?"

Like you really care.

"I'll tell you all about it later. Good luck with the general manager; I hope all goes well."

Hanging up, I look down at my list, which seems to be getting longer by the second. I decide to get a few items in gear for the following day before I head home: put photos in order for presentation; confirm video conference call; gather notes regarding locations, caterers, lighting, rentals, and entertainment. A massive yawn escapes my mouth. Knowing that no more work could possibly get done in the state I'm in, I shut down my computer and grab my bag. It's time to feed and put this tired body to bed.

I make a beeline for the sushi section of my favorite organic market and pick up a couple of spicy tuna salads—one for me and one for Marla in the unlikely case her evening is cut short, even though most nights she's stuck at the hotel taking care of one emergency or another.

One night she was heading home and received an urgent call from the on-duty manager who said that a group of drunken convention-goers had stolen a few of the golf carts and were playing "cart polo" with tennis balls on the streets of Beverly

Hills. Needless to say, slamming into a Phantom Rolls cost them dearly.

On another occasion, we were on a double date at the Hollywood Bowl when she was called to the hotel on behalf of an elderly couple accidentally ingesting their grandson's "little purple pills." When she arrived, they were running around the lobby naked, flapping their arms, convinced they were birds hunting for prey. Unfortunately, the husband got a little too close to a former heavyweight boxer visiting from Philadelphia. In one punch, the guy knocked him out cold. The wife kept fluttering about until she was eventually found on the front lawn, hugging a palm tree. The pills wore off after a few hours and the couple was fine, aside from being more than horrified.

Back home, I relax into my favorite comfy chair, spicy tuna salad in tow. I could not be happier at this moment. I dig in, taking as big a bite as my chopsticks will hold. I'm not even halfway through chewing when, lo and behold, Marla marches through my front door, slams it behind her, and begins ranting. "I am through with the hotel industry! They can go to hell! I don't need them! I am a great hotel manager! Believe me, I know the truth. What pigs I work for...I give them decades of my life and this is how they repay me. Fuck them!"

I lean back, finishing my glass of water, wishing it were wine. I gotta say, watching her tirade is fabulous entertainment. No need for television—I have all the drama I can watch right here in the confines of my living room. Suddenly something occurs to me. "M, if paparazzi are not allowed near the hotel, how did they get the photo?"

She stops in her tracks, placing her hand on her hip. "Oh, you're going to love this one. Jake, the new bellman has a girlfriend whose father happens to own one of those stalkarazzi companies. So our beloved Jake wanted to prove how valuable he is to his possible new father-in-law. Needless to say, I fired him on the spot."

Standing, feeling that same hangover jet-laggy thing, I beckon her to the kitchen.

"Wow. You almost need to have the secret service do the hiring these days. I take it Corporate wasn't thrilled about the photo?"

When Marla doesn't respond, I take that as my cue to hand her the other salad. I'm sure all that rage has worked up some sort of appetite.

She plops herself down in a chair at the kitchen table. "Got any wine? I'm thinking the biggest glass you have will be just about perfect right now."

I walk over toward the under-counter wine cooler on the kitchen island. "Well," I say, "I have the Day from Hell glass…" I point at a fourteen-ounce glass on the rack next to the cooler. "But if you really need something big, allow me to introduce you to the granddaddy of them all. I always thought I'd need this baby one day." I point to a pair of Riedel thirty-seven-ounce glasses.

"Wow! I've never seen one so big." She snorts. "Whatever should we pour in it?" I follow her gaze as she stares up at one of my prize possessions, the magnum which sits on top of my cabinet.

"Marla, that's a 1970 Château Trotanoy. A client gave it to me ten years ago. I was sort of waiting to open it for something like, I don't know, my wedding."

"By the time you get married, it'll be vinegar. Come on, open it. Open it!" Marla pleads. "Here, I'll help you get it down."

I roll my eyes. There's no stopping Marla when she wants something. And I must admit, I'm actually excited to finally see what Bordeaux from the seventies tastes like. She opens the bottle with gusto, pulling out the cork, then reaches down to grab the fishbowls.

This had better be worth it.

Over a half of glass of wine for me (and three for her), she tells me that her boss had seen the photos in the tabloids, which his wife had been reading, and concluded that she was having an affair with Mr. Santiago. When asked how long it had been going on, Marla assured him that it wasn't what it seemed, and filled him in on Jake the bellman. She thought this would be the end of the story, but her boss then proceeded to fire her. She'd been driving around Beverly Hills all day abusing her credit cards in one store after another.

Marla slurs out, "It's the currrrrrrssssssse, I tell ya, the Santiago cuuuuurrrrrssssse. Stupid, sexy Santiago!"

Setting my fishbowl down, I help Marla up. It's time to cut her off and walk her downstairs. Unfortunately, Marla chooses this moment to pass out on me.

Like every time before, I go next door to enlist my slightly cranky seventy-five-year-old neighbor, Mildred, to help.

"Oh for heaven's sake, Eve, can't she just sleep it off on the floor?"

"Mildred," I say, sliding Marla's dead weight out my door. "I think she'll feel better in her own bed, don't you?"

"Honestly, honey, I don't care!"

We do our best to hold her up until we hit the second set of stairs, and then we lose her. She rolls down a few steps, her head bouncing against the last one.

That's going to hurt in the morning.

Finally getting to her door, we open it and drag her in. I pray no one else from the building is watching us. I can just imagine it—a neighbor peering through the blinds, talking in an urgent whisper to 911...

Marla's phone is ringing as we enter. We drop her in front of the sofa, and I run over to pick up the receiver. "Hello. Marla Wells's residence."

A rough, older male voice says, "This is Frank Zapetti. Is this Marla?"

Oh no! Unless there is another Frank Zapetti, this guy is the owner of the hotel. Her hotel.

What do I do? Why is he calling?

Making a snap decision, I disguise my voice, trying to sound like Marla. "This is Marla. How may I help you?"

"Are you sure this is Marla? Marla Wells?" The man isn't buying my impersonation.

I drop my voice another octave, "Yes."

"Well, Marla, this is Frank Zapetti. Besides our general manager, I've never telephoned any of our employees, ever, but my wife demanded I call—she apparently thinks you are terrific. Your GM at the hotel told me that he let you go earlier today. And…well…"

His wife must be standing right next him, because I think he's holding his hand over the phone so that I—I mean Marla—can't hear what she is saying.

"I'm telling her. Stop bothering me. I'm telling her," he says. Then, "Well, he made a mistake. He didn't mean to fire you. He meant to tell you that we are raising your salary and benefits. That's what he meant to explain to you."

My jaw hits the floor. Holy Mother! I start to do a happy dance when Mildred creeps up behind me, whispering loudly, "Whatta we gonna do with the body?"

"Excuse me?" Frank asks, sounding startled.

"Nothing, sir… It's just HBO."

"Oh, yeah. My wife refuses to have extended cable." He grumbles, clearing his throat. "Okay, so, we'll see you tomorrow

at the hotel, and Ms. Wells—you're doin' good work. Keep it up
and take care of that cold."

I get Marla tucked in and thank Mildred for her help. Mildred
thinks she pulled a muscle in her hip, so I help her back up to the
third floor.

"Would you like to come in for a glass of wine, Mildred?"
I still have plenty.

Before she can answer, my phone rings.

I shrug my shoulders. "I better get that. Thanks for your help."
I wave, running inside to answer the call. It's Peter and he sounds
desperate. "Oh Eve, I thought I was going to get your voicemail.
I'm glad you're home safe. I need a huge favor from you. I mean
huge."

Last time he asked me for a huge favor, I found myself at a gay
bar downing Jell-O shots in the middle of the night so that he
could let off some steam after a conversation he'd had with one
of his brothers.

I'm exhausted but I force myself to sound enthused. "Of
course, as long as it isn't for tonight."

A nervous laugh comes over the phone. "No, silly, it isn't for
tonight. It's for the weekend."

Please tell me he doesn't mean this weekend.

"This weekend? You mean two days from now?"

He's crazy for asking and he must know it.

"Listen to me, Eve," he continues frantically. "My brother is
getting married this weekend in Montecito, and it turns out that
I'm in the wedding party. I wasn't planning on showing, but I
changed my mind. You know how my family criticizes every
little thing about me. I need you there with me. You are my
rock. Please, please, please. I need you."

Perhaps he isn't hearing the complete and utter exhaustion in
my voice. Maybe I should try harder. "You do know that I just
got off a plane from Europe this afternoon? And you do know

that I have just two months to organize two events? That's eight weeks. That's sixty...sixty-something days. I'm sorry, Peter, I'm going to be working around the clock to get them done. I don't think that I can even fit in a workout, let alone a weekend getaway."

But when do I ever get to fit a workout in?

No feedback. Not even a whimper—just complete and utter silence. I wait.

After twenty seconds, our silent standoff ends. Slowly he speaks, "I knew it was a long shot, but you are my best friend. When I need someone in a crisis, which isn't often, you are the one I turn to, and I can't think of a bigger crisis than seeing my family."

Is he crying? I hope he isn't crying. I should be the one crying! I'm past the point of fatigue, and this conversation is draining the last bit of energy I have left in me.

I must be having an out-of-body experience, because I hear myself say, "Well, I guess I can do some work in the car while you're driving. And I'd like to meet your family. I know they can beat you up mentally, so I guess I can help with some of the blows."

"Thank you, thank you, thank you, Eve. I will spend the rest of my days on this earth making it up to you. We'll leave Saturday morning. The wedding is early on Sunday, and we can drive home late in the afternoon. Eve, you are my lifesaver. Bring a nice dress for the rehearsal brunch and something formal for the wedding. I'll pick you up at six o'clock on Saturday."

Six o'clock...A.M.?!

"Wait, Peter...six A.M.?"

"Yes! See you in a couple days, Eve."

He hangs up before I have a chance to back out.

Why is it so hard for me to just say no? Just say NO, Eve! I better write this down as another item to address with my future therapist.

I go back downstairs to make sure Marla is okay, but I'm shocked to find her missing. Only moments ago we dumped— I mean laid—her body inside her condo. Running around her place, I start to feel panicked. Opening every door in her apartment, I find her slumped over a pile of clothes in her laundry closet, facedown, fast asleep.

Hey, at least it's more comfortable than the shower.

I lay her on the floor, pick her up by the underarms, and drag her into her bedroom. I'm barely able to get her over to the side of her bed when I remember that it's three feet off the floor. This is going to be tougher than I thought. Going to plan B, I make a makeshift bed with a couple of comforters and sheets on the carpet and roll her on top, covering her so she'll stay warm.

"Oh, M," I say, placing a pillow under her head, "I hope if I'm ever in this situation, you'll remember this moment and take good care of me."

I see a mental picture: Marla leaving my body on the sidewalk outside of a trendy nightclub in some big city and telling others, "Nah, don't worry, she carries mace."

Reevaluate my relationship with Marla—check—another item to add to my ever-growing list for the therapist.

I should probably leave her a message about her promotion in a place she will find it when she wakes up. I walk around her room. The dresser? Maybe. Her door? She might see it. Ah . . . the mirror in her bathroom. Considering how much time she spends in front of it, I know she won't miss it there. Taking pen to paper, I notice a motion in the mirror. I look back to see nothing. I continue writing and again see a blurry image behind me.

"Eve, whattarrrr you doin here?" Marla stands in the doorway, swaying back and forth, somehow managing to keep her balance. "My head hurts," she says rubbing the exact spot where her head hit the stair.

Deciding not to bring up the fall, I opt for, "Well, you drank a lot, sweetie. You're bound to hurt for a couple of days." I switch gears: "Hey, the owner of the hotel called and said that they made a big mistake and want you back with a raise and better benefits. I went out on a limb and told him you'd take the offer. Want some champagne? Just kidding."

She gives me a blank stare.

"How about some water?"

Again, no answer. Instead she leans against her candy-red vanity, holding her head. I grab two aspirin from her cabinet and fill a glass.

As she sips, I ramble on. "I also got an interesting phone call this evening. I'm going with Peter to a wedding in Montecito this weekend."

Coming to life, she looks as if I'm smoking crack. *"Are you crazy?"*

Wow, didn't think that was the comment that would wake her up.

She slithers down to the floor, and I take a seat next to her. "Yeah, I might be crazy, but you've heard about Peter's parents. They treat him like the black sheep and his brothers like the golden boys. I feel sorry for Peter; they can't seem to be happy for him. You know, this may be the first time he has seen them in years."

When she begins to snore, I notice that her glass of water is half-empty. I yawn, then nudge her awake. "Come on, M. I'll help you get to bed."

Her eyes flitter open. "It's nice to know I can afford all of those shopping bags in the car now."

Marla calls me the next morning to check in. She sounds remarkably alert for having consumed as much as she did last night. So I jump on the tiny window of opportunity to tell her about Sebastian. As much as I've fought the urge, he's been on my mind.

There's no denying I'm wearing a smile the size of the Pacific Ocean. "It was one of the best nights of my life."

I hear a low whistle. "You don't mean Sebastian Von Alt, do you, Eve? The German billionaire playboy who goes through women like I go through underwear?"

She goes through a lot of underwear?

"I don't think I got his last name..."

"Google him. He's stayed here at the hotel a few times. I always wonder who he's going to show up with next."

My smile suddenly shrinks to the size of, well, nothing. It's gone.

After describing what he looks like, she reads a couple captions from hellomagazine.com: "Von Alt Is Von On It" and "No Von Alter for This German Billionaire."

I have a hard time not stuttering. "That's him."

"Well, let me tell you about your knight in shining armor. He's usually seen with European or Hollywood skanks—you know, the women who can't keep their legs shut for the paparazzi? I wouldn't be surprised if he travels with prostitutes. Classy, huh?"

I listen as she continues to shred my heart, my pride, my child-like enthusiasm for happy endings and everlasting love.

"I've heard that when he flies to meet his two-hundred-foot yacht in different ports around the world, he asks for a lineup of women to stand on the dock. He'll then choose two or three of them to spend time with while he wines and dines his clients."

And there goes my last scrap of dignity.

"Oh, but the best story I've heard about Mr. Von Alt's antics is from my own insider's network." She pauses as if for effect. "He was at one of our sister properties in the South of France. After his stay, his bodyguard was found naked in his suite with four women passed out around him. If my memory serves me right, drugs and sex toys were found all over the room." She ends as if she's making a closing argument in front of a jury of my peers. Slamming her hand on what must be her desk. "That, my friend, is your new lover boy."

She could've left the last part out. I'm already convinced I was just another victim of his serial charm, but to retain some element of self-worth, I say, "I don't know, M—I for one don't believe everything I read in the gossip pages. I'm surprised you do." I hang up, deflated.

Is there something to these stories? I mean, where there's smoke there's fire, right?

I feel sad and disenchanted. This doesn't seem like the man I met, but here I am, five minutes later, reading article after article that says otherwise. I have such a crater in my stomach.

Marla calls back. "Hello?! We weren't done talking. Have you talked to Miles?"

Ugh! This is not a good time to talk about her love life when mine feels... well, nonexistent once again. "No, not yet. Sorry. I have a lot of work to do, M. I have to go."

Three hours later, I'm sitting at my desk in my office with a phone on each ear, listening to two different phone conversations, when another line comes through. I quickly wrap up one call and glance over to the monitor to see who's on the line. My jaw drops—it's Sebastian. Familiar butterflies explode in my stomach, but after hearing what Marla had to say about him, I let the call go to voicemail. No butterflies for you, Sebastian! I consider ripping off the ribbon from my wrist, but there are more important things to do right now—*my job.*

My current to-do list is three pages long, with two pages that need to be addressed today.

Adrenaline courses through my veins as I start one phone call and finish another. At this rate I could make another fifty calls before day's end. I'm about to jump on another one when I look up to find Blaine standing in the doorway wearing jeans and a plain white T-shirt, looking like he's been working on cars, not events.

"Hey, Blaine," I say, signaling him to sit down. "How's working with the team?"

He weighs his answer, taking way too long.

"So..." he says as my phone lines light up. "Um...do you need to get those calls?"

I do. I smile, nod, and without looking, pick up the phone. "Eve Walker, how may I help you?"

"Hello, Eve, it's Sebastian."

My heart begins to pound, and I swear my arm feels numb. I try to cover, making my voice sound casual, unaffected, slightly inconvenienced. I mean, I have a lot of German billionaires calling me daily, and frankly, you all sound the same.

"Hello, Sebastian."

"Well, you are one tough woman to get ahold of. Eve, I can't stop thinking of you. You made such an impression on me. You have my head spinning. I want to spend more time with you. I'm thinking about flying to L.A. to see you. What do you think?"

Oh boy.

I cover the phone, whispering to Blaine that I need privacy. He leaves the room but doesn't go far; out of the corner of my eye, I notice him peeking in on me, like a protective little brother...interesting.

For being such an international playboy, I swear Sebastian sounds almost nervous. "I am so glad that we met at the concert," I say, "but honestly, I have too much going on. We have eight upcoming events, with two of them my own, in the next couple of months. At this point, I don't have time to eat between now and then, so I am very sorry, but I won't be able to see you."

"Okay, maybe I'm wrong, but I got the impression we had started something special."

Special?

"It was a wonderful evening, Sebastian—let's leave it at that. I have two other calls coming in; I really must go."

Don't give in. You know all forbidden fruit is tempting.

I hang up, place my hands over my face, and try to still my pounding heart. I had no idea how the call was going to unfold. And now I'm glad it's over. I look up and again see Blaine milling around the hallway, shooting glances my way.

An alert on my computer pops up reminding me it's time to meet Miles on a video call. I pick myself up, dust myself off, and make my way down the hall toward the conference room. I didn't think I could place Blaine in front of a client, but given my state of mind, I ask him to sit in on the meeting. On our way, I grab a freshly pressed blue uniform shirt out of the storage closet. Handing it to him, I ask/order him to slip it on.

Obliging, he looks at me, concerned. "Is everything okay, Eve?"

"Thanks, Blaine. It's nothing I can't handle." I'm doing my best to hide my emotions. I'm in the office after all. Sitting down at the large glass table, we greet Miles as his disarming face pops on the screen. Smiling from ear to ear, he cuts right to it. "Do you have some good news for us? Oh, and by the way, welcome home, Eve. I hope the trip went well."

Ah, I must say, his deep voice is soothing.

"We do, Miles," I say, feigning that I'm as cheery as cheery can be. "But before we begin, I would like you to meet Blaine Stone, the newest member of our team. He will be working with me on your events."

"Nice to meet you, man." Miles nods. "Let's get crack–itch–ton."

Blaine tosses a what-the-hell look my way. I ignore his gesture.

Instead, I pull out the large touch screen to share photos of the trip. "Okay, starting with Amsterdam…" I point at a photo on the screen. "Allow me to introduce de Oude Kerk, and guess what? It sits right next to the red-light district. I'm thinking we can easily attract a diverse crowd here. While I was there the idea of Creation came to me, emphasizing the bizarre, the sexy, and the unusual. We'll have searchlights swaying back and forth along with the name of the event lit up in the large stained-glass windows, and the outside of the building will illuminate in deep, rich tones.

I look to the screen to get an idea of what Miles is thinking. He's relaxed, sitting with his legs crossed, listening intently. "Very avant garde, go on."

"Here are a few photos of the inside. I envision a fantasy of sorts—"

Blaine interrupts. "With a hologram of a sun rising and setting as guests walk in, and interchangeable lighted patterns on the ceiling."

Um, whoa. Where did that brilliant idea come from?

I flash Blaine a grin and continue, "Yes…"

Just like every pitch before, I feel a rush of adrenaline as my heart picks up speed. "And as the event begins, an opera diva makes her way down the spiral staircase in the background, here." I point to the far back of the church. "The perimeter has an array of Cirque du Soleil–like entertainers and deep colors that will shed light on each of the large stone columns. A living statue, transvestites transforming from male to female, playboy bunnies walking around, and of course, my favorite—the fashion police issuing citations to those attendees committing crimes. In the middle of the church, between the pulpit and the pews, is where I imagine the main stage. Keeping with the circus theme…"

I'm pulling tricks from my hat now. I'm on fire.

"Chinese acrobats, African tribal drummers, and a cappella singers. We'll finish up the night with a couple of the hottest DJs, like Boot in Box, French Mansion Mob, or Grey. We'll see who's available."

I can't seem to stop. I grab the laser and keep going. "Off to one side, away from the main stage, is a smaller stage with, let's say, a martini bar and a lounge singer. We can use someone kind of sleazy, old-Vegas style, wearing something like a leather jumpsuit, who can really work an audience."

A quick glimpse at the screen: Miles's dark brow is furrowed in concentration.

I point to the blueprints of the church. "Here is where I would like to have the VIP room. A few Persian rugs, some low lighting with hurricane lamps, living-room seating, and large screens so these guests can watch what's happening on the floor. And speaking of the main floor, we can sprinkle a few photo booths and video games around. I think we should offer a light menu of appetizers and desserts, since we don't want the guests getting inebriated. And I imagine having large bars in each of the corners. Oh, and one last thing... because the floor is actually gravestones, no high heels allowed. Safety issue. There's no way around it."

Miles stands up and begins to pace around the room, his head tilted to the side, thinking and nodding.

My stomach sinks. Miles is never this slow to react.

He turns sharply toward us. "It's risqué. It's strange. It's even more out there than I could imagine. It's perfect!" He smirks and says, "I knew you could do it, Eve. See, and only in a couple of days! Imagine if you had a year..."

Before I can respond, a young blonde woman takes a seat next to Miles.

Blaine takes this moment to interject, "For admission to the event, we can have hologram badges made with a logo design for the event."

And I thought he was shy. And even more to my surprise, he keeps going: "So we can finish up the details over the next six weeks. If you send us the guest list, we will get the invites out to their phones and email." He stands with purpose. "Also, I was thinking if we want to make this the must-have ticket, we can mail out an electronic teaser this week. Everyone at the show will want one."

Who is this person? He certainly doesn't seem like the same timid, introverted guy I met last week.

Miles seems to share my confusion about Blaine, but his enthusiasm is undeniable. "Great! I think we have a plan, and I'm looking forward to seeing it come to life. Let's gravalate!"

"Gravalate?" Blaine asks, taking his seat.

"I got this, Miles," I say, explaining this Miles-ism—"Let's get to it."

"Right-ti-o, Ms. Eve—now Berlin. You're on, Cathy," Miles exclaims as he struts out of view.

Hold on a second. Miles, you better not leave me with...

Cathy, who has been sitting next to Miles for the last few minutes fidgeting with a pen, smiles obnoxiously at us, grabs the camera, focusing it on her. "It's my turn, Eve. What do you—"

"Sorry for interrupting, Cathy, but I didn't realize Berlin is your event?"

I mask my frustration as much as I can, but come on! Not Cathy!

I've worked with Cathy in the past. Once the CEO's assistant, she's bubbly and sweet, and has the common sense of a fried egg. Working with Cathy will make my job exponentially harder.

A side message pops up on our screen. "Sorry, it wasn't me who assigned her to you." Aha! I knew he scrambled out of there for a reason.

"Cathy," I say, pretending to be delighted, "this is Blaine Stone." I look over at Blaine, who is drooling like a dog in heat at the sight of her. I give him a snap-out-of-it kick under the table. "Blaine, this is Cathy Williams-Smith, our client for the Berlin event."

Cathy leans forward, studying Blaine. "Blaine, you have good energy. Your aura is a wonderful blue pattern."

I roll my eyes, but Blaine eats it up. He's completely mesmerized by Cathy's oversized ta-tas, which is somewhat understandable since she's wearing a low-cut, knitted striped sweater that's one, maybe two, sizes too small and is giving us quite a show.

I need to find a way to make this meeting somewhat productive. "Cathy, would you mind placing the camera a little closer to your face so that we can see you better?"

Blaine throws an incredulous look my way.

"Oh, you can't see me? How's this?" She zooms in so close only her eyes, nose, mouth, and a sample of her blonde locks are visible.

"That's perfect, Cathy. You look so perky today."

Blaine makes a face at me as he implodes in a silent whimper.

"Thanks. You know, I feel pretty perky."

Now that that's out of the way, time to get this show on the road. Sadly, the truth is, I haven't had time to think about this event since I got back. And when this occurs, there's really only one thing I can do: unleash the B.S.

"Have you ever been to Berlin?"

"No, but I think my ex-boyfriend's sister's ex-boyfriend used to live there. Or was that Beirut?"

Huh?

"Well, I'm glad you'll get to experience it. It's a great city with lots of energy, and I've found the perfect place for a sixties-style party."

She looks mystified. "Like the 1960s?"

Um, yes.

"That's right, the 1960s. And Cathy, I have to tell you, I am so excited about this event."

That is, I will be so excited once I have some idea what to do with it. I glance over at Blaine, who is intently studying the blueprint of the club and the stills on the table. Buying a little time to come up with something fabulous, I choose a photo of the inside of the nightclub, flashing it up on the screen. I do have photos of the exterior, but why unnecessarily concern her with the minor challenge of the façade.

"This is just the place for people to let loose after the conference. It's um, wild."

Think, Eve, think.

Blaine jumps in, noticing how desperate I must look. "You are in for a real treat, Cathy. The lucky invitees will begin their journey by entering a multimedia tunnel built specifically for your event. The tunnel will have projections of scenes from the sixties, like the Stones, MLK, flower power, Diana Ross and the Supremes, The Who, Jimi Hendrix, and Woodstock."

Cathy screeches, "I love MLK! They're such a great band!" By the look on his face, Blaine is temporarily stunned.

I smile, not saying a word.

"I meant Martin Luther King, the African American civil rights leader. You know... 'I have a dream.'"

"Does he have his own show?"

"Never mind." He moves on, pointing to the inside entry of the club. "Here, you can see there is a crossroad. On the west side of the club we will have a live band and dance floor that will be surrounded by dancers. A feast of lights, including strobes and black lights, will illuminate the posters and psychedelic back-drops around the room."

Listening to Blaine, I find myself relaxing as I marvel at who he really is. He is a master, a natural, a prodigy, a boy wonder, the Bobby Fischer of event planning. I need to write Amanda a thank-you card.

From the look on Cathy's face, she too is in awe. In fact, she is so wound up, we keep losing her on the screen as she bounces around. "And I'll be one of the dancers? I do Zumba all the time."

I stifle a giggle. The last time I saw Cathy dance—during the ten-minute version of "Thriller"—she cleared the place out in three minutes flat. When the song finally ended, she blamed the exodus on the fact that people couldn't keep up with her. "They're just jealous of the way I move," she claimed. The truth? The guests thought a rabid animal had bitten her.

And now she wants to dance again.

"You may be busy with everything else going on that night since it is your event, but if you want to get out there before the party starts, knock yourself out."

"Okay, I will. You know I love to dance. Do you want to see my latest and greatest?"

Without hesitation, NO!

Before I can protest, Blaine cuts in, "Yes, please." This time I send him a much heartier kick under the table.

She gets up from her chair, changing the camera to full view, and gyrates her body around the room, going in and out of camera range.

Blaine claps away, encouraging her to do more.

Enough is enough.

"Wow, Cathy, thanks for sharing, but as you know we are in a time crunch, so how about we finish the meeting?"

Out of breath, she takes her seat, unaware that her dance moves made her look like an oversized bobblehead with too many jiggly parts.

"That's okay, Eve. I'll get you out on the floor during the party. You know I will."

Not in a million years.

Blaine collects himself, transferring his attention back to the blueprints. "Okay. Well," he continues, "on the east side of the club is the lounge area, where guests will be able to go and learn about 1-2-1 TV in a very cool way. There are six framed inlets on the walls; we will project each inlet to demonstrate an application of the software that you offer. To make it even more appealing, sixties music will fill the room, and oversized lava lamps will hang from the ceilings and adorn the tables. The furniture will be fashionably low, minimalistic, and reminiscent of the era."

Blaine, now almost ahead of himself, completes his presentation. "Even the bathrooms will be embellished with large bubble lights, neon flowers, and blow-up furniture."

Bouncing around in her chair, Cathy squeals, "I absolutely love it! It will be soooo much fun!"

She's acting as if this is her own sweet sixteen party.

"To wrap it up, the club can hold five to six hundred, so the four hundred you have planned should be quite comfortable."

We can't waste any more time. I want my clients to know that I care for them, and generally I spend more time interacting, but on this late afternoon I find myself focused on all the other things I need to do. Top of my list—head home to pack for my trip to Montecito.

"Alright, Cathy, I'm glad you like it. Give us a few days and we will discuss details such as invites, guest list, transportation, staff, catering, and costumes," I say. Blaine and I stand, collecting our laptops and notepads. A sudden urge takes over and I add, "We hope you have a great weekend. Do you have some fun plans?"

"Oh, you know me, Eve. I spend my weekends in Reno looking for a good man to marry."

"Why Reno?" Blaine asks under his breath.

I smile, shaking my head. "Have fun and good luck with the search."

I switch the video screen off and turn to Blaine. "Is this the real you? How were you able to jump in like that? I thought you were going to take baby steps but no . . . you just threw yourself into the lion's den and survived!" I pat his shoulder. "That was great, Blaine—you saved me today."

"Thanks, you know I'm not quite sure what just happened. I've been writing scripts most of my life. Scripts are like puzzles. You need to bring all the pieces together—the story line, characters, atmosphere, arc, a twist or two, and a resolution. If I'm given something that really needs to be solved, like a puzzle— or like today, an event—then I guess I go into troubleshooting mode." He pauses. "Yeah, that's it, troubleshooting mode," he says, delighted with himself.

"That restaurant owner you were working with was a fool not to see this quality in you. But it's his loss." I turn off the lights in the conference room and head toward my office. Blaine walks in the opposite direction, but I call after him. "Hey, you know you have to put all of these great ideas into action now, right?"

He turns back, looking a little taller. "Got it."

I chuckle. Who would have thought?

"Hey, Eve?"

I look back.

"How do you come up with all these great events? Don't you ever run out of ideas?"

I hesitate. Part of me really wants to tell him, but not yet. I know it's crazy but I feel like the mystery behind my creativity has taken on an extraordinary life of its own.

I smile. "You wouldn't believe me if I told you." Turning, I call over my shoulder, "I'm so glad you're part of the team, Blaine. Good night."

It's been a long day. Grabbing my stuff, I head straight home to pack. I'm surprised to find a note from Marla and a large white floral arrangement on my kitchen table. *"Hope you like the flowers. Leftovers from the Women in Film luncheon. It must be a full moon. Have to run back to the hotel. Gabriel Santiago is there for some reason. Ciao."* It was written at seven, and it's now a quarter to nine.

I open the fridge to find nothing to eat. Instead, I drink a large glass of water, then slip into a comfortable pair of rust-colored yoga pants and a gray tank top—much better attire.

Swiping my carry-on luggage out of the laundry room, I bring it to my bedroom. I haven't even had time to unpack from Europe. Opening the case, I find the backstage pass from the concert in Berlin; I sit on the bed holding it for a minute, then toss it toward the trash can. It misses, but at least it's out of sight.

I open the dresser, full of bits and pieces reminding me of the last ten years. There are collector's pins from past Olympic Games, photos with former Presidents Clinton and Bush, and original speeches I helped write for several Fortune 500 CEOs. Beneath them I see menus from Noma in Copenhagen, Le Pont de Brent in Switzerland, The French Laundry here in California, El Bulli in Spain, Alain Ducasse in Paris, Vivendo in Rome. I shuffle further down to find two of my most treasured keepsakes: a white silk kata scarf given to me from the Dalai Lama on my first trip to Tibet, and a small silver horsehair purse from the princess of Japan I received as a gift during a summit in Tokyo. All great memories... of work.

It takes only a moment to realize the concert was uniquely different from all of the other memories in this drawer. I spent a magical evening with a handsome billionaire and relished every delicious moment of it. I'm going to remember this night with fondness and appreciation, because for a brief time I was able to enjoy life beyond work.

Picking up the badge, I place it in my dresser drawer among my other special memories.

Is that a knock at my door?

I walk out to the living room to see the front doorknob turn open. Before I can react, Marla appears from behind the door, dazed, muttering to herself, "Why me, why my hotel?"

"M?"

She doesn't acknowledge me as she walks by, tossing her satchel, keys, and handbag on a kitchen chair and making herself comfortable in another. I can tell she had a doozy of a day. I decide not to ask her if she wants a glass of wine, I just pour.

"I can't begin to talk about my day yet," she exhales. "So tell me, did the schmuck call?"

"Yeah, he called, but I don't think I'll be hearing from him again. I actually got a little Marla on him." Marla gives me a round of applause as I set the glass in front of her.

"So, why the frown?"

It's been awhile since I've seen Marla look this wiped. It could be a result of last night's drinking binge, but my intuition is telling me otherwise. Her eyes are glossy and she looks stunned, which is strange since she has seen so many bizarre hotel situations in the past. I can't help but think she might be rocking some sort of stress disorder.

"A shit storm doesn't even begin to explain the day I've had." She slides another chair over and puts her feet up. When she reaches for the glass of wine, she hesitates, not picking it up.

Too much last night?

"It all started this morning when Gabriel Santiago's camp denied the rumors that he was having an affair with me. At lunchtime, I hear he's checked into the hotel...again!"

"Well, he does have a right to stay there," I say, getting the feeling this is just the beginning of the story.

"He does. You are so right. He does." She takes a long pause. "However, in the afternoon, he was joined by a few of his team-mates. Over a period of fifteen minutes, security received more than a dozen phone calls," she says, cringing. "Our precious Mr. Santiago and his animalistic friends started *a food fight!*"

She has my full attention now.

"When the guards arrived, it got even worse. One of them threw a whole rack of lamb, catching one of our guys off balance, sending him into the swan pond."

"The one with the killer geese?"

She hangs her head. "It wasn't pretty."

"Eve," she says, standing up, "I had to have them arrested. Arrested! An arrest at my hotel."

Marla is clearly shaken, but I can't help wanting to crack up.

"Ohhhh . . . and that's not all." She takes on a very serious tone. "This story isn't even close to being over."

More? More than having a rack of lamb thrown at a guard, sending him into a pond of assassinating birds?

"So I thought my day had finally finished after all of this nonsense. We had to have the cabanas and pool areas bleached clean; I mean, it looked like a slaughterhouse out there. Can you believe the poor guard went to the hospital and had seven stitches sewn on his forehead? Anyway, I think we're in the clear, when Gabriel calls security this evening from his room."

"Didn't he get arrested?"

"No, just the three friends who wouldn't stop throwing food."

She half-whispers, "Sooo . . . what I am about to tell you is incredibly sensitive information and goes no farther than this room, agreed?"

I nod my head.

You know that feeling when you are watching an overly dramatic movie and the background music plays to get you all worked up? I'm there.

"Okay," she says hesitantly, "so the call that Gabriel makes to security is one of a scandalous nature. When the guard arrives at his door, he answers it naked with a blow-up doll attached to his private parts. Apparently, he thought he had rubbed some sort of lubricant in the doll's hole, which turned out to be some kind of *delayed drying superglue.*"

We both explode in laughter.

Marla can barely breathe, doubled over. "I phoned our hotel doctor, who removed the apparatus with god-knows-what. The scream of what sounded like a young girl was heard throughout the hotel. Gabriel was mortified. We found out later his friends gave him the doll and glue, as a practical joke." She snorts and gasps for air. "I don't think the bastard will show his face at the hotel again."

"Or his girlfriend—I hear she's a huge airhead." We both break down laughing all over again. I hold my stomach; my muscles hurt, as if I did a thirty-minute Pilates routine. I didn't realize I was going to be working out this evening!

"This one may go down in the hotel history books, Eve."

"Under, the 'don't get caught with your pants down' section?"

"Or 'it's a sticky situation' section."

Marla is now air grunting, and I'm trying not to pee my pants. "Oh M," I cry out, "you have some great stories. You need to write a book."

As tears stream down my face, I see the time on the microwave. It's getting late and I still need to pack. I could spend all night chatting it up, but I really need to choose my wardrobe for the wedding.

Marla wipes the tears and mascara from her face. "I needed that. Thanks for being my personal vault." She picks up her belongings and starts heading toward the front door. "Alright, I gotta go pack for boot camp."

"Boot camp? I didn't know you're going to boot camp. Have you ever been? Where is it? What is it like?"

M laughs at my inquisition. "I don't know; my assistant booked it for me and told me it's a good place to get rid of some bottled-up tension. I'm looking forward to working my butt off and getting some intense personal training." She grabs for the door but doesn't quite reach it. "All I know, it's in Laguna Beach and the activities are scheduled early morning to late night. I'm packing a bag and staying the weekend."

"I guess we should both get packing then," I say with a smile.

Marla opens the door and yelps, startled to find a woman with a large, puffy white hat standing there about to ring the bell.

"Marla," I say, peeking at the woman, "I think this one's for you."

"Hi there! I am looking for Evelyn Walker." A voice underneath the white hat spills out with a twinge of a Southern accent.

Marla and I exchange looks, completely confused at the sight of the woman dressed in chef's attire. "I am the off-site manager on call this evening, but come on," M says sarcastically. "I get it's a tough job market right now, but coming here is a little over the top, don't you think?"

Wait, didn't the woman with the funny hat ask for me?

I interrupt: "Hi, I'm Evelyn Walker. What can I help you with?"

"Nice to meet you. I'm Trish." She reaches out and shakes my hand, then M's hand too. "I was told you don't have time to eat these days, so I'm here to make your meals for you." She pushes her way through the two of us, marching over to the kitchen, assessing it.

"Wait a second," I demand. "Where are you from and who sent you?"

"Are you hungry or not?" she snaps back.

"Yes, I'm famished actually, but…"

"I'm starving, too," M chimes in. "But that doesn't give you the right to barge into my friend's house and take over."

The chef turns around and faces the two of us. She stares us down with a determined gleam, then heading back to the front door, she picks up two large boxes filled with knives, dishes, vegetables, seafood, breads, and pots and pans. She places them on top of the kitchen table and starts setting up.

"To answer your questions," she says, while pulling out a bamboo cutting board, "I am a private chef. I have my own business here in Los Angeles, but I travel the world for my clients." She grabs a large knife from the box and begins slicing a rather plump sea scallop. She picks it up and shows it to us. "See here," she says, pointing at a small piece of muscle on the scallop. "If you don't remove it, it will be chewy, and you don't want a chewy scallop."

That's interesting, I didn't know that.

"This is all fascinating, but why are you making us a meal?"

She looks at me with a blank stare and answers back with another question. "So there will be two of you tonight?"

Marla doesn't cook. She heats and reheats, so she gives in: "Well, if you're making dinner anyway…"

Trish snatches a sauté pan, a bottle of olive oil, some fresh garlic, and a juicy, deep red tomato from a box. The gas stove turns on with a flick of her hand, and within seconds, the aroma from the garlic, onions, and olive oil fills the room.

I'm in a strange sort of heaven.

"Trish?" I ask, inhaling the sensational aroma. "For the last time, why are you here at my place, cooking us dinner?"

"Do you like truffle oil?" she asks.

Harmoniously, M and I answer, "Yes!" while licking our lips.

Trish has multiple pans cooking on the stove and is moving so fast around the kitchen that our heads are almost spinning.

"Ladies," she says, stopping in her tracks for a brief moment. "May I have thirty minutes to finish your dinner and then we can talk?"

M and I give each other a sideways glance, shrug our shoulders, and walk away.

In my bedroom, M whispers, "Who sent her?"

Thinking cap on, I whisper back, "Well, there's that new restaurant on La Cienega. They've been trying to get our event business for months. But I can't imagine they would send us a private chef and not one from their own kitchen. Are you sure that Trish isn't trying to get the prime position at the hotel?"

M doesn't hesitate in responding. "Not possible. Chef Michel has been with the hotel since inception. Every chef in L.A. knows he isn't going anywhere."

I'm done thinking. "Well, then, I have no idea, but her food smells tantalizing. I'm going to finish packing, and you need to start. See you in thirty up here at the kitchen table." My shoulders hit my ears again, then drop. "Let's enjoy it."

As Marla leaves, I allow my mind to wonder. The truth is, I have a feeling Sebastian is behind this.

Thirty-five minutes later, in her Southern voice, Trish asks us to return to the kitchen where the table is set for two. We find a stunning saffron silk-and-French-linen tablecloth perfectly positioned on the table. The matching napkins are laid on top of the dining chairs. Italian hand-painted majolica plates have been set at both place settings along with handcrafted blue-marble-and-silver flatware. A simple transparent emerald-green vase sits in the center with yellow ranunculus tightly gathered.

"How beautiful, Trish!" I say, as both Marla and I glide into our seats.

"Okay, little miss cheffy poo, I don't get it." Marla pounces. "Who set you up to this?"

"Please, ladies," Trish reassures while pouring glasses of Pavillon Rouge du Château Margaux 1988. "I was instructed to have you enjoy your meal. Once you've finished the last chocolate truffle, I will identify the responsible party."

Course after course, we indulge, savoring every bite, barely talking, appreciating each mouthful of pure delight. Trish places before us an artisanal polenta, with cultured butter and truffled pecorino, followed by pan-seared sea scallops in a saffron-potato aioli. The handmade Italian breads are perfectly seasoned, melting in our mouths.

When we have taken our last sinful taste of the chocolate ganache and pecan truffles, Trish hands me an envelope. "This will answer all of your questions, Ms. Walker."

I have trouble opening the card gracefully, so Marla grabs it and rips it open. "For god's sake, Eve, it's Sebastian." She reads the card aloud. *"Since you mentioned you have no time to eat, please use the talents of Trish as long as you need them. I hope to see you soon. And he signs it S."*

It is Sebastian.

I look to Trish. "So you know him? You know Sebastian?"

Marla looks at her with disgust and pretends to spit off to the side of the table. "Yeah, give us the dirt on this master manipulator."

"Um, M, may I remind you he sent us Trish and this incredible dinner?"

"I'm not certain that we should have eaten it now," she says, placing a finger in her mouth as if she's about to regurgitate.

"All I can tell you . . ." Trish breaks in as she finishes cleaning a pan in the sink, "is Sebastian Von Alt has been nothing less than a true gentleman, and I have worked for him now for more than five years. And for what it's worth, he has certainly done *nothing* like this for anyone that I know of before."

I blush as the tiny butterflies return inside my stomach. "But M showed me a few websites that talk about what a playboy he is. They even have photos."

"Don't believe everything you read and see," Trish suggests.

"So true," Marla admits.

"Trish," I say as I help clear the table, "I know Sebastian hired you to take care of my nourishment, and I thank you for such an amazing meal, but I don't feel comfortable having a chef at my beck and call. I hope you understand."

Her eyes soften. "I like you," she says.

Marla and I help Trish pack up the boxes and load them into her car. "The table linens and settings are yours," she says with a smile. "Sebastian wants you to have them."

Trish hands me her business card, and I give her a hug goodbye. "Please keep in touch," she says. "You never know when a private chef will come in handy."

CHAPTER ELEVEN

I'M HAUNTED BY a ghost I call sleep deprivation. I can try and run from it, but why bother? It's as if I wear it loud and clear on my sleeve, written out for everyone to see. What does that say on your shirt? "I've worked an eighteen-hour day and had four hours of sleep, how about you?"

Six o'clock in the morning comes way too quickly. Four hours is not enough. Our government should change the number of hours in the day. We need more. There simply isn't enough time to get everything done.

Peter is knocking on the door, ready to go, and I am lying here in bed, unable to get my weary body to move.

Can't he hear my muffled voice through the sheets begging him to go away?

As the knocking grows louder, I imagine Peter morphing into an oversized gorilla trying to take out my entire condo. Perhaps it's time to slide one leg off the bed.

I zombie it over to the front door. Flinging it open, I nod, then drag myself back toward my room. Mildred, in a full head of curlers, has now made the trip from her condo to mine, shouting, "You're going to wake up the whole place, Eve!"

I can't even muster up the strength to care. "Sorry, Mildred, but you must be mistaken. I wasn't the one trying to bang the door down." She turns, disgruntled, clasping her robe tight and shuffling away.

"Eve, we need to go." Peter follows me to my bedroom and plops himself down on my bed. He looks sharp, wearing a nicely pressed indigo shirt with a black sports jacket, designer jeans, and loafers. "Please tell me those pajamas are not part of your ensemble for today."

"Thanks, Peter. So nice to see you this morning," I say yawning and stretching my arms. "How about you take my bag out and I'll jump in the shower. I'll be ready in five. I can do my makeup and hair when we get there." Moments later, he takes a seat on top of the toilet. I grab a towel and step out. Drying my hair with the towel, I peek over at him, noticing he's checking out my body. Hang on...

"What are you looking at?"

Peter stands up and points. "Is that *cellulite*?" He breaks out laughing.

I take my towel and snap it at him. He yelps when it makes contact.

"Well, that teaches you to not come into someone else's bathroom when you aren't invited! Now get out." Wrapping the cozy white towel around me, I grab my new favorite pair of Italian jeans. "By the way, if *that* grosses you out, then you certainly don't want to see me pour myself into these skinny minis." Rolling his eyes, Peter heads for the kitchen.

It takes me two minutes to finish dressing. I pin up my hair, slip on a pair of sandals, reach for my white linen jacket, and we're on the road.

We aren't more than fifteen minutes up Pacific Coast Highway when Peter's usual antics begin. "Have you ever thought of having plastic surgery?"

Okay, it's going to be one of *those* days, huh. "Look," I say firmly, "I understand that you're nervous about this weekend, but I'm the good guy here, remember? I'm here for you, so you better be nice." Frowning, Peter looks over at me but doesn't apologize.

Okay, I guess it's time for the pep talk.

"Hey, turn that frown upside down!" Okay, maybe a little much. I start again: "Look, this is not the Peter I have come to know and love. The Peter I know is confident, well meaning, strong, courageous, sarcastic, and sometimes when he is nervous, even downright rude to me in a loving way. He is a sensitive human being. He is the master of his universe, the mighty dog of his generation. The—"

Peter leans over and gives my shoulder a squeeze. "Okay...I get it."

We pass Zuma Beach, where a group of surfers are already out taking on the waves. I watch, remembering the many times Peter and I sat on the beach, staring out at the ocean, talking about life.

"We've had some wonderful times together, haven't we?" Peter asks, as if he just read my mind.

I smile, recalling a particularly unforgettable experience. "Do you remember not long after we met, the event in Barcelona when we worked together on the Pfizer incentive trip?" Peter shoots me a blank look. "Come on, you have to remember," I insist. I rub my forehead trying to recollect the entire situation. "We had nine hundred people departing for a city tour and the motor coaches were a no-show. You were brilliant. You got in touch with our local contact and had eighteen coaches there in ninety minutes. You even wrangled all of the hotel's on-site entertainers and had them performing for the crowd until the buses arrived. You didn't seem nervous at all, but you must have been shaking in your boots. You were incredible, Peter"—I poke his chest—"you were the hero of the trip."

He turns to face me. "I remember wanting you to be proud of me."

He did?

"I was, Peter, I was very proud."

His eyes suddenly tear up. I quickly switch gears. Driving down PCH with blurry eyes is never a good idea.

"We've been through some wild adventures, too," I say, gently grabbing his arm. "Do you remember that CEO golf outing in Scotland? Over the radio you said, 'We're on our way over to St. Andrews, and I believe we have a corpse on our hands.' I thought you were using some kind of travel-director code. But nope, you actually had a dead body on board the bus."

He snickers. "Everyone got off the coach and kept tapping him on the shoulder as they walked by. 'Oh, that Bob, he can sleep through anything,' they were saying."

"But that wasn't all," I quip. "Do you remember his wife and how she didn't want his body flown back to the States? 'You can bury the fucker there at the first hole, I don't give a damn.' It was so very strange. You flew back with the body. That must have been difficult. I couldn't have done it."

All of a sudden Peter nods, his face darkening. "Do you remember the safari in Africa with the executives of that big furniture company?"

My voice softens as I recline the seat back slightly. "You mean when you heard your grandfather had passed?"

Peter's eyes glisten again. "You stole a jeep to catch up with my group. You had the driver screech to a halt in the middle of a pack of wild zebras. You grabbed my hand, switched TDs, and drove me back to my hotel room. You stayed with me all night."

His eyes are misty when he looks over at me. "I'll never forget the ceremony you held for him on my bed. You lit candles on an old antique silver tray. One for each decade he lived. Then holding our hands in prayer, you said the most beautiful wishes for his passing, even though you had never met him."

I reach across the front seat and place the back of my hand on the side of his neck. "And you stayed on the trip, Peter—I don't think most TDs would have done that."

For the next half hour neither of us speaks. I have my arm placed around his shoulder, watching the waves in the distance coming in and crashing on the shore. With no surprise, my thoughts trickle their way to work. Taking out my iPad, I start making notes. *Review invite and contract with hotel, check invite list and outline of program. Book airline tickets for staff and 1-2-1 clients. Send deposit checks to vendors, contact local staff for both events, start rooming list.*

Done with my list, I refocus my attention on the drive, but this time the silence feels uncomfortable, like eye contact that lasts a second too long. Sitting up, I look at Peter; he rolls down the window to get a feel for the moist ocean air. "Peter, I'm so thankful you're in my life. You don't have to say anything; I just want you to know that's how I feel."

Peter takes a long pause and then meets my gaze, "I'm counting on it."

Not long after, we arrive outside an apartment building in Santa Barbara, where I come to find out Peter owns a unit. An apartment that, up until this moment, I had no idea existed. Taking this in, I'm again reminded of the vast amount I don't know about Peter. But that's his way—the way he likes it. Unlike

Marla, who will blurt out everything and anything without editing first, he has always been far more reserved and introverted.

Grabbing my hand, he leads me inside. I have to say, I'm impressed. After Peter tells me he decorated the place himself, my theory about my dear friend is once again reaffirmed: he has to be gay. All the signs are there.

He is always well dressed, he has immaculate taste, and he can criticize until the cows come home. I originally caught on years ago when we were doing a program in Hawaii. Late one night, after teardown, he asked me to the beach. We sat on the damp sand, looking up at the moon. It was breezy, and noticing that I was getting cold, he wrapped his arms around me. I remember, in that instant, feeling a little *something* as he looked deeply into my eyes. But he snapped his head away and quipped, "Boy, your hair looks awfully thin in the moonlight." In that exact moment, my something evaporated, and I saw him as a brother.

His sexuality is simply none of my business. But I can't help thinking about it.

"So what do you think?" Peter looks at me, standing in the foyer.

"Give me a sec. I'm still in shock that I didn't know this place existed!" I walk farther into the apartment, taking it all in.

It's small yet expertly put together. Red walls, white wainscoting, large coffee-table books placed thoughtfully around. A custom crystal Schonbek chandelier hangs over the small cherry dining table. As we make our way around, I see that the marble bathroom has a two-head shower and steam. Interesting. The grand finale, however, is the centerpiece of his entire place—the mahogany Louis XIV bed, complete with hand-carved florals on the headboard and turned, fluted columns. It's stunning. Covered with what appear to be crisp, expensive linens, the bed looks like a cloud on a throne. And finally, right next to it, sits a Lalique crystal vase filled with white irises. This place is truly better than any hotel room in the area but...there's that small, tiny little matter which is staring me in the face...one bed. Hmm...how is that going to work? I guess we will handle that little matter later since he isn't bringing it up. But I do prefer my sleeping partners to be men I'm dating. When I date. Which happens to be never.

This place is so different from his minimalistic condo in Santa Monica. I can't help but ask, "So why have you kept this lil' gem a secret?"

"I want to take you on a drive before we meet up with my family. I will tell you why then." He pours us each a glass of water in two beautiful Baccarat glasses. "Cheers," he says as we clank the glasses, toasting, "To your undying support."

"And new discoveries." I wink back.

Just then, Peter receives a text from his brother asking him not to be late. Immediately his face clouds over.

"We better get dressed and get going," he says, peeling off his jacket. "Do you want to use the bathroom first?"

"Only if I can have some privacy this time," I say, teasing him as I pick up my overnight bag and make my way to the bathroom.

Peter takes another sip of his water, which smells a lot like vodka, then starts to undress. "Of course. I want to see the big reveal; I'll be waiting with bated breath out here for you."

Thirty minutes later, I open the door. Peter is standing near a window, close to the front door. He looks dashing in his bold white suit, pale pink shirt, and matching knit tie.

I took my time in the bathroom, creating an elegant up-do, applying my makeup perfectly, and picking out the right diamond earrings and bracelet. After slipping on a light-plum chiffon *Gone with the Wind* dress, I add just the right touch of sexy with a pair of gold-and-crystal-studded heels.

I must say, I feel like a princess.

"Wow. That dress..." Peter says, his eyes bulging.

"I know...isn't it beau—?"

"Makes you look like an oversized pastel mint! What else did you bring?"

And good-bye little bit of confidence I built up in front of the mirror moments ago.

"It's fine, Peter, let's go." I collect my purse and we head toward Peter's energy-saving, high-mileage little car. He may hate my dress, but he loves treading lightly on the planet.

"Do you know anything about Montecito?" he asks.

"Not really, but it's beautiful up here." I sigh, settling into the passenger seat.

Driving to the southern end of Santa Barbara, Peter tells me the story of the area. "Most people think it was the Spanish who inhabited this land first, but it was actually the Chumash Indians. They farmed here and fished the local creeks. It has also been said that they discovered hot springs that healed the sick. You know how you like to hike?"

"Of course, when I have the time," I reply, gazing out the window.

"Well, many of the horse and hiking trails here were developed by the Indians and are still being used today. Maybe we'll have time tomorrow and I'll show you one."

"That'd be great!"

He seems to be in full guide mode talking about the area. "The Spanish arrived here in the 1700s, which was when Montecito was chosen as the site of what would be the tenth California mission, though it was never built here. They moved it to Santa Barbara to be closer to the Presidio."

He pulls the car over to the side of the road and points at a beautiful estate. "There used to be a large polo field here. My father once told me that, in the early 1900s, a Mr. Bartlett had them built. He not only developed the field, but he had grandstands, stables, and a lavish clubhouse built as well. Unfortunately, the Great Depression got the best of it."

Wow, he is painting a fabulous vision of the era. "You really know your stuff—tell me more."

He throws the car back in drive, heading up a beautiful, shady tree-lined street. "The Italians followed suit with the Spanish here, but it wasn't until the 1800s that wealthy Americans became interested in the area and began building their West Coast hide-aways and grand estates."

Peter stops the car alongside a block-long adobe wall, then inches toward the large, arched wooden gate. "Take for example this home here. The owners likely purchased it from farmers and built a fortress, which no one can really enjoy from the outside."

"What a shame," I say, gazing at the wooden entrance, notic-ing the electronic cameras above, scoping us out. "Um, maybe we should go now."

Peter waves, looking straight at the device, which most likely will be the reason why we spend the afternoon in jail.

"Come on, Eve, wave to Carlos and Juanita!"

I look at him, confused. "Who are Carlos and Juanita?"

"Our housekeepers," he replies as he continues to wave.

"Our?"

He sighs. "Yesssss. This is the family compound, where at this very moment the setup for tomorrow's wedding is taking place on the very grounds where my brothers tortured me when I was young. Ohhhh, and the place where my father overindulged in gin and my mother hid behind her interior design work. Yes, this is the very place. I believe they are using the rose gard—"

"Compound?" I ask, more confused than ever about who my friend is.

Peter moves the car forward as a large truck carrying event rentals passes through the gate. He turns and looks at my stone-cold face. "I know this must be a shock, but when I was growing up, I wasn't sure if someone liked me for my family's money or if they liked me for... well... me."

He grabs both my hands. "Eve, you have always accepted me for who I am. This place, my family, isn't me."

"We have known each other for ten years, Peter! Ten years! A decade, for crying out loud! It isn't like we met a few months ago! You couldn't have told me, like, I don't know, year two? Or three?!" I feel mad at him, but then again, I get his hesitation, but then again, ten years?! "Can I just have a moment to take this all in before we meet everyone?"

"I'll drive slow. We do need to get to the brunch at the hotel," he responds.

As slow as he goes, we arrive at the hotel in three minutes and thirty-two seconds. I guess I did only ask for a moment, and that's what I get. Opening the door, I take in the San Ysidro Ranch, all the while doing my best to compose myself.

Calm down, Eve. You've been through far worse.

"Let me show you where JFK and Jackie honeymooned," Peter says as he escorts me from the car, acting completely indifferent. He seems disconnected. Uncaring. And certainly not even remotely concerned with how I'm feeling.

You've hit me over the head with a shovel of news and I'm supposed to bounce back as if all is normal? Why does he seem so nonchalant about it all? Is he suffering from some sort of emotional disconnect? Hello, Peter... are you in there somewhere? Not that the money is a big deal, but at the very least, I could have worn a better dress!

"Um... okay."

I thought I knew him as well as anyone could know Peter. And now that I know I don't, I feel crushed and disoriented. Who is he really?

I must look like I've been hit with an emotional stun gun. I sure feel like it with my strange masklike smile. As we walk along the small gravel path, Peter holds me by the arm, not saying a thing.

"This place was my playground when I was young, my sanctuary," he says, escorting me into the gardens. "I would run through here to reach the trailhead into the mountains. I remember once when I was sitting over there, on the old wooden bench, this large black lizard came crawling up and sat right beside me. At first, I was scared, but he just sat there looking up at me. I ended up talking to him for over an hour." He pauses and stares away, then with a tiny smile he mutters, "Animals don't judge."

The sloping grounds are exquisite, sprinkled with white guest cottages draped in bougainvillea. The fragrance of lavender and lemons fills the air.

"As many places around here were, this area was a citrus ranch in the 1800s," Peter continues, robotically. "To this day"—he points up to the mountain—"they chose not to alter the landscape from the mountains to the sea, wanting to keep the California coastline natural." He presses my arm. "Look up there on the mountain at the fuchsia milk thistle. See the yellow primrose and the red and green Indian warriors? Aren't they beautiful?"

I try hard to be present, but I'm still dumbfounded by the talk in the car. As Peter plays tour guide, I find my attention swinging in and out of the conversation, deciphering what it all means. Has he lied to me all of these years? I mean, that's what it is, right? Lying by omission? Omission of an entire life that I didn't know existed. What did he have to gain from it all?

I need to stop my brain from all the swirling questions. But the one I can't seem to stifle is how does this affect our friendship?

Stop, Eve, stop! It's not the time. Turn off your mind and focus on Peter; you'll have plenty of time to give him a piece of it later.

With that, I vow to put on a good show for the brunch. "This place feels like home away from home. It's timeless," I say, warming my voice.

"That's exactly how they want you to feel. Come with me." Peter places his hand on my back and moves me up the path toward one of the cottages on the hill.

"What does San Ysidro mean?"

"San Ysidro was a patron saint from Madrid. They say he was extremely kind and caring," Peter answers.

Oh, how nice. So where's San Ysidro when you really need some of that kind, caring energy. Hmm...

Peter walks up to the door of a stone cottage and begins to turn the knob.

"You can't just barge in there, Peter! What are you doing?" I whisper-yell.

"Relax," he says. "My parents rented out the whole hotel for their guests. This is the Kennedy cottage, where Jack and Jackie spent their honeymoon in 1953."

The bungalow's interior has a simple yet eclectic European country charm. "Come over here," he says, making his way across the living room. "It even has two master suites. No wonder celebrities like to stay here."

I do have to agree with him. "It's tranquil and beautiful."

Grabbing my hand once again, Peter heads up the hill to the Warner cottage, which is known as the pièce de résistance of the hotel. We walk through the suite, passing the stone fireplace and antiques, heading to the large patio overlooking the grounds. In the far distance, the vast Pacific Ocean appears to have been painted to provide the voluptuous backdrop.

Just as he reaches for my hand and looks at me as if he has something serious to discuss, Peter's phone sounds off. It's a text from one of his brothers: *"where r u? ur late."*

Peter sulks. "I guess we better get down the hill."

At the word "hill," I immediately reach down to sling off my heels. There's no way I'm about to ruin them descending from the grass, dirt, and stones to the brunch.

"You shouldn't do that, Eve. The ground is hot. Your feet will get burned."

So I'm supposed to break my ankle instead? Blistered feet or twisted ankle? It's a toss-up.

I put my heels back on, and Peter walks in front of me so that I can hold his shoulders to help balance myself. As a child who grew up here would do, he takes a shortcut around a large hedge and pool, down a steep hill, and up a stairwell that leads us into the restaurant. We arrive, unscathed but parched.

Inside we are greeted by one of his elder brothers. With one look at his stance, I know his type: the obnoxiously loud know-it-all who loves to play bully. "Hey man, good to see ya—is this the little lady?" He slaps me on my back. "Mighty fine. You've got yourself—"

"Brriiaann," Peter interrupts, before his brother has the opportunity to make an ass of himself, "this is Eve. Nice to see you." He nods at Brian and shepherds me along. We step not two feet away from brother number one only to run into brother number two.

Brother number two is not much better when it comes to manners, but he is far more pleasing to the eye. Tall, with dark hair and messy bangs, his baby face makes him look much younger than his forty-some years.

"Wow, man, I didn't think you were actually going to make it. Thanks for comin'. Can you believe I'm actually going to do this tomorrow?"

"No. No, I really can't," Peter responds, shaking his head in what looks to be genuine disbelief.

Is his brother high? His eyes are half-open, and the lazy grin on his face hasn't moved since he walked up. And now he's nodding for no reason. Peter looks over at me with an embarrassed grin.

After meeting both brothers, I can honestly say, neither of them rivals Peter's good looks or charm.

Plastering on a "happy face," Peter moves me along, right into the belly of his father—at least right in front of it, which is a mound of white cotton. With thick curls of salty hair, his father wears a blue-and-white pinstripe suit, complete with an ascot and a drink in each hand. Two things become instantly clear: his dad likes his drinks, and he likes them strong. I can smell the gin from where I'm standing.

"Michael Norton," he says with a deep, burly voice, wrapping his arms around me, spilling an entire martini down my back. "And you must be Eve?"

"Yes, Mr. Norton, I am."

He chuckles loudly. "Well, it's about time we met you!"

Peter places his hand on my back, feeling the dampness of the situation. "I'll be right back—looks like you need a refill, Pop," he says, shuffling away. I pray he's using that as an excuse to rescue me some napkins.

"Has Peter told you about his cousin Lori?" Mr. Norton asks, oblivious to the fact that I'm dripping like a wet dog. I can't help but be amazed. I mean I'm about ready to shake and spray everywhere.

"Lori? No, I don't think so…"

"I ask this because your business could use her. She put on the best fortieth birthday party I've ever seen!"

Be gracious, Eve.

"Wow. Really?"

Nod like you care, Eve.

"And the parties she organizes every year for those six kids, well, I tell you…"

"I guess I should speak to Peter about her," I muster, forcing a smile.

As his father takes a wobbly step toward me to give me another bear hug, a petite older woman takes his arm away and gives me a welcoming peck on both cheeks. "Mrs. Norton?" I ask, thankful for the interruption.

"Of course, darling. Who else would I be?"

Um, is this a game?

Peter's mother is sharply dressed in a carnation-pink silk crepe dress and hat to match. She stands about five feet tall in her three-inch heels. Her face has been pulled back so many times that it sports a permanently surprised expression. And I can't help fearing that her eyeballs might launch themselves in my direction the next time she blinks. Between her eyeballs and the gin and tonic that has made its way down my back and is now dripping from my crotch, I may be more uncomfortable than I've been in, oh, ever.

"Oh dear, you have a problem," she says, noticing the small puddle at my feet. "Let me take you to the ladies' room and we will get you all cleaned up. You know, I too am starting to have that problem. But I would have thought you're much too young...Oh, but what do I know?" She scurries me toward the restroom as a young woman approaches us.

"Oh, you must be Eve," she says, grinning through tightly clenched teeth.

"Not now, Brenda," Peter's mother insists. Then she adds with a whisper, "Eve is all wet *down there*—we have to get her cleaned up."

Does *everyone* need to know?

"I'll come in and help," Brenda says gleefully as we cross the threshold into the bathroom.

"I'm Brian's wife," she explains. "I don't believe there is one person here who truly believed you existed until this very moment."

"Excuse me?" I respond, as Peter's mother wipes my dress clean and I wipe my legs dry.

Suddenly, from outside I hear Peter's voice: "I have soda water. Let me in."

Well, if this hasn't become a circus.

"What do you mean, Brenda?" I ask.

"Not now, Brenda! Eve's here, that's all that matters. Right, darling?" Peter's mom touches my cheek affectionately, a gesture that should feel nice, but instead feels downright odd.

Tall and thin with straggly red hair and lots of freckles, Brenda rolls her eyes and changes the subject. "Have you seen Marjorie Cortez?" she asks her mother-in-law. "She looks fantastic! I think it's all due to her leaving that horrible husband of hers. Do you think she had her nose done? And that outfit of Julie Monahue's—where does she think she is, a beauty pageant?"

I see a definite dynamic operating in this family, a dynamic that is starting to concern me.

"So, Brenda—back to what you were saying before—about me not existing?"

Brenda shrugs, glancing at Peter's mom. "Peter told us about you a few years ago when you started dating."

Dating?

She leans back on the rustic wood vanity, stretching her long torso longer. "And then when you took him on as a business partner, we thought he was making the whole story up. But the news last month of you two getting engaged and you showing up today...well..."

Peter's mother jumps up and hugs me tight. "Welcome to the family, sweetheart!"

Business partner? Engaged?! What the...?!

I stare back at them; despite their excitement, all I can think about is ways to shred Peter. Peter, my lying, secretive, supposed best friend.

"Well..." I begin with a painful smile, searching for the right thing to say next. Nothing comes to mind. I really am absolutely speechless. He lied to me. He's been lying to me. No, he's been lying to *all of us for years*. I jump up. I suddenly could care less about looking like a plumbing fixture gone awry. I need to get out of here and fast.

"Will you excuse me, please?" I open the door, almost knocking Peter over. He's heard the whole thing.

"Eve, let me explain."

I glare at him. "May I have the key to the car, darrrrling? I left something in there that I need."

"Sure, but let me come with you to get it," he breathes.

"That's okay, *honey*," I say, seething. "Stay with your family."

I send a fake smile to the women behind me and clutch Peter's hand that holds the key. I squeeze it with such force, I'm surprised and somewhat disappointed to see—as I rip the keys from his sweaty palm—that I didn't break his fingers.

I run—no, sprint—to the car, get inside the driver's seat, and lock the doors.

Throwing the car in reverse, I tear across the porte cochere, leaving a cloud of dust behind me.

As I make my way down the long drive, Peter appears in the rearview mirror, waving frantically at me. "Eve, stop!" he shouts. "Please! Please let me explain."

I slam on the brakes, stopping before the turn on the road. Rolling down the window, I yell with such force my voice cracks, "No more lies, Peter. No more. I'm done!" Pedal to the energy-saving metal, I hightail it out of there.

As I descend the long street, heading toward the ocean, tears flood my face. Thoughts...memories...confusion. The apartment, the family compound, my business partner, engagement, all of these lies. A cornucopia of photos from all the times and places we've shared spills from my mind. What has been real? What has been a lie?

Pulling off the side of the highway, I park the car and throw open the door. Then I kick off my shoes and sink into the coarse sand of the beach. There's a boulder the size of a small chair in front of me, and I lean against it. Having so much happen in the last few days... finally, I let it all out.

I don't cry often. I'm the person everyone cries to. I should have rented out my shoulder long ago because I could have retired by now. I give advice. I'm the mother figure: I organize, clean up after, and encourage. I'm not the one who cries. I don't have time for it.

But here I find myself in unfamiliar territory, bawling like a baby, uncontrollably. I gasp for air and blow my nose. I yell at the top of my lungs—things that don't make any sense and probably aren't even in English.

Finally, I catch my breath. My throat sore, I hold my stomach and rock back and forth. I'm crushed.

I feel so betrayed. I always thought I could tell the difference between people who mean what they say—people I can count on—and those who don't. And most of all, I thought I knew Peter. I realize that he wasn't very open, but I chalked it up to him not knowing himself. I just can't believe I was so naïve. How could I be unaware of his secret life? Was I so busy with work that it simply passed by me?

An hour goes by, and I wipe the remaining tears off my face. I desperately need to talk to someone, and Marla is the only person who comes to mind. I walk back to the car, grabbing my phone, which tells me I have ten missed calls. My eyes are so swollen I can barely read the number pad. I opt for Siri: "Call Marla cell." Seconds later her phone starts to ring. She doesn't answer. I dial it again, and again, and again, and still no answer. I let out a string of swear words, then remember she's at the boot camp.

Distraught, I crawl into the cramped quarters of the backseat, if you can even call it a backseat, and wait for Marla to call. I awake to tapping on the car window. A family of beachgoers is peering into the window. When I open my eyes, the father yells, "Are you alright?"

Wonderful.

I climb out of a fetal position, exit the car, and assure them that I'm fine. But the minute they get a whiff of my alcohol-saturated dress, the parents shepherd their kids away. Not one of my finer moments.

I slip back into the driver's seat to get my bearings. Taking a catnap helped, but it doesn't erase what happened with Peter. I need an outlet for these explosive emotions I'm feeling. I need...I need...I need boot camp! That's exactly where I should be, working off some of this rage!

I speed home, hoping Marla left behind some clue where said boot camp is located. I grab the hidden key in the normal spot and quickly survey her condo. Jackpot! I find the name of the place written on one of her gazillion Post-it notes stuck on the front of the fridge. I sprint upstairs to my place, jump in the shower so that I don't smell like a five-hour happy hour another second longer, change into my best gym attire, pack another overnight bag, and GPS the directions on my phone. Heading for my car, I pass Peter's Prius where I left it outside the apartment building. Well, it will just have to remain there until he gets back...somehow. Forcing myself to take the high road, I leave his car key in our secret hiding "rock" and head out. As I merge onto the massive moving parking lot, aka the 405, toward Laguna Beach, I'm hit by a wave of excitement or adrenaline—not sure which one—knowing at least I'll get in a killer workout and see Marla.

An hour and a half later, I find myself in the middle of what feels like nowhere. Or rather Japan. Surrounded by vegetable gardens and acres and acres of natural habitat, I arrive at a beautiful

Japanese-style temple. I check the signs again to make sure I'm in the right place, and to my surprise, I am. When I pictured boot camp, this was not the picture that came to mind. Where are the drill sergeants? And their whistles? And all the sweaty people pleading for death? This place is far too serene.

Deciding I've driven too far to turn around, I park and get out. After mastering a hefty flight of stairs, I am greeted by a woman with creamy white skin in a black monk robe whose haze of gray stubble shows where her silver locks have been shaved off. She gives me a warm and welcoming smile, then hands me a broom.

A broom?

"Hello and welcome," she says calmly, bowing her head. "Please note, it's chore time. Use the broom and sweep the porch."

Um, okay. Can she not see that I have a bad case of anxiety oozing from my every pore? Does she seriously want me to sweep right now?! "But I am here to see—"

"All in due time," she insists with another warm smile. She waves her hand toward the porch, dismissing me.

Well, at least she said please.

Putting a lid on my boiling pot, I march around as directed. I try to decide between breaking the broom over my knee, tossing it back at her, or actually sweeping, when I notice the porch is spotless. In two seconds flat, I'm back in front of her, handing her the broom. "Someone must have already gotten to it because it's already clean."

"Please," she insists.

I don't know why I listen to her, but I do. I guess I figure with the amount of pent-up tension I have, sweeping the deck will take me only a few minutes.

But I guess I hadn't actually seen it . . . Walking around, I notice a large connecting deck at the back. It takes me a half hour. But if I do say so myself, I actually made it cleaner and it felt good to do some manual work. I hand back the broom and complete the necessary paperwork.

Out of the corner of my eye, I spot a familiar figure cleaning a window. Marla must've seen me at the same moment because she mimes a silent squeal. Giving me the just-a-minute-finger, she turns back to the window. A few minutes later, after finishing her chore, Marla joins me on the deck.

The first thing she does is give me a much-needed hug. "What are you doing here and why aren't you at the wedding?"

The floodgates open. I begin to pour out my crazy story when a gong rings.

"Oh shit, that means silence!" she says, cutting me off. She grabs my arm, leading me to another building across the lawn.

"But—"

"Shhh."

She doesn't understand! I'm ready to burst! I need to get my story out!

We walk slowly into a large hall where Marla whispers, "It's called a zendo." People dressed in comfortable attire sit on the floor among monks wearing long black and gray robes roped at the waist. I later learn their robes are called *kassaya* and represent the humbleness of Buddha. Marla grabs two square cushions for us and places them on the floor in the center of the room. She shows me how to use it under my pelvis, but it feels awkward, so I stuff it behind me and try to lean back on it instead.

I start to feel guilty about all those times I'm on an event site, unreachable when Marla really needs to talk. It's a terrible feeling not being able to spill the beans to someone.

Three more gong rings and the consequential silence becomes deafening. The only sound now is the smoothness of the group breath. Innnnn...ouuttttt.

Marla looks over at me. She has her mouth wide-open and is sticking her tongue against the roof of her mouth, then moving it down and up. Then holding it there, she closes her mouth.

Huh?

I move my cushion closer to her as the instructor, in front of the room, begins a collective meditation.

"Ommmmmmmm, Ommmmmmm."

I whisper oh so softly in Marla's direction: "I really need to talk to you, M."

"Not now," she whispers back. "We can talk at dinner after the meditation."

"Ommmmmmmmmm."

This really doesn't seem like her thing. Why did she choose this moment to become all Zen on me?

"M, really," I plead, noticing that the instructor has one eye open, scanning the room for the offender.

I bow my head and continue chant singing, "Ommmmmmmmm." Then, "MMMMMcanwejustgooutsideforafewminutes-pleeeeeezandtttaaaallllllllkkkkkkkkk?" I exhale.

The instructor with his wise eye flashing at me responds for Marla. "Pleeeeeezzzzzzzzbesilentifyouwanttoremaininthetemple-withussssssss."

"ButtttIamgoingtoburstifIdon'tspeakwithmyfriendsooner-ratherthanlaaaaterrrrr."

No one in the room is flinching except for me. I can't keep still.

"Thennnnnnnnnntakeyourfriendoutoftheroomsoyoudon'tdis-turbusanylongggggggggeeeerrrrrrr."

I pull Marla up off the floor, accidentally stepping on the monk next to me. Luckily, he must have transcended to another spiritual plane, since he doesn't look up or budge. We leave the room with our heads bowed, palms together, apologizing the entire way.

Marla steers us toward a beautiful footpath. Together we walk the grounds as I tell her what happened with Peter. Eventually we come to rest at an old wooden bench surrounded by tall grass overlooking the water.

"Eve, like I've always said, all men are unworthy of our attentions. Peter's no exception. For god's sake, not even my father is worth my time."

"I just can't believe that, M. I can't. But then again, I didn't think Peter would have been so deceiving. Are there any good, honest men out there?" I glance at her, seeking any sign of hope.

"Yes, there are," she responds. "They are called Buddhist monks and they are celibate."

Not quite what I was looking for.

"Who would have ever guessed Peter?" I say, deflated.

"I would!" Marla rips.

I'm not certain how much a weekend here is going to do for her—her spicy demeanor needs at least a year of backbreaking manual labor.

"Look," she says, bending down to pick a wildflower, "perhaps you need to look at Peter differently. He is as good as they get, and he has been a good friend to you."

Maybe my last thought was too harsh; she probably only needs six months.

"Marla, I have no idea who Peter is. Everything he said to me was a lie."

"Then screw him!" she spits, kicking a rock.

Nope, definitely a year.

"Why are you here, M? This kind of thing doesn't seem like your kind of thing."

"Well, I know it sounds cheesy, but I'm here to find balance, and who knows, maybe a man. You probably haven't spoken to Miles about me, and I guess I realized if he was interested in me, he would have been in touch."

Hang on. *A man? Here?* Didn't she just get done telling me they're all celibate? And good, it looks like I'm off the hook with Miles.

Marla stands, brushing off her pants. Typical M—the moment she feels vulnerable, she dashes off. "They're short on help today, so now it's my turn to scrub the already-clean toilets before dinner, so we better head back to the lodge."

"Do you mind if I stay here and think for a while?"

"No, go ahead. Take all the time you need." She hands me the flower she's been twirling in her hand. "They may even have a bed or a sleeping bag if you want to stay the night. We can check later if you do."

I watch Marla walk down the hill until she's out of sight.

I get in lotus position, reveling in my solitude. I'm about to attempt meditation again when an elderly Asian monk walks by. He stops just after he passes me, sitting in prayer position on the ground, his eyes closed. He begins to whisper.

"In order to find peace in the world, you must first find peace within."

He falls silent for what seems like eternity. My thoughts drift, ebbing and flowing with the wind. As if adding a soundtrack to the moment, my gentle companion begins softly humming. And it's mesmerizing. I don't mind not understanding what his chant is about; I just want to stay here on the hill where life feels safe and I feel calm.

When he finishes, I ask what the chant means. He looks out at the setting sun. "There is light within darkness and there is darkness within light. Find your truth and don't waste time."

A single tear escapes, running down my face. "That is so beautiful and so true," I say as the frail man disappears down the path like a ghost in twilight.

Sitting in silence once again, I ponder my life. There are some serious questions I need to face. I need to not waste my time. I need to know what I truly want and go after it. This is why I am here! In some cosmic way, Peter, of all people, sent me here to learn this lesson.

I hear the gong ring and guess it means dinner is ready. Standing, I head back to the temple with my stomach growling.

Marla and I dine on tandoori tofu, sweet potatoes, sautéed kale, kidney beans, and salad at a communal table. We learn that complete thought and consideration are given to each meal. From the care of the soil (which is mixed with clay and cultivated by hand), to the regard while gathering, skill in preparing, and artistry in presenting each leafy piece—all make for a gift of nourishment to our bodies and souls. I swear I feel myself becoming more spiritual with each bite.

After dinner and full of fiber, we take the short walk back to the living center. Marla is quiet, which is rare. "What's wrong?" I ask.

"You know the dorm room? Well, there are twelve other ladies sharing it and the windows have no drapes."

I stop. This is kind of a problem. I wish I didn't have to have complete darkness and utter silence to sleep...but I do.

"Oh, are there any private rooms?"

One of the visitor coordinators must have overheard our conversation, because she looks right at us, interrupting: "As a matter of fact there is. We have an isolated cabin up on the hill. It takes about fifteen minutes to walk to it."

I could jump for joy. And relief. I don't have to drive home, and I get my own room. "I think I saw it on our walk this afternoon. Is it available? Can I sleep there?"

"It is and you can," she says, excusing herself. A few minutes later she returns, handing me a set of sheets and toilet paper. "It's all yours. We ask only for a donation before you depart the grounds tomorrow. Someone will knock on the door in the morning and wake you up for the mandatory meditation session. Good night."

Marla and I exchange hugs, then I head off into the darkness, a borrowed flashlight illuminating the way. Arriving at the old crate-sized shack, which could very possibly have been a former outhouse, I wonder if this really was a good idea after all. Full of second thoughts, I head inside and conclude that this isn't a room but a closet, and a very simple one at that. The twin bed has a straw mattress. Well, at least it feels like straw. There is an old kerosene lamp on a short hand-hewn wooden table, a small sink, and a sad old toilet.

As I try to get comfortable on the straw mattress, feeling as if I'm paying an involuntary visit to the acupuncturist, I wonder if this is another lesson. After a short time, I move the sheets off the bed to the more comfortable hardwood floor where I find a strange kind of comfort at last.

Nothing could have prepared me for the wake-up knock on my door. Nothing. I answer the door half-asleep and ask the monk standing in front of me what time it is. Silence is the only response I get, so I grab my phone: 4:30 a.m.

The monk continues to say nothing. I ask him where I should take a shower, and still nothing. He simply points toward the zendo, then places his index finger over his lips, which I can only assume means silence.

"I'll be right back. Will you walk me down the hill?"

Nothing.

I shut the door and grab my clothes in the dark cabin. Opening the door seconds later, I bring my palms together and bow. I thought that I'd get some reaction from that, but no. With a sigh, I walk with him like a prisoner to the zendo. No makeup, no brushed hair, no clean mouth. We all appear just as we were when we awoke. The only consolation is we are all in the same boat. I mean, zendo.

Not a single word is uttered before breakfast. The morning's meditation is silent. I wouldn't know anyone else was present if it wasn't for the occasional clearing of a throat or the whiff of offensive flatulence.

When we hear the gong signifying breakfast, I couldn't be hungrier. An explosion of happy fireworks erupts inside of me. We get to eat breakfast! And again the food is delicious, with abundant fresh fruits, baked goods, roasted coffee, and home-made herbal teas.

Marla and I plop down at a table for four and are joined by one of the coordinators. She has thick salt-and-pepper hair shaped in a bob and wears loose hemp clothing. "Is this your first visit to the temple?" she asks.

Marla covers her full mouth of food with her hand. "Yes."

"Welcome. I'm so pleased you could join us this weekend. I find this to be a place of wonderment and tranquility."

I take a sip of tea. "Thank you. Do the monks own the land?"

"Interesting you should ask," she says, grabbing a blueberry scone from the center of the table. "They don't, but they are trying to purchase it. It has changed hands many times in the last few decades. The owners past and present have graciously allowed us to continue our practice on this property, but we want to buy it soon before some developer pays top dollar for it and changes its character."

Marla snorts, "Yeah, who needs another strip mall?"

"Is there an immediate risk?" I ask.

"Well, there is someone in Germany who wants the parcel but hasn't convinced the existing owners to sell it, yet."

Gulp. I feel an odd guilty sensation.

"Do you happen to know his name?"

"No," she says, taking the last few sips of her tea. "But I do know the initials are SVA."

I feel a swift kick to my gut.

Marla must have misunderstood. "Did you say FBA?"

"No," I say, "S...V...A."

"No way! We know that jerk!" Marla exclaims, her eyes wide. "Eve has dated him."

"No, no, no. I have not," I say, shooting imaginary poisoned darts at Marla.

"I met a man with the initials SVA in Berlin last week, but—"

"It would help us tremendously if you could find out if he is the interested party. If he is, the monks would very much like to speak with him."

But...but...but...

How does this man keep popping up in my life? I can't seem to get rid of him, even when I am actually trying.

"Okay," I say quietly.

The coordinator stands up. "Thank you so much," she says, bowing to us as she leaves the room.

As I watch her go, a heavy unease settles over me.

Thanks, Marla.

After breakfast we are permitted to take a cold shower. Once clean and refreshed, we meet in the living center where we are given one last task and told we will have a meal before we leave the grounds. A young monk approaches us, informing Marla that she has been chosen to ring the gong signaling lunch.

Marla squeals, punching the air as we follow him into the courtyard, home of the gong. There, he shows her how to stand in order to achieve the proper angle to hit the metal.

No sooner does the young monk excuse himself when I turn to find Marla cranking up for what she calls "a practice round."

"I don't think that's—"

A deafening hollow-bucket sound rips through the air. I can't cover my ears fast enough.

She doesn't just tap the metal, she slams the mallet into it as hard as she can.

Marla winds up for another. Again and again she hits the gong. I watch in horror, sure she's lost her mind, until a monk runs and grabs the mallet from her hands.

"Can I take one of these home with me?" she yells over the thunderous bell, out of breath, sporting an adrenaline-fueled grin.

Looks like Marla got to work out some of that aggression after all.

We slowly turn to see the entire congregation, mouths agape, staring at us. As the sound dies down, Marla shrugs. "Come on. You know you all want to do it too." No one says a word, including me. In fact I don't even breathe. Marla looks around and laughs, rolling her eyes. "Oh whatever, people," she says. "Kale gives me gas, I've been craving a hamburger since last Thursday, and I killed two spiders in the dorm this morning. Obviously, I don't belong here. Come on, Eve, let's go get our bags." After picking up our bags from the welcome center and placing money in the donation urn, we head toward our cars with everyone still standing in what looks to be shock.

"I'm sorry. Namaste. Be one with your breath. I'm sorry about the spiders, and I love vegetarian food," I call, as Marla drags my arm.

It's clear how Marla feels about this place, but as we pull away I realize I want to return someday. I'll never forget that sense of peace on the hill. Even though this weekend did not go as planned, one thing became clear: my life is changing, whether I like it or not.

CHAPTER TWELVE

Even though most people think the life of a meeting and event planner is glamorous, this career does have its drawbacks. And traveling with clients on long overseas trips can be one of them.

September snuck up on us sooner than I could have imagined. Now, on the day of our departure, I am not only unconvinced I can pull off either event, I find myself needing to take extra and unexpected care of my client. Yesterday I had arranged for a car to pick Cathy up at her home so that we could meet at the airport. The car service I use is very dependable, but unfortunately, my client is not. I'm at the airport and Cathy is nowhere to be found, with time before the flight departure ticking away. After trying numerous times to get ahold of her, on the eleventh attempt she finally answers.

"Eve, where is my car?" she asks, sounding more like a diva than a professional.

I stifle my annoyance. "The car has been sitting in front of your home for thirty minutes, Cathy."

"Uh-oh..." she says. "Did I forget to tell you that I moved last week?"

The answer is an overcooked, charred-on-the-bottom, crisped as hell yes! After the last few weeks of working with Cathy, I've had to exercise remarkable patience. The capper was her request to bring to Europe a cake that she and her mother baked. "Eve, you're gonna die when you taste it."

After I told her it wasn't a good idea to transport it all the way to Berlin, she brought it into her office instead. Miles later confessed everyone had the runs for two days.

"No, you did not tell me you moved. What's your new address?"

"You know, it's so new, I don't even know. Hold on, I'll walk outside and take a look at the numbers on the building."

This is going to take too long.

"Wait, Cathy, have you received any mail at your new place yet?"

"Yes," she says, making a sound as if she is smacking herself on the head, "of course!" I hear her flipping through papers. "The address is 18973 Oak Knoll Lane, apartment seven. You know the number seven is lucky, right?"

Not for me today.

"So I've heard. And what city are you living in?"

"Oh, silly me, I'm in Glendale."

Glendale? Glendale!

"Okay. That's across town. Let me think. We have a limo company that works out of Pasadena; they can be at your apartment in fifteen minutes if they have a car available. Sit tight, I'll call you right back."

"Eve, wait!" she insists. "Why don't I drive and meet you there."

My mind floods with all the horrendous scenarios this could entail: (1) she gets lost driving to the airport, (2) she drives to the wrong airport, or (3) she makes an unexpected stop along the way to the airport, most likely for food or a last-minute blowout.

Um, I'm going to go with "not a good idea."

"You know, with traffic the way it is, you're better off being picked up."

Hanging up, I call the Pasadena limousine service. Maybe seven is lucky after all because they have a driver who just finished a run in Glendale. Relieved, I call Cathy and let her know the car will be there in five minutes.

With the problem solved, I move on to the bigger one. I need to somehow stall the plane. Walking up to the counter, I ask to speak with a supervisor. In this industry, sometimes it pays to plead with the person in charge.

"Hello, sir."

"Sir?"

A robust woman with a Burt Reynolds haircut, whom I unfortunately mistake for a man, steps out from the door behind the counter. Her stern voice is enough to scare even the fearless away. "What do you want?"

I can already tell she needs to brush up on her customer service skills.

"Wow. Are you wearing a forty-year service pin?" I ask with all the sugar I can muster.

She rubs the pin that sits atop her right breast. Her masculine face relaxes. "Yes, yes it is. You're the first person who's noticed it in a few years. What can I do for you?"

Time to lay it on thick.

"Hi, I'm Evelyn Walker. I own an event-planning company," I say, shaking her hand. "I have a client who is joining me on the flight to Berlin today. We also have most of your business-class and first-class seats booked in a couple of days. I want to introduce myself and thank you and your staff in advance for the outstanding customer service that you always seem to deliver for us."

"Well, thank you—that is refreshing, Ms. Walker. Most of the planners we meet have some kind of special request or complaint. It's nice to hear when things are going well. I'll pass on your message to management."

She reaches out to shake my hand again. "Thanks for stopping by, I appreciate it."

Better get to it before she walks away.

"Well, speaking of . . ." I confess, my voice squeaking a bit.

"Yes, Ms. Walker, what is it?" One of her brows climbs to her hairline as she looks at me skeptically.

"My client is on her way from Glendale, and I'm afraid that with the security line as long as it is, she may not catch this flight. Is there anything we can do to expedite the process?"

She looks at her watch. "You do realize that the flight takes off in forty minutes."

Refusing to give up hope, I push on.

"I know." I let out a large sigh and I give her my please-help-me eyes. "What can you do to save this situation?"

"Well," she grumbles, "we can escort the two of you to the front of the line, but you will still have to go through security. I can also ask the pilot to delay by ten minutes. That's the maximum we will allow."

"That will be wonderful. I am so grateful. Thank you. Thank you so much."

The driver makes surprisingly good time. In exactly twenty-five minutes and fifty-two seconds, Cathy's car reaches the door of the airport. But not straying from her usual antics, Cathy lingers, finishing her one-sided conversation with the shell-shocked driver. The look of relief in his eyes when I approach is unmistakable. He hops out, throwing her luggage at me as fast as he can.

"Cathy," I say, hurrying her along, "the airline staff is escorting us to the front of the security line, and the pilot is holding the plane for us. We not only need to go, we need to run!"

Due to Cathy's plump figure and the fact that she loves to wear four-inch heels, our "run" feels more like a slow-motion shuffle. "I can't run in these shoes!" she cries. "But I can't take them off because they make me look skinny."

Am I being punk'd?

Noticing an abandoned luggage cart against a wall, I seize it, plopping her in and our luggage on top. Four-inch disaster averted. The escort, now sprinting, beckons me to follow him to the security checkpoint. Our bags clear, but each time Cathy walks through the detector the alarm buzzes. First it's her belt, and then it's her large, gold rope necklace. After a full scan, with minutes to go, I throw her and her belongings onto another cart and rush down a long corridor toward the gate. I have to wheel her up a steep ramp, which is no small feat, only to see the jetway door closing.

"We're here!" I scream. "Please, please open the door!"

I pant the entire length of the jetway, thinking about the long days and nights it has taken me and my staff to organize these events for 1-2-1 TV. As I try to catch my breath, I feel an immense appreciation for the majority of my clients, grown-ups who are independent thinkers. Not like this one, who needs her hand held, or rather pulled, dragged, and plopped. We're on the plane!

At Cathy's request, we are seated next to each other. This is her first international flight and she is... well... freaking out. She death-grips my forearm, to the point of almost puncturing my skin. "You know," she squeaks, "I'll be fine once the plane is up in the air, but it's the taking off that worries me."

"Look," I say, catching her saucer eyes, "I used to be scared of flying too." I slow my words down in order to calm her nerves.

"Trryy and prreetend that youuu are drriiving the plaane." I motion at her to take my lead. "Take your hands and place them on the steering wheel in front of you and use your feet to press the pedals."

"I can do that," she replies with a nervous giggle.

"Great. Now, as we move toward the runway, slowly push your accelerator toward the floor. Wait until we turn the corner here, and...now, press full throttle and get this plane flying!"

I watch Cathy firmly gripping her pretend steering wheel, her right leg pressing down as far as she can stretch it. She leans her body backward and her face freezes, as if she's fighting gale-force winds.

I give her a few seconds to relax after takeoff, but I notice she hasn't moved. Her hands are still clutching at the imaginary helm.

"You did it!" I say with a congratulatory smile, hoping she'll break character. "How about a glass of champagne to celebrate?"

"Sure," she responds, trembling. I lean back, settling into my chair. If this is how the week is starting out, I'm in for a world of stress. My stomach clenches just thinking of the enormity of Amsterdam. If I can get through these two events unscathed, it'll be a miracle.

A couple sips later, my faithful companion is back to being chatty Cathy. "So then I got a mani-pedi—you know, a girl's hand's always gotta look good in case someone wants to put a ring on it. And I ran into Charlene, who's in my Zumba class. She told me Macy's was having their huge weekend shoe sale, so I went and got three of the same style pump in different colors. It's like I robbed the place." She finishes her glass, slamming it down. "So what about you? And what's up with Peter?" She turns to face me.

If she had slapped me across the face, I wouldn't have been as surprised.

"Oh!" she cries, registering my reaction, obviously remembering the news about the wedding fiasco was something she's not supposed to know. Red-faced, she quickly changes the subject.

"Oh, I have to tell you about these two guys I met in Reno a few weeks ago. One guy, Ricky, was so into me he begged to take me home to meet his parents. They have this great double-wide just outside of Truckee. When we were there, his brother, Wade, started crushing on me too, so they asked if they could share me. Believe me, Eve, I didn't know what to do...so I made out with them both. Can you believe it? Two! Not just one. I am so lucky! We're going to meet up in Flagstaff for a keg party when I get back. You should totally come!"

This is going to be a long flight.

"That's sweet of you to invite me, but you know we're crazy this time of the year..."

"You don't know what you're missing! They're sooo hot, and they look like twins."

Wow, two for the price of one.

She raises her newly filled glass of champagne, her head wobbling like a broken pendulum: "To two smart, intelligent women who know what they want and are going for it!"

True...by completely different tactics, but nevertheless, very true.

Cathy snuggles into her chair. "Sooooo, what do you want to talk about? Oooh, we could watch a movie together! Do you like scary movies?"

"How about going over the details for the event?" I ask.

She makes a face.

"Or we could talk about your trip to Santa Barbara? Tell me. Tell me," she begs.

Sadness surges through my body.

"It was fine," I mutter, not wanting to involve her in my personal life.

Even though our relationship wasn't romantic, it feels like Peter broke my heart. I still haven't spoken with him since. I haven't answered his phone calls, returned any texts, or answered any emails, especially the one he sent me shortly after that weekend.

I look at her with a half smile. "I need to get some work done." I grab my laptop, pulling up Outlook. After five weeks, Peter's message still sits in my inbox. I can't seem to discard it or file it away. I keep waiting to reread it, but now I realize I may never be ready...I open the email.

> Eve, I don't know why you left me just when I needed you the most.

I notice Cathy trying to sneak a peek, so I turn the screen, shielding it from her nosy eyes, and start reading again.

> Eve, I don't know why you left me just when I needed you the most. I was so upset when you left the brunch without discussing things with me. I guess my family and the conclusions they have jumped to over the years must have hurt your feelings. I want to get one thing completely straight—I never told them you were my fiancé, but they kept pushing me to get married and it just seemed easier to let them assume than to disappoint them. After you left, I explained to them that we are not a couple nor are we business partners. I was hoping you could have cleared this matter up, not me. Perhaps it was for the best. I think for the first time in my life, my family may actually care. My mother told me that I need to go to family counseling. She may be right, but before I do, I need to talk to you.

Is he claiming it's my fault he's lied to his family all these years?

I didn't tell you about my family and my apartment because I just want people to like me for me, not because I am a Norton. You seemed to be different, and the money wasn't important to you. I didn't want to ruin things by telling you and anyway, the right time never came up.

Over ten years the *right* time *never* came up?

The message ends with: *"I just want things to be the way they used to be."*

What *used* to be was all a lie and I won't go back to it, and I can't believe he would propose to. I write back saying that once he gets the help he needs, I will be happy to discuss it with him. As for me, I am more confused than ever. I was sure he was gay or at least asexual, which made me feel safe around him. Like big-brother safe. Now I'm second-guessing every aspect of our relationship.

There is a long pause as I sit and contemplate Peter: his motives, his actions and reactions. But in actuality, I shouldn't just blame Peter. Maybe I was too closed off and he didn't feel comfortable telling me the truth. But still, I was completely open about my life with him; how could he not do the same?

A flight attendant interrupts to ask us for our dinner preferences. I choose the vegetarian plate; Cathy goes right for the steak. Scarfing away, Cathy, who has been glued to the latest installment of *Soap Opera Digest*, asks, "So, are you dating anyone?"

I utter an elusive, "Kind of."

"Oh, tell me more!" Cathy claps.

I have a vision of myself as a celebrity and Cathy snitching to the tabloids the entire scoop on me, like Marla's bellman.

"There is this one guy, but..."

"Duh," Cathy says, rolling her eyes, gnawing on a buttered roll. "Pretty people always have dates."

Um, should I say thank you?

Before I have the chance to open my mouth, Cathy pulls out her headphones and turns on her personal entertainment center, signaling she doesn't want to be bothered anymore.

Apparently I'm no longer interesting.

That's okay. What she doesn't know is that Sebastian and I have spent hours on the phone. The man I have grown to care about isn't even close to the person that the media and Marla have made him out to be. As it turns out, his publicist thought it would be "cool" for him to have a playboy reputation, when in fact Sebastian is quite noble, compassionate, and deep. I was surprised to find out he was a soldier for East Germany before the wall came down. He lost both his brother and his best friend to what is now referred to as *friendly fire.* His family and most others still live with pain and suffering caused by those horrific events. It's no wonder he has such little tolerance for injustice.

After reassuring me he was not the same SVA interested in the Buddhist retreat, he said he would get back to me.

He called back a couple days later to inform me that the initials SVA do not belong to a man, but to a woman by the name of Samantha Von Andel, a real-estate developer who combs the world for prime properties, then turns them into mega-resort marketing machines. Based on her reputation, she'll stop at nothing to get what she wants.

I didn't hear from Sebastian again until mid-August, and when I did, what he told me sent me soaring. Taking a sip of water, I get tingles just thinking about it.

Cathy, who has remnants of sauce speckling her chin, looks over at me. "Why are you smiling, Eve?"

Please don't ruin my blissful state.

I close my eyes, recalling the night he phoned to tell me that Ms. Von Andel was a shrewd woman who was indifferent to the monks. And from the tone of his voice I could tell this didn't sit well with him. It so happens, years ago, Sebastian spent a month at the same camp, learning and appreciating the ways of the monks. Drawing upon their teachings, he kept his cool when he met with SVA, offering a proposal. It took hours, days, and weeks of negotiations, but she finally backed out of the deal, and Sebastian purchased the land for the monks. They will never have to worry about their peaceful oasis falling into the wrong hands again.

Needless to say, my feelings for a certain Von Alt have changed considerably, and I hope to see him during this trip. All those nights I listened to his romantic voice, I imagined the two of us walking hand in hand down a crowded cobblestone street, snowflakes falling, as if we're in a perfect little snow globe. Just thinking of our reunion is overwhelming. But because he knows how hard I've been working on these events, he's made it clear he doesn't want to get in the way, so we haven't made any plans. But I can hope...

After finishing up my to-do list and eating a little breakfast, we land in Berlin. It's misty and the streets are cluttered with autumn leaves. Much to my chagrin, Cathy insists on seeing the nightclub venue as soon as we drop our bags off at the hotel. And I mean, we literally drop the bags off with the doorman and head off. No rest for me.

Before we left Los Angeles, I had told Cathy multiple times that the building is a warehouse, with damage on the façade from years of Germany's strife. But as we pull up, she loses it nonetheless. "I have worked so hard to get where I am and now you are trying to get me fired!"

"Calm down, Cathy."

"Calm down?! Calm down?!" Her arms flail all over the place as we step out of the car. "Look at this place. It's a dump! We can't have our event here! This is a fucking mess!" She starts swinging and pointing her finger at me. "I'm going to lose my job and it's all your fault!"

I really don't like the finger thing.

Cathy begins to cry hysterically.

"Cathy, please...please calm down and let me explain." I sit her down in the car, facing the building. "Like I told you, the exterior of the building is going to be awash with moving gobo lights. It'll have a pattern, so you won't be able to see the defects that you see now. None, I promise."

I hand her a tissue to wipe her eyes. "Please come with me inside and take a look."

Reluctantly she gets up, and we walk inside to meet Wolf. He greets us with a huge smile. "Please come in and sit down for a minute," he says, escorting us through the lobby to the lounge.

Usually, I have time to assess a location before my client gets to see it, but today is a different story. When I was here for the site inspection, I noticed that there was gum stuck all over the carpet and that the walls were filthy; clearly, the place had not been cleaned in years. Unfortunately, this time around it's worse; the room not only hasn't been cleaned, but now there is an added stench of stale cigarettes and urine.

Cathy doesn't waste a minute. She points at both Wolf and me, screaming, "I hate you, Eve, and you, dog boy!" She runs away, screaming an "f" word here and an "s" word there and a whole lot of words in between. I try to stop her, but she jumps in the car and takes off.

I spin around. "Wolf, what happened? You promised me the club would be sparkling by the time we arrived. This is far from sparkling! I am so incredibly disappointed."

"I'm sorry, Eve. I have no excuses other than we have been very busy." He scratches his head. "I promise you, though, we will have this place like new in two days."

"I don't want it smelling like urine or fresh paint, Wolf." I turn around and take a good look at the wood veneer in the demo room. "You'll have all this polished as well, right?"

"Yes, and we will have the bathrooms scrubbed, the carpet torn out and replaced, and the filters cleaned. Everything will be great, I promise."

"I'm sorry, but your promises don't mean much to me right now. I need to see some big changes or heads will roll." Heading toward the door, I throw a menacing "I'll be back tomorrow" over my shoulder.

I walk back to the hotel, convinced that taking on this event on-site was far too ambitious. Maybe all of it was, but right now, this event is in the danger zone of becoming one of my worst events ever. I need additional recruits. I need help. I need Blaine. I start running toward the hotel as soft raindrops pelt my eyes, texting him: *"Need ur help. Get here ASAP."*

Even though I know he's scrambling, he writes back a simple *"ok."*

As I walk back into the hotel, damp and frizzy, a short bald man with a blue suit and blue leather shoes walks up to me and extends his hand. "Good afternoon, Ms. Walker. I am Mister Gratzreicht, the general manager of the hotel. Welcome. My staff and I are here to make certain that you and your clients are well taken care of. Please let me know if there is anything you need."

How does he know what I look like?

"Thank you very much," I say, shaking his hand. "I appreciate it."

"Yes, of course. The pleasure is all ours," he replies, beckoning a young man holding my luggage. "Please follow the bellman to your room. I hope everything is to your liking."

I don't need to check in? Okay...

The bellman escorts me to the top floor, opens the door to a small entryway, then a few feet farther stops in front of a set of doors marked with *Präsidentensuite*.

This can only mean one thing: I am being escorted into the Presidential suite.

"Here we are, Ms. Walker."

I would have never dreamt of requesting the Presidential suite, but I have a good idea who did. I gaze around, feeling all tingly from my head to my toes.

When I travel for on-site inspections or familiarization trips, the hotels often arrange for me to stay in a suite. It's smart on their part. They want the group business that I can bring them. But never have I stayed in one as grand as this. I feel like the orphan girl in *The Little Princess*.

But as spectacular as this is, I do have a rule. When on-site working, it simply isn't appropriate to stay in a room nicer than your client's.

My eyes absorb the word on the door as I stand paralyzed, reading it over and over again. Okay, maybe just this one time... I'm not paying for it nor is my client. In fact, they don't have to pay for my room at all, and I do feel oh so special...

The bellman says, "Mr. Von Alt has asked us to bring a meal to your room every few hours. He wants to make sure you eat."

Blushing, I giggle, "Of course he does."

He points at a large crystal bowl on top of an antique credenza in the entry; it's filled with apples, oranges, and bananas. "You can see there is plenty of fruit. The hotel wants to make sure you're as comfortable as possible. Would you like a tour of the suite?"

"Yes, please," I say, placing my satchel on the baroque-style gold-leaf bench in the entry.

The hallway to one of the guest rooms of this huge suite has high cherrywood ceilings. The walls are desert beige, which lightens up the windowless corridor. As I follow behind, I recognize a Goya, a Rembrandt, and a Rubens projected on the walls.

The bellman explains, "We display artwork depending on the guest preference."

Very cool.

"Will you change it to Impressionists for me?" I tease.

"Yes, madam," he says with a smile and a slight bow of his head.

"I'm kidding, you don't need to change it for me."

He smiles and bows again, making me question if he gets my American humor.

The chandelier is a large glass plate full of multisized blown-glass sculptures, mainly in corals, blues, and browns, with a sprinkling of asphalt black. An unusual color combination, but it works from where I'm standing.

"Over here," the young man says, directing me into the dining room. "This antique dining set has traveled to some of the most famous people in some of the most famous houses around the world. It is now back home in Germany where it, um, how do you say, or-ig-inates."

I stand, admiring the magnificent piece of craftsmanship, most likely designed and built for royalty. The table and twelve chairs are of black lacquer embellished with marquetry of tortoiseshell, mother-of-pearl, brass, and copper, placed atop a scarlet Persian rug. The icing on the cake on a nearby wall—an original O'Keeffe.

I'm struck by how well they have mixed the contemporary work with all these fabulous antiques. It's simply stunning.

He leads me through a short hallway to another room. "There are two additional guest bedrooms should you require them. You may also close them off if you like."

"One bedroom will be enough, thank you."

He shuts the door behind me. "They are part of the suite, so should you need them, they are yours." He heads back to the entry and down another hall. "And last but not least we have the master suite," he says, turning the corner. Before I'm even inside the room, my eyes fixate on the mahogany bed with its high, beveled headboard and canopy upholstered in rich cream linens. This bed is the closest thing I can imagine to sleeping on a cloud. Tearing my eyes away, I notice a writing cabinet and chair edged with gold leaf and silver.

"The entertainment center is located behind the large painting on this wall." He grabs a remote, pushes the button, and away goes the painting, replaced with a large flat-screen television.

Entertainment center. Entertainment!...Oh my goodness, *the event*! I'm not here on vacation; I'm here to work! Why does that all of a sudden not feel so fun? I need to contact Cathy NOW!

"This is wonderful," I say, quickly escorting him back to the front door. "Thank you." I hand him a gratuity with one hand and shove him out the door with the other.

"If there is anything we can do to make your stay..." comes from the other side of the door.

In a room like this, Sebastian and I could...well...I need to make sure work is my first priority. I'll call Sebastian later.

I dial Cathy's room.

From her raspy voice, I guess she's been sleeping.

"Hi, Cathy, it's Eve. I want to assure you all will be perfect for your party. I spoke with Wolf, and he understands the importance of the event and how you need to showcase your company to your clients. In fact, I'm personally overseeing it. I promise you will shine like the star you are."

"Thank you, Eve. Sorry for the breakdown earlier. I may have overreacted. I have faith in you. I mean Miles said you were a miracle worker. I would offer to help..."

Uh-huh.

"But I just had a mani-pedi and well, you know. Hey, before I forget," she says, completely switching topics, "the bellman told me that there is a really great museum nearby. Do you wanna go with me?"

Does she think we're on vacation, too?

"Wish I could, but you go and have a good time. I'll see you tomorrow morning."

I take a good look around the suite, walking from room to room. Who sat in this chair? Who ate at that table? Who had sex in the bathtub? Or on that table? I wonder who was the last person to stay here—a certain rock star maybe or a soccer player or a prince? Letting my mind wander to all the escapades that must have occurred here, I shudder.

And yet I want to speak to Sebastian. I grab my phone, listening as his phone rings.

"Eve! You're here! I've been waiting to hear your voice all day."

I love his sexy voice. I love his enthusiasm. I love the thought of all the things we could do in this room...

"Sebastian," I breathe, "thank you for this fabulous suite. I'm almost speechless. Since you insist on having meals delivered to the room, will you fly over and have dinner with me?"

"Darling, I would love to, but Madrid needs me right now. This media deal is moving slower than we expected. Would you be upset if I delay our reunion by a couple of days?"

In the background I can hear a mélange of television shows running. He must be in some kind of a production facility.

"Not a problem," I say, feeling a trace of disappointment. "I have a production schedule to work out myself."

"*Auf wiedersehen, meine Schatzi.*"

I hang up the phone. Before I have the chance to Google what "Schatzi" means, the doorbell rings. It's the young bellman, looking concerned.

"I'm so sorry to disturb you, Ms. Walker. There is an upset gentleman downstairs who is demanding to see you."

"What's his name?" I'm sure no one else is supposed to arrive today.

His eyes blinking profusely, the young man replies, "Mister Howard. His name is Mr. Chuck Howard."

What? The CEO of 1-2-1 TV is here? Today?! How can that be? He isn't supposed to arrive for another two days!

"Please tell him that I will be down in just a moment."

I scurry about, grabbing the event file and slipping on my shoes, then rush to the elevator, where I meet up with the bellman. "I guess you won't have to tell him anything after all."

"Thank you." He blinks, relieved.

On the way down I have a few seconds to gather my thoughts. Mr. Howard runs a successful television software business. He likes to think of himself as one of the big players in town, when in reality he has a medium-size company that does well. He is short with a round belly. The patches of white hair on each side of his head, coupled with his wispy comb-over, make his unusually large ears look even bigger. He resembles a cartoon character, a goofball who likes to throw his weight around. And now he's *here*!

As we disembark the elevator, Mr. Howard lasers in on me.

"There she is." He strides over with one of the front-desk representatives who clearly looks disturbed.

"May I have a word with my client alone for a moment?" I ask, taking Chuck by the arm to walk a few steps away from the desk.

"Eve, the people at this hotel have no idea who I am and what I'm doing here."

That's because they have no idea who you are and what you are doing here, TODAY.

"Chuck, it's nice to see you again. Why don't we take a seat over here in the lobby? May I get you something to drink?"

"No, thanks," he says with a flick of his hand as we sit.

"In no way is your arrival a problem. We didn't know it would be today. Did you decide—"

"I contacted Cathy a couple days ago from London to tell her I would be in Berlin early. Didn't she tell you? And where is she?"

"No, she didn't pass that information on, but she has a lot on her plate right now." I turn my head away from him long enough to roll my eyes. Turning back, I smile sweetly. "How about we get you to your room so you can settle in?"

"But the front desk told me there is someone occupying the Presidential suite. Can you believe how disorganized this place is?"

No, but I can believe how disorganized a certain someone from your staff can be.

"Why don't you have a cup of coffee and a snack in the restaurant, and I will see what I can do, okay? I'm sure we can work this out."

He sighs. "Alright, Eve. You'll come and get me?"

"Of course, Chuck. Everything will be fine. I'll be right back."

I rise, smile at him as if nothing is wrong, and head over to the front desk posthaste.

The young woman behind the counter greets me. "Hello, Ms. Walker, how may I assist you?"

I place my forearms on the counter, leaning in to whisper. "I am going to need to switch my room for another and have Mr. Howard occupy the Presidential suite for the duration of our stay."

"I'm sorry, Ms. Walker. That's impossible."

"Impossible?"

"Yes, ma'am," she says, now leaning toward me. "Mr. Von Alt has specific instructions to keep you in this suite throughout your stay. We are prohibited from moving you."

"May I speak with Mr. Gratzreicht, please?"

"One moment please," she says, picking up the phone. She speaks fast and fluently in her native tongue, so I only understand every fourth word. She hangs up and smiles. "Mr. Gratzreicht will be down shortly."

I pace the lobby. Pacing is my go-to when I have to think fast. Having multiple plans is a must, but sometimes I have to come up with them on the fly. Like right now. As I turn to pace back toward the front desk, I almost collide with Mr. Gratzreicht.

"Ms. Walker. You wanted to see me? What may I help you with?"

I'm still pacing, and he follows along. "Mr. Gratzreicht, I understand that you have a firm policy when it comes to Mr. Von Alt's request that I stay in the Presidential suite."

"Yes, madam, we take this very seriously."

That's what I'm afraid of . . .

"Of course you do, which is why I need your help."

He stands to attention, as if he has just been enlisted in the armed forces. "I am here to help you. What can I do, Ms. Walker?"

"Mr. Howard, the CEO of 1-2-1 TV, has arrived earlier than expected. I realize you didn't have the Presidential suite set aside for him and we had not asked you to . . . but I would very much like to give him the suite as a goodwill gesture. Do . . . you . . . understand?"

He grits his teeth. He understands far too well.

"Ms. Walker, I am very sorry, but we are under very stringent orders from Mr. Von Alt, and he's a very important client of ours."

"I appreciate your loyalty and your business ethics, but Mr. Gratzreicht, is there any compromise we can make?"

We continue pacing together.

I stop when the bright light inside my head switches on. "You know, there are two separate guest rooms attached to the suite that can be blocked off from the main area. If I take one of them, I am technically still in the suite, right?"

His pace picks up to a march. Jaw set, he finally stops and faces me.

"Is this what you really want, Ms. Walker? You know this could mean my job? This is a real predicament that you are placing me in."

"Please, Mr. Gratzreicht. This could mean my job as well."

There's a pregnant pause. He bites his lip, stomps his foot, and shakes my hand.

"Done!" he says boldly. "We will have your bags moved immediately and Mr. Howard's moved up. Please give us ten minutes."

I can't help but lean down and kiss him on both cheeks. "Thank you, Mr. Gratzreicht, thank you!"

I run into the café and give Chuck the news. He's eager to get settled in his room, but because we need to wait, I join him for a drink.

"Do we have time to see the venue tonight, Eve?"

"Actually, the club is doing some maintenance repairs this evening and tomorrow, so it's best we stay away for a couple days."

I look up to see Cathy walking in from outside. She doesn't recognize the back of Chuck's head as she beelines straight toward me.

"Eve, can you believe the museum was full of pictures of *dead* people? It was so awful and depressing. It made me cry and I had to leave."

"Well, most people who visit the places that depict the Holocaust tend to feel that way. It was a horrific part of history." I point to Chuck as she walks up.

"Chuck!" She cringes as if she forgot something.

"We've been having a nice chat," I say. "All is set up for his room, which he's about to head off to now."

"Yes," he says, winking at me as his short legs rise from the chair. He faces Cathy. "I'd like to see you in my suite now, please, Cathy."

She squeaks, "Yes, sir." She looks over at me with a classic "oh shit" look and mouths, "I'm sorry." I can't help chuckling as I watch them leave, looking like a young daughter sulking behind her father.

I glance at the time. I still need to unpack, update my to-do list, and most importantly get some rest. Since I average four to five hours of sleep a night, less when I'm on-site, I steal all the rest I can get before it all begins. Strategically, I travel with earplugs—the wax variety. They are really my only defense against partygoers, street noise, or the occasional sex hounds who bang the headboard in the next room. Hours later and scribbling the last note on the roster, earplugs are in and I'm out for the night.

CHAPTER THIRTEEN

I WAKE UP THE next morning feeling refreshed. Despite a scream I thought I heard in the middle of the night, I slept well.

My doorbell rings. "Who is it?" I ask before opening the door. A cheerful aging butler with a breakfast tray enters and hands me a newspaper.

Like I have time to read it.

"*Guten morgen,* Ms. Walker." Placing the tray on the desk, he hands me a note. "Mr. Gratzreicht would very much like to see you first thing this morning."

"Thank you."

"Also, both Mr. Howard and Ms. William-Smith would like to have a word, and Mr. Von Alt requests that you phone him as soon as possible."

"What's going on?" I ask, grabbing a bran muffin.

He opens the door and looks back at me. "There was a bit of an altercation last night," he says, swallowing what looks like a smile. "I don't know the details."

The door closes behind him. *An altercation?*

I phone Cathy's room, but she doesn't answer. There's no way she would be up and out this early in the morning. Something's up.

Who to call next? Mr. Gratzreicht or Sebastian? It's a coin toss. I *actually* need to toss a coin. Grabbing one out of my purse, I decide heads for Mr. G and tails for Mr. V. The coin goes straight into the air, lands on top of the bed, and then falls behind the headboard. I'm about to get down on my hands and knees when the phone rings. Well, that settles it. It's Mr. Gratzreicht.

"Guten morgen, Ms. Walker." I envision his cheeks taking on the look of a blowfish from the way he's breathing on the other end. "I told you I didn't think it was a good idea to move your room. Now I must insist that you come down here immediately and have a word with me."

"I have no idea what happened, Mr. Gratzreicht, but I will be there momentarily. Do you want to tell me what's going on?"

"I will see you in a few minutes."

He cut the conversation awfully short. What am I walking into here? It feels like this recurring dream I have where I find myself naked in the middle of the Louvre. The doors fling open, and there are thousands of tourists staring at me as if I'm a piece of artwork on display. Needless to say, I'm feeling a bit exposed.

Knowing full well this is a situation that requires my immediate and undivided attention, I dress quickly, dabbing on a touch of lip gloss and sweeping my hair into a ponytail.

Eight minutes later, Mr. Gratzreicht's assistant escorts me into his office. They both have that I-haven't-slept-more-than-two-hours look about them.

He's pacing in his office. Not a good sign.

"Ms. Walker, please take a seat." I look at his puffy red cheeks. In fact, his whole face is red and swollen. He must have high blood pressure.

He finally seats himself in a black leather chair behind his desk. "Obviously you know nothing about last night's incident."

Incident?

"No sir, but I'm quite anxious to hear."

His assistant walks in. "Would either of you like a cup of coffee or tea?"

"Thank you. I'll have tea," I say.

"Coffee for me—make it another triple, please." She returns a minute later with our drinks. She's fast. It must be that German engineering.

"Now that we are alone, I can explain to you why I am going to lose my job."

"Why would you—"

He holds his hand up to stop me.

"Please, Ms. Walker." He takes a good hard look around his office as if it will be the last time he sees it. "At approximately 2400 hours, I received a phone call informing me that Mr. Von Alt was taking the security elevator up to the Presidential suite." He points at me as if he is a member of the Gestapo. "I would think to surprise you!"

Sebastian flew over to surprise me?

I get up from my chair, "But—"

He gestures for me to sit down, "Please, Ms. Walker."

I sit back down again.

"Now, if you were in the room, this would not have been a problem, but when he exited the elevator in the kitchen of the suite and found a naked blonde woman in front of him eating an apple, then it became one."

Naked blonde woman? Naked blonde woman!

And in the kitchen? *What kitchen?*

"I wasn't shown a kitchen in the suite."

"Of course not. It is primarily used by staff. We don't generally show the kitchen facilities to guests. One of the two refrigerators is actually a secured elevator with its own entry from the back of the hotel."

"That's a rather clever idea."

"Thank you. Back to the issue. The blonde woman screamed and threw fruit at Mr. Von Alt and called him a pervert and other profanities."

Ah, the scream I heard last night. Okay.

"Mr. Von Alt tried to calm her down while Mr. Howard apparently was tied up in the master suite. As you can imagine, he and his wife were quite upset."

Hang on a second. Chuck arrived alone.

"There has to be a misunderstanding—Mr. Howard didn't bring his wife, who happens to be brunette."

Both of us take a mental pause. He must be thinking prostitute, but I'm thinking in an altogether different direction. Cathy. It has to be Cathy! When I heard she was promoted, I knew there was more to the story. I knew it! And no wonder Chuck flew in early. This is all making sense now. I'm an idiot for not putting two and two together.

"Mr. Von Alt had me called from bed at half past midnight after he was kicked and shoved out of the suite he is paying for!" He gets up, pacing the room again. "Do you have any idea how angry he was?" His cheeks are ballooning. "He spent an hour screaming and yelling at me. I will not repeat what he said because you are a woman and I am a gentleman, but let me tell you that I have never been insulted or humiliated like that in all of my career."

Hmm, that's not the Sebastian I've come to know.

Seeing Mr. Gratzreicht getting choked up, I reach for a tissue, handing it over. He waves it away, pulling out a handkerchief instead.

"I'm sorry this happened, but—"

His assistant opens the office door. She looks over at her boss wiping his eyes and she too chokes up. "May I get anything else for you?"

All of a sudden the three of us hear running footsteps in the hallway. A desperate-looking Cathy appears, dressed in a night-shirt, her hair a tangled mess, which as I understand is a sin where she comes from.

"Eve," she cries, pushing the assistant out of her way and crouching down beside me, "what has this man told you?"

"Everything Cathy, he has told me everything."

She takes a seat in the chair beside mine, facing Mr. Gratz-reicht's desk. "I need some time alone with Eve."

Mr. Gratzreicht and his assistant hesitate for a moment and then shuffle out of the room.

Cathy runs her long, fake red nails through her hair. "Okay. I need to explain to you what actually happened."

"Where do you want to start?" I ask, not expecting too much new information.

"Late yesterday afternoon when Mr. Howard asked me to come up to his room, I thought I was in trouble for forgetting to tell you about his early arrival. But noooo"—her voice drops to a whisper—"he asked me if I could help him find someone to entertain him that evening. Well... I wasn't going to do that, so I did what you have always told me to do in that kind of situation."

My lips twitch ever so slightly, "What exactly is that Cathy?"

"I told him that he needed to talk with the bellman and they can arrange female companionship for him. That I am a profes-sional marketing coordinator and not his pimp."

She may have more chutzpah than I give her credit for.

"So, a little after midnight I got a phone call from him saying that he was in some kind of trouble with the woman he had in his room. Her name is Heidi. She had tied him up in the bedroom and robbed him. I guess she worked up an appetite because she was in the kitchen when your Sebastian arrived."

"If Mr. Howard was tied up, how was he able to phone your room?"

"I guess he freed one of his arms?"

He's stronger than he looks.

"That's when he heard Heidi scream. He didn't want to contact the front desk because of the embarrassment of it all, so he called me. When I arrived, Heidi had nothing but a towel around her and his wallet in her hand. Security took her away."

"So what happened with Sebastian?"

"I have no idea. He was gone before I got to the room."

My cheeks blush. "Does Chuck know about Sebastian?"

"Well, no." She twists her hair into a knot. "I figured he was here for you, and I didn't want to get you in trouble, so I didn't say a word to Chuck." She leans over and pinches me. "Sebastian's kinda romantic, huh?"

"Cathy," I say. "I owe you an apology. I thought that you were the naked blonde in the room."

"Me? Oh gross, no! Do you really think I'd...with *Chuck*?"

I can't help but laugh at the horrified look on her face. "You're right, I don't know what I was thinking. Sorry, Cathy."

I get up and we hug.

She starts out the door. "I better go get dressed and put some makeup on before I scare the other guests, plus I need to meet with Chuck later. He says he has an idea for the party."

"Speaking of the man of the hour, how do you want to handle this situation?"

"Well, my feeling is Chuck got himself into this mess, so I think he needs to deal with it on his own without any help from us."

Brilliant idea! Cathy is steadily climbing on the scale of likability in my book.

"See ya," she says, tossing her hair over her shoulder, passing Mr. Gratzreicht as he zips back in the room.

I start walking out the door myself.

"But Ms. Walker, we're not done."

"Yes, but we both have jobs to do, and I have to get back to mine and you have to get back to yours. Please don't worry. I will speak with Sebastian. Rest assured, you will still be running this hotel when we leave in a few days."

I reach for his hand to shake it, but instead he takes my hand and kisses the back of it.

Cleaning up unexpected affairs, pun 100 percent intended, is a skill I am still working on. "I apologize for my client's behavior. You may deal directly with him regarding it. Your job and the jobs of all others involved are intact. From this point on, it will no longer be discussed. I ask you to be discreet. Do I have your word?"

He straightens his tie and stands tall. "And exactly what matter are you talking about, Ms. Walker?"

"Precisely!"

After saying a prayer begging for no more catastrophes, I tackle the rest of my meeting-filled morning. First up is a discussion with the hotel's front-desk manager about our room block. We have one hundred rooms set aside for this event. I need to make sure that each is cleaned to our satisfaction, not just to the hotel's guidelines. I am a stickler about cleanliness. Especially when it comes to the air we breathe. I believe that all rooms should have better than adequate air quality; I've been in too many hotel rooms over the years where gunk hangs down from the ventilation systems. It's maddening! And I won't stand for it. Take any hotel's checklist and multiply it by ten, then you'll have mine.

Next I meet with the catering manager. We ask that a gift of locally made German chocolates and a plate of fresh fruit be delivered to each room before our guests arrive. It's imperative I check the gifts, confirm arrivals, and go over the timing of every delivery.

Finally, my last meeting of the morning is with the representative of the transportation company and the bell captain. We have four mini-coaches arranged to pick up our attendees. I want to confirm that the coaches each have beverages on board, and that the four drivers have the same directions and are all equipped with GPS. The drivers need to look presentable in business suits, the coaches should be clean, and each driver must have the appropriate signage reading 1-2-1 TV.

These business travelers travel light, so they most likely won't need the bell staff's assistance. As long as we have a few staff, we should be covered.

Glancing at my phone, I realize it's almost lunchtime. I better call Sebastian. I was going to call him after my meeting with Mr. Gratzreicht, but frankly I thought it might be best to give him a little extra time to recover from last night's encounters.

Before I get past the first three digits, I hear—

"Heyyyyyy girrrlll!"

As much as it makes me cringe to hear it, I'd know that Peter impersonation anywhere. I turn around to see Miles's beautiful smile lighting up the entire lobby, followed by his bright aqua jeans, and his red patent-leather loafers.

Miles wraps his arms around me. Over his shoulder I see Blaine, twenty steps behind, with two large boxes he's trying to balance on top of his carry-on. I'm sure he's wearing the same plaid shirt and jeans I saw him in the last time we were in the office together. Having him here suddenly gives me some peace of mind.

"I am so happy you're both here! Did anyone else catch the early flight?"

"It's just us, so let's get cheetah-chic," Miles says, beaming.

Blaine reaches out and shakes my hand firmly. Kind of like a financial advisor who is just getting to know you would.

"Here are your keys. Why don't you drop your bags off and get refreshed. Shall we meet down here at the café in a half hour?"

"A half dash it is, sister." Miles whips his body around and heads to the elevators.

"Okay, Miles. Should I expect you to continue channeling Peter over the next few days or will this end soon?"

Miles just snaps his fingers, ignoring me.

Blaine, in another unlikely moment, mimics Miles, snapping his fingers and tossing his head back. "See ya round sis-ta."

Doesn't quite work for him, I'm afraid.

Forty-five minutes later, the three of us are sipping drinks in the hotel's café. The men look exhausted, so I quickly fill them in on last night's shenanigans. Looking dazed and confused, neither Miles nor Blaine reacts. Perhaps it's a little too much to hit them with after they just flew ten hours.

Miles hasn't even flinched. Strange.

"Any questions?"

"Not a one," Miles answers. "Seems like the norm."

Huh?

"I mean, he's Chuck." Miles rolls his eyes. "Need I say more?"

Blaine raises a finger. "Where were you when all this happened?"

"I was in my room sleeping. Where else would I be?"

Both guys look around the room as if their answer is just going to fall from the ceiling.

"Any other questions or shall we move on?"

A unanimous "let's move on" issues from their mouths.

"We need a strategy since we only have a few hours until the other flights land, and of course, tomorrow night is the event."

"Give it to us, girl," blurts Blaine.

Blaine imitating Miles imitating Peter is just too much. I shoot him a look that immediately shuts him down.

"Here's a list of items that we need to get done in the next few hours: Blaine, call Olga, the head housekeeper, and inspect each room with her. The rooms are generally clean, but we have higher standards. Take this checklist. You need to make sure she has her staff ready to clean right behind you.

Miles, please check in with Cathy to see if she needs any help with welcome letters, add-on meetings, preparing credentials, assembling gift bags, etcetera..."

Miles shoots me a forced smile.

"What's wrong?" I have to ask.

"Nothing..." he says covering. "I'm just so happy to be here. Put me to work or leave me forever."

Men certainly are a different breed.

"I am heading over to the club to check on Wolf. Each of our cell phones has a walkie-talkie. Let's use these to stay in touch."

Blaine breaks into a megawatt grin. "Should we test them?"

"No need," I respond. "They've already been tested." Blaine gives me a look that makes me feel like I dashed all his hopes and dreams. "But, we will be using them a lot starting in just a few minutes."

His face lights up like Christmas Day. "Oh good!"

"Let's plan on meeting for dinner in my room about, oh...1930 hours."

"Pajama party!" Miles whispers with a wink. Everyone is overly tired and turning giddy.

Why is it that when he talks softly, Tyrese comes to mind?

"Sorry, no pj's. Please come dressed—you never know who may drop in or when we may have to head out."

"You mean we aren't going to be jumpin' on the bed and eating popcorn..." Miles teases.

"And...and..." Blaine can't seem to find the words to follow. "And...and...watch old episodes of *The Big Bang Theory?*"

This time I give them the I-mean-business glare. It's not that I don't want to have fun, but...

"I'll order up the chow," Blaine pipes.

Miles stands, clicks his loafers together, and salutes me. "And I'll make certain that everything stays calm on the home front, *el capitán*."

We are in Germany, not Spain.

Blaine stands to attention as well, saluting just like his new role model. "Ay, ay, *el capitán*. You can count on us—we're L.A. chic dogs."

And on that note I'm now positive it's a good thing to keep Blaine separated from Miles for a while.

I jump in a waiting car where the driver whisks me off to the club. I have high hopes for the space and the changes that Wolf promised to make...

"Eve! Eve! Don't leave! Let me explain!" Wolf sprints after me as flames shoot from my mouth.

What am I going to do? We can't use this dive! It's still a complete wreck! I feel ill realizing how disastrous this could actually be.

Wolf stops to catch his breath. "Eve, I forgot we had an event scheduled for last night. I have twenty guys coming in to help today within the hour. Look"—he points around the room—"the painting has already been done and we are going to air the place out all night."

"What do you want me to say, Wolf? That I feel comfortable with this situation? Because I don't! This place has to resemble the hottest club from the sixties that you have ever seen in less than a day."

"I know my promises don't mean anything to you, but you will see. I will be here all night with my team and will personally clean each room down on my knees if I have to."

I consider sending our team over, but I know that we have other details to handle at this point.

After reviewing the cleaning that has to be completed by morning, location of the catering stations, boxes of supplies, indoor and outdoor lighting, staging, audiovisual, reception area, gift bag station, staff and their responsibilities, among other details, I still don't feel very secure about the venue. But as we finish testing the outdoor lighting, I see with colossal relief all twenty men arrive ready to get to work. I head back to the hotel with the tiniest tinge of hope restored.

My phone reads 2130 hours; I'm now late for our staff meeting.

I open the door to my room and discover three silk-pajama-clad tricksters throwing my lace underwear at me. *So much for coming dressed.* Miles, who is kneeling on the bed, holds up a sexy black bra to his chest and places the G-string on his lap. "Is this the one you're wearing tomorrow night? Because it's my personal favorite."

"What do you think you're doing?"

Blaine blushes and points at Miles and Cathy. "It was their idea."

I notice that Blaine is wearing just a large pajama shirt over a plain white T-shirt and a pair of boxers, his skinny white legs jutting out like toothpicks. He must have borrowed the top from Miles. I feel a real bromance growing between the two of them.

"I have no doubt."

"Hope you're hungry!" Cathy shouts as she runs up to give me a hug.

Are we bonding over my lingerie?

Blaine can hardly meet my eyes in embarrassment. "Do you want help picking up your personals?"

"Thanks, Blaine, I've got it and don't worry. I know you aren't the instigator here."

I look over at Cathy as her face morphs from all smiles and giggles to one of concern. "So how is the club? Everything on schedule?"

Okay, I'm going to fib just a little here. It's for the sake of her sanity; I certainly don't want her to come unglued again. "I think you're going to be very pleased. It's all coming together as planned. All we need to do is move our production in tomorrow morning. In fact, let me change into my pajamas and we will go over the schedule."

I head into the bathroom, continuing to talk. "Cathy, how is the group? Did they have a nice trip here today?"

"Well," she says, standing outside the bathroom door, shouting as if I'm getting dressed down the hall, "the plane had some mechanical problems and had to land in New York. They've since changed planes. Everyone's fine but they aren't getting in until one o'clock in the morning. Blaine offered to stay up and meet the group."

I open the door and come out in my nightshirt and socks. "Okay, not the best of situations, but they're on their way."

I glance over at Blaine working away on his laptop. "The rooms are all spotless and ready to go. Room service is staying on late to deliver the welcome gifts, and I have requested additional registration and bell staff for the 1:30 a.m. arrivals."

Miles jumps in with his news: "I have updated the transportation company, and the gift bags are assembled. I also updated the contact list and sent it out to everyone with local numbers. Chuck was so busy with work today that he never left his room."

"Yeah, well, that's what I'm worried about," I whisper, since he has the room right next door. We laugh gleefully. "At least the master is on the other side of the suite."

Cathy is sitting next to Blaine at the top of the bed; she and I exchange knowing glances. I grab a piece of chicken off the worked-over serving cart and sit on the chair at the desk, my legs curled sideways.

"Any updates, Cathy?"

"After Chuck and I finished composing the welcome letter this afternoon, I followed behind Blaine and placed them in the guest rooms myself, along with tie-dyed T-shirts for everyone!"

Miles looks troubled. "I thought they nixed those hideous things. I can tell you right now, I'm not wearing one!"

"No worries, Miles," Cathy says, picking up a few large shopping bags. "Chuck asked me to make certain all of the staff are dressed very mod-like, so I went shopping today and had so much fun!" While she squeals with delight, the rest of us look at one another blankly.

She pulls out a pair of white patent-leather high-heel boots, a balloon-sleeve, low-cut tie-dyed blouse, and a blue miniskirt. As I'm trying to figure out which piece is more hideous, she hands them to me. "This is for you, Eve—don't you love it?"

"I ... don't ..."

This is NOT a Halloween party!

Happy as a clam, she hands Blaine a pair of red bell-bottoms, an Afro wig, flip-flops, and a tie-dyed T-shirt with a large peace symbol on the front. Blaine, eyes wide, sits with his jaw on the floor, speechless. He shoots me a this-is-not-part-of-my-job-description look.

Last but not least, she tosses Miles a pair of brown bell-bottom cords, a floral print shirt with buttons that begin halfway down, and some fake gold necklaces, which he refuses to catch.

Miles stands up as if to revolt. "The only way I'd be caught dead in these clothes is if I was literally caught dead. Someone would have to kill me and physically put them on my body. Cathy, you got any screws left?"

"Do you want to see my outfit?" Cathy beams, seemingly unaware of the horrified expressions we all share.

"Cathy," I begin, treading lightly, "the vendors, the on-site staff, and the employees have to be recognizable at the party. That is why we agreed beforehand on staff uniforms."

"But Chuck—"

"Chuck will understand. Trust me, you did a great job with all of the outfits, and it's a real shame that we won't be able to wear them—right, guys?"

"Such a shame," Blaine blurts.

"Right," Miles adds.

"Can I still wear my outfit?" Cathy asks.

"Of course you can!" we all reply.

I move on before Cathy can say anything else. Reaching over from the desk, I hand the production schedule to Blaine, who is dabbing his brow sweat with his napkin. I don't blame him. Just the mere thought of wearing bell-bottoms to a corporate event...

Everyone takes a moment to review the schedule.

11:00	Setup begins (Eve and Blaine arrive).
12:00	Miles and Cathy, technical crew and local staff arrive for setup.
16:00	Run-through of streaming.
17:00	Run-through all technical equipment and demos.

"Okay, okay, wait," Cathy says, mouth full of cupcake. "Do I need to be around for the run-through? Because I have a hair appointment at four thirty."

"Oh for heaven's sake, Cathy," Miles spews, "this isn't the fucking prom."

"We'll have plenty of people around," I interrupt. "It shouldn't be a problem."

"See!" Cathy playfully flips off Miles.

"Back to the schedule," I insist. "1800 hours the caterer arrives for setup."

"Speaking of food," Blaine says, picking a few grapes off the room-service cart. "Do we need to bring any food with us for lunch and dinner?"

"Good question, Blaine." I smile. "No, we have the club providing a sandwich spread for the entire crew at lunchtime, and behind the club the caterers have a small tent set up for staff to have dinner."

"I hope it's not German food," Cathy says.

"What does it matter?" Miles scoffs. "You are going to be so hungry by the time it's set up, it could be cow brains and you'd eat it."

Cathy makes a face at him.

"All right," I quip. "Look, I know it's late and everyone has put in a full day, but let's just try and get through the rest of this schedule and then we can hit the sack, okay?"

19:00   Review "Run of Show" with host, DJ, AV
         staff and 1-2-1 TV VPs.
20:00   Review game with all staff, demo managers
         and 1-2-1 TV VPs.

Blaine stands, looking as if he's going to make a speech. "Hey Blaine," I say giving him the cue, "do you want to fill the group in on the game?"

"My pleasure. The idea of the game is to get everyone at the event interested in the 1-2-1 TV software program. At each of the demo stations there will be a different element of the software that will be discussed by a technical team member of the 1-2-1 TV staff. After the guests rotate through and understand how each element of the program works, they get a card stamped.

Once it's filled in, they drop it into the bowl on top of the DJ stand, and toward the end of the evening some real cool prizes are given away."

"Wow! Fun! Can I play?" Cathy asks.

I knew that was coming.

"I'm sorry, Cathy, employees and staff are not eligible to win a prize, only the guests."

She shakes her head. "Low blow, Eve."

Miles covers me. "You do understand that the prizes are an incentive for the guests to play the game, right, Cathy? That's why we asked Eve to come up with it."

Blaine smiles at Cathy. "Remember, you're going to be dancing the night away. You don't need to be playing the game."

20:10   Photographers arrive. Reiterate expectations with photographers. One professional photographer and four Polaroid digital photographers.
20:15   Complete run-through of procedures with registration staff.

Cathy springs from the bed, placing her hand on her tilted hip— her version of a classic model pose. "Should I pose like this for the cameras?"

"Yes!" Blaine says.

"No. Hell no," votes Miles.

I choose to stay out of this one, but I do agree with Miles.

Miles mutters under his breath, "She's not a complete idiot; there are just a few vital parts missing."

Miles doesn't seem his suave, composed self this trip, and judging by the dynamic between he and Cathy, I'm guessing she's the reason. With lack of sleep and stress-filled days, she can get the best of all of us.

20:30   Registration staff, entertainment and bartenders in place, outside gobos on. Event should be ready to go!

20:50   Doors open. Game cards handed to each guest by hippies. Demo managers in place and ready to begin. Polaroid photographers to have stacks of photo frames. Gobos on walls, psychedelic patterns changing colors behind stage. Sixties theme music to be pumped! Lively and welcoming. Go-go dancers in cages and on boxes, dancing. Pro photographer taking random, candid shots of guests and entertainers. Emcee and band to be dancing onstage. Food stations and bars open.

21:05   Emcee to welcome guests, announce the object of the game and prize drawing.

23:00   Emcee to encourage guests to make their way to each of the four demo stations to get their game card stamped and to place completed cards in the large vase on the stage.

Cathy downs another glass of red wine and starts jumping up and down on the bed. It's apparently that time again, when Cathy feels the need to be the center of attention.

"You know," I say, "it's getting late. Why don't we resume this meeting first thing in the morning. Breakfast at the café?"

"Fabu-licious idea, Eve!" Cathy claps her hands in delight.

"That, my dear, is a Miles-ism and you cannot use it," Miles informs her as he and Blaine help her off the bed, only to have her fall flat on her face.

"Oh, are you all right?" I ask.

She cups her hand, waving like a pageant queen who has just had a mishap down the catwalk. She stumbles to get up as Miles pushes past her to get out of the room. Blaine hangs back, escorting Cathy out the door, calling over his shoulder, "I'm going to make sure she gets back to her room, Eve. Don't worry about her."

I'll try not to.

I reorganize the room and call room service to come pick up the serving cart. It's time to rest this weary head of mine.

Oh how good it feels to be in bed! The clean sheets, the dark room, the way the mattress hugs me just right. But just as soon as I get comfy, I realize I still haven't spoken with Sebastian. I better call.

His phone rings and rings—no answer... maybe he's out to a late dinner? I turn off the lights and close my eyes.

It normally takes me awhile to get to sleep when I'm on-site. My mind moves in tortuous circles, thinking about what the client expects and whether I forgot any to-dos. I run the items through my head like an old cash register, ringing them up one by one. It's a good thing I keep a pad and pen next to the bed for moments like these or I would never get any rest.

My brain settles on the unfortunate circumstances surrounding Wolf's empty promises. What if he doesn't come through for us? I better run over there again first thing in the morning. But for the sake of sleeping soundly tonight, I pick up the phone to call.

"HELLLLLOOOOO?" Wolf yells over the loud construction noises in the background.

As a wave of partial relief washes over me, I find myself blaring back, "It's Eve. I couldn't go to sleep without knowing how things are coming along."

"EVE?! I CAN'T HEAR YOU, BUT I THINK IT'S YOU. EVERYTHING IS GOING AS PLANNED. SEE YOU IN THE MORNING."

That's all I needed to hear.

I fall asleep thinking about Sebastian telling me how much he loves me in the middle of a grassy field on top of a mountain overlooking the ocean. He's just about to kiss me...he leans in close...opens his mouth ever so softly...and...BRRRRIIIIIN NNNNGGGG!

I shoot awake to the hotel phone ringing louder than a fire alarm, remnants of the dream clinging to me. Wow, it had seemed so real. I swear I could feel his touch. I refuse to open my eyes, hoping Sebastian will reappear. No luck. And the phone's still ringing.

My tongue is sticking to the roof of my mouth. "Eeeehhhh-Vvvvaheerrrrrre."

"Eve? It's Blaine. We have a problem."

"Blaine? Problem?"

"I'm here at the front desk where the staff is walking our guests to another hotel. What do I do?"

Another hotel? I need to snap out of it...fast!

"Um, okay. First, don't panic. They can't do that because we have a contract, and second, don't let them do a thing until I get down there. Have the guests take a seat in the café, and get the hotel staff to make them as comfortable as possible. I'll be two minutes."

I generally keep some kind of comfortable outfit for emergency situations like this one. I grab the black yoga pants, a basic tee, my Nike Frees, and I'm out the door. But then my body freezes. Better brush my teeth and hair. The last thing I want to do is negotiate with bad breath and bedhead.

I head directly to the restaurant. "Welcome, everyone, to Berlin," I say, trying to sound chipper. "I apologize for the delay with your rooms. I'm sure you're ready for some much anticipated rest. Let me assure everyone, you will not be walked to another hotel. Please allow me a few minutes to sort this out with the hotel staff, and in the meantime, please order anything you like from the menu."

A guy off to the side with a seaweed-green long-sleeve shirt and black slacks shouts back. "How are we supposed to order anything when this place is closed?"

Another man toward the back of the café yells, "I'm tired and I want a bed."

I can't help feeling their frustration, but I have to keep them calm. "I'm hoping if you order a bite to eat, by the time you're done with it we will have answers. I ask you for your cooperation and patience for a few more minutes." As I finish, the café staff arrives to take orders.

Oh good, no one threw anything or screamed at me. I made it through that crisis virtually unscathed. I figure I have thirty minutes max to resolve this minor catastrophe before that happens.

I sprint over to reception. Blaine, his face cupped in his hands, is standing with a gentleman who I'm guessing is the front-desk manager. I walk up. With no time for introductions, I jump right in. "Please tell me you have a very good reason why you are walking our group to another hotel, because if you don't, I will want to see Mr. Gratzreicht here within the next five minutes."

The young man in his twenties looks cocky, and speaks perfect English. "Pardon me, madam, but we are not walking your entire group, merely one-fifth of it. They are late in arriving, and after 2300 hours we have the right to distribute the rooms to FITs. You know, Free Independent Travelers."

Blaine groans. And I would too if I wasn't heating up faster than a thermometer in Buenos Aires. He's making me upset and no front-desk staff should ever encounter an angry meeting planner. Really, they *really* don't want to experience it.

"May I inquire why Mr. Gratzreicht is not here assisting with this matter?"

"Madam, Mr. Gratzreicht is sleeping and does not like to be disturbed in the middle of the night."

I'm like a boiling pot. I'm tired, Blaine's tired, and the rest of the group is in the café falling asleep wherever they can rest their heads. I lean over the desk with a piercing eye. "Am *I* here in the middle of the night? Would *I* rather be sleeping?" He looks at me as if he doesn't know quite what to do. Then I use the voice I can only describe as the deep, dark place where all my anger lives. "Get him here in FIVE MINUTES!"

The color seems to drain from his face as he slowly utters, "Excuse me, please," turns around, and walks through the door behind him.

I don't like getting upset on-site or for that matter ever, but give me a genuine reason and not only will I stand up to the situation and face it, I'll grow a few inches, too!

Five minutes later, Mr. Gratzreicht appears in his pajamas, robe, and slippers, and not too happily. I wouldn't take him for a satin kind of guy, but here he is standing in front of me in royal blue looking like a large, well... round, oversized floor vase.

"Ms. Walker, I have been apprised of the situation, and my staff is working on resolving it. I'm sorry for the inconvenience."

"Mr. Gratzreicht, your staff wants to walk our group, and I will not stand for this. We have a contract and your staff has had our manifest of arrivals with updates. There is no reason this should have happened. Our group is tired and they want to get to their rooms. Now, how can we make this happen pronto?"

"Will you please excuse us for a moment, Ms. Walker?" He takes the manager and pulls him into the back room. A couple of minutes later they return.

"Ms. Walker, I apologize for this mess we have created," Mr. Gratzreicht humbly states. He peers over at his front-desk manager before addressing me again. "Are there any of you that can double up for the night? And then later today we will straighten this matter out."

I sigh and take a deep, exhausted breath. "Cathy can move to my room, and Blaine, would you mind moving in with Miles for the night?"

Blaine is standing next to me in stiff sleepwalker mode. "No problem, I'll move now."

"Call Miles before you move." I watch as he slowly gravitates to the elevator. "Don't fall asleep in there."

"Let's also call Mr. Howard," I suggest. "How many beds are in that suite?"

"Well, including the sofa, another five people could sleep in there." The GM then adds, "I can also move out of my room and another five people can move into my suite."

"That's very generous of you."

By the time the clock rings 3:30 a.m., all the guests are in rooms and, my guess, sleeping.

Just before I head up myself, I turn back to Mr. Gratzreicht. "First thing this morning we will need to meet on how best to rectify the damage. I'll see you at nine o'clock in the conference room."

"Yes, Ms. Walker, and thank you for working with us on this matter."

It remains to be seen if he thinks I am "working with him" when we meet in a few hours, but for now I'm dragging myself to my room and going to bed.

I open the door to find Cathy spread-eagled across the bed, sound asleep, and snoring so loudly that I'm surprised the neighbors aren't complaining. The hotel must have good soundproofing! Grabbing a blanket out of the closet, I decide to sleep in the bathtub. At least I've upgraded from a shower this time.

Between last night's disaster and, let's say, the "rough roar of the seas" coming from the bedroom, I sleep only an hour before the alarm blasts at eight o'clock. Stretching my aching body, I hoist myself out of the bathtub and walk into the room to see if Cathy is awake. Of course she isn't. Lying flat on her stomach, she is still sprawled, with one foot dangling from one side of the bed.

"Cathy," I say as I poke her shoulder, "it's time to wake up."

"Really?" she rasps, rolling over to reveal a pink, sparkly eye mask. "Man, I was so excited about tonight I wasn't able to sleep a wink."

Huh? The woman would have slept through a jackhammer drilling through her room.

She sits up and stretches. "I didn't sleep more than an hour. I kept thinking about my outfit for tonight and which pair of shoes I'm going to wear."

"Well, it's game day and we have a lot to do. We're going to have to push back the staff meeting until ten o'clock. I have a meeting with the general manager about the rooms situation."

She shrugs and yawns, as if she could care less. Ignoring me, she bends over, picking out an outfit from her suitcase. It's a low-cut red rayon shirt. "Do you think this dress will look cute on me?"

Dress?

I need to get ready and out of here—the last thing I need to be doing is playing dress-up with Cathy.

"Do you have a blazer to go over it?"

"Oh, do you think it's too much to wear by itself?"

Anyone would.

"Since you're here on business, you should probably wear a jacket if you have one."

"Good point," she replies.

I get ready in a jiff and fly out the door. I have five minutes before the meeting begins with Mr. Gratzreicht. Thankfully, Blaine is waiting outside the conference room when I walk up.

He lights up. "Good morning! I thought you might need a little moral support this morning." He opens the door, hanging back. "Beauty before brains."

"Excuse me?"

Blaine grins, not moving. "Fine, brains before beauty."

I roll my eyes as we walk in, surprised to find twenty-five or so people sitting around a rather large meeting table. I certainly didn't expect this many people, but it's a good sign the hotel is concerned about the situation. It's time to draw upon the one hour of sleep I've had and the adrenaline running through my veins.

Mr. Gratzreicht, who I spot at the far end of the table, invites us in. *"Guten morgen,* Ms. Walker und Mr. Stone. Please come take a seat near me."

I would feel better near the door, but my body apparently disagrees since it slowly makes its way toward him, smiling along the way, passing people, shaking their hands.

While everyone in the room gets settled, I notice Chuck Howard entering the room. What is he doing here? Another curveball.

I'm much better with a one-on-one meeting; the larger the crowd, the higher the stakes—and nerves. My only defense is a good game face. And by the looks of it, others in the room seem to be feeling the same thing.

Mr. Gratzreicht starts the meeting by introducing Chuck and then myself and Blaine. "We are here to apologize formally for the mistake our hotel made early this morning with your group. Please let me say this is not normally how we operate our group business, and we will have a full investigation on the entire process of what occurred. Meanwhile, we would like to know how we can remedy this situation so you will have complete confidence in us for the rest of your stay. Not to mention for future stays with our hotel brand around the world."

Since Chuck is in the room, I look over at him, assuming he's going to address the question. He shifts uncomfortably, wearing a lifeless stare. "Mr. Gratzreicht," he begins, clearing his throat, "thank you for the apology. I do appreciate it. As for our concerns, I would like Eve to answer your question."

Mr. Howard is a coward.

"Thank you, Mr. Howard." I turn, looking each person in the eye, my throat thick. Blaine grabs my hand under the table and squeezes it. His gesture is just the support I need. With that, I focus on Mr. Gratzreicht. "I thank you, too, for the apology, Mr. Gratzreicht, and for the show of support from your entire team, which is represented here this morning." I look down at my notes; my eyes are so tired that I can't seem to read them.

I can feel everyone's eyes locked on me, waiting for my next move.

"Due to the inconveniences to our entire group having to double, triple, and"—I glance at Chuck—"in a couple cases even more...I think it is only fitting that we are compensated accordingly. I would like to see the following as a consolation for last evening..."

I blink, finally seeing my notes clearly.

"First, a one-night free stay at any of your properties worldwide with no blackout dates for those who had to double up. Second, a two-night stay for those who had to share with multiple people in their rooms, and third, along with a note of apology to each guest, a $100 American Express gift certificate." I pause for a moment to see the dropped jaws around the room. "It also goes without question that we will not be paying for those rooms last night."

Mr. Gratzreicht's head hangs low. He may be on the verge of passing out. "Will you compromise and pay 50 percent of the rooms for last night?"

"I think that's fair," I say, after looking over to Chuck for the "okay" nod.

Mr. Gratzreicht gets up slowly from his chair, comes over and shakes my hand. He whispers in my ear, "You run a tough bargain, lady." I find myself grinning through my annoyance. "If you hadn't asked Mr. Howard to be here, you would have gotten off much lighter." I wink at him and then whisper again, "I had to make an impression."

CHAPTER FOURTEEN

IT'S EVENT DAY. Event day is unlike any other day. It's the day when I have to be at my very best, when all of the hard work comes to fruition. We have to make it look flawless. There are no second chances. It's do or die. It works or it doesn't. I never know what's in store. I'm like a maestro conducting an orchestra, making certain that all of the instruments are playing just perfectly to make a beautiful, harmonious musical masterpiece. And even though today is nothing compared to what's to come in Amsterdam, hopefully, all of the players show up with their instruments tuned and ready to play.

It's eleven in the morning. I kept the staff meeting short, then headed to the venue. Now, making my way through a tunnel that is only halfway erected, I call out, "Hello? *Guten morgen?* Is anyone here?"

Not a peep in response.

I continue through the club, bracing myself. To my elation, the new paint and new carpet look great, the woodwork is nicely polished, and the furniture is clean. My mind turns to Miles. It's cheetah-chic! But where is everyone? This place should be jumping with people setting up for tonight. I walk to the kitchen where a door leads me to a back patio. Here I see Wolf and a crew of twenty carpenters eating.

"Hey guys," I say, walking onto the deck. "How's everyone doing?" A collective grunt fills the air since most of their mouths are full. A guy sitting down with a stuffed sandwich in his hand holds it up in the air. "Hey, *danke,* for the meal. We appreciate it."

"You're all very welcome. *Danke,* for working through the night. Where are we in the process, Wolf?"

Wolf looks over at me, smiling proudly. "Well, we got it all done, and it's ready for setup today."

"Great!" I respond, more relieved than I'm letting on. "We'll get started with setup when the rest of the crew gets here. Thanks again, guys." I high-five a few of the men sitting close.

Ten minutes later Blaine finds me sitting on the floor in the main space just "feeling" it. He hesitates, then interrupts. "Eve, I have the rest of the boxes outside and the prop company is here. Should I let them in?"

From my lotus position, I open my eyes and smile. "Yes, proceed."

Those quiet moments will be the last calm ones I'll have until I get to sleep sometime tomorrow morning. Stillness is the key to thinking more clearly. And in the midst of all this impending chaos, getting a chance to realize my inner peace is more valuable than words can describe. That weekend at boot camp must have really affected me.

Who would have guessed?

Most of the crew is now arriving. Blaine is here with the boxes of extra tie-dyed T-shirts, and Miles and Cathy walk in with the audiovisual crew and prop guys. Things are starting to roll.

Miles struts over and gives me a kiss on the cheek. "I understand that you kicked some major patoo-tay this morning."

My cheeks flush, not from his compliment, but from the reminder of this morning. I'm not a fan of confrontation and that meeting sure felt like one.

"I did what I felt was fair."

Cathy, oblivious to the moment, interjects, "How do you guys like my outfit?"

A few men in the crew ogle, whistle, and clap at her while she struts around the room.

I throw a stop-egging-her-on look their way and the room goes quiet.

So inappropriate! I'll deal with her clothing issue later.

Time to take charge and get everyone working. "Okay! Blaine, you work with the band on the main stage in this room, and if you could oversee the décor, that'd be great." I hand him the outline and the blueprint. "You should have everything and everyone here that you need. Rehearsal is scheduled for 1600 hours. Thanks."

"Miles, I'd like you to supervise the demo station in the lounge and the music for the afternoon. Keep us movin' and groovin'."

Miles extends his arm, giving me a snap and a finger point. "Pop and lock it, baby."

I turn to Cathy, who again looks upset. "What's wrong, Cathy?"

She stomps her foot. "This is my event. I should be ordering people around!"

I can't believe she's serious.

"Of course, it's your event, Cathy. You hired us to make you look good, right?"

"Well, right, but..."

I give her a reassuring hug. "So that's what we're going to do. We're going to make you the star tonight."

She pouts. "Okay..."

"Well, if we're going to do this, then we need your help. Are you in?"

I get back an unenthusiastic shrug.

This is exactly the kind of attitude that can destroy an event. And I don't have time for her to make a scene. I need to get everyone to work, including her since she's here. "Great! Why don't you set up the registration area, the Polaroid backdrop, the gift bag station; and even more important, make sure that everyone has water and eats lunch. That way we'll make sure they don't run out of steam later on."

I head off, looking around. The place is coming together. We're creeping up to rehearsal time, and the Beatles tribute band should be arriving soon. A few hours ago they flew in from London. They should be at the hotel now.

The computers are being unpacked for the demo stations, and all of the demo managers are here from L.A. getting down to business.

The lighting was tested last night, the audiovisual guys are working away on the stage trellis, speaker system, and tunnel entrance.

The furniture and décor are being set up. And as soon as they're through, we will have a cleanup crew come in and finish the job.

An hour later the band members arrive for their sound check wearing jeans and T-shirts. The emcee trails in after them, a cool cat dressed right out of the sixties, sporting a silver silk suit, white shirt, and black tie. His pants are too high by four or so inches. It may not be authentic, but he sure does look the part.

"Wow," I remark, checking him out. "Lee, you look like you're all set for tonight—fabulous costume."

He has a beautiful English accent. "What do you mean, beauty queen? This is brilliantly new. I'm going to change to a jumper for the party."

Jumper? I was told once that means a sweater. I hope that's not what he's talking about.

The setup crew is getting a good feel for the room. I hear one of them say, "Wow, it's quite posh in here, really. Nice digs."

Lee and the band members all jump onstage to test their mics. Lee introduces the band, and they begin to play. And as luck would have it, not five minutes later, all of the power goes out and the room fills with smoke.

Not a good sign.

"What just happened?" I ask, keeping my voice as even as possible.

One of the AV guys runs in. "We blew the entire grid!"

What?!

"Oh no. How do we fix it?"

Lee jumps off the stage, walks over to me, and pats me on the shoulder. "I'm afraid this means no rehearsal, darling. You need to find a generator in a jiff."

"Generator?" Now my voice cracks.

I look to the AV team who all look fried. "Shit!" one of them yells.

Think fast, Eve.

Lee and the band members need to rehearse—there's no question about that. I turn to the bandleader. "Can you do a run-through without your instruments? This performance is too important to not do it at least once."

As they jump back onstage to run through the act, my main focus is on finding a generator. The AV guys are calling, Blaine and Miles are calling, and Wolf has his team on it too.

Unfortunately, it's Friday evening and past five o'clock. I look down at my phone to see Sebastian calling and cringe. There's so much to talk about, but stealing away for even a moment is just impossible right now. I go to place the phone back in my pocket when my thumb accidentally hits the answer button.

Perfect!

"Sebastian," I answer, frantic. "I really want to talk to you, but we have a bit of a situation happening right now. The electricity blew and we desperately need to find a generator."

There's no doubt he can feel the nervous tension coursing through the phone.

"Hi, Eve." His tender voice envelops me. "Can you put your head AV guy on the line with me, please?"

After chatting a few minutes, the guy hands the phone back to me and yells, "We will have power shortly. A large generator is on its way!"

I hold the phone to my ear, stunned. "Sebastian! You found us a generator?"

"It's the least I could do, Schatzi. I'm well aware I've caused some trouble for you this week. We'll talk later, but go do your thing. And good luck."

I feel all warm and fuzzy as I hang up with Sebastian.

Screams of joy resound throughout the rooms. I join in. "I love you, Sebastian Von Alt!"

I stop in my tracks, covering my mouth. Um, where did that come from?

Everyone in the main room stares at me, then breaks into laughter. It's a good, hard laugh we all needed to help us let go of the day's stress.

One of the AV guys in the back of the room shouts, "You can't do better than Von Alt."

I couldn't agree more at this point.

Once again I guess I won't get to talk to Sebastian, but just as soon as this event is over, I will find him, grab him, and give him a great big kiss. And maybe more... we'll see.

A couple hours into the thick of it, the caterers arrive. The food smells wonderfully fresh. I pull up the menu on my laptop since I can't quite remember all of the delicious morsels I chose for the buffet. I do remember I wanted to keep it light since it's a late-night party and guests have most likely eaten dinner already, but we also want them to keep eating if they're going to be drinking.

Barbecued pork short ribs, savory stuffed mushrooms, sirloin tips en brochette, vegetable egg rolls, super-size prawns with cocktail sauce, chicken-curry lettuce wraps, an assortment of pâtés, veggie-and-fresh-fruit platters, and a selection of the chef's pastries.

Miles glances over and winks. "Eve, you're a genius. You have grapes, melons, and strawberry fields forever."

"Very clever, Miles."

Of course, this isn't our menu. The staff menu is set up out back, and we get to it when we can. Ribbon pasta with chicken parmesan, house vegetables, green salad, and a roll. Sounds more like an authentic 1960s menu than the one for our sixties party.

"Do you want to catch a bite now?" Blaine asks, patting my shoulder.

"You and Miles go ahead. I'll hold down the fort."

Blaine looks around as he heads to the back door. "Where did Cathy go?"

One of the crew answers him. "Oh, I saw her leave a couple hours ago."

Miles stops in his tracks. "*What?* What did you just say? She left a couple hours ago?"

"Miles," I respond, getting in his face and whispering. "Cathy is most likely better off where she is, if you catch my drift. Okay?"

"You'd think this would teach Chuck a lesson for hiring such a ditz," he sighs, "but it won't because you will save her." As he walks away he shouts, "For the love of...!"

I hear a voice calling from the front of the club. "Evelyn Walker? Is there an Evelyn Walker here?"

I run to the front where I find two men dressed in gray worker khakis and striped short-sleeve shirts. One guy looks as if he hasn't showered in days. Smells like it too. Keeping my distance, I wave. "Yes, I'm Evelyn Walker. How can I help you?"

"Yeah, we're here with the generators," the grease monkey says.

"Generators? There's more than one?"

"Honey, you got three here. You can have a whole damn block party with these babies. The guy who ordered them for ya wanted us to make sure that you have everathin' ya need, so where do ya want 'em?"

"You guys are from the States, aren't you?"

"Workin' here a decade now, ma'am." They both look at me impatiently. Not that they're rude exactly, but sometimes you can just tell it's best to get to the point.

"Let me introduce you to the AV lead, and he'll be able to give you further direction. Follow me, and hey, thanks for saving us. We're so grateful."

As the generators are set up, the entertainers arrive. Fifty or so people are scurrying about finishing details and cleaning.

With the music playing louder and the excitement building, the go-go girls glide into the room, ready to go. Three of them are wearing short-shorts the size of a thong, and another two sport pasties over their nipples.

Okay, we're not in Amsterdam yet.

And of course, the guys are all gawking. The dancers are definitely too much of a distraction. It seems as if Cathy's going to have a little competition here tonight.

"Um, hi, ladies. Do any of you speak English?"

Only one of the girls raises her hand. She's tall and slim with a black bob. "Are you Eve?"

"Yes," I reply, shaking her hand. "And your name is?"

She gives me a proud smile. "Alina. I am your connect-tion with zee girls. De oders do not speak *Engleesh*."

Oh, great.

"Okay, Alina. Let's move the girls to the back room and find something appropriate for them to wear tonight. Did you happen to bring any other costumes?"

She looks at me confused. "Vat? I donut under ztand."

This gets better by the minute. My connect-tion's English is about as good as my German.

I opt to try: *"Folgen Sie mir bitte. Haben Sie andere Hühner mit Ihnen?"*

I now have them following me, but they're also laughing their heads off.

Alina walks alongside me down the hallway. "Vee donut have aneeee cheekuns vith uz."

That's great. Ha. Ha. Ha.

As we walk, I notice that Cathy has returned looking rested and refreshed. Isn't that nice? I watch as she falls in stride behind the girls, checking them out one by one, a disturbed frown spreading across her rested and refreshed face.

"Um, Eve, we may have a problem with these costumes?"

No, really? Wait a minute . . .

"You are so right, Cathy. And since you have such a great sense of style, how about you work with them and get them dressed?"

I don't give her the time to answer. There are too many other things to manage and not enough time to get this worked out. Not to mention, this is right up Cathy's alley. "This is Alina, your contact. She speaks a little English, but the other girl's donut. I mean do not. I need to run and see what's happening with everything else. Come to the registration desk in thirty minutes, okay? Okay, perfect."

As I run off, I hear in the distance behind me, "But what do I do? Where are the other costumes?"

She can figure this one out. I hope.

I need to do a last-minute check of the entire event starting with where the mini-coaches are going to drop off guests out front. I grab Wolf to join me on my way out.

Standing on the curb, looking back at the building with only a few minutes until the doors open, Wolf shouts, "Wow! This looks great!" The entire building, sidewalk, and street are splashed with a black-and-white checkered pattern. Covering the middle of the building is the 1-2-1 TV logo. At the bottom of the building near the registration desks, the building is flooded in patterns of bright colors: hot pink, orange, and yellows. It looks magnificent.

As we slowly walk back to the entrance, the registration staff gives me the thumbs-up and yet I get a feeling something is not quite right. And I know what it is! I look over to Wolf. "The human lava lamps who are supposed to stand on the platforms lining the front door are MIA. Also there's a bump in the black carpet leading up to the entrance."

"I see it, Eve, and I'm on it." Wolf radios his staff to fix the carpet. I radio Cathy.

"Cathy, come in, Cathy?"

Nothing.

"Cathy? Are you on radio? Cathy...Come in, Cathy?"

Nothing.

"This is Blaine. What's up, Eve?"

"Have you seen our human lava lamps? We need to get them in position and illuminate them ASAP."

"I'll find them and also get a radio to Cathy."

Wolf and I enter the club and make our way through the beaded curtain and through the sixties media tunnel. It's our last chance to make sure everything is a go. Every detail matters. We need to comb this place like we're looking for a needle in a haystack.

The entrance walls are awash with bright-color flower power, the music is blasting sixties theme songs, and a small group of "sixties hippies" are ready to hand out game cards.

Wolf's head is spinning as he surveys the three main rooms. "I have never seen this nightclub look *so good!*"

Cathy runs out with an outfit she purchased for Blaine yesterday. "Okay, the girls are ready to go!" she exclaims, self-assured and proud of herself. Each girl struts out wearing an element of the clothes she purchased. One has the white patent-leather boots, another wears the short miniskirt, while a couple of the women are sporting extra-large 1-2-1 TV tie-dyed T-shirts as minidresses, belted at the waist.

I have to admit, she did a great job.

But no time to linger in admiring them. "They look great, Cathy! Let's get them in place."

Wolf and I stand in the middle of the main room on the shiny white dance floor that reflects a kaleidoscope of psychedelic patterns. The girls climb into metal cages flanking the stage and on high risers around the perimeter of the room. The band is stage right and Lee, sporting a smart suit looking like James Bond, is already dancing with a few of the girls onstage.

Very dashing indeed.

The cyclorama backdrop features two spinning gobo patterns front-projected, one on each side, while shadow dancers are backlit. A scattering of illuminated Lucite cocktail tables around the dance floor are topped with stacks of sixties vinyl records.

Behind us on the back wall is the disc-jockey booth and above him are sixties beach-babe movies playing without sound.

In the "demo room" the computers are turned on at each of the stations. The room has been converted into a very cool lounge. Gorgeous models are dressed in tight-fitting silver and gold catsuits serving up martinis from a bar disguised as an oversized ice sculpture. Behind each of the stations are cycloramas with sound-activated music projections, while lava lamps sit on top of the classic sixties furniture.

"We are T minus five," comes across the radio.

I'm excited about the evening and proud of how it has come together. I almost feel like I can take a breath as I press down on my radio to talk. "You have all worked hard to get us here. Thank you so much for all of your efforts. Our clients and I thank you in advance for an outstanding party. If you have a good time, everyone else will too. Now, everyone in place, please. We're ready to rock."

I grab Cathy, Miles, and Blaine, walking them out front and then through each room. Not a word is uttered among them. They simply smile while Cathy sheds a tear.

"I didn't think we could do it, Eve," Cathy says, astonished. "Oh my god, it's incredible!"

Where did "we" come from? She certainly can't mean that she helped in any way, shape, or form, minus the dancers' costumes. Yet it is her party and we are here to make her look good. After her meltdown when we first arrived, her change of tune is music to my ears.

"I have one last surprise for you," I say, leading them back through the dark hallway into one of the bathrooms. I hold up my arms, revealing black lights and a multitude of fluorescent paints covering the walls. Miles can't keep his cool any longer, cracking up. "Maaaannn, some drunk guest is going to come in here and think he's havin' an acid blast from the past." He shakes his head back and forth. "This is cheetah-chic, Eve. That's really what it is, cheetah-chic!"

A few minutes later we are ready to open the doors. Cathy's voice comes over the radio: "The buses are here—or am I supposed to say the eagles are landing? Well, what-ev-er! People are walking toward us! They're here! Yay, they're here!"

The party is off to a great start. People are moving to the sixties music, guests are playing the demo game, and the martinis are a big hit. I'm feeling more confident until Chuck comes up to me whispering, "What the hell is this? This is not what I had in mind!"

Uh-oh.

Luckily five or six people happen to pass us, one guy fist bumping Chuck. "Great event, Chuck—this is amazing!" A woman sashays by with a drink in one hand and stilettos four inches high. "Chuck, we have to work together. If you can produce something like this, we need your software!" The others follow suit, and suddenly Chuck is the man of the hour.

I'm going to chalk that up to divine intervention or simply perfect timing.

"Like I was saying, Eve," he clears his throat, "this is not what I had in mind for this event. It's much *better* than I could have imagined! Wanna drink?"

"No thanks, Chuck, but have a good time and let us know if you need anything."

"Thanks, Eve. Right now I need one of *those*!" he says, strolling toward a group of girls. "Yeah, baby!"

Whew! That was a close call.

I enter the main room, pressing the talk button on the radio. "Someone needs to talk to Alina—tame the girls a bit. They're go-go dancers, not exotic dancers."

"This is Blaine, Eve. I copy, and I will personally work with the dancers to tame them."

I chuckle. "I bet you will, Blaine. Tough job, but someone's gotta do it."

We're at the halfway mark of the event, and it's time for prizes. I ask Lee to introduce the band, and after the second song, give away the first prize.

Once the band starts playing, no one wants to stop dancing. I decide to change the schedule and just flow with it. After the band plays for forty-five minutes, it's clearly time to give our sweaty guests on the dance floor, go-go dancers, and hippies a break.

"Oh mommy, spank me," comes over the radio.

"Who was that?"

"Uh, Eve? Blaine here. Sorry, a guest took my radio for a moment. Looks like we have a problem with the restrooms, over."

"What's the problem, Blaine? Over."

"Well, groups of people are going in and they aren't coming out."

"What?"

"And there's a line of people who really have to go!"

"Have you tried knocking on the doors?"

"Yep and nothing is happening. No one is coming out. I'm afraid the natives may break down the doors. Oh! Wait... Wolf is here now with the keys. We're good. Over."

It seems the bathrooms are a hit!

"And the first prize of this evening..." With Goldfinger playing in the background, Lee bends down on one knee, pointing the microphone, shaped like a revolver, at the audience—like Bond scanning the crowd for the sultry temptress he's going to take home and ravage. A few seconds pass as the packed room follows his gaze. He brings the microphone to his chest, blowing the smoke off his fake gun.

Cathy, who has been dancing the night away, runs up to the stage, stumbling on the first step. "I wanna pull the card! It's my turn. This is my job!"

Lee pulls back and steps away from the large, blurry mass coming toward him. Clearly, if Cathy ran into him, she'd take him down, linebacker-style. Instead, she hits the large vase, knocking it off the stage. The cards go flying. Chuck picks one up and hands it to Lee.

Standing as far away from Cathy as possible, Lee reads the card. "Our first prize of the evening goes to Michael O'Reilly from Ireland. Michael, join me onstage, ol' chap. Michael?"

"Uh, yeah, this is Blaine again. For all those who can hear me, Mr. O'Reilly, I believe, is lying here on the floor in the hallway at my feet. Um, I can tell you right now that he's not going to make it to the stage. Over."

Lee, who heard Blaine's radio call, addresses the crowd. "Yes, okay, riiighttttt. Ummm, Michael is a bit detained at the moment, but we will make certain that he receives his brand-new ultra-deluxe…" he looks at the package… "viiiibraaaatoooor!"

The crowd cheers and laughs hysterically. He unwraps the box. "Sorry, sorry. I was confused. It's a vibrating musical sound machine. That's what it is!" He holds the package high in the air. The crowd roars, and I can't help wondering if our emcee has had a martini or two himself?

I notice the food station hasn't been touched, which means people are not eating. The last thing we want is to clean up after a bunch of drunks at two o'clock in the morning. I ask the catering staff to start tray-passing food. "If they want to get loaded, let's get them stuffed."

After the first set of prizes are given, the lucky recipients step off the stage. "Well, party people," Lee announces with his best Austin Powers impersonation. "We have a very exciting announcement to make tonight…"

We do? Wait a second… I have nothing in my notes about an announcement. Has he gone rogue?

200   Janee Pennington

"Ladies and gentleman, a man after my own heart, a man who needs no introduction..."

Chuck? Is he introducing Chuck? And who wrote this intro?

"A man of great distinction and charisma..."

Okay, can't be Chuck.

He lifts his martini as if to toast someone.

"The new European media king himself... I give you... Mister... Sebastian Von Alt!"

SEBASTIAN?! Where is he? Why didn't I know about this? *What?*

I scan the room, connecting eyes with Miles, who shrugs, looking as confused as I am. Searching again, I can't seem to find Cathy, and I know Blaine isn't around, so how... wait. I whip around to see Chuck wearing a smug, pleased-with-himself look. Unbelievable—Chuck of all people! Chuck who has no idea Sebastian was the one in his suite the other night, and vice versa, for that matter.

Oh god! How do I look? I haven't brushed my teeth in a few hours! And my hair! My hair hasn't been brushed since early this morning! Ah! And my face must look like an oil well! But there he is climbing onstage. He catches my eye and winks. And just like that all my insecurities melt away. I feel myself falling even more for him, awestruck by his presence. Really, I mean I can't seem to move, and why do I feel as if I'm going to fall over? And those pesky butterflies! Wow!

I kind of like it. Scratch that—I like it... *a lot!*

Sebastian reaches out to shake Lee's hand. Lee does another James Bond action move before exiting the stage.

"And thank you, Chuck, for inviting me here tonight." He bends over and shakes Chuck's hand from the stage.

Yeah, and thanks for not letting me in on that little surprise. I still can't seem to move.

"I met Chuck this afternoon at the conference. We shared stories and a few laughs. He heard about the possible merger of the Spanish media group and my company here in Germany." He pauses and takes a few steps around the stage. He looks wonderful in his dark suit. "Well, I am very pleased to announce that as of late this afternoon, this merger is final. This means great changes for European television."

Resounding applause.

"There will be more information to come, but meanwhile, let's bring the band back to the stage and celebrate!"

As he hands back the mic, his eyes are focused on mine. They are more radiant than I remembered. And the feeling they're giving me... Someone help me. He's coming down the stairs, beelining straight toward me. Still, I can't move, my smile frozen in time.

And then he's in front of me. His eyes alive and his breath on my skin. Without saying a word, he grabs my hand. I follow behind as he leads me down the hall toward the bathrooms, closing and then locking the door behind us. The room is small, but the moment feels so big. "Wow, nice job," he says, pulling me toward him.

I sink into him. Enveloping myself in him. Wait, how did we pass the long line to get in here without waiting? Did he have someone standing outside the door for him?

Now I get why people weren't coming out of the bathrooms. In all its psychedelic glory, it is seriously a great make-out room. He leans me back against the wall, not letting me go. Slowly untucking the back of my top, he touches my skin. I look up at his chiseled face and lose myself again in those deep brown eyes. "Eve, you are unlike anyone I have ever known," he says, running his finger softly up my spine.

My body melts. "I had no idea you were coming here, and if I had—"

He kisses me. It isn't a stale peck or even the ram-your-tongue-down-my-throat kind, but a simple, magical kind of kiss, his lips delicately caressing my top lip, holding on for a moment and releasing. Shivers of ecstasy course through my body, and I feel alive. Oh so alive!

What a kiss!

I don't wait for him this time. I grab the back of his head, pulling it down toward mine, pressing myself into him. And he doesn't stop me. We stay like that, making out like teenagers, not breathing for what feels like eternity. We may have suffocated that way, but a knock at the door rips us back into reality. My reality. Where I *should* be working.

I break away.

"We'll have to continue this later, Sebastian . . ."

"You go outside. I'll be right there."

Hmm . . . I can't imagine why. I look down at his zipper, feeling my face flush. Oh boy . . .

Straightening my, um, everything, I open the door, only to walk right into Chuck, who is pressed up against it. Devoid of any social graces, he flies into the bathroom.

"Chuck? Were you listening to us?"

"Do you know this guy, Eve?" Chuck ignores me, eyes on Sebastian.

"Yes, Chuck."

He stares right at me, incredulously. "But why are you two in here . . . together?"

Sebastian decides to take this one. "Chuck, I happen to care very deeply for Eve, and we do not have the opportunity to see each other very often. Please excuse me for taking her away from her duties."

Chuck hurls a disappointed look my way.

"Well, yes. Eve is our event planner, and she has done a wonderful job with this event, but it isn't over yet."

Okay, I am thoroughly mortified.

"I apologize, Chuck. I promise, this is a first for me ..."

"No need to apologize, Eve—just get back to work."

I glance back at Sebastian, who's still "composing" himself.

"I'll see you in a bit." He winks, giving me an I-can't-wait-for-more smile.

Leaving the room, face flushed, I press down on my radio. "All posts check in, please, over."

"This is Blaine, Eve. All is going well with the game and the demos. In fact, I've been relieving posts so managers can have a little fun, too, over."

"You know how their software works? Over."

"I learned throughout the day, and I've been teaching myself the little tricks of the trade, over."

Is there anything he can't do?

"Evelyn Walker?" A sultry voice floats over the airwaves. I smile; the drunken voice of Miles is as sweet as honey. "Evelyn Walker, where are you, fierce lady?" I walk into the main room, where he is taking photos with a gaggle of girls. He's in heaven, true heaven. Not wanting to miss out on this moment, I get closer.

Miles leans his head on a woman's bosom. "Oh baby, baby."

He's gone. It's good to see him having a little fun.

"Cathy, come in. Cathy?"

Nothing. Why did we even give her a radio?

"Alina, come in Alina?"

Nothing.

"Oooohhhhhhhh, she's going to regret that tomorrow," I hear a woman saying on the dance floor. I look over and it's Cathy on her back, scooting across the floor.

As she goes by she yells, "I'm crawlin', I'm crawlin', watch me crawl, I'm crawlin'!"

Startling yes, surprising no.

I check my watch, shocked to see how late it is. People will be leaving soon. The prizes have been given away, and the band is on their last set. We need to get the gift bags ready to hand out and make sure the drivers are ready to transport guests back to the hotels.

"Blaine, come in, Blaine?"

"What's up, Eve?"

"Will you round up our hippies and get them to start handing out the gift bags as guests leave, please? And check that all the coaches are out front ready for departure?"

"Didn't Cathy want to give the bags out? Over."

"That's a ten-four, but her twenty is down-and-out, over."

"Got it, Eve, I'm heading to the lobby now, over."

"Thanks, Blaine, over."

"Oh, and you may want to get the security guards to help load some of the guests that didn't get cut off from the martini lounge when they should have."

"Will do."

CHAPTER FIFTEEN

ONE THIRTY ROLLS around and everyone but the staff has left. "Okay, everyone, let's pack it up for the night... or morning if you prefer."

Sebastian, watching from a distance in the demo room, signals me over. The computers are being torn down and there are crews all around us, but somehow it feels like we are the only two people in the room. I cozy up next to him as he gently slides my hair behind my ear. "When can we head back to your room? I have a bottle of champagne waiting..."

"Not anytime soon, Sebastian," Chuck interrupts, standing in front of us, hands on his hips.

Now what does he want?

"I stayed on L.A. time, so it's just about dinnertime. Don't you think we need to talk about Amsterdam since it is happening in just a few days?"

Can't he give me a few minutes to enjoy the success of Berlin?

"Chuck, it's one thirty in the morning; I doubt any restaurants are open."

"I checked with the concierge. There just happens to be a restaurant on the other side of town. It'll only take thirty minutes to get there. They supposedly have the best German sausage around."

Oh, that's tempting. He knows all too well that I'm mainly a vegetarian. But then again, he is my client.

"I have a taxi out front ready to go. I'll see you in five... oh, and will you send a bottle of Jack Daniels to my room?"

One word—no, two—yuck, Chuck!

Chuck walks away as if he just won something.

I cringe, turning back to Sebastian. "Will you be upset if I postpone? I honestly don't know how long this supposed meeting is going to last..."

I stand up, but he grabs my waist, pulling me back down onto his lap. "Well, Schatzi, I want to spend time with you, but if it means waiting, I will wait."

"But you know we're leaving for Amsterdam tomorrow."

He smiles, quite aware of my plans. Again he renders me speechless. I get the feeling if I open my mouth, something silly is going to spew out. So I kiss him on the cheek and walk away fast.

Where in the hell is Cathy? I've checked every room, passing the strike crews, caterers, bodyguards, and Miles. Where is she? I'm not going with Chuck alone.

"Can I get a twenty on Cathy?" No response. "Anyone? Has anyone seen Cathy?"

"Yeah, Eve, this is Blaine. Cathy left here thirty minutes ago, over."

Great.

"Blaine, I need you to wrap up whatever it is you're doing. We're going to dinner with our client."

This is most likely the last thing Blaine wants to do after a long day, but I can't fathom getting into a taxi alone with Chuck.

"I just saw Miles leave, over."

"It's with Chuck. Get a cup of coffee. We have another couple hours to go."

Dinner after an event at two in the morning? Unprecedented, but I can handle it if Blaine is with me.

A few minutes later, I step outside. Chuck is waiting with the taxi door open. "After you, Eve," he says with a hint of slime in his voice.

"Oh, I'd like to get in after you, Chuck, if you don't mind?"

He crawls in, happy to oblige. I bend over to look inside the cab where he is patting the black vinyl next to him. "Let's go, Eve."

"Oh, wait just a moment, Chuck. Here comes Blaine. He said he was hungry too."

I watch as Blaine runs to the car with the dwindling energy of an Olympic athlete who is on his last lap. "Hey Eve," he pants. "Whew, that's a long run. Whew!"

"I hate to tell you, but it's not even fifty yards."

"Well, it felt a lot farther," he smiles, shrugging.

Chuck looks impatient. "Thanks a lot for a great job this evening, Blaine, but I'm hungry, and Eve and I are going for dinner."

I give Blaine the stay-with-me-or-else look.

"Dinner? That sounds great. Do you mind if I join you? I'm famished. That was a long run."

Chuck hurls him a forced smile.

Blaine holds the door open for me and I slide in, Blaine following behind. We sit, one uncomfortable Eve sandwich.

"So I'd say you had a very successful event tonight. Congratulations. You must be very happy," Blaine declares as the taxi pulls away from the warehouse. Chuck places his hand on my left knee and replies, "Yes...yes, I am very happy."

Before I can do it myself, Blaine surprisingly leans over and swipes the top of Chuck's hand. "Holy cow, did you see that bug on your hand? That thing looked nasty!" He's hamming it up good, and I couldn't be more proud. He even proceeds to open the privacy screen, yelling, "Hey man, do you realize that you have nasty little critters in here?"

Well, I know of a big one sitting next to me on my left...

I turn my head to Blaine and mouth "thank you," then bring up the most diversionary question I can think of. "So, how are Cynthia and the kids doing, Chuck?"

I'm certain this is not the direction Chuck was hoping to go in. After seeing me with Sebastian, I have this weird feeling he thinks I'm fair game. He mumbles dejectedly, "Yeah, thanks. They're doing well."

Twenty minutes later we arrive at the sausage stand. Yes, stand. There are no places to sit. Just a few highboy tables covered with flies. And Chuck looks so happy. "Let's order!"

We sidle up to a window screen where a graying man with far too few teeth takes our order. I guess eating outdoors is a good thing considering the grease covering everything in the kitchen is the main décor.

"I'll have some french fries, please," I say, trying my best not to show how nauseated our surrounding condition is making me. Chuck and Blaine, on the other hand, order the biggest, most disgusting sausage plate on the menu.

What's wrong with them? The smell alone is threatening havoc on my stomach.

I lean against the wobbly table, trying to relieve my throbbing feet.

Chuck turns to me, sausage juice trickling from the corner of his mouth. "So Eve, tell me, how do you like Berlin? And how do you like L.A.? Where do you work out? Do you like to go out on the weekends?"

Does he think we're on a date?

"Well, that's a lot of, um, personal questions."

As he slowly nods, licking his lips, I can't help but notice his resemblance to a predator in heat. *Is he forgetting Blaine is standing next to him?*

I take a deep breath. "I think Berlin is great. My first trip here was during college when I studied abroad. As for L.A., I grew up there and feel comfortable near water, so I've never moved far away from it."

I force a french fry down, aware both their eyes are trained on me. This Eve-show-and-tell is becoming more unpleasant by the second.

"I try and work out as much as possible, but I don't have a routine. If I am home on a weekend, I would rather catch up on my sleep and maybe read a good book. I'm afraid I'm boring if I'm not working on an event somewhere."

"I don't believe that for a second," Chuck insists, downing his beer in one giant gulp followed by a rather nasty belch.

My, my, isn't he the charmer.

Both men finish their plates. I watch as their eyes grow heavy, food comas setting in. "I think it's time to head back to the hotel..." I encourage, eyeing a nearby taxi.

First to the car, I slide in, making sure to score a window seat. I don't want to take any more chances with Chuck and his wandering hands. But to my relief, both guys fall asleep on the way back, their heads magnetized to each other.

When we pull up to the hotel, I ask the bellman to assist Chuck to his room. By the time we reach the lobby, Blaine is running to the nearest restroom. I patiently wait outside. After a few minutes he stumbles out with his hand on his stomach. "I need to go to bed." I say good night and watch him hobble to the elevator.

"Hey Blaine?" He looks back at me. "Thank you. Really, thank you for coming out here. You've been a big help."

Exhausted and weak, he smiles.

"No problem. It's good practice for Amsterdam."

I feel that familiar knot in my stomach. *Amsterdam.*

"Feel better, Blaine. Good night."

Finally alone and operating on fumes, I head upstairs to wake Sebastian and spend time with him. The door opens quietly; the lights are out and it's pitch black inside. I tiptoe in, feeling for the small lamp. When the light comes on, my stomach sinks. No Sebastian. Sitting on the bed, where my handsome German should be, is a little card instead: "This isn't how I want this to happen. Please call me tomorrow. *Liebe,* Sebastian."

I sink onto the bed, admiring his handwriting and cursing him for being so noble, but then again, I am so exhausted there's a good chance I'd fall asleep before we could round first base.

Thankfully, my flight to Amsterdam is in the afternoon, so I have a few hours to catch up on some sleep. I set my alarm, allowing for enough time to wrap up the accounting with the hotel before leaving and saying our thank-yous and farewells. Now all I need is some sleep!

My eyes close...

"Eeee...eeee...vvvvv!" Am I dreaming or is someone knocking on my door at four thirty in the morning?

Form a sentence, Eve. You can do it—put the words together.

"Who is it and what do you want?"

"Eeee...eeee...vvvv, it's Chhhhuck." I can barely understand his slurring cries. "Dare's a parteee go-ing on and yer in-viii-ted."

Will this guy ever give up? To say I'm annoyed right now would be the understatement of the year.

"Chuck, did you drink that bottle of Jack?"

"Well...yah."

"Chuck...go back to your room and go to bed!"

"But...the party?"

"Where's the party, Chuck?"

"In my room."

"And who's there?"

"Um, ME!"

"Chuck, you have a flight in a few hours and you may want to get some sleep."

"The party's in my pants."

"Yes, I'm sure it is, but you need sleep. Go to your room and close the door."

"I need help getting back to my room. I need you to help me."

"Not even a chance, Chuck. Go next door. I am not listening to you any longer. Good night!"

I just want some sleep!

Chuck makes it back to his room, and I know this because now he is pounding on the wall between our rooms. "Eve, save me! Eve!"

I crawl back into bed hoping he'll pass out when the phone rings. Only one guess who it is.

"Chuck, go to sleep!"

"Eve, I want you."

"Yes, Chuck. I know you want me..." Pause for a moment. "To be your event planner, but in order for me to do this properly, I need some sleep. Good night." I hang up.

A minute later, another call.

"Eve, no, I mean *I want you.*"

Now I'm mad. "Look, I'm too tired for this, and we both know this isn't going anywhere, right?"

Dead silence. Fifteen seconds go by, thirty, forty-five and then ...finally...relief...the porcine grunt of a snore.

Hanging up, I realize I have never seen Chuck hit DEFCON 5 before. I pull the covers over my head, praying never to see him like this again.

CHAPTER SIXTEEN

WHEN I AM given a short lead time, a large attendance, and an international destination, it automatically turns into the Olympics of event planning. Even with a normal event, there are so many details and often not enough time to organize it all. But give me an event like Amsterdam, and we're no longer talking the Olympics. It's now survival of the fittest, take no prisoners, do or die—Hunger Games–style. Every detail counts. Every nano second counts. *Everything* counts!

"Hey, M. It's Eve."

"Hey! Where are you?"

"I'm sitting at Tegel airport in Berlin waiting for my flight to Amsterdam." I take the phone, placing it up to my other ear. "I wanted to call and check in."

"I wish I could chat for a while, but it's nuts here!"

I can hear the clangs of large metal items being thrown around in the background.

"M, where are you?"

"I'm in the kitchen. We have a kosher group in-house, and the rabbi is due here in just a few minutes. Can you hold on a sec?"

I get up and take a walk over to the window, pressing my nose against the glass as I did when I was a young girl. Staring at the sea of planes, I wonder where they're all heading, knowing that all I really want to do is stay here and get to know Sebastian better.

I shake off the daydream, overhearing Marla's conversation in the kitchen.

"Yes, Ms. Wells. They were all boiled yesterday."

"All the meat and dairy are in separate refrigerators?"

"Yes, ma'am."

"All of the countertops?"

"Cleaned with boiling water. Truly, Ms. Wells, we are ready for the rabbi."

"Okay, ladies and gentlemen. Good job. I'll be right back."

Back with me, she says, "You know, I can't complain. This situation is nothing compared to what happened the other night."

"What happened?"

"Well, from all accounts, some crazy old guy decides to try a daredevil dive off the roof of the hotel. He was going for a reverse somersault with a double twist, I think."

"Oh my god, M! Is he okay?"

"No! And that's what I mean. He does a stunt like this, and we have to deal with the police all night. Can you believe? How selfish."

"But... he died?"

"Duh. And do you know how many people were affected by his fall? We ended up giving free hotel packages to at least ten guests and had to call in grief counselors. Even removing the body from the premises was complete drama."

I hope she talked with a counselor, but from the sound of her insensitive tone, I'm guessing she did not.

She goes on. "What an idiot! Who does such a thing?"

"I don't know...maybe a man who is so depressed that dying sounded better to him than living."

"Yeah, yeah..." she mutters, seeming to block out any reasonable explanation. "So how did the event go?"

"It was full of surprises. I don't even know where to begin."

"And you didn't call me for advice?"

"I think I handled it well."

"Yes, yes, I'm sure you did. So was your client happy at least?"

I feel my cheeks warm.

"I'll put it this way—I feel lucky we pulled it off. But since we haven't had enough time to review all the Amsterdam details, coupled with the fact that I haven't slept much in days and I'm running on low energy, it'll be a miracle if we can get away with it again."

"I've never heard you like this before, Eve."

"Yeah, well, I'm feeling like a cast member on *Project Runway* who is getting ready to send a model down the catwalk with all the hemlines undone."

"No!" Marla cries. "So what did Seb—shit, Eve, the rabbi just got here. Have to go. More later, okay?"

"But—"

"Gotta go!"

I guess my Sebastian storytelling will have to wait.

"Ladies and gentleman," floats over the loudspeaker, "Flight 122 to Amsterdam is now ready to board."

Taking my seat, 4A, on the plane, I settle in, watching the other passengers. For some reason I always like to watch the people boarding. I look at their faces and wonder where they are going or who they are leaving behind. But today seems different. It seems to be taking a lot longer to board everyone. I notice what look to be the same people boarding the plane over

and over again. As if they are walking down the aisle to the back
door, exiting, and re-entering again. Quite bizarre. I think it's
safe to say I'm spent!

Thanking my lucky stars I have the inside seat, I prop my pillow up against the window, then rest my head down. I watch as
the last few passengers shuffle on, noticing at the back of the line
someone with a rather large head, standing at least three inches
taller than everyone else. There is a wide gap between him and
the person walking in front. As he turns the corner making his
way down the aisle, a hush of silence settles over the cabin. I
watch, awestruck. He's the size of a sumo wrestler! Please don't
sit next to me, please, please don't sit here! With every step he
takes, I can feel my heart racing, intuition telling me he's going
to be my companion on this flight.

He reaches above me and places his luggage in the bin, then
lo and behold, takes the seat next to mine. After he maneuvers
himself into the seat, he turns to me. "Hi, I'm Sammy."

Sammy?

"Hi, Sammy, I'm Eve. How are you?"

"Do you really want to know?"

To be honest, no. I really don't have the energy right now.

"Sure."

"I'm beat, man. I used to be a sumo wrestler..."

*No! With your hair tied up like that? My powers of observation
haven't deserted me yet.*

"I am now a peace representative for the U.N. We are pro-
moting peace around the world, but I have to tell ya, I'm tired.
We're only halfway through this trip, and we have another tour
planned throughout Asia after we're done here."

I'm leaning on the divider, my eyes as heavy as lead, trying to
stay awake.

"Wow, but you are doing such a wonderful thing."

"Don't get me wrong, I love what I do, but I need a break. A day off or so, ya know what I mean?"

I adjust my pose so I can read his face better. "I hear ya."

Sammy has a great big smile. It's huge. I love his energy.

I just hope he doesn't ask...

"So..."

Oh no...

"What do you do, Eve?"

I am so close to telling him that I sell tractors for a living when the truth comes pouring out of my mouth. "I'm a...I'm a...I'm a meeting and event planner."

He belly laughs. "No way!"

Way.

He tries to turn to face me in his seat, but he can't. He resigns himself to just turning his head. "You aren't going to believe this..."

Oh, I'm certain I will.

"That's exactly what I want to do!"

Okay, he got me with that one. I wasn't expecting a long shot like that coming from him. A cousin, an aunt, maybe even an uncle or a girlfriend, but certainly not the big guy himself!

"Events are my thing!"

I start to worry that his bun is going to burst from excitement. If he was tired before, he isn't now.

No nap for me.

"So what type of planning are you interested in? Social? Incentive? Corporate? Association?"

He stammers, "Oh geez, I don't know. I guess I didn't think about it that far ahead." He takes a long sip of his soft drink and places his glass on the tray, which is resting on top of his belly. "I didn't realize there are so many different types of planners." He processes the information for a minute and then smiles real big.

"You know, I guess I'm going to have to think about it. I'm so lucky doing what I'm doing right now."

I smile back, "Yes you are, Sammy. And so am I."

Thankfully, now I have a few minutes to close my eyes.

I arrive at the hotel De L'Europe feeling beaten down and withered. On the upside, I have the evening free to get some rest so that I can wake up refreshed and ready to go. The dark wooden door with its antique silver handle could not look better. It's as if it has a sign on it that reads, "Silent Zone—Ms. Walker Only." I want to pet the door. Okay, I am petting the door. I slowly lean in and open it, anxious for the moment I can fall into bed.

"Hello, sexy, welcome to Amsterdam." I peer in to find Sebastian, wearing nothing more than a white terry cloth robe and matching slippers, smiling from ear to ear. My heart explodes.

"How...?"

Two steps and a stumble, I fall into his arms. "I thought you might need a little pampering tonight," he says, placing his hands on my shoulders, rubbing away.

No suites, no chef, no flowers...just him standing in the entry massaging my neck. Looking up at him, I notice lust in his eyes. The energy between us is so intense, so strong, so...euphoric. He leans toward me, his lips finding mine.

His kiss is soft and warm. My hand crawls up the back of his head, through his thick, soft sandy-blond hair. He takes my arm and brings my hand to his face. I leave it there, on his cheek.

He's holding me with such passion and yearning. His robe is slightly open, exposing his strong, tan, sculpted chest. Not a word is said between us. He talks with his hands as he slowly undresses me, revealing my black lace lingerie. I close my eyes, savoring the moment as he kisses one part of my face, then another, feeling myself getting swept up in the love storm that's brewing.

The radio blares a Maroon 5 song as I awaken in a haze on the carpet in the entryway, with drool running down the side of my face, my luggage beside me, and no one lying next to me. My black patent purse, however, looks like it got some action last night, with lipstick and tongue prints all over the side of it.

It seemed so real. I was here. He was here. I roll onto my back, deflated, fully dressed, wondering if I have a serious problem. My body and soul are like starving orphans begging for a life beyond event planning. I'm creating fantasies when I need realities.

But at this moment I have a reality to get to, and that's right here in Bangkok—I mean Amsterdam.

My schedule today is not about rushing around from one appointment to the next. Okay, it is, but not like normal. We have three days before the big event, and if I'm going to pull it off, I need to pace myself. Glancing down, I take a moment to review my schedule for the day:

9:00   Check on setup and staff at hospitality office.

10:00   Meet with Chuck at the 1-2-1 TV booth, RAI Convention Center, to go over the entertainment for the party.

11:00   Meet local staff who will be handing out credentials along with lanyards to the event. Go over details on how to make this party the "hottest ticket in town."

13:00   Meet with Robert from the lighting company at de Oude Kerk.

14:00   Finalize the walk-through arrangements with the caterer and de Oude Kerk representatives.

20:00   Meet Miles, Cathy and Blaine for a dinner meeting on board canal boat.

After a long-deserved shower and a change of clothes, which look similar to the ones I wore yesterday, I head downstairs to the Clubzaal Room where we've set up our hospitality office. Entering, I see eight or so staff working on last-minute details, forming lists, updating manifests, and confirming vendors. Good sign, everyone's busy. Surveying the room, I notice a rather large box. A young travel director hands me a note from Peter. Ah, the box of uniforms I presume.

I tear the envelope open to find a four-page handwritten letter inside. Despite the frenzied atmosphere of staff rushing in and out of the room, the words capture my full attention.

> My dearest Eve,
> I understand why you haven't wanted to speak with me. I do hope in time that we will be able to sit down and discuss what happened. I thought I should start here in a letter with nothing but honesty and love.
>   Let me go back to when we first met. I thought our laughter and compatibility was a sign that you found me attractive. When you asked me to be more involved with the company, I took that as a sign we were growing closer together. But when you started referring to me as your "brother" and "best friend," I knew you didn't share the same feelings I had for you. This devastated me. You are the only woman I have ever really cared for.

But Peter is gay . . .

> I hope that didn't shock you too much. I know you thought I was gay. In fact, I let you believe that think-ing I could get closer to you that way. I thought it was

the only way you could trust me, especially because men have hurt you in the past.

Oh my god, I've been naked in front of him! More than once!
According to my therapist, I was criticizing you because of my own insecurity. I thought if I could make you feel more self-conscious, then I could feel more confident in pursuing you.

I knew something was up there!
Looking around the office, I notice all eyes in the room are on me. Somehow I've become the center of attention, and I'm guessing it's related to the steam coming from the top of my head. I clear my throat and pretend to be mesmerized by something to do with work. "Let's have the opera singer at the top of the stairs. Will someone call her and let her know?"

Yeah, from the look on their faces, no one is buying it.

I'm surprised Peter would send such a letter to me on-site, but then again, maybe he thought it was the only place he could be assured it would personally reach my hands. I am grateful he put such thought and emotion into his penmanship, but I'm going to have to save the rest to read later. I need to digest what I read so far.

He's *not* gay?

He wants me?

He likes me?

In *that* way?

No. It can't be...He's not gay?

Come to think about it, I have never seen him with another man. I haven't ever seen him try and pick up one, either. We have gone to gay nightclubs together, but he seemed to have always wanted to dance with me. Me?!

I thrust the letter into my pocket, determined to keep my mind focused on the day's agenda.

After answering a round of questions in the office, signing off on a few invoices, and making a few last-minute adjustments on décor, I stand up to leave when a travel director makes frantic eye contact with me, mouthing "Emergency!" as she hands me the phone.

You can use just about any other words in the English dictionary with me without getting me too riled up, but "emergency" and "disaster" are two words I prefer not to hear before, during, or after an event.

I grip the phone, bracing myself for the worst. "Eve Walker."

"It's Saartje, Eve." Her voice sounds shaky and scared.

"Saartje. What's wrong?"

"Eve, I am so very sorry, but we will be unable to cater your event."

"What?!"

"Last night one of the chefs preparing for your event left a stove on. The entire place went up in smoke in the middle of the night. And unfortunately, it gets worse. I've phoned every decent caterer in a one-hour radius, and they are all booked solid due to the convention. I am so, so sorry."

At a time like this I normally go straight into plan B, but in this case there is no plan B. Instantly I transform myself into a meeting-planning computer, processing data from years gone past. Fortunately, I won't have to go back that far.

"Saartje," I say conjuring up a scheme, "did you call Agneese and Adrianus?"

"Who?"

"They're a mom-and-pop operation here in Amsterdam. They come highly recommended by a friend of mine. If you can work with them and bring your staff, there's a good chance we can pull this off. I can also see where Trish McCall is at the moment. She's a fabulous chef from L.A. I know it's less than perfect, but with a little creativity and a few kitchens around the city, we can still make this happen."

All I hear is silence.

Please agree!

"I don't know what I'm signing up for, but count me in. The on-site staff hasn't been cancelled, so we'll just keep them on. I'll start making calls to the food wholesaler, rental company, and the team." Now that's the Saartje I know! She continues, "We'll get this together! If you need me, call my home phone number. I'll check in later, Eve."

Seconds after hanging up, I leave messages for Trish on her home and cell. All I can say is, "There's been a fire in the kitchen of our caterer here in Amsterdam. I have no idea where you are in the world, but if I could persuade you to help... Please call me ASAP!"

An hour later I receive a text from Trish. *"In Greece teaching American cuisine. Just rcvd ur vm. Will refig my sched and catch next flight."*

Twenty minutes later I receive another text from her while I'm sitting in a cab going over to the exhibition center. *"Will be there in a few hours. Hold tight... I'm bringing my six students w/ me... all will be fine."*

Well, I put out that fire—no pun intended—but now I need to get the staff to find a few rooms somewhere in the city as well as a large kitchen for Trish.

Heading down the long aisle in the convention center, I see Chuck in the distance, his usual pompous self. But the second he catches a glimpse of me, he withers, avoiding eye contact. I'm sure I'm a sharp reminder of how he's *actually* feeling today.

"Hey, Eve," he says, stepping down from a small stage in his booth. The booth, which has a chalkboard background and a few desks scattered around, reminds me more of a schoolroom gone bad than a professional place to make contacts at a convention.

He should have asked for our help. Instead, he wanted to do it himself, and unfortunately, it shows.

"What are you doing here?" he says.

I keep my distance from him, still able to smell the Jack on his breath. "You asked me to meet with you this morning about the entertainment for the party. What would you like to discuss?"

Chuck is not the organized type. He makes sure he has people around him to do it all for him, but for some unknown reason, whenever he's on-site, he feels the necessity to be more involved, often to his detriment.

He shifts in discomfort, eyes glued to the floor. "I want to address the circumstances of what happened in Berlin."

"Yes, please do," I say, staring at his forehead until he finally makes eye contact with me, revealing utter shame. "Well, yes." Others in the booth are looking over, wondering what's going on. "Let's take a walk," he says, moving toward the long aisle of booths being set up.

"Eve," he begins, studying me as if to see how bad the collateral damage is. Remembering he still is my client, I wipe any sign of judgment off my face. "All I can say is that I'm sorry. I have never lost control like I did after the party, and not that you aren't attractive or anything, but you could have been almost anyone and the same thing would have happened."

That's flattering. Mixed emotions flood my psyche. A little vanity at realizing I was just a "body" to him, and a lot of relief that I don't have to worry about it in the future, I hope.

I stop in my tracks. "But you called me by name, so if that was true, wouldn't—"

"I call Cynthia by her name, too, but—"

"But she's your wife!"

In some ways I feel sorry for Chuck. After he married Cynthia and they had their two daughters, she lost interest in him. It has probably been years since he's seen any affection from her. She loves to order him around and spend his money. I've been told that the only reason they haven't gotten divorced is he doesn't want her to collect half of 1-2-1 TV, his baby.

We take a walk over to the convention center café and take a seat in a booth. My gut tells me I should still be cautious, so I take a seat facing him rather than beside him. "Shall we talk about the event?"

"Yes," he says, looking to see who's around. "How's it shaping up? How much staff do we have working?"

"Well," I say, pulling the information up on my phone, "myself and Blaine along with four TDs, fifteen local staff, two on-site managers, your staff of two, one production manager and his colleagues, one projectionist manager and his staff. We also have four off-duty police, two paramedics, twelve security guards, four traffic guards, the catering staff, de Oude Kerk representatives, and the vendor reps. Of course this doesn't include the dozens of entertainers. Does that sound about right to you?" I ask, knowing that he most likely didn't hear a word I just said.

"Uh, yeah. Yeah, yeah. Yep, that sounds good."

Miles appears, taking a seat next to Chuck. His presence alone makes me smile and I do have to say, he's looking sharp in his 1-2-1 TV polo and slacks. I feel my whole body somehow relaxing. He seems pumped that it's his turn to show off, and he obviously wants to take the opportunity to do it in front of Chuck. I plan to help Miles in whatever way I can, so if he wants to show off, more power to him.

Miles starts by running down a list of to-dos, then hammers me with questions regarding the attendance and the teasers. He even asks if we should send another reminder to people to come by the booth tomorrow to pick them up. I tell him it's a great idea, but only if the booth isn't busy first thing in the morning. I also inform the two men that I have arranged to have two gorgeous models, dressed in 1-2-1 TV attire, assist their booth staff in handing out the credentials over the next couple of days. Chuck's eyeballs pop out, matching his stupid, overexcited grin.

What they don't know is that I intend to make this the hottest ticket of the conference. I've created a plan to have our staff hand out credentials only to the people whom Miles and Cathy have designated on our attendee manifest. In the past, Miles has always instructed us to hand out tickets to the invitees and give them as many additional ones as they want. Not this time. I'm going to make certain that this party is hyped up and "exclusive." Everyone will want a credential when they think they can't have one.

I sure hope this works!

We go over additional details such as the menu and the food-to-alcohol ratio. I assure them that our waitstaff will encourage guests to eat more and drink less. Even though we can't force people to eat if they don't want to, having a delicious menu to choose from should make eating more enticing. I'm certain I don't want what happened in Berlin to happen at this party.

Miles runs through his notes, staying on top of his game in front of Chuck as he asks me for an updated Run of Show. We go over the minute-to-minute agenda of the evening, from the time guests arrive to the time the party ends.

And as he always seems to do at the last minute, Chuck adds a VIP room. Luckily, we were prepared for such a request; Miles had already set it up with us. He faces Chuck. "And we have arranged for a live feed of the party and two large HD screens. Is that sufficient?"

"That's cool," Chuck replies, looking off to the distant sea of conventioneers walking by, placing the finishing touches on their booths.

Out of nowhere Miles loudly blurts, "FRICKOL!"

Immediately I go into Miles-ism translation mode. Frickol...let me think, Frickol?

"It's frickin' cool." I point at Miles. "You're right, Miles, its frickin' cool."

Chuck looks at both of us, perplexed.

I start collecting my stuff. "Well, if there isn't anything else, I had better head over to the church to check in."

"As a matter of fact, there is one other thing, Eve." Chuck stops us from leaving the booth.

"And what is that, Chuck?"

"Do you think the church will allow me to play their organ during the party?"

Excuse me? The organ? Really? That seems like a strange request. The organ?

"I don't know, Chuck, but I can ask. When were you thinking of playing? You know we have a full lineup of entertainment."

"No...I know," he says. "Maybe as guests are leaving?"

"Well...if I may suggest," I say, as Miles looks at me more fricked-out than frickol-ed, "if the church allows it, why don't you play a score from *Les Miserables* or *Phantom of the Opera* when the party is beginning, kicking off the evening's festivities?"

And...explanation time.

"There are two reasons for this. First, the evening is going to be high energy. We don't want to bring people down just before they leave. We want them to leave on a high, right?"

Both men nod.

"Secondly, what a fantastic way to start the party with the host heading off the entertainment."

There is a third reason, too, but I won't say it. Most likely, Chuck will have too much to drink, and the last thing we want him to do is make an ass out of himself up in the organ loft after he's already tied one on.

Chuck seems euphoric and anxious. "Great, it's settled. Shall I go with you to the church to work this out? I'll need to practice."

He jumps out of his seat, excited despite the fact that I'm not certain the church will agree to his request.

"If they approve it, I'll try to set up a rehearsal time for you this evening. What time would be good for you?"

Chuck takes a look at his BlackBerry. "Shoot, I have dinner with clients tonight."

"What if we set it up for after your dinner, around midnight?"

"Well, that's perfect!" Chuck leaves the table, almost skipping back to the booth.

Miles, on the other hand, doesn't look thrilled. "He's going to ruin my event!"

"Miles," I respond, keeping my cool. "He's going to play as soon as the doors open. He'll be harmless."

With Miles still moping, I leave the center for de Oude Kerk, where preparations for the event are in full swing. I spend two painstaking hours going through all the final details with Robert from the lighting company and the carpenters who are erecting the stages and large props. I'm going to have to wait to make any concrete decisions on the outdoor colors until after dark. And of course the representatives of the church want to be involved with every facet. My staff has outlined it all in a Run of Show that they can follow along with me.

Having a moment to myself, my thoughts shift back to Peter's letter. It's felt like a rock inside my pocket since I put it there. This weight—I'd like to toss it far away and yet hold it close. I'm torn. Should I meet with him when I return to the States or forget about him entirely? I really should be concentrating on the most challenging project of my career. I vote for thinking about it later. Funny, how I am missing Peter's dog more than Peter; in my head I can hear Charlie's cute little bark, trying to get my attention. Maybe it's my way of handling the hurt and pain.

Spending most of the afternoon helping Saartje and Trish find restaurants that will allow them to use their kitchens has proven my begging skills are in good working order. By early evening, the chefs are in place and ready to cook.

The dinner bell rings in my head, or was that the alarm on my phone? Regardless, there's no time to run back to the hotel to get changed. I do a little arts and crafts project on my face in the taxi en route to meet Miles, Cathy, and Blaine for dinner on the canal boat. My driver tonight is a young black man with a contagious smile. He is nicely dressed with a vest over a polo shirt and is well versed in English. He drives carefully slow. That is until a man in a tuxedo storms the car at a red light, pulling the door open. "Please, please help me!" he says, sliding in next to me.

What the hell?

The man is sweating bullets, literally. "I am supposed to be getting married in thirty minutes and my car never showed! Please, please, it is only a few miles away. Will you please take me?"

When I find out the church is in the opposite direction from where we were heading, I jump out, relinquishing the car to the penguin in need.

I knew the car and driver seemed too good to be true.

The next cab I catch I can't even talk about.

Taking the walkway down the side of the canal to meet the boat, I shake my head from sheer frustration.

My staff has arranged for us to dine on *Her Royal Highness*, a beautifully designed vessel that is set to cruise down the canal, showing off the sights. Looking down, I feel underdressed in my black uniform slacks and periwinkle sweater.

Miles is waiting for me. Like the gentleman he is, he takes my hand, helping me onto the boat. "Thank you, Miles," I say, shooting him a flirtatious smile.

This time he doesn't return the favor. "I still can't figure out why you're allowing Chuck to play the organ at the party! Are you crazy?"

And hello to you too, Miles.

"Miles," I say, leading him over to the table where Cathy and Blaine sit engrossed in their own conversation, "Chuck is harmless, and honestly—"

"Can he even play the damn thing?"

"It doesn't matter. We'll have him play before the doors open. Besides, if he can't play, he wouldn't want to get up there in the first place, right?"

"One word, Eve: Bermuda."

Oh yes, Bermuda. Well, well, well. In the five years since it happened, no one from the company has attempted or dared to bring up the disaster that Chuck created there. The signs warning swimmers not to swim near the large rocks due to a swarm of men-of-war were clearly posted on the beach that fateful day. But Chuck, in a rather bold move, decided to remove the signs and take a group of his employees out for a whirl. "I know what I'm doing," he announced to Miles. "Don't worry. The hotel is taking away the best swimming spot and trying to scare us with those stupid signs." He jumped into the water. "I'm not falling for it. Come on, guys, let's go."

After a few minutes of frolicking, twelve people were stung, five of them so severely that they were sent to the hospital to be treated for toxic poisoning. One almost didn't make it.

"The man isn't right in the head! Are you really going to allow him to possibly destroy the event before it even begins?" Miles turns around seeking support from Blaine and Cathy.

"It was Chuck who created the idea for the hideous booth at the convention center," Blaine reminds me.

"Eve, this event means everything to me," Miles pleads.

"Um, ditto, Miles."

I can't help but sympathize with Miles, but in reality it's Chuck's company, and he is the one paying for the party.

"It's all going to work itself out, Miles. I promise you it will."

Miles only answers with a nod and a resigned sigh.

Moving along the canal, we pass house-arks, barges, the Palace, and the old city gate. After a couple of hours, and a couple bottles of wine, we have talked, laughed, and cried over event stories, and what transpired in Berlin. Like water under the bridge, Miles has calmed and moved on. This event is challenging enough without any added stress from my client!

Back at the dock, we are all clambering to leave when out of nowhere Cathy blurts, "So Eve, how was Sebastian? Is he good in bed?"

A couple glasses of wine for Cathy and I never know what is going to spew from her mouth. Of course, I would love nothing more than to answer that most awkward question when I'm saved by an incoming text: *"Test in 15. C u asap. Thx Rob."*

"I hate to cut the evening short," I say, "but I have to go check out the lighting setup at the church."

"I'd like to come along," Miles says. "Me too," Blaine and Cathy chime in together, then "jinx" each other like schoolkids.

Climbing off the boat, we thank the fine staff and walk briskly through the narrow streets and alleyways toward the church. The streets seem narrower once we reach the red-light district, and darker too. Passing the "storefronts" where women are selling their bodies and sleazy men behind dirty doors are selling drugs, I can't help feeling sad and agitated. A few more minutes of walking and this dark world almost begins to feel strangely normal. Almost.

As we're called to by the women inside, I can't help feeling sorry for them. I wonder how they got into the position they're in. Not literally—figuratively speaking, of course.

"Look!" Cathy booms, stopping in front of a row of lingerie-clad women licking their lips and making suggestive poses. One young woman has a whip in her hand, ponytails on her head, and is dressed in a little girl's outfit. She holds up a sign reading, "I've been a real bad girl."

"They're dancing! They just want to have fun, like I do."

We shepherd Cathy along, certain that if we left her, we'd find her working in one of the windows when we returned.

My heart skips a beat when I first see the illumination of the church from blocks away. As we get closer, I notice it has already attracted a large gathering of curious onlookers. The church is awash in royal blues and forest greens. Rays of gold from inside shoot out from the stained glass, giving the whole place an ethereal look. The crisp Creation logo, plastered on the side of the church in white, pops, giving passersby, most of whom are attending the convention, a reason to come here tomorrow night. Even though I didn't think about it beforehand, it's a great marketing strategy.

We give the thumbs-up to Robert, who is having a good time impressing the crowd, and walk inside. There we find his team lighting the columns in a deep red. Unfortunately, it's taking on a demonic look—not exactly what we want for a church. I nix it and ask them to go with a mixture of softer colors, including the gold lights, which are shooting up and out the windows.

Since Robert is going to be working all night, I let him know that Chuck, who did in fact obtain permission from the church representatives, will likely be coming soon to practice.

"You know," Cathy says with her eyes closed, arms in the air, swaying back and forth. "No one has asked for permission to be here. *They* want us to ask for permission, Eve."

I look to the guys for help, but they both shrug. "*Who* wants us to ask for permission, Cathy?" I ask.

"The people who lie beneath. You need to ask their consent. I can help you do this tomorrow." Instantly she switches gears: "I heard there is a great bar nearby. It's supposed to be a lot of fun! One of your staff told me about it, Eve."

After our long day, and with no good reason not to, we all decide to join Cathy for a nightcap. As we walk into the crowded club, we almost collide with a group of men, some belonging to 1-2-1 TV, as well as many other convention-goers. A sort of reunion ensues. We make small talk for a few minutes, building the hype for the party tomorrow night, and then move on.

Taking the stairs up to the second floor, we find a horseshoe bar that resembles a small stage. As Blaine orders drinks, we hear hooting and hollering coming from the back edge of the stage. Craning our necks, we see two women wearing only high heels and red lipstick climb onto the bar. As we ply our way through the rowdy crowd to get a better look, I notice one of the women onstage eyeing Cathy. She hands her a bottle of baby oil, and Cathy, as happy as can be, takes the bait. Downing her drink in one fell swoop, she cracks open the bottle.

"Cathy, I think it's time to go."

Most of the other 1-2-1 TV guys from downstairs have now joined us and are egging her on along with the rest of the crowded room like we're at a wet T-shirt contest at a fraternity house. I almost can't watch as she fills her hands with oil and starts lathering the woman, even caressing and fondling her breasts.

I turn to Miles and Blaine who are fixated on the scene. "Guys! We need to get her down from there."

They don't even blink. And the crowd is going crazy! I guess I'm on my own with this one. Turning back, I see Cathy, fully dressed in her too-tight, low-cut, glued-on dress and red stilettos, lying on top of the woman, with her tongue down the woman's throat.

I swear I hear Miles scream to me, "We'll put 'dignity' on her Christmas wish list."

When Cathy crawls off the bar, Miles and Blaine get the group to start shouting my name, encouraging me to repeat Cathy's act. The roar of the crowd is deafening as they cheer me on, "EV-EL-LYN! EV-EL-LYN! EV-EL-LYN!"

I turn to face the riled crowd of partygoers. "Thank you, guys, but honestly, it's not my style."

Just then the naked woman calls Cathy back and asks if she would like a postcard to send back home. "Oh my gosh, how sweet of you. I would love a postcard!" Cathy squeals. I literally just about fall over when the woman places a pen between her legs, then squats and swiftly writes her a note on the card.

Miles can't stand it any longer and walks out of the room. Blaine on the other hand starts clapping. "Wow!" he yells. "That's a real talent!"

Needless to say, I can't find the front door fast enough.

CHAPTER SEVENTEEN

When I walk into the church the next morning, a rather large woman in a brown polyester suit greets me by yelling, "Get him down from there!"

"Well, good morning to you."

"He won't stop!" she screeches, pointing above the altar toward the organ loft. "Get him down from there! He's been playing for over an hour!"

I glance up, knowing full well who is responsible for the deafening sound ringing from the organ. And Chuck isn't just playing—he's pounding away on a Bach fugue. Oh no! Miles was right. What have I done? I nod to the woman as I climb up the stairs, covering my ears. "Chuck, it's time to come down," I scream.

I wave my phone at him, showing the time. "And you need to get over to the convention center, don't you? The booth will be open soon."

Chuck pauses, glances at his Rolex, then hops up from the bench and runs down the stairs. "Thanks, Eve, I have a meeting in a few minutes I almost forgot about."

"No problem. What happened to practicing last night?" I ask, my ears still ringing.

"Um, I was busy," he says, avoiding my eyes.

I bet you were.

Not saying another word, he takes off out the door. As he goes, I swear I hear hissing coming from the church rep in the dark suit.

Glancing down at my phone again, I notice a text from Miles saying the line for the credentials is a row of booths long. And it's only ten o'clock! I'm not one to jump to conclusions, but that's a good sign. I'm hoping we have the food to feed all of these people.

Moments later Saartje arrives, looking the complete opposite of her professional self. She's in sweats, obviously hasn't had a wink of sleep, and there is no trace of the smile that is usually plastered across her face. "We are going to need another prep area, Eve. Where are the rooms?" She obviously wants to get down to business.

Since there are very few actual rooms in the church and they have already been claimed for other uses, we are using an area off to the side of the altar, sectioned off by pipe and drape.

"Do you think this will work?" I ask, noticing that the rentals have yet to arrive.

She takes a good look around. "You know, Agneese and Adrianus use much more room than we do. They are going to need a separate area of their own."

Is there an issue here that I am unaware of?

"Okay," I say, reviewing the blueprints and not finding any additional space. "We can set up a tent outside. Will that do?"

"Perfect," she says flatly. "That will work fine."

I get the feeling something's up, so I press a little more. "So, how is it working with Agneese and her family?"

She makes a mélange of faces before answering. "It's good . . . it's good . . . it's all good."

"Really?"

She looks as if there's some kind of battle going on inside, to dish or not to dish. "Well . . . it's all good except for the fact that Agneese drives me crazy with her singing all the time, and Adrianus whistles. I feel like I'm working with Snow White and the seven dwarfs!"

Oh the joys of working with multiple companies.

"So besides that, we're good?"

She sighs, writing notes on her tablet, and glances back at me. "We're good."

I'm glad she could get that off her chest. But let's face it, there's not too much I can do about two happy-go-lucky caterers.

"The rentals should be here by noon and a delivery from the beverage company by two. Trish will be working with my team today, and Agneese, Adrianus, and their family, including their grandchildren, will be working at their kitchen. Half the team will be here tomorrow at noon and the other half at six in the evening." Saartje nods along, taking all the information in. I leave her, hoping she'll power through, but with the stakes this high, I better start crossing all my fingers, knock on a pile of wood, and find a few four-leaf clovers!

After ordering the extra tent, I'm surprised to see Cathy wandering around the furiously working vendors, looking lost. I stop her. "I thought you were handing out credentials this morning?"

"I did. But they were gone in an hour. Miles sent me over here to help you."

Remind me to thank Miles later.

"Gone? Already?"

"Yep, and all these desperate people are begging for tickets at the booth. I have never seen Chuck this charged!"

Cathy quickly changes her expression as she scans the huge church from floor to ceiling. Her voice drops. "It is time, Eve," she whispers oh so seriously.

"Time for what, Cathy?"

"It's time to ask the ones that have left us for permission."

"But if they've left us, Cathy, then can we assume that they are not here?"

I'm really not trying to be sarcastic . . . really.

"They're still among us, Eve," she says. She takes hold of one of the lighting engineers, calls a few carpenters over, the disc jockey, two electricians, three random worshipers, and four reluctant staff from the audiovisual team. "Please, everyone, sit on the floor in a circle, hold hands, and close your eyes."

Sounding like a medium leading a séance, Cathy starts softly: "We are mere strangers here, asking you who live amongst us for your guidance and permission to have our event here tomorrow evening."

I better keep one eye open just in case this is a hoax or on the off chance a ghost appears.

Cathy begins to sway back and forth as if transported by the energy emanating from the place. "Please, if any of you object to this request, please show us a sign now." Right on cue, a spooky, cool breeze swoops in from the door. My eyes snap open, as do everyone else's.

"No need to worry," she says softly. "That's just their way of telling us that they know we're here."

She asks us to close our eyes again and remain holding hands. The hand of the carpenter next to me is sweaty, and even though I would rather not, I continue holding. "Thank you, great spirits," Cathy concludes. "Thank you for your patience and understanding. We hope that you join us at the party and that you have a good time."

In all my years as a planner, this is a first.

My phone rings. What perfect timing. Wiping the carpenter's sweat onto my pants, I stand. "Excuse me, I have to take this call."

"Eve, it's Blaine. I'm in the 1-2-1 TV booth at the convention center."

"How's it going over there?"

"It's, uh, going well." His voice is muffled as if he has his hand over the mouthpiece. "They have a minor situation happening, and I hope we can help."

I hope it is "minor" since I'm not there to do anything about it.

"Every time Stan Mickelson, their hired emcee, stands up at the podium, the audio goes berserk. The AV guys have changed out his mic three times, and we've tried the standing mic at the podium too. Do you have any ideas?"

Luckily, I've actually had this experience with other speakers.

"Try changing the mic's position."

"We have."

"Try repositioning the speaker output so that—"

"Done."

"Try equalizing the signal—"

"Done."

"Have you tried a noise gate or filter?"

"Yep."

Okay . . . I've listed anything it could be. Wait . . . there once was a situation . . .

"If it happens again, replace him. I know this sounds crazy, but I've had this happen before and he may be the problem. The static from his body's energy isn't meshing with the sound system. You really don't have any other choice unless he wants to go without a mic. Is his voice powerful enough that he doesn't really need it?"

"Oh, that may not go over well. But no need to worry, I'll figure it out. Thanks, Eve."

I can't help thinking how much Blaine reminds me of me when I first started out. I flash back to my first job when I was thrown into four back-to-back events of a thousand people each. "What exactly should I do here?" I asked nervously, having been flung a clipboard with only a mere sampling of the details. Without much assistance, I took a calming breath, straightened my navy-blue polyester suit, and relied on my common sense. I wasn't sure how I was doing until a few weeks later when the client requested that I work with them on all their events going forward.

"Okay," I say, feeling more confident than ever about having hired Blaine, "check in with Saartje and Trish when you're done there and see if they need any additional help. I'm going to stay here at the church all day."

"Will do. Later."

Thankfully, the rest of the day continues without too many glitches. The tent arrives and is erected, while the rest of the lighted highboy-pedestal tables are delivered. We had received the bulk of them yesterday, but some of the tables were the wrong height. Now, having been changed out, each of the tables is wrapped with white spandex linen that will be illuminated in hues of orchid and royal purple. The carpenters continue to build the stages and props, the lighting continues to be installed indoors, and a few of the entertainers rehearse.

Besides the dozens of phone calls from people pleading for credentials, the day is finishing up nicely.

So why do I still feel so uncertain whether we'll be able to actually pull this event together?

CHAPTER EIGHTEEN

IT'S SHOW DAY! The excitement and nervous energy that accompanies such an event is unparalleled. Not only are the clients eager but also the vendors, staff, and most of all, the guests. There was such a flurry of calls and requests for credentials at the booth yesterday that Chuck, Miles, and the entire 1-2-1 TV staff had to close it down. They were even followed back to the hotel by convention attendees. Today isn't too different; there are a couple hundred people outside the church, who have been waiting for hours, hoping to get a last-minute pass tonight. In light of the situation, Chuck decided to close the booth for the entire day.

And now, as Miles, Cathy, Blaine and I, along with the entire team run around prepping, Chuck walks in through the church doors.

"Okay, Eve," Chuck says, sidling up to me. I know he loves all this attention. "Where are the extra credentials?"

I shrug my shoulders. "What other credentials?"

His face turns white. "Aren't you holding a hundred extra credentials for us?"

I keep a straight face. "No, I'm not."

Beads of sweat appear on his brow. He takes a hanky from his pants pocket, patting his forehead. He appears to be on the verge of hysterics. "I thought you said you were holding an extra hundred credentials for us." He points to the door and raises his voice. "The people outside are my colleagues. I told them to be here today to pick up a badge. Now what?"

I look him straight in the eye, forcing myself to sound apologetic. "I told you I was holding a hundred badges, Chuck, but in reality...I am holding two hundred." I pick up a box with the credentials. He's now smiling from ear to ear, looking as if he could kiss me, which is exactly what I don't want. I hand him the box before he can make any sudden moves. "Here, go be the hero that those people are expecting you to be."

Chuck takes the box and shakes his head, "You got me, Eve. You got me." He and his gleeful team run outside to distribute the contents.

"Eve!" I hear from behind me. I turn to find a frowning woman approaching me. "We need to talk."

"Hello, Mary," I say, shaking the hand of one of the church representatives, who is wearing a beautiful red cardigan and a ruffled white blouse. She reminds me of a favorite aunt of mine who lives in South Dakota and always wears extra-wide non-slip Velcro walking shoes with knee-high stockings and her signature apron. I love that aunt. She makes the best pies in a four-state region.

"What can I help you with?"

She looks at me, distressed. "Eve, we aren't feeling comfortable with the number of people invited. We haven't had this large a group here before."

Could we have discussed this *before* the day of the event?

"So I'm afraid that we are going to have to insist on metal detectors."

"Metal detectors?"

"Don't worry about trying to find them. I already have." She hands me a paper written in Dutch. "Oops," she says, "I meant to hand you the one in English. Here you go."

"Are you serious?"

"Yes, I am. The good news is that we have staff that can help you with the wands and pat-downs. Twenty or so nuns from the convent are coming over to lend a hand." She starts to walk away. "The wands are being delivered in a couple of hours. Thanks for understanding, Eve. I'll get working on the details right away."

"But how much is this going to cost us?"

She turns around with a grin. "A nice donation to the church is all we ask."

I meant the cost in relation to wands, not the nuns.

Amid the chaos of my name being called every few minutes, inside an alcove I sneak into what looks like a giant rock, but what will be the casing around a living statue later tonight, to take a few bites of a protein bar. Sometimes I don't even have time to eat, but I need something to get me through to the start of the party. After the first sensation of the nutty, rich taste of peanuts and sesame seeds hitting my taste buds, I hear Chuck calling for me.

"There you are, Eve." He points to a far door. "There is a Dutch dance troupe that has arrived out back. I think they said they want to rehearse? They don't speak very good English. Anyway, they're looking for you."

"Thanks, Chuck," I reply, having no idea what he's talking about. One thing I do know, we have no Dutch dance troupe performing tonight.

I walk out back to find Agneese, Adrianus, and the entire motley crew, including Trish and her students, dressed as old-fashioned folk dancers, setting up in the tent.

Trish is first to beeline over to me. "Well," she says under her breath, "if I had only known beforehand that these were going to be our uniforms tonight..." She leans a little closer: "Can I look any more like a dressed-up Kewpie doll than I do right now?"

I smile at the others in the tent as I softly answer, "Obviously, someone did not get the 'all-black' memo."

I overhear a beaming Agneese asking one of her nephews to start playing the accordion as they set up.

"Wow!" I say approaching Agneese, who even after two and a half days of cooking day and night is ready to kick it up to the music. She gives me another one of her bear hugs. "Well, hello, Agneese, these are very colorful outfits. Did Saartje happen to inform you that I requested black shirts and slacks? I mean, Creation is the theme tonight, and I'm not certain these costumes are appropriate."

She giggles and dances about as she lays out a few trays of appetizers needing final touches. "No, no, we did receive, but they not show our Dutch heritage, so I decide to use our outfits." Her broken English is better than I remember.

Maybe I should use them as a dance troupe this evening after all... the evening is all about the bizarre and unusual anyway.

"Better get to it," I retort, stealing a piece of melon wrapped with prosciutto from the tray as Saartje and her team arrive in all black.

"What the hell is this?" Saartje asks, looking over at Agneese with disapproving eyes. "I thought we were supposed to come in black. Who took the drapes down from the Von Trapp Estate to make costumes?"

I take Saartje by the hand and walk her over to the side of the tent. "It's okay. They wanted to give the party a little Dutch flair. It's not going to hurt anyone, and really, they're just going to blend in once the party gets started. In fact, let's begin with your staff on the floor and only utilize their staff if needed." There's a long pause until I add, "We're lucky to have them. Come on... will that work?"

"Okay," she says, gritting her teeth and making a face. "I'll call a truce, this one time." She heads back over to the table to take a look at their work. Adrianus hands her a plate of appetizers. "Thank you," she says, then adds how surprised she is by the beautiful display of appetizers resembling a Van Gogh... She takes a bite of their homemade chicken sausage, and I watch as her eyes light up while she savors every chew. "That's divine!"

Saartje is back in front of me in a second, newfound respect written all over her face. "They look ridiculous, but they sure can cook. You never know, Eve—after this event, I may have to go work for them!"

It's eight o'clock and time for an all-hands-on-deck gathering. The bartenders, waitstaff, chefs, singers, dancers, strolling entertainers, disc jockeys, production staff, audiovisual guys, lighting crew, church representatives, security nuns, off-duty policemen, paramedics, traffic guards, and clients, along with my staff, are standing around waiting for direction from me. However, it doesn't look as if that's going to happen. Just as I'm about to open my mouth, Chuck taps my shoulder. "I've got this."

"But Chuck—" He has no idea what to say and how to say it. He doesn't usually show up until after an event has already begun, for crying out loud.

Please trip.

He makes his way over to the stage in the middle of the room and jumps up on it. "Hey everybody, how ya doin? Thanks for coming tonight."

Is he trying to address event workers, or does he think he's doing a stand-up routine at a comedy club?

Please don't start off with a joke. Please.

"So I was headed here tonight..."

What's he talking about? He's been here *all* day!

"And I got to thinking: I bet no one's heard the joke about the woman reporter who visits the Indian reservation?"

That's enough. Miles and I must be thinking the same thing since we both jump onstage at the same time.

"Ladies and gentleman," I declare, politely taking the microphone from Chuck, "I would like to introduce you to our clients for this wonderful event—Chuck Howard, CEO of 1-2-1 TV, and Miles Emerson, Director of Marketing." Without giving Chuck the opportunity to speak any further, I continue with the agenda.

"Mr. Howard and Mr. Emerson are delighted you are here to assist them this evening in what will most likely be one of the most visually spectacular and well-attended events of this conference. We all feel honored to have such an incredible group of people to pull off such a feat like this. Please give yourselves a round of applause."

I walk across the stage, making sure that I make eye contact with as many people as I can. "Tonight we are expecting two thousand people, and our goal is to make sure that each person walking through those doors has a good time. I want to empower all of you to make decisions that are reasonable and make good sense. If you should require additional assistance, please see a team lead who will have a headset. They can radio for help if need be.

"To all of the twenty nuns that we have here tonight, thank you for helping us with security." The nuns wave the metal detectors over their heads like foam fingers at a sporting event. "I want to remind all of the staff working outside tonight that no high heels are allowed, so if you see someone wearing them, please politely ask them to change and return without them on."

A set of bright red lips shouts, "We fabulous entertainers are the exception to the rule because we couldn't bare our souls or our clothes without the power of the heel." Bunny lifts her size 14, sexy black leather Christian Louboutin five-inch caged-ankle boot high in the air for all of us to gawk at.

"Yes," I say, acknowledging Bunny and the other entertainers. "Good point, but I ask all of you who have to wear high heels to be extra careful." I look down to glance at my notes. "I realize that we still have work to do, and we have a few entertainers still missing at this point, but it's important that you eat if you haven't already done so. There is a great menu of food for you in the tent behind the church. I know it goes without saying, but please do not use the buffets this evening, which are for our guests inside the church.

"I am standing on the main stage, between the pews and pulpits, where the main acts and our two disc jockeys will be performing this evening. Let me point out to you how the rest of the evening will work. Guests will enter through the main doors over there." I point to the scrim, a lightweight fabric floating above the entrance doors, steps from the arched entrance. "This material will have a projection of a sun rising and slowly setting."

The nuns hoot, knowing this is going to be their territory. "That's right," I say as they wave their wands again. "This area is where each person will be searched before entering." I point farther down from the entrance. "The coat check is here in this room, and just off to the right is the VIP room. Guests will have to show ID in order to enter. This is where Chuck, Miles, and their team will be able to conduct business. A complete, separate waitstaff will work in there with a full bar and buffet. There are also video screens so they may view the entertainment without leaving the room. Unless you are scheduled to work in there, there shouldn't be any reason to go in. Mr. Howard requests this room be dedicated to holding business."

More like "monkey business," but I'm not saying a thing.

I point to the far corner. "As many of you have already found out, the last set of rooms on this side of the church are dressing rooms for the entertainers or for any staff who feel the need to use them."

My eyes are directed to the front of the church and the "holy moly" area. I jump off the main stage and walk over to the smaller stage between two large illuminated mojito bars. "This is the lounge area of the event. We have a great singer who will perform while the six floating screens above me are going to project a montage of life. Think seeds springing to life, animals...you can see on the screens now, a lioness giving birth."

Many of the female staff gasp and cringe.

"Okay, well...that's a little graphic. We may need to fix that," I say, eyeing one of the AV guys who immediately takes off running to the control center.

I walk to the back wall as everyone follows me. "Here, among the sea of lighted tables, bars, and buffets is an array of interactive games and digital photo booths for the guests to indulge." I make my way back to the main stage, walk up the stairs, and point to the back of the church. "In this corner, we have the inside catering prep area, and on the opposite side of the room in the alcove is a living statue, with more buffets and bars. Does anyone have any questions?"

Cathy raises her hand. I dread what her question might be.

"I don't have a question, but I do have a comment." She walks up the stairs to join me. "I just want to say unless you're a transvestite transforming yourself..."

People start to giggle and laugh.

"Please keep your clothes on."

An audible gasp comes from the nuns' direction.

"Well," I say, trying to cover up that disaster of a comment, "speaking of our entertainers tonight, we have an array of performers who will be strolling, singing, dancing, etcetera all night. The best thing I can ask of all of you is to have a good time. If you have a good time, everyone else will too. Thanks in advance for helping us make this party a huge success."

Please, please, please let this party be a huge success.

A large round of applause fills the hall. "I will ask you now to finish up the last-minute details, grab a headset if you are a lead, and let's get this party rolling."

Everyone scatters about. The lights are turned on the tables, the food is placed out on the buffets, the bartenders open bottles to air, the professional photographers snap a few last-minute photos of the décor, and everyone is in place.

My heart is pounding loud enough to wake the dead beneath my feet!

I press the button on my headset. "We are T minus five, people. Do we have a go?"

"Go with catering," Saartje responds.

"Go with security traffic and crowd control," Miles replies. "We have a mighty anxious crowd out here."

We have a "go" response from the VIP room.

"Go with entertainers and music," Blaine blasts back.

"Where are we going?" Cathy sounds up.

Anonymous laughter comes over the airwaves. "Sharp-ketlen!"

Oh no!

"Miles, come in. Miles."

"This is Miles Cap-do-yang."

"Miles," I begin, wanting to calm his nerves, "everything is all set, everyone is ready to go. You are an amazing client. Let's have a good time, over."

"I'm a go, Eve. Open-wasp-dil."

Okay, he'll calm down after the party gets going.

I take a quick look around the entire room, then give Chuck the cue to start playing the organ. "Let's open the doors!"

You would think a department store was going out of business, given how the people rush in. Some of the nuns look like they're having a hard time keeping up with the zealous crowd; and one or two of them seem as if they're having too much fun with the pat-downs. "Oh my..." I hear one of them exclaim as she reaches below the belt of one of our male guests.

Chuck, meanwhile, is playing a piece from *Phantom of the Opera*. I glance around to see that everyone is astounded by the strong, beautiful, haunting music. He isn't pounding on the keys like he did earlier. Guests stop in their tracks to listen. It's soft yet powerful—undeniably the best way to begin an exotic evening of entertainment.

Oh sweet Mary in heaven... Thank you!

Within half an hour the place is filling up and the lights are dimmed. A single spotlight reveals the shimmering platinum dress of a woman perched above the spiral staircase on the back wall. Her hair slicked back and a yellow boa constrictor draped around her neck, she begins to belt out the aria "Caro Nome" from *Rigoletto*. And she is spectacular! I stop, taking her voice in, and notice I'm not the only one. Miles radios, "Eve, the church may be full, but we have a rather large crowd outside as well, and they can hear the music. This is so amazing!"

As I cruise the venue, I pass the "fashion police" dressed in short black skirts, white shirts with rolled-up sleeves, fake badges, black ties, and handcuffs hanging from their belts. They are handing out one fashion citation after the next and, not surprisingly, already have their first arrest. I see them hauling away a man who is wearing shorts, a blazer, a bow tie, and dress shoes.

The suntanned girls with faux fur bikini tops and white leather pants seem to be catching quite a few eyes. "Keep smiling, ladies," I remind them as I head toward the back.

The place is packed. The lighting trellis around the large stage starts flashing as the disc jockey kills the sound. "Ladies and gentlemen," the disc jockey cries, "get ready for the sounds of tribal heat from Africa!"

The crowd roars while the dozen African tribal drummers, dressed to the nines in their colorful sarongs and beads, beat away on their traditional *djembe* drums. As I move about the room, I find myself swaying along to the primal beat.

"Eve, come in, Eve."

"This is Eve, over."

"Our lounge singer for the small stage is MIA, over," Blaine announces. "He was here fifteen minutes ago and now we can't find him."

"Do we have someone else to replace him, over?"

"Open-the-front-door! This is Bunny. Let me take a shot at it, doll. I am the ultimate performer, you know."

She scuttles up to me, snapping her fingers around her "bad" self.

Does she sing with a male or female voice? I smile at how ridiculous my thought is. "Bunny, you're a go."

"Eve, come in. This is Miles." Miles is outside with the crowd. "We have two or three thousand people still out here waiting to get in, over."

Gulp.

"Miles, we are at capacity. These people can't possibly have credentials for the event, over."

"No, but they're dying to get in. I can't believe the size of the crowd!"

"Miles, do you need more security for crowd control, over?"

"It's okay for now but wow!...The size of the crowd is unbelievable...over."

"Ask the off-duty police to call for backup if they need it. I'll see you back inside, over."

It suddenly occurs to me I should check in with Chuck. With this many people, it's going to be almost impossible to find him.

"Chuck, come in, Chuck?"

Where may he be lurking?

"This is an APB on the whereabouts of Chuck Howard. We need him out in front of the church immediately. Has anyone seen him?"

Dead silence.

I hope he isn't in trouble. "Will someone please check the VIP room?"

"This is Saartje, Eve. Not a soul has been in here, over."

Not a surprise. He always insists on a special room, and inevitably, it never gets used.

Where can he be?

I come up behind the faux-fur bikini suntan girls and am shocked that their pants are actually white leather chaps, exposing a thong on their backsides. Masses of men are following closely behind, but no CEO. Time to check in with Cathy.

"Hey, Eve, what's going on?"

"No time to chat at the moment, Cathy," I radio back. "I'm trying to find Chuck."

"No probs. I haven't seen him, but I'll keep an eye out for him, okay? Over and out. See ya later, alligator. In a while, crocodile."

"Stop pressing the button, Cathy."

"Okey dokey, smokey."

I pass a woman I recognize but can't place my finger on how. "Hello," I say hurriedly, "do you happen to know Chuck Howard?"

"You mean the man who was onstage before the party started?"

I nod.

"Yes," she says disgruntled. "He tried to get fresh with me by climbing into the casing of my living statue, so I played along until I could show him how it works, and then I locked him in it!"

Oh no.

"Where is he now?"

Her posture tells me she's laying down the law. "That's where I left him and that's where he belongs, locked up!" She runs off with what I'm thinking may be the keys.

I run over to see Chuck's silver-painted head and arms popping out of the living statue. "Eve," he begs, "please get me out of here, I'm cooking."

Standing there, looking at him, I'm sure I will keep this mental snapshot for a long time to come. I so want to laugh in his face and tell him that he deserves to be right where he is.

"Okay, Chuck," I say, taking my sweet time assuring him, "I have a little situation that I have to handle, but I'll send someone over to get you out."

Not that I really want to let him free, but it's the right thing to do. Isn't it? Before I do, I'll have one of the photographers snap a couple of photos.

I run toward the entrance, pressing the button on my radio. "Blaine, Chuck needs help in the alcove. Will you please assist him, over?"

"Eve, this is Blaine. Will do after I get the a cappella group over to the main stage, over."

I turn to go out the front door, noticing a packed crowd that has gathered around the small stage. Bunny certainly knows how to draw people in as she belts a sultry, sexy version of a Tina Turner song.

I hit the entrance at lightning speed and run straight into a man's well-defined chest.

"Schatzi!"

"Sebastian?"

He puts his arms around me, planting another fabulous kiss on my lips.

"This is incredible, Eve. I haven't seen anything like it." He holds me to his side, looking up at the rays of light emanating from the stained-glass windows. "Wow," he says, "you really know how to throw a party." I look over at him, dangerously close to losing myself in those eyes...But no! Not right now. There's work to be done.

"How about you go in and get a drink," I say, softy planting another peck on his lips. "I'll find you in just a bit." He squeezes my hand and maintains the grip for as long as our arms can reach. Oh, how I wish everyone else would disappear. *The effect Sebastian has on me!*

"Eve, the crowd is barr-daw," Miles yells over the noisy crowd as I make my way to him.

"Miles, I have an idea. Why don't we send some of the entertainers outside to perform? It will keep the crowd distracted so they aren't trying so hard to get in."

"Fab idea, Eve. Have Blaine send the opera diva and the African tribal drummers out here. I'll meet you inside in a few minutes."

"Will do, over."

"Blaine, come in, over."

"Go for Blaine, over," says Blaine, out of breath.

"When you're done with Chuck—"

"I'm done, over."

"Send out a small stage and any performers to Miles. We need to keep the crowd outside under control, over."

Now that I know Chuck's back on the prowl, I better find him. I turn to find him helping Bunny wrench her heel from between two gravestones. "Not the Christians!" I hear Bunny gasp. She may lose a shoe, but at least she's keeping Chuck out of trouble...for now.

From a distance I see Trish doing her best to keep her students and Agneese and Adrianus's family members tucked inside the tent, only allowing Saartje and her team to serve inside the church. The two seem to be working well together. As a server passes by, I see what looks and smells like a delicious garlic-and-onion-stuffed mushroom. Yum.

After making sure everything is going according to plan, I find Sebastian watching the Chinese acrobats from a pulpit off to the side of the main stage. I sneak away for a moment to watch with him, keeping one eye on the performers and one eye on the event. The troupe is amazing—with stunts on top of stacked chairs; a man juggling atop a human pyramid; and two young female contortionists dressed in sequined body stockings, weaving effortlessly between each other, bending their bodies into shapes and positions that look impossible. Sebastian whispers with a seductive tone in my ear, "Can you do that?"

I turn around and hit him playfully. "No! But I do have some signature moves that may surprise you. Maybe I'll show you sometime." I flash him a naughty smile, then rush off, leaving him with that thought so I can check on the other end of the church.

We must be getting to that time of the night when people are feeling relaxed, some more than others. I round a column to find Miles singing along with Bunny, the two of them rubbing their bodies together in between the mojito bars on the small stage. When the song finishes, he turns to her. "Shall we sex it up, Bunny?"

I stand there speechless. Should I tell Miles "she" is a "he"?

I mean, he's really getting into it. And I had no idea he could sing Barry White.

Oh my! Bunny shimmies down the front of Miles, feeling his abs while he belts out the song.

Oh well, if he doesn't know now, he will soon. Why break up the fun?

But come on! The Adam's apple! It's a dead giveaway!

I shake my head and move on. Ah-ha! I had been wondering when the fashion police were going to finally catch up to Cathy.

I imagine they could cite her on a dozen counts of violating the codes of fashion ethics. The women take her wrists and place them behind her back, swiftly snapping the handcuffs on her. She screeches as she's taken away.

Just then a loud drumroll sounds and a spotlight beams above the guests on the dance floor. All eyes shift to the high-wire troupe, dressed and painted as wild animals, walking across the entire length of the church, forty feet off the ground.

There is complete silence as one by one a lion, tiger, elephant, and zebra glide from one end of the nave to the other. I radio Blaine, "What happened to the nets?"

"At the last minute they asked us to remove them, over."

"*Who* asked you to remove them?"

"The performers, over."

Okay, now I'm as shaky and nervous as the rest of the crowd.

Suddenly the elephant performer teeters and falls, grabbing the wire with one hand! A collective inhale is heard as some of the men in the crowd form a human chain underneath the performer, moving tables as needed. I ask the paramedics who are standing nearby to get ready as I see two of the nuns faint.

Holy cow! I mean elephant. Not now!

"What next?" One of the performers yells down, teasing the panicked crowd. Moments later, after we are all on pins and needles, we watch as the elephant performer swings back up and they finish the act. The crowd goes wild as Blaine gives the disc jockey the signal to turn up the tunes and get the mesmerized guests dancing again. I let out a huge sigh of relief.

Miles runs up to me. "Did you do that for me?"

"Well, you did ask for a live-animal high-wire act. This was the best I could do."

"I have to say it had quite an effect. I'm impressed," he beams.

We both turn to see Cathy, looking rather... well, different. Miles doesn't even wait to ask; he hightails it away.

"Cathy," I say, trying hard to keep a straight face, "why are you dressed like a man?"

She looks down, admiring her transformation, and then back at me with a shrug. "I wanted to see what it would feel like to be a transvestite."

Of course you did.

I watch as she sashays off toward the dancing guests. The energy on the dance floor is contagious. Even Trish and her students are out there dancing to the techno beat. Normally, I would never allow the staff to join in on an event, but the party is so huge, I doubt anyone would even notice.

It's two in the morning and the party hasn't thinned out at all. I check with security to see what's going on.

"Miles, come in, Miles."

"Go for Miles, Eve."

"Have you checked the counter at the front door lately?"

Miles sounds preoccupied. "Umm, the last time I checked, we were at two thousand four hundred and twenty-two people, over. But I will check again, over and out."

A few minutes later, he radios back. "Eve, the counter is at three thousand eight hundred and fifty-six! I don't know what happened?"

I can hear Miles ask a traffic guard to explain.

"When your guests were leaving," says the guard, "they were giving their credentials to people standing around the corner."

Miles radios all leads: "We are closing entry to this party, over."

There is no way I'm letting this event go under in the eleventh hour.

I run up to Chuck, who is at the top of one of the pulpits, surrounded by admirers. I have to shout to get his attention. "Chuck, we are already an hour overtime with a full house. The crowd is getting wild. I think you should shut the party down now. You've had close to four *thousand* guests."

His head is bopping with the beat. "Okay, Eve, whatever you say. You tell them the party is over."

Sprinting to the stage, I tell the disc jockeys to play a last song. "Hey," the disc jockey announces, "This is the last song of the night. Chuck and the entire 1-2-1 TV team thank you for joining in on the fun, and we hope you had a real good time."

The crowd goes ballistic until the disc jockey slows the mood.

Just then Sebastian grabs my hand. *What a strong hand.* He leads me to the side of the stage and wraps his arms around my body. As we sway back and forth, he whispers in my ear, "I have missed that smile of yours." I pull back to look at him: "And I've missed those eyes." We embrace each other for the rest of the song, our bodies touching. At the song's end, I glance around and see that no one is leaving. In fact, people are standing on the pews, in and around the dance floor and the perimeter, beginning a dance revolution, stomping and yelling: "We want more...We want more...We want more!"

Hating to leave Sebastian, I nevertheless excuse myself and sprint over to Chuck, who is up in the pulpit with six women draped around him, all yelling along with the crowd.

"CHUCK!" I scream, waving him down from the pulpit, "you're going to have to ask this group to calm down and leave the premises."

He shoots me a you're-a-party-pooper look. Chuck reluctantly makes his way over to the DJ stand and grabs a microphone. He can't hear himself over the noise, so he uses his hand to get the crowd to ease up. "Hey, did you guys have a good time tonight?"

The crowd roars.

What is he doing?

"If you did, and you want to do it again next year, you're going to have to wrap it up for tonight, and we'll see you next year with a bigger and better party. Good night."

And with that he puts the mic down and heads out, with the entire posse of guests behind him cheering and whooping it up as they go. Chuck the pied piper of his own event. He was so worried about getting a crowd in; who would have guessed it would turn out to be all about leading them *out*.

All I know is that if it's bigger next year, I'm going to insist we start planning the second we touch American soil.

Watching people jump down from the pulpits and get out of the pews and photo booths, I make my way around the large hall. There is Miles, dressed from head to toe in a blue body suit, stuck to the Velcro wall in a horizontal position while Bunny lies on the floor at his side, panting as if she's in heat.

"Help..." Miles murmurs.

"Bunny," I wink, "be gentle with him."

Sebastian pulls me aside from the games to give me a quick kiss. "Shall I meet you back in the room?"

"I'll be there shortly." I smile, melting all over again.

I hear, "Owwwwww!" coming from behind one of the columns. I turn to see Trish and her students attempting to cram themselves into one of the photo booths. It looks like they're trying to put the contortionists' moves to shame.

"Be careful!" I giggle, heading toward the catering area.

I find Saartje, Adrianus, and Agneese inside the tent toasting to the event. "We pulled it off!" Saartje exclaims as I walk up. Adrianus hands me a glass of champagne. "All of you must be so exhausted," I say, raising my glass with them. "To all of you and an incredible feat, you are all miracle workers! What a fabulous night and undoubtedly one of our most unusual events ever!"

"Eve, come in, Eve," comes blaring over the headset.

"Hey, Eve," Blaine calls, "I'm in front of the game area, and Miles is here in a rather precarious position... thought you might want it on video before I help him down." I catch a snicker in his tone. "He's spewing out one Miles-ism after another and I have no idea what he's talking about, over."

Probably time to unstick him from that wall.

"Already saw enough—go ahead and get him down. Do you need some help, over?"

"Oh, I think Bunny will be more than delighted to help me. We're covered, over."

Since Miles and Blaine are accounted for, the only one left is Cathy.

"Cathy, come in, Cathy?"

"Did someone call my name on this thing?"

At least she answered.

"Cathy, you sound *really* tired. What's your twenty?"

"The fashion police and I are in the VIP room enjoying some brownies."

Brownies... Amsterdam...

"Stay where you are. I'll be over in a few minutes. Don't eat anything else!"

I grab a couple morsels off a tray in the back, gulp down a glass of water, and thank the entire cast of catering characters. Agneese and Adrianus's family members are all asleep on top of one another in the truck adjacent to the tent. I giggle at how they look like a toy chest full of colorful Dutch dolls.

Moments later I'm in the VIP room where I find Cathy welcoming me with a brownie. "Here, Eve, try one!" Six women in scanty fashion-police outfits, sprawled across two sofas, smile lazily up at me. Amsterdam or not, this is not okay! "Really, ladies!"

One of them who is already in the "zone" looks up at me. "Cathy's the best. She can't dress worth shit, but dude, she can party with the best of us."

"Yeah, that's great," I reply, taking away the special brownie that Cathy is biting into. "You don't want this, Cathy."

She tugs on my arm. "Yes, I do, Eve. I've only had one."

"A *whole* one, Cathy?"

"Yes, and they're so good. You should try one." She takes the brownie from my hand and takes a large bite. And then passes out.

"We need to clear this room, ladies, and get it cleaned up." Even though it shouldn't take any time to clean since it wasn't used during the event.

"Pick up your things and head out. It's time to go."

I radio Blaine. "Blaine, when you're done getting Miles unstuck, will you bring Cathy back to her hotel? She's in the VIP room, over."

"Is she conscious?"

"What do you think?"

"Got it. I'll get help, over."

I finish wrapping things up around the hall. The crew is taking down the games, the photo booths are being wheeled out, the recycle bins are full, the rentals are being stacked as well as the linens, and finally it's time for me to leave.

I decide to walk back to the hotel. After two hellish months of frenzied preparations, we actually pulled off both events. And not just pulled them off, we blew the lid off both of them! Two events with eight small weeks of planning! Especially Amsterdam. I couldn't be more proud and amazed. But strangely, I don't feel the same way I used to when I'd pull off something crazy like this event. Usually I feel on top of the world, but not tonight. What has changed? Am I just tired? Or is it something else? Is this what I want to be doing for the rest of my life? Because if

I'm going to be completely honest with myself, it can get pretty lonely on planet Eve. And for the first time, in a very long time, I'm not okay with it. I need more. I need balance. I need a life. And...I think I know where to start.

The door creaks as I slowly walk into my hotel room. I find Sebastian fully dressed, sleeping in the lounge chair next to the television console, with a single red tulip lying on his chest. The floor lamp next to the lounge chair gently illuminates him in a soft glow. One of the French doors leading to the balcony is open, letting in a crisp, refreshing breeze.

How can he possibly sleep with the noise of the city so loud?

Slipping off my shoes, I stand next to him. I greedily stare at the stubble on his face, his long eyelashes, and his coiffed hair; he is unbelievably handsome. He looks so content here in my room, so relaxed. I'd like to think it's because we've spent so many hours on the phone getting to know each other over the last six weeks. He, of course, is why I've had to increase the number of minutes on my phone plan and why the phone company keeps calling to see if my phone has been stolen as the minutes climb astronomically high.

"Hello, handsome," I whisper. As he slowly opens his eyes, I stretch out next to him on the chaise.

He hands me the floppy tulip. "This is for you, Schatzi."

I take it from him and lean in for a kiss. "How very sweet, thank you."

"What you do is incredible, Eve. Tonight I was so proud of you. Watching all those people...they were mesmerized. And the transformation of the church...it came alive, it was magical. How do you do it?"

As his fingers run through my hair, I wonder what he would say if I told him the truth—how I actually come up with the ideas. Will he laugh? Will he believe me? Perhaps another time. "I don't know, Sebastian, it's just what I do."

He looks at me, lightly tracing my lips with his finger.

He has that same hungry look in his eyes—a look that can mean only one thing.

I jump up, afraid that I must smell wilted from the day I've had. I can't get intimate with him right now. I refuse to have our first time happen when I feel all gritty and grimy.

"Will you hold that thought for just a few minutes? It's been a long day and I need to take a shower."

In the bathroom I'm surprised to find half-burned candles placed all over the room and fragrant peony petals strewn about.

He walks up behind me and places his head on my shoulder. "May I join you?" he asks, turning me around and looking at me with those same ravenous eyes.

We slowly unbutton each other's shirts, then gain speed as the lust intensifies. I whip off his belt, unzip his pants, and we both slip our underwear to the ground. He's a briefs guy; I would have guessed boxers, but what does it matter?

Standing among the pile of clothes in the candlelight, his mouth on mine, wet and moist, I break away, only to take his hand and lead him into the marble shower.

He presses my back against the tiled wall, his body strong, his gaze not leaving my eyes. He slithers a stream of liquid soap across my chest and fondles my breasts as I gasp in sensual oblivion.

As he's lifting me, I wrap my legs around his waist, then lean back to feel the cascade of warm water as it runs down my hair, all the while Sebastian's lips kissing my wet skin.

Oh, how I have wanted him! How I have fantasized about our first time—where it would be, how it would feel. Would it be on a bed, at a venue after an event, or on a late-night train heading to a faraway place? And here we are, ravaging each other's bodies, making passionate, uncontrollable love in the shower.

CHAPTER NINETEEN

MY EYES UNSTICK at the sound of an obnoxious honk from what I assume is a large truck outside the window. "*Guten morgen, Schatzi,*" Sebastian says, leaning in to give me a kiss.

Propped up on one elbow, he stares down at me with a mischievous smile.

I soften my eyes and reach over to feel his face, just to make sure I'm not dreaming. "Good morning." I smile. "What time is it?"

He kisses me again. "I have no idea." He gets up to look outside. "But I was thinking, since it's Sunday I should take you to Paris for the day."

I must still be dreaming. Did he just say *Paris*?

I wrap the bedsheet around me, tripping over it as I make my way over to him. "What did you say?"

Sebastian takes me in his arms. "Let me take you to Paris today. We can stroll through the Bois de Vincennes, have a picnic lunch, and I'll show you my penthouse."

Before I have time to think, I'm interrupted by the ring of my phone—the mood assassin. I pick it up. "Eve, you may want to get over here."

It's Blaine and he doesn't sound happy.

"What's up?" I ask, looking over at Sebastian.

"The church has a service today, and they need us out of here by ten."

"Ten? We had discussed noon. I'll be right there. Give me a few minutes."

I hang up the phone to see Sebastian's sorrowful pout. I'm sure my face reflects the same. "Paris sounds…amazing, but I am here on business. How about a nap at lunch?"

"You better be careful, Eve," he forewarns me, a twinkle in his eye. "I may buy your company and have my staff *run* it for you. Then I can have you all to myself." He gives me his best "understanding" smile. "I should get back to Berlin, get some work done. When do you leave for L.A.?"

I sit on the edge of the bed where he joins me. "In a couple of days," I respond, placing my hand on his muscled thigh. "But I can be back here by noon, and we can spend the rest of the afternoon together."

"Please, Schatzi, do you really think it'll be noon?" he asks, as doubtful as I feel.

I place my sheet-wrapped legs in his lap. "Probably not…"

He wraps his arms around me. "I will visit you in Los Angeles as soon as I can. You need to concentrate on your clients and finish up your business here. Plus," he says, kissing my neck, "we both want some much-needed sleep!"

Not much later, I meet Blaine and the upset church representative at de Oude Kerk.

"Ms. Walker," she says, taking me by my arm and pointing at the stacks of wood and metal around the hall, "all of this has to be removed. Do I have your word that it will be done?"

I look at my mobile phone to see that it's already eight thirty. Luckily, there is a team of workers busy disassembling the décor. "I'm sorry for the inconvenience this is causing you and the church. I know that our workers are tearing down as fast as they are able to..."

Think quick, Eve.

"If we are not able to move everything by ten, may we place it to the side or outside of the church for pickup later?"

Her nose flares, dragon-like.

Not pretty.

Pausing for a moment, she deflates her nostrils. "I guess so, but what about the broken pews, the door knob that was stolen, and the lifted gravestone?"

What?!

Blaine steps in. "I thought it best not to fill you in on this part of the situation until you got here."

"The pews have been here for hundreds of years," she continues, pointing out the destruction, "and the door knob is from the seventeenth century."

My heart sinks. *Who would do such a thing?*

Shamefaced, I have to ask the inevitable. "And what about the gravestone?"

She leads us over to the far corner of the church where a stone slab has broken chips scattered around it. "Lucky for us, they weren't successful, but you can see they used some kind of instrument to try to lift the slab and dig up the grave."

I am so embarrassed and upset. "I can assure you," I say, taking her hand, "we will take care of this and make it right...how do you place a price tag on such items?"

"I will get back with you after speaking to our board. I will also need to get bids from the stonemasons for the work."

"Please do," I say, with a mortified sigh.

Blaine and I grimace as she heads back to her office. I can't have her walk away with such a pit in my stomach. "Excuse me, please!" I exclaim as she turns back around. "I just have to tell you how abashed I feel. We have never had any intentional property damage like this occur during an event before, and frankly, I am thoroughly horrified."

"Thank you," she quips, with a palpable scorn.

I need to call Chuck, but first things first: we need to finish clearing this place out.

Blaine and I, along with the few additional staff he was able to wrangle up after the long night, help where we can, stacking the staging, décor, and trellis off to the sides. Parishioners begin to enter the church right as we finish. "Is this someone's bikini top?" asks an elderly woman, in a paisley print dress with a dainty lace collar, as she sits down on a back pew. "If no one claims it, it's mine." She tucks the small dangling top away in her purse.

"Blaine!" I blurt.

"Already on it, Eve. I'm checking the rest of the aisles and the floors in between."

"Great, I'll call Chuck."

Chuck surprises me by answering on the first ring. "Yep. What's up?"

Why should I expect a "hello" or a "how are you" from him? I should know better.

"I'm at the church, Chuck. I'm afraid that some property damage occurred last night."

"Can they prove it?"

Let's see, between the wee hours of the night and this morning, do you really think a group of hoodlums came in and ruined their priceless treasures?

I can't help but growl. "You witnessed the dancing on the pews, a seventeenth century door knob was stolen, and believe it or not, they tried to dig up one of the graves!"

"Wow!" Chuck yells, and judging from the loud chatter in the background, I'd guess he's arrived at the convention center. "Sounds like we had one winner of an event to me!"

"Chuck!"

"What?"

"These items are *priceless*. They may be able to be fixed, but they certainly cannot be replaced."

He grumbles, "Oh Eve. Don't worry. We'll take care of it." I can picture him rolling his eyes. "Let me know how much and add it to our invoice."

I can tell he's not paying attention any longer—probably shaking hands with all the hungover people he passes. I can hear the comments on the other end of the line, "Great party last night" and "You are badass, man."

"Gotta go, Eve—great job last night!"

I'm seriously considering charging a million dollars just for his outrageous behavior.

Blaine and I walk back to the hotel. "Do you want to get a bite?" he asks, making our way to the elevator. My body is shaking from exhaustion.

"Thanks, Blaine, but all I need right now is sleep." I give him a hug. "Thanks for all of your help." I yawn. "I'm sorry, I'll see you in the morning in the office."

When I reach the room, I notice a paper hanging from the door. "Please call extension 104 should you require housekeeping service today," the note reads.

Huh. I guess I better call. I thought it would be cleaned before my return.

I remove the card key from the door to see a bare leg peeking out from the bed. Sebastian is sound asleep, looking like one of those male models in a cologne ad just before the sultry young woman sinks in beside him.

I run into the bathroom, turn off my phone, slip off my clothes, and stagger back over to the bed. He moves, stretching his leg in between mine as I pull the sheets over my undressed body to spoon him.

Seconds later I drift into deep reverie.

Twelve hours elapse before we wake. It's two o'clock in the morning, and we are starving for food and each other. Our bodies intertwined, I whisper, "You didn't leave."

He holds me tighter. "I couldn't," he whispers back before rolling on top of me. "Do you really take me for a fool?"

I hadn't thought about it like that, but...

After such a long rest, there's no doubt I have desert mouth, not to mention I have to use the toilet—desperately. "I'll be right back," I say, trying not to open my mouth as I glide out from beneath him.

One startling look in the bathroom mirror and I realize my breath is the least of my concerns. I quickly brush my hair and remove the black lines from under my eyes. I'm surprised he didn't scream when he woke to see me looking like a member of some satanic cult.

After cleaning up, I applaud myself for having left my lingerie bag in the bathroom. I love the feeling of soft silk or lace against my body. Forget the high fashion on the outside; my favorite designers are the ones that make me feel special from the inside out. Aubade, Carine Gilson, Lise Charmel, La Perla, and Cotton Club are tops on my list. And hoping that I was going to spend time with Sebastian on this trip, I came well prepared.

I slip on a black form-fitting bustier, matching thong, and stockings. Grabbing a double strand of pearls from the vanity, I snap them around my neck. A little lip gloss and a pair of pumps, and I'm standing in the doorway waiting for Sebastian to catch my eye. Okay, maybe not my eyes...Being here in Amsterdam is making me feel a little naughtier than normal.

Sebastian is lying on his back, reading the late-night room-service menu. Catching a glimpse of me from the corner of his eye, he tosses it to the floor. His jaw drops. "So that's why you took so much time in there," he says, shaking his head with a devilish smile, biting his lip. "I guess it's my turn." Hopping up, he passes me by, throwing me a teaser of a kiss before closing the bathroom door behind him.

The moment the door opens, I turn on the MP3 player. "Love on My Mind" by O.n.E. is playing a come-hither, seductive beat. "You and me and what could be...I wish that you'd come closer to me." Sebastian looks at me with intense eyes as he crosses to the bed and reaches for my hand. I can't help chuckling. He changed from his briefs into a pair of navy silk boxers, combed his hair, and is shining that dazzling smile my way. We dance around the room in our underwear until he dips me down onto the bed and kisses me at the end of the song.

And we're off again...

Stretching out to cuddle Sebastian, I find the other half of the bed empty. I start to daydream about last night when the intrusive ring of the phone shatters my fantasy. "Ms. Walker, would you like your breakfast served before lunchtime today?" a pleasant voice asks.

I must have slept in. Where is Sebastian?

I lean over to find a note on the pillow next to me. "*Schatzi, you were sleeping oh so beautifully and I didn't have the heart to wake you. I need to get back to Berlin, but I took the liberty of ordering breakfast for you. I'll call you later today. Love, Sebastian.*"

"Ma'am?"

I wipe the sleep from my eyes. "Yes, please deliver it and thank you for keeping it for me."

The digital clock reads 11:45 a.m. I better call Blaine to see what's happening in the staff office downstairs.

"Everything is fine here, Eve. The crates and boxes for L.A. are packed and labeled, the office supply company will be here soon to pick up the printers, Chuck asked Miles and Cathy to work the booth today. The last day of the convention is going great, and I have met with the hotel staff, arranged to get cash, and made a list of people who provided us outstanding service and deserve gratuities."

"That's great, Blaine. And what about—"

"We will collect as many of the invoices as we can, but we'll have a few outstanding bills, including both caterers, a few of the performers, the lighting company, the rentals, and of course, the church. We touched base with all parties and requested to have these invoices sent to you within ten days."

"That's wonderful," I state, pleased with what he and the team have accomplished in my absence. However, there's something else on my mind. I smile, dangling a little carrot in front of him. "But that wasn't what I was going to ask you."

"It's not?"

"No, it's not."

"Really?"

"Really."

"I wanted to find out if everyone received their invitation last night for the event I have set up for our clients, vendors, and staff this evening?"

"Uh, yes, I think we all have. But, um, no one knows anything about it..." He seems utterly confused.

"Well, I guess it wouldn't be a surprise thank-you event if you did, would it?" I tease, slipping on a robe in case room service arrives while I'm chatting. "I have a few things to do, so I will meet you and everyone else downstairs in front of the hotel at five o'clock."

I go to hang up, but Blaine stops me. "Eve?"

"Yes?"

"Is Sebastian still with you?"

"Um, no. Why do you ask?"

He clears his throat. "I thought you would be here directing us this morning. You know we are *all* completely wiped."

That's straightforward.

"I know I overslept this morning. I apologize for not being there, but it sounds like you and the rest of the team picked up the slack. Great work, Blaine."

"It seems like you are a different person when he's around."

"I don't think I need to discuss my personal life with you, nor do I feel I want to."

"When it starts getting in the way of business..." he pauses for a moment, "then I think you should know."

He needs some sleep or to get laid, or both.

"Do you need me there right now?" I ask, with a mixture of annoyance and understanding in my voice.

He sulks back. "No, but I thought you would be here and it was disappointing—all of us feel that way. That's all."

"Call if you need me, Blaine, and I will see you at five. I need to run."

Who is he, my mother? And what's this talk about me being a different person around Sebastian? Maybe this so-called different person is who I'm actually supposed to be. Someone who is in love and enjoys life rather than the overworked, run-down event planner I've embodied all these years...

Speaking of events, what Blaine and the others don't know is that I asked Saartje for a venue in which to hold a dinner this evening. Agneese and Adrianus overheard me and suggested Muiderslot Castle. They live in Muiden and promised it would be a special place for our group to spend our final night in Holland.

I hang up the phone as someone knocks on the door. "Room service," I hear a gentleman call out. He rolls in a cart with three covered plates on top, a glass of fresh-squeezed orange juice, and a basket of muffins.

Sebastian must have really thought I was going to have quite an appetite this morning!

"May I?" asks the nice man holding a napkin over his forearm. "Please do."

Sitting on the edge of the bed, I take a sip of the juice as he lifts the first cover. I guess I was expecting eggs or pancakes, but under the cover sits a beautiful pair of pearl earrings with a note: *"To complement the necklace you wore last night."*

"For me?" I ask, as the man looks at me with a shy and embarrassed grin, as if he's the one giving them to me.

I blush.

"May I lift the second cover?" he asks.

"Yes, please," I say, tightening my hold on the glass in anticipation.

He lifts the middle cover. "Oh my goodness!" I exclaim, after he exposes a photo of what I'm presuming is Sebastian's yacht. I grab the card: *Looking forward to taking you on my new boat aptly named... Schatzi.* I look up to see that the older gentleman is as stunned as I am.

"Are you ready for number three?" His hand hovers over the cover.

"No, not really," I say, half-kidding, pausing to take in the yacht and wonder for a moment if it's true. I sit up again on the bed.

"I believe it's your breakfast, Ms. Walker."

Under the cover is the best gift of all, a green drink. I haven't been able to find a juice store since I arrived. "Oh," I say grabbing it. "There could not have been a better gift than this!" I down the vegetables in one large gulp.

He leans over to pick the earrings off the table, then hands them to me.

"They are beautiful," I say, holding my hair up in the mirror to take a peek.

"Very beautiful," the waiter says.

I phone Sebastian as soon as the cart is wheeled out. "You'll just have to see," he says as he answers.

"See what?"

"If the boat really exists, of course." He chuckles. "I miss you already, Schatzi. The boat is moored in Monte Carlo. Stay a little longer and we can sail the Mediterranean."

The conversation with Blaine just a few minutes ago flashes through my mind. I'm a professional. I've been a professional for over a decade now. Would it be so bad if I took a time-out? If I let myself get swept away in this magnificent dream he has created for me? Would it?

"That sounds lovely, but I have a business to run in L.A." I cringe, not even sure I mean it. "In fact, I have eight or nine programs in just the next few weeks."

"I need to go," he says, sounding impatient. "I will call you soon, but I do hope you pamper yourself this evening."

"It should be relaxing at the very least."

"Until later, Schatzi."

"Until later, Sebastian."

Throughout the rest of the afternoon, between my daydreaming of what our wedding will be like and what we'll name our future kids, my phone rings off the hook, my email inbox overloads, and the number of texts I receive is practically unheard-of in most countries. Despite all of this, I need to concentrate on the matter at hand. I want to keep the plans under wraps for tonight, and everyone attending wants the scoop about it all. "Eve, it's Chuck. You should tell me what we're up to tonight. Call me. I may have other plans."

Miles: "Hey Eve. We're getting a lot of great feedback from the party. I knew you could do it. So, what's up with tonight? You should let me know, I won't tell a soul."

Cathy: "Chuck asked me to...Oh, uh, I mean, hi, Eve, it's me. Just thought I would call and see if you want to chat about tonight's plans. Call me."

Trish: "I don't know if we are going to be able to stay. Give me a call and fill me in on what you have planned."

Bunny: "Umm, umm, umm. Girl, what kind of rabbit are you pulling out of that magic hat of yours? You know I don't wear comfortable walking shoes. Check your Twitter."

The one message I receive that I want to return is Marla's. It reads, *"Met someone that might be worthy of my time, will introduce you when you return. Your condo isn't the same without you."*

Who is this guy and what is she doing using my place when she has her own?

As I write back to Marla, *"Can't wait to hear about him,"* I receive another text...from Peter. *"Were you able to pull off the events? Bet you missed me."*

How unnerving. Funny thing is...I haven't.

A few hours later, two mini-coaches pull up to the hotel right on time. Blaine is the first one to arrive outside the lobby. "Can I help with anything?" he asks casually, masking his desperate desire to know what's going on.

"No, but you can make yourself comfortable on one of the two buses. There is an ice chest on the backseat"—I gesture for him to climb aboard—"so help yourself to a cold drink."

Chuck and Cathy arrive next. "So what is this all about, Eve? Where are we going?" Chuck seems uneasy. Cathy, on the other hand, loves playing games. "I just love this. It's like we're all blindfolded and we're being led into a dark room where the lights are going to be turned on and a whole bunch of people are going to yell 'surprise!'"

"This isn't someone's birthday party," Chuck reminds Cathy. Smiling, I just say, "Welcome aboard!"

A few minutes later Miles walks up followed by a very handsome Asian man wearing a T-shirt, jeans, and plaid loafers. The mystery man gives me a big hug, grinning. "Hi, Eve!"

I pull back, looking at him carefully. "I'm sorry..." I say, glancing down at my list of guests, "have we met?"

He stands on top of his toes, twirls around, and trills, "Everyone knows Bunny!" He places his feet down flat on the ground. "But they don't know Adam."

I'm stunned. That's right, I never did see him transform himself the other night.

"I simply didn't know what to do when you asked us to wear comfortable walking shoes," he says, flinching. "So I thought coming as a boy would work best."

I have to hug him again. "Well... *Adam,* we're so glad you could make it. Please take a seat on board."

I can't help but watch his cute little tush shimmy up the steps.

The guys from the production team file in, followed by the rest of my staff, the travel directors, and finally, Trish and her students. I glance down at my list, checking one last time to make sure we have everyone before we take off.

Wait a second...

"Has anyone seen Saartje?"

Just when I call her name she jumps on board. "I'm here!" she says huffing and puffing. "Traffic was horrible coming into town. I had to leave my bicycle at the train station and run from there."

Blaine hands her a cold beer. "Here," he says, "Eve has informed us it's time to relax."

She tosses back her thick black hair. "So where are we going?" she asks, catching my eye, and winks.

A resounding "We don't know!" issues from the group.

And with that, I send Agneese and Adrianus the signal to emerge from their hiding spots conveniently located around the side of the hotel. Dressed in medieval costumes, they each jump on a bus, belly laughing.

Once on the bus, I watch as Adrianus stands in the front, speaking on the microphone. It's a little hard to understand his thick Dutch accent. "Halo everyone and velkom aboard. Agneese and I, vee live in Moudin, spelled M-U-I-D-E-N. Moudin is fifteen kilometers from Amsterdam and ist home to Mouderslot Castle, spelled M-U-I-D-E-R-S-L-O-T."

I can hear someone in the back of the bus say, "We aren't going to *their* house, are we?"

Someone else says, "Eve wouldn't do that to us . . . would she?"

Oooh, what they don't know won't hurt them . . . much.

Along the way, Adrianus realizes that he's lost the crowd, so he starts to speak louder. "THE CASTLE VAS BUILT IN ZEE YAR 1280 BY COUNT FLORIS ZEE FIFTH VEN HE BUILT IT TO ENFORCE A TOLL ON ZEE TRADERS WHO VERE TRAVELING TO AND FROM UTRECHT.

"IN 1370, ZEE DUKE OF BAVARIA REBUILT IT, BUT ZEE MOST FAMOUS OWNER OF ZIS CASTLE VAS P. C. HOOFT, A WRITER, POET, AND HISTORIAN. HE EXTENDS THE GARDEN AND PLUM ORCHARD. IN ZEE EIGHTEENTH ZENTURY, ZEE CASTLE WAS USED AS A PRISON."

Unfortunately, not even his loud voice can get him very far with this group: most people are trying to talk over him now. I signal to him to let it go as we pull away from the hotel.

Twenty minutes later, the driver stops in front of a large stone castle. "Enjoy your evening," he says, opening the door.

A frazzled Adam, aka Bunny, must have been trapped next to Cathy because he's waving a scarf as he exits the other bus, crying, "I surrender . . . for god's sake, I surrender." She, on the other hand, exits the bus looking like a kid in a candy shop. "Is this your house, Agneese? It's beautiful!"

"Really, Cathy?" Miles sighs.

Cathy obviously wasn't paying attention to Agneese's commentary.

I look around, pleased. Everyone is in awe as we cross the drawbridge, passing over the murky water in the moat below. I feel giddy when I see the castle staff have gone all-out. Men in suits of armor hold long swords crossed before us, barring our way. We all stand, unsure about what to say or do, until they release their swords, a sharp ping cutting the air, signaling we may enter the courtyard.

We are met by a lovely-looking woman with straight, pinned-back black hair, dressed as a medieval princess. "Welcome to Muiderslot Castle. I am Margriet and I will be your hostess. The castle is yours this evening. Here is a map," she says, handing us each a brochure. "Feel free to explore the gardens and the castle grounds. We will all meet in the dining room in one hour."

I hear exclamations of excitement as the group disperses throughout the grounds and castle. As they leave, I ask Margriet if I can see the dining room. She drops into tour-guide mode the moment we walk up the brick staircase into the exhibit rooms, giving me highlights of the castle. Rounding a corner, we pass a mannequin dressed as a jester in red and yellow.

Wow, that sure looks like Blaine.

"Blaine?"

"I thought I should properly welcome everyone to our little party." He turns around, laughing hysterically. "What do you think?"

How best can I tell him that he looks like a mustard-and-ketchup-laden fairy? How was he able to change so fast?

My eyes travel to a naked mannequin in the corner. Oh Blaine.

"You are quite the jokester, Mr. Stone. Are you going to stay dressed like that all evening?"

"No. Look!" he says, removing the Velcro sides of his costume in one quick swoop.

Next thing you know he's going to blow fire from his mouth.

Moving on, I'm surprised to see that the dining room is more modern than I expected. It has the feel of the seventeenth century more than the twelfth, when the castle was built. I notice the floor first, with its striking black-and-white tile pattern, and then my eye is drawn to the massive brick fireplace and many-paned windows. The long banquet tables have been arranged in a large X shape, filling the room. Emerald-green velvet tablecloths rest atop the tables, with tall pewter candlesticks. Wooden bowls of fruit serve as centerpieces along with a large pewter urn that's filled with multicolored flowers, leaves, branches, and fruit. Old silver chargers mark each place setting and are complemented with crystal glassware.

I turn to Margriet. "This is perfect, absolutely perfect." I shake her hand. "Thank you so very much. I know that I gave you no time at all to prepare, but this is wonderful. Since we still have a little while until our guests are escorted in, do you think we can light the candles now so that they have the dripped effect in an hour or so? And can you turn down the lights to create the right mood?"

She nods. "That will be fine."

The sun is sinking in the distance. The turrets and brick walls glow with fire from the burning sun. The flags atop the castle are gently flapping in the warm breeze. Two costumed trumpeters in the courtyard begin playing to announce that dinner will be served.

We adjourn to the dining room where everyone chooses a seat. I take mine at the head of a table so that I can see all the faces.

When everyone has a glass in hand, I stand up to make a toast. "Thank you, everyone, for your efforts, talents, and energy in making these events such a big success. I realize we are all exhausted, so I thought we could use a release from work. Honestly, if it wasn't for all of you, we could have never pulled off these two extraordinary events." Everyone stands and lifts their glasses. "So cheers to Team 1-2-1 TV, who made two events come together better than we could have hoped or expected."

Everyone cheers as we all sit down, hungry.

We feast on delicious pheasant, marinated chicken, and fresh vegetables from Agneese and Adrianus's organic garden. Every few seconds, I catch the echo of stories fluttering around the room—what everyone discovered about the castle, the gardens, the architecture, the location, and the river.

Across from me, Cathy can't wait to spill out her own experience. "Did you see me with the eagle owl the falconer showed me?" She leans across Blaine's plate to share more of the story with Adam. "An eagle owl—does that mean the owl is half eagle?"

Adam grabs his glass of wine. "You are getting on my last gay nerve, girl." He shoots back with his palm. "Back off."

"Wow, um, *moooody!*" she snaps. "You are no longer my friend."

Adam shakes his head in disgust and mimics Cathy, "And you are no longer my friend." Miles cracks up, almost shooting wine out his nose.

Agneese and Adrianus get up from the table when they hear one of their young-adult children playing the lute off-key. "No! Zhis is not how it ist done," says Adrianus, grabbing the instrument from his son and beginning to play it himself. Agneese, meanwhile, retrieves the violin from the case in the corner, and soon, the couple are playing a beautiful medieval medley.

As the dinner comes to an end, Margriet rises from the table. "As your host, I want to know if anyone believes in ghosts?"

Cathy jumps from her seat. "I do!" she cries, spitting the rest of what she is chewing into her napkin so that she can talk about the subject. "I have a great relationship with ghosts and their families."

"Would you like to follow me to a room that very few people have ever seen?"

"Nope. Not interested," Miles immediately replies, leaning back in his seat.

"Yes!" Cathy screams. "Which king or queen will we be meeting?"

"Unfortunately, there are no kings and queens. However, there were many prisoners here when they used the castle as a jail, and many of them died tragically. We believe some of them still have not transitioned over to the other side and are living among us here in the castle."

"I'll ask them why they want to stick around," Cathy says, as if she's an expert ghost-whisperer.

Margriet invites any of us who are interested to join her. We pass through rooms with old furniture, tapestries, paintings, swords, maps, and shields. Then we head up a winding brick staircase to a turret room complete with small windows.

"Take a peek out the window," she says softly, "and tell me what you see."

Cathy looks first. "I see water and green."

Blaine is second. "I see lots of boats."

Adam is next. "I see that I am getting claustrophobic and shouldn't be up here." He twists around and heads back down, only to climb back up the stairs right behind me after hearing a creak, clutching my waist as if holding on for dear life.

Chuck continues up the stairs to the small window. "I see a tall ship in the harbor."

"I do, too," I say, following the group.

Inside the cold, small circular room are numerous defense weapons and a few dusty suits of armor.

"What you just saw out that small window was more than most of the prisoners were permitted to see in the years before they were eventually executed," Margriet says. She waves her hand around the room: "This is where he lives, Cathy. If you can bring him out, he can be quite playful."

Cathy shuts her eyes and lifts her hands above her head as if reaching for the sky. "Oh, great soldier," she calls, "prisoner of some great crime...or injured soul...please come forth and make your presence known."

She opens one eye to look around the room, only to find nothing changed.

"Well, that didn't work. I'm out of here," Chuck says, unconvinced that Cathy has any special powers.

"Wait!" she shouts after him. "Over there." She points at a pile of shields and suits of armor. "He's in there."

Chuck walks over to the pile and picks up a couple of shields. "See, there's nothing here. Cathy, I'm sorry to tell you this, but..."

Out of nowhere, one of the suits moves toward Chuck and grabs him!

An eerie voice issues from the armor, "You dare to come to my house and disrupt my sleep!"

We all scream except for Margriet, who looks down at the steel pile without flinching.

"I just peed my pants," Adam screeches, running down the staircase.

Something's not right. I charge over to the suit and rip off the headpiece. Exactly as I thought: Miles stands there smiling.

"Miles!" I cry, not knowing whether to hit him, which may hurt me more than him, or hug him, glad there really isn't a ghost in the room.

Cathy storms out. "Miles, you messed up my conversation with the dead! Now the ghost isn't going to show himself!"

Ignoring Cathy, he looks down at the suit of arms encasing him. "Hey, help get me out of here, guys. I'm roasting!"

Chuck's the first one to leave after Cathy. "You're on your own, man." He heads down the stairs, raising his voice: "You almost gave me a frickin' heart attack."

Blaine is standing in a corner holding his chest. "What the . . . I thought I was in some kind of bad made-for-television ghost encounter." He looks around the dimly lit room, catching his breath.

"Since you gave us all quite a fright, Miles, you deserve to stay up here until we leave the room," Margriet says as she follows me out the door. "Oh, and Miles, his name is Johan and he really isn't a nice ghost, but you seem like a nice strong man. You'll survive."

After she closes the door, we giggle as we hear Miles shouting, "Okay, this isn't funny anymore, guys."

We take a few steps down. "I assure you, I will send someone up in a few minutes to help him remove the suit and get down. After all, it was his idea to set this whole thing up."

Twenty minutes later Miles comes in, boasting, "Hey, that ghost is cool. I'd hang out with him all night."

We all look him over, doubtful, when I notice he's perspiring. "So you must have gotten all sweaty making your way down the stairs then, huh, Casper?" I hand him a beer. "I think it's safe to say we're even now." I clank my champagne glass against his stein of beer and wink. "What a fun evening!"

"Indeed," he says raising his stein. "To you, Eve, for making the impossible possible." He bellows, "Everyone, a toast to

Eve and her team. We at 1-2-1 TV secretly questioned whether she would be able to pull these events off…and she did, with unmatched creativity and execution."

"Here, here" echoes throughout the room.

Then Miles leans in: "So, Eve. Now that Amsterdam is finished, will you finally tell us how you come up with these ingenious ideas? Don't leave us in the dark anymore!"

I gaze around, looking at some of my favorite people. I did agree to tell him, but for some reason my tongue feels heavy, my secret refusing to be spoken.

I shake my head, wink at him, and reply: "You never told me you were going to want the answer in a public place, and if I recall, I told you that I *might* tell you." I take a look around. "I'll need another year to think about it."

CHAPTER TWENTY

THE DAY AFTER the dust settles can be difficult. Once in a while I experience PESD, Post-Event Stress Disorder. It's the in-between space of knowing an event is dead, never to come to life again, while also realizing there are others in the future that will soon be born. It's a grieving of sorts, which I have to deal with before catching my plane back to L.A. this afternoon.

I wonder why Sebastian didn't try to get in touch with me last night, especially since I thought we had an amazing time together.

After my limp arm manages to pick up my cell, and my eyes clear from the fog of sleep, I read a text from Marla: *"The guy is history. Couldn't keep up."* Followed by one from Peter. His reads: *"Are you home yet? We need to talk."*

Perhaps I *will* take Sebastian up on his offer to sail the Mediterranean. I place the phone down and cover my mouth with a pillow and scream. I don't want to go home!

After taking a shower, dressing, packing, and eating, I feel better. It's incredible what a green drink full of vegetables and some raw cereal will do for you.

An hour later we all pile into a van that Blaine had ordered to take us to the airport. Buckled and ready to leave, we are about to pull away when pounding on the back of the car stops the driver.

Blaine opens the side door to find Adam, holding a designer shopping bag. "This is for Miles," he puffs, handing it to Blaine, who hands it to Miles. "I'm your biggest fan, Miles," he swoons, striking a model pose. "Don't forget about me."

Bunny—I mean Adam—waves and blows kisses as we pull into the street.

There's an awkward silence until Blaine asks, "So what's in the bag, Miles?"

Miles peeks in and chuckles. Inside are bundles of posters and photos of Bunny. "That's hilarious." He laughs as he distributes them around to us.

Did I just see Chuck shove one in his backpack?

"Well..." Cathy spits, stepping on the one she was handed, putting her heel through the middle of it. "Now that I look at her...I mean, *him*...he's not that good-looking, especially as a girl."

Miles hands the half-full bag to Cathy. "Here, Cathy, you'll get more enjoyment out of these than I will." Cathy tugs on the bag, only to have the contents fly out the window. "Don't worry," the driver says, "I'm sure someone will collect them."

We arrive at Schiphol airport, where an agent reminds us to get our passports and identifications ready.

"My passport?" Cathy looks at the agent, eyebrows raised.

"Yes, ma'am. You need your passport as a form of identification if you are traveling abroad."

"Oh no!" Cathy says. "I was told to place my passport in the safe in my hotel room, and I think it's still there. I need to go back and get it."

"Oh, you did not." Miles sends her a look that says "I'm about ready to strangle you for your stupidity."

"Shut up, Miles," Cathy says.

Miles pushes Cathy aside and says to the agent, "It's her first overseas trip and she isn't quite used to the process yet. Will you please excuse us?"

We all get out of the line. Glancing at the time, I see that we have a couple of hours until departure.

"I have an idea," I start before Chuck interrupts me.

"No, I have an idea. Have the van return for Cathy and me. You take the rest of the group to the gate, Eve."

He hands over their four carry-on bags, but Miles reminds him we are only allowed one, along with a purse or laptop bag. He takes them back. "Alright. We'll head back to the hotel, pick up the passport...and we'll see you back here in about an hour."

"But—" I begin to say.

"No buts about it, Eve. You've done your job. This isn't your problem to solve." Chuck grabs Cathy's arm and they take off toward the doors.

Well, so Chuck is capable of some responsibility after all. Good to know.

I say a silent prayer that they'll make it back, and then Miles, Blaine, and I head toward security.

Two hours later Miles puts his hand on mine as the plane taxis down the runway without Chuck and Cathy. "Don't worry, Eve."

I know he's trying to console me, but it's not working. I still feel responsible.

"Think about it this way"—he grabs my chin and turns my face in his direction—"we get to have a peaceful flight back home." He smiles, closes his eyes, and rests his head back on the seat as if he were lounging on the beach in Hawaii. All he's missing is a Mai Tai. Oh, and of course, the flight attendant is coming down the aisle to hand him one right now.

Blaine, who is one row ahead of me, reaches back his hand to hold mine with such comfort I can't help but feel better. That is, until I glance over at the two empty seats.

Miles and I drift in and out of sleep, but every time I sneak a peek forward, Blaine is working. "Really, Blaine, the paperwork can wait until we get home. Aren't you tired?"

He whispers back so as not to wake Miles: "I'm fine. I'm just writing some ideas down. I'll tell you about them later."

"Well," I say, straightening the blanket around my legs, "don't feel like you have to do anything right now."

"No, I know. It's just on my mind, and I want to get it out while it's fresh."

I stretch and let out a loud yawn, waking Miles up.

Still half-asleep, Miles asks, "Is everything alright, Eve?"

"Besides not knowing about Chuck and Cathy, everything is fine, Miles."

I watch as he drifts back to sleep. But I'm awake now, and with Miles out and Blaine working, I decide to read the rest of Peter's letter. Since I'm here and it's here, maybe this is the time.

> I knew it was wrong, but I truly love everything about you and I couldn't bear the idea of you with someone else. I had a feeling before my brother's wedding that the lies and half truths were coming to a head. When we arrived at my place in Santa Barbara, I thought it was the best way to start anew and tell you the truth. I want to assure you that my family knew nothing. I have kept my secret not only from you but also from all of them over the years. I can't tell you that I'm

proud of myself, but I guess once I started this mess, I was committed to following through with it until I could convince you that I was the right man for you.

Do I have to remind him that he pretended to be gay!

I thought if I told you the truth that you, like many others before, would fall in love with my family's money and not me. I know now that you are different.

It took you *ten* years to be sure I wouldn't go after your family's money? I'm skipping to the end of the letter.

I want to sit down with you and begin our friendship anew. I know it will take you a long time to trust me again, but I want to earn your trust and I want to earn your love.

Please, Eve. I ask for the chance to win your heart. You may not love me now. You may not even like me, but can we start over again and have a fresh beginning?

I promise I will be a respectful, kind and honest person in your life. I'm ready, are you?

Well, before I'm ready I'm going to need to hear more of an explanation—one he can do in person. Not that I'm looking forward to the confrontation.

Oh, how time flies when you are contemplating a conflict of a friend who has completely betrayed your trust. I don't even realize we are landing until we touch down in L.A. And to my surprise, Blaine can't seem to exit the plane fast enough.

"Will you hand me my bag above you?" he says so quickly all the words run together.

"What's up, man?" Miles asks, as he lifts the bag down.

Blaine is slightly twitchy. "I'm fine," he says, passing us by, excusing himself to reach the front of the line. He turns back and shouts, "I have an appointment I need to get to, and I'll be late if I don't leave right now."

Miles and I give each other clueless looks.

"Maybe he's worried about Cathy. I think he might be interested in her," he says.

"And," I say, as we walk through the jetway, "he's probably going to do some sleuthing to see which plane they caught."

"Whatever it is," Miles says, "I hope the guy is okay. You may be worried about Chuck and Cathy, but I'm worried about him. If he is in fact interested in her…"

It's a scorcher of a late September day. As I drag myself and my luggage up the terra-cotta steps to my condo, I can't believe how happy I am to be home. After the top step, I survey the scene, feeling as if I reached the peak of Everest. I open my door, only to be smacked by a blast of heat from the steamy, unconditioned air. Given how I'll sweat till it cools off, I won't need a facial this week.

Marla has stacked my mail in a post office collection box on the kitchen counter. It's going to take me days to go through it. A note on the refrigerator says, *"Hi Eve, welcome back. I'll be home around 8ish. Will you make us that delish kale salad that I love so much for dinner? See you soon. M"*

She must have meant this note for someone who has relaxed by a pool this afternoon or who has a fully stocked refrigerator or someone who has a bottomless store of energy and would love to do nothing more than cook a dinner for a friend. She couldn't have meant me.

I glance at the time, 5:00 p.m. If I'm going to readjust my internal clock, I need to stay up for a few more hours, even though my body is saying something completely different: "Go to bed, get some rest, you're overtired...lie down and see what happens." I give in to my body, placing my bag in the laundry room, take a quick shower, and don my nightshirt. I'm brushing my teeth when someone knocks on the front door. "I'll get it," I say out of the blue as if I'm not the only one here. Another indication that I am 100 percent exhausted.

I open the door to find Peter on my front doorstep with a dozen red roses in hand and a pleading face.

His timing couldn't be more off.

"Look, Eve, I know you're upset and you asked for time to think about what went down with the two of us, but you are truly one of my best friends and I need for us to be okay."

Knowing now that he isn't gay makes me suddenly very aware that he is seeing me in an oversized nightshirt with nothing underneath. I cross my legs and arms to cover up my lady parts, which of course aren't showing, but you know, just in case he has X-ray vision.

"Come on in, but only for a minute," I say cautiously.

He hands me the flowers. "These are for you. A, uh, peace offering."

"They're beautiful. Thank you. I'll put them in a vase." He follows me as I move toward the kitchen, where I place the flowers in the sink with some water.

Then I feel an overwhelming need to change my clothes.

"Will you excuse me for a minute?" I walk out of the room, pulling my shirt down further.

On my way to my bedroom, I pull a pair of drawstring sweat shorts off the top of the dryer, swipe a tank top from the second drawer of my dresser, and change in the bathroom.

"Much better," Peter exclaims as I make my way back to the kitchen and finish arranging the flowers, opting for a cheap turquoise vase from Target instead of my favorite oval cut-crystal vase that he gave me years ago for my birthday.

"Would you like something to drink?"

"I guess a gin and tonic is out of the question, huh?"

A picture of his father holding drinks in both hands crashes through my mind.

The nice, forgiving part of me wants to laugh, but the still-hurt, betrayed side refuses to allow it. "Yeah, probably not the best idea." I hand him a glass of ice-cold water. "Shall we move to the couch in the living room?" The matching ottoman has my name on it.

"So, that wedding weekend was, um, really hard on me," I say, wanting to cut to the chase. "I'm guessing your family was pretty confused."

He looks comfortable relaxing in the chair, but I'm sure he's freaking. "Yeah, I had to come clean with them. Ironically they also thought I was gay. I guess I played the part too well."

"You fooled me."

He drops down on one knee in front of me. "Look," he says placing his glass down on the floor. "It took a lot of convincing, but they have forgiven me for all the lies, and I hope that you have it in your heart to forgive me, too."

"It isn't as easy as that, Peter."

Without notice, Marla barges through the front door to see Peter kneeling on the floor, holding my hand. "There is no way that Eve is going to marry you, Peter! You are a liar and a fraud. She will have nothing to do with you!"

She picks him off the floor and manhandles him over to the door. "It's time for you to leave, buddy. You have no business here any longer."

"Eve?" Peter struggles.

Marla slams the door on him. "Hit the pavement, you worthless bag of flesh!"

She turns around from the door and air-cleans her hands. "I brought dinner tonight."

"Don't you think that was a little harsh?"

"No. Do you?"

"Well, kind of."

She picks up a bag that she dropped next to the door. "The chef at the hotel made a super healthy organic chicken salad with tarragon today. I thought you'd like it."

"You know me so well."

Maybe it's best Peter left. Even though I wasn't as angry when I saw him as I thought I'd be, it was still disturbing. For now, I guess that was a good enough start to salvaging whatever is left of our friendship. Baby steps...

M dishes up the salad and we sit at the bar in the kitchen.

"So, who was the guy you dated while I was away?"

She wipes her mouth clean of her first bite. "He's not worth talking about other than he is a real-estate investor who drives a Rolls Royce and has only one thing on his mind...himself."

"That sounds boring."

"All it took was two dates. He had nothing else to talk about except how much money he makes and how much money he spends."

"Did you happen to tell him you are *Italian*?" I can't resist a little sarcasm.

"Actually, I told him I'm Mexican."

"And?"

"He didn't seem to mind."

"Interesting," I say, hoping she may be having an aha moment.

"Eh, whatever," she says, taking a sip of water. "Let's cut to the chase. What happened with Mr. Billionaire womanizer? Did you get together with him?"

"Marla!"

"What?" She goes over to a cupboard, pulling out the salt grinder. "I'm just calling a spade a spade."

"Well, as far as I'm concerned, you are referring to the wrong card in the deck."

She shrugs, wearing a smug smile. "Well, time will tell." She sits back down. "So I'm guessing you saw him."

"I did."

"And?"

"And... it was magical."

"Oh, so you slept with him. That explains the dreamy, come-on-you're-making-me-nauseous look in your eyes."

I give her a guilty smile. "M, he showed up in Berlin and we made out, and then he surprised me in Amsterdam at the party even though he was busy with his media deal. And then he asked me to sail the seas with him on his yacht."

She wipes her mouth with her napkin, staring at me. "So basically, he crashed your party and wants to kidnap you. That's great."

Jealous?

Okay, it's becoming clear Marla does not want to hear about my Sebastian escapades. And frankly, if she isn't willing to listen, I don't want to tell her about the man I think I'm falling in love with.

We spend the rest of the hour catching up on my events in Europe and her ever-bizarre hotel happenings.

"It's good to have you home," she says, leaving with the left-overs. "I hate to admit it, but you know I miss you when something like the Mr. Wilson story happens and you are away."

"Hey, I'm sorry that you had to close off a few rooms because he left the bathtub running for six hours, but think of it this way"—I pat her shoulder—"at least you didn't have Chuck as your guest." She simply stands there for a minute and sighs. "True. Very true."

Then, in a very unexpected move, she reaches out and gives me a hug. A real hug. Not the insincere versions I'm used to, but a genuine squeeze. My time away must have meant more to her than I guessed. Normally, she acts as if she hardly noticed I was gone. But this time she seems different. Like what a true friend should be.

CHAPTER TWENTY-ONE

"**E**VE, I HATE to bother you, but will you please sign these checks?" Jessica, my young assistant, comes into my office to find my head planted on the desk.

"Sure," I say, lifting what feels like a lead ball. "What time is it?"

"It's two o'clock. Also Miles Emerson is on the line for you."

My PESD, along with sleep deprivation, adrenal fatigue, and the fact that I have forgotten to eat any meals so far today have caught up to me. Mustering a smidgen of energy, I pick up the phone.

"Hey Miles," I mumble, with one iota of enthusiasm. "How are you?"

"Where in the world do you get your drive? I'm wiped and barely functioning, and you answer the phone like you have just come back from a holiday."

It's called, faking it.

"So I found out last night that Chuck and Cathy were able to catch a flight this morning," I say.

"Yes, well, that's why I'm calling." He clears his throat. "I received a phone call from Cathy at the airport, where she is waiting for Chuck."

"Waiting for Chuck? What do you mean?"

"It turns out that customs was conducting random searches of carry-on luggage today and chose Chuck's bag. He began dishing out snide remarks such as, 'Is this really necessary?' and 'Do you know who I am?'"

Sounds like a classic Chuck move.

"The officer asked him to step aside. Cathy was next to him and you can imagine how riled up she got. You know how she can exaggerate a situation? Well, for some reason she thought they were going to jail and started to cry. Two guards escorted them to a table near the exit, and they opened his bag to find it full of—well, sexual paraphernalia."

"What? How embarrassing. No wonder he tried to pawn his bags off to us yesterday."

"You're so right! I forgot about that! Well, Chuck swore he had received them as parting gifts at the parties hosted by companies during the convention. Cathy told me he said something like, 'My little lady here and I are really going to have fun with them tonight.'"

"Cathy must have loved that comment."

"Needless to say, she flipped out. The agents let her leave, but Chuck was detained. Now she's waiting in baggage claim for him to come out."

"What charges are they holding him on?"

"I don't know, but I contacted his wife to see if she can help get him out of Dodge."

"Good move, Miles. It's never a dull a moment in the life of Chuck Howard, huh?"

"Never! And he needs to learn that if he plays, he pays."

I am so proud of Miles. He is keeping his cool and not playing into Chuck's peculiar antics. He's coming into his own power and wisdom. In fact, I won't be surprised if he stops using "isms" soon.

"I need to go, Eve, and get caught up. I want to thank you again for making us the hit of the conventions. Let's meet next week after you have time to send us the invoices and discuss the post-con notes."

"It was our pleasure, Miles, and as always, we'll look forward to the next set of adventures with you and your team."

Not to mention seeing that handsome face and body of yours walk by.

"Take care."

And my head flops back down on the desk where it belongs.

"There's a group of people here saying they are your two-thirty appointment. It's not on the books..." Jessica says, popping her head back in.

"Appointment?" I burble, keeping my head up where it belongs.

"Yes, Eve. Do you want me to send them in?"

My wrecking ball of a head won't stay up any longer.

"I never schedule myself to see anyone the day after I return from Europe. You know that. In fact, I don't schedule any meetings for a few days."

Did I forget about something?

"Well, I guess since they're here..." I grab a protein bar from a drawer. "Send them in, please, but give me a few minutes to at least get out of my comatose state."

Five minutes later, four beautiful women and two hunky men walk into my office wearing white medical coats.

"You're here to take me away, aren't you? I knew this day was coming. But seriously," I say, looking over at my staff, who give me clueless shrugs, "did we have a casting call today for an event?"

One of the women steps forward. "No, madam. We are from Avotre Sante Spa here in Beverly Hills. Where may we set up?"

"For what?"

"Your day of beauty."

"My day of *beauty*?"

"Well, technically, it's for your entire staff." She glances down at her phone as if to read notes or a schedule. "Yes, you have us for the rest of the day."

The woman asks me to pick up my mobile phone. "You have a message waiting for you."

I look down, and sure enough, it's Sebastian. I listen as he tells me he feels guilty for not pampering me enough, and so he sent Inga's staff to help us relax. They are the spa team of choice when he comes to town. He then suggests I try the synchronized Ayurvedic Samvahan massage with two of the women.

I look around the office, noticing for the first time Blaine's absence.

"Where's Blaine?" I ask.

No one can answer my question. I wouldn't blame him for taking the day off, but he is normally so good about filling me in on his schedule.

Oh well, he's a big boy. Bring on the hands!

A menu of spa services is presented to each of us. Inga steps into my office. "Madam, are you ready for your facial?" she says delicately.

I was ready last month!

Though Sebastian was unaware of my PESD, he knew exactly what I needed—a little TLC. As Inga's firm fingers clean, exfoliate, and massage my face, I drift away to consider what life might be like with Sebastian if we were to get serious. Where would we live? In Berlin? On the yacht? In Paris? Everywhere and anywhere? Images flash through my mind of me lounging on the yacht, the staff bringing another pitcher of iced tea because my friends and I are too warm from lying on the deck to get it ourselves. Another flash has me on his private jet with friends heading to the Monaco Grand Prix just because we can.

But these images, none of which show Sebastian and me together, cause me to wonder what they mean. Are they memories of boyfriends past coming back to haunt me? I'll chalk them up as yet another topic to discuss with my soon-to-be therapist. The list just keeps getting longer. I'll be in therapy for years at the rate I'm going.

As I sit in the lobby wearing a robe and slippers, awaiting my next treatment, Blaine blasts through the doors, unaware of the quiet sanctuary our office has become. "EVE!" he shouts.

Then he stops in his tracks when he sees our receptionist pull off a cucumber eye mask. "Yes, Blaine?" I ask, opening an eye for a split second. "Where have you been?"

"I have some exciting news that I need to share with you," he says. He brazenly takes my arm, lifts me from my chair, and leads me into my office and shuts the door.

"Why are you and everyone else in robes and slippers?"

"One word," I respond. "Sebastian."

He makes a face. "All six of us... really?"

"The whole staff. That's how he does things."

I take a seat in my ergonomically designed desk chair and nosh on a plate of mango and strawberries as he bounces around in the chair opposite me.

"So tell me what's up?"

"I drove over here to tell you that you... are my muse."

I stop chewing, "I'm your what?"

"Let me explain," he says, springing up from his chair. "You were the one who got me out from under the cloud of depression that hung over me for years."

He leans on the desk, his hair flopping with each move that he makes. "Don't you see? It took you to unleash my power."

I suddenly envision Blaine turning into the Hulk. I hope I don't look panicked, but I'm starting to feel that way, and it won't do me any good since the rest of my staff is passed out in the lobby.

"Go on," I say, conjuring up my best non-emotional face.

He sits down again, crossing his legs one way and then the next.

"Are you okay?" I ask.

He smooths his hair back as if to clear his mind. "You know what?"

"What?"

"This isn't the time or place for this to happen." He gets up and walks over to the door, leaning against the doorjamb. "Will you meet me at the Park Ranch tonight for dinner around six o'clock?"

I pick up my phone to look at my calendar, buying myself some time. "Oh darn, Blaine, I'm tied up here until five thirty or so."

"Okay," he says, opening the door. "Is seven better?"

Despite his erratic behavior, I do feel that I should listen to whatever he has to say. After all, I don't want to be like his former boss, who refused to. Besides, if he suddenly turns crazy, at least Marla will be there.

"Seven it is."

I text Marla: *"Coming to dinner with Blaine at 7, reserve a table for me?"*

My phone dings in reply. *"Blaine? What the hell? I'll set aside a table inside since it's so warm. I'm sticking around for this!"*

Marla expressed how she doesn't care for Blaine from her school years, but those feelings are from years ago. I must have mentioned to M that his behavior has been strangely irrational over the last couple of days. Still, it's nice to know she has my back.

It's 6:55 p.m. when I pull up to the hotel, feeling like I've just returned from a short vacation—a very short vacation. "Welcome back, Ms. Walker. How are you this evening?" the young valet asks, opening my car door.

"Thank you, Devon." I smile as I step out, handing him the keys. "I'm exhausted but feel remarkably refreshed."

Inside I notice a friendly face. "Pierre!" I say, greeting the maître d' with the usual L.A. air-kiss to both cheeks. Pierre leads me to our table, where Blaine already sits, on the balcony overlooking one of the lighted pools. I try to keep my cool, even though I'm feeling anxious about what Blaine wants to tell me.

Sitting down, I notice how nicely Blaine is dressed. He's left the jeans and plaid shirt at home and exchanged them for an untucked, long-sleeve dark-striped dress shirt, a pair of khakis, and a light sweater that's wrapped around his neck.

"I know," he says, clocking my reaction, "I brought the sweater for you." He pauses a moment, taking a look out at the grounds. "I wasn't sure what you would be wearing, and just in case this warm weather turned suddenly cool... I wanted to be prepared."

"You are quite the gentleman, Blaine Stone," I reply as the waiter comes to take our drink orders.

"Champagne," Blaine insists. "And your finest bottle, please."

"Sir, that would be a Jeroboam of Dom Pérignon White Gold, currently priced at just under twenty thousand dollars."

Undeterred, Blaine waves him off. "Then make it a regular, uh, normal bottle of nice champagne."

"So what are we celebrating, Blaine?"

He doesn't answer right away since four people are being seated close to him at the next table over. I take a quick glance at them. It's obviously a business dinner, with four men dressed in suits. One of the men catches my eye. "It's you!" he exclaims as if he is starstruck. "It's the church lady!"

One of the men squats down beside me. "Hi there. We are a group based in London. Pardon my intrusion..." He glances at Blaine. I grin as the man continues, "But we would like to discuss with you some ideas for our own events."

I take his business card and smile. "Thank you for stopping to say hello. I will have someone from my office contact you soon." The man shakes my hand before making his way back over to the table next to us; the rest of the men smile and wave.

"This is exactly what I mean," Blaine says as the sommelier pours the champagne, setting the glasses in front of us. "You just can't write this stuff."

Blaine picks up his glass. "To you, Eve. You have changed my life from black-and-white to Technicolor."

"And to you, Blaine," I say as our glasses touch. "You are a wonderful asset to our team. Someone with your organizational skills, tech savvy, common sense, and creativity does not come along very often." I raise my glass again: "To our new superstar."

"What are we toasting to tonight?" Marla asks, strutting up to our table with a disgusted gleam intended for Blaine.

"Blaaaainnnne Stooooone!" Marla stretches his name out, taking a chair from another table to join us. "God, it's been ages. Are you still living under a rock?"

"Marla!" I say, shocked at her rudeness.

Blaine motions to me that it's okay.

Marla studies him intently; surprised she wasn't able to intimidate him the way she most likely did in school. "Sooo tell me! What are we celebrating?"

"Well, over the last week, whenever I could find a moment, I have been taking notes," Blaine begins.

"I told you he's a creep, Eve. I told you!" Marla slaps the table.

I pretend-laugh, acting as if she's joking. "M, stop!"

Ignoring Marla, Blaine leans in: "Eve, I pitched a screenplay to Amanda Schwartz—a dramedy inspired by you and your events. And she was very interested." His excitement grows. "I haven't been this passionate about something in years."

Inspired by *me*? *My* company? *My events?*

"What do you think, Eve?"

I honestly think this is the last thing I was expecting to hear tonight. And apparently, so did Marla.

Marla jumps in: "No, no, no. You obviously don't know Eve if you think she wants a tell-all out there. She's way too discreet. Eve is a behind-the-scenes kind of person. She won't buy into it, and I don't blame her. You need someone much more outgoing."

I look back and forth between Marla and Blaine. This is far too much to think about tonight—even after an afternoon of treatments—in the exhausted, jet-lagged state that I'm in.

After a short dinner filled with Blaine's ideas and story line for the movie, including how he'd develop "my character," and Marla's occasional snorts, my head is spinning. I am just too tired to take in Blaine's project. Excusing myself early, I leave the two of them to finish up dessert.

The next morning I awake feeling better. My head is clear and my eyes no longer ache the way they have been the last week. I'm even able to get ready and leave for the office earlier than usual.

"Well, you certainly look chipper today," Blaine says, peeking into my office.

"And I feel pretty good, too, if I don't say so myself. Come on in and take a seat—I just need to finish up this email..."

> My darling Sebastian,
> Thank you doesn't seem quite enough for your gener-
> ous gift yesterday. You were so right about the mas-
> sage. I feel radiant all over this morning. My staff

cornered me as soon as I walked in to ask if we could
make a spa day a monthly ritual. What have you done?

It's my turn to pamper you. How long do I have to
wait until you come to L.A.?

I miss you. Don't keep me waiting long.

Your Schatzi

"You were the lucky one to leave early last night."

"What do you mean?"

"Once you were gone, Marla had a lot to say…"

Oh?

"Aaannd, she spent more than a couple of hours telling me
stories about the hotel."

"You have to admit—"

"Well, I'm not looking to write about the shenanigans that
happen at a hotel. I'm looking to write a screenplay about your
world. I want stories from you—experiences with clients, hotels,
and vendors. I read Marla like a bad book as soon as she heard
'screenplay' come from my lips…"

He certainly has Marla pegged.

"Blaine," I say, taking a turn around my office, "I'm not the
person who likes to be out there flashing myself about. I don't
need that recognition. I feel comfortable making our clients
shine—not me."

He moves over to my desk and plops himself down, facing me.

"No one needs to know it's you."

"Oh, I don't know. There are things that can only happen
once in this lifetime." I shoot him the trust-me glance. "Not to
mention we are busier than ever. This is my passion, Blaine, and
I thought it was becoming yours, too."

"Don't get me wrong, I really do enjoy the events industry,
but I have to be honest, my true passion is screenwriting."

He does look so different from the first time we met. He looks alive. Passionate. Excited. I really wish I could help him.

"Blaine, with all the events that we have scheduled, I'm afraid I just don't have the time to dedicate to such a project. But I'm happy to give a reference and help in contacting the other big names in town."

He shakes his head in frustration. "I don't want the names of other companies or the names of people who run them. I want *you*."

"That's flattering, but all I can say right now is...I'm sorry."

He hangs his head. "I'm sorry, too. I'll stay and help you through the next few events, but I need to let you know...this is my notice."

"I expected that. I don't like it, but I expected it. But you know," I say, trying to smile, "it may help you with your research."

"Amanda wants the screenplay in three months. It'll be hard, but I can juggle both." He walks over to the window behind my desk, seeming to contemplate my idea. "You know, I was really hoping the studio would hire you to organize the premiere..."

There's that little carrot dangling in front of me again! I've desperately wanted the studio business, but I never thought this would be the way to get it.

Without meaning to, I let out a short groan. Blaine immediately turns back around. "Eve, I can assure you no names of clients will be divulged. I will exaggerate all the events—I just need the story lines."

I can't help but laugh. "I doubt you'd have to embellish. If anything, a little taming would be in order."

Blaine sits down opposite, facing me. "Please reconsider, Eve. I know this will be a success. I feel it in my gut. You've got to trust me."

I take a long pause. Would it be so bad to share my stories with the world? Especially if no one knew it was me? Maybe not. *Probably* not. But that's not what I'm actually worried about. The thing that I can't seem to get past is the promise I made to myself in Amsterdam. I need to make time for myself. I need to have a life beyond my work. I need to know who I really am. How is it remotely possible to work, sign on to a project where all I do is talk about work, and still have any spare time left for myself? So that's what it really comes down to. I'm sticking to my guns this time. I have no choice.

"I'm sorry, Blaine. I really, truly am. I can't right now."

Blaine lets this soak in, sadness reflecting back at me. "It's okay, Eve. At least I tried." He turns to go, then says, "You know, you've changed my life. Thank you for that."

I feel myself warm. As hard as it was, I know I made the right decision. "You're very welcome, Blaine."

As he leaves, I get a text from Marla. *Which A-list movie star do you see playing me in the movie? Let Blaine know I'm up for anything. I'm an open book.*

Open book? For god's sake, M, you tell everyone you're Italian.

De-lete.

The day is almost over, and I still have a slew of to-dos to get through when Cathy calls.

I pick up the phone, only half-listening. "Cathy?"

"Hi, Eve," she whimpers across the line. "Chuck may be in trouble, and I don't know what to do, so I called you."

"Tell me what happened..."

"Cheryl, Chuck's wife, came to the airport yesterday, and he denied that the bag full of sex toys and drugs was his."

"Drugs? What drugs?"

"The sex toys were filled with what he called medicinal marijuana. He changed his story as soon as she arrived and told the customs agents that the items must have been planted in his suitcase, and he thought he was being set up."

"So basically, he isn't having a good day. Is that what you're trying to tell me?"

"I wanted to give you a heads-up that you may be called to testify or something."

Or something.

"Cathy, I know how concerned you are for Chuck—"

"And Miles doesn't seem to care!" she pouts.

"Look, have you thought that this might be Chuck's path? Maybe in some small way, he was crying out for help. Maybe now he'll get it."

"But what about his marriage to Cheryl?"

"Well, don't you think they must have other things to talk about if something like this happened? I think you should just step away from the situation now, concentrate on your work, and let Chuck figure this whole mess out. And anyway, you have better things to occupy your time, don't you? Like, what are you planning to wear on your big date this weekend with the brothers?"

"I need to work on that! What do you think? I have a really tight-fitting halter jumpsuit?" she says giddily. "I'm going shopping for strappy wedges later today."

May the fashion gods be with you.

"Knock, knock." I look up from my half-checked list of post-event to-dos to find Blaine now wearing a suit. A brown suit accented by a crazy purple tie and dark wood suede OluKais.

"Isn't the Meeting Planners International reception this evening?" he asks, noticing that I'm noticing him.

"Oh! Yes. Yes, it is. I can't believe I almost forgot. Want to drive over together?"

"It'd be my pleasure. Except I took the bus to work today, so you're going to have to drive."

I shake my head, smiling, as I organize the remaining papers on my desk. I hate leaving my office a mess, even if it's just for the night.

Thirty minutes later, as I swerve, narrowly escaping a car that came way too close to taking out my rear bumper, I ask Blaine, "Is there a full moon tonight?"

"Geesh!" Blaine says, giving the guy a less than polite gesture. "Want me to drive?" he asks.

"No thanks, I'm fine. We only have another ten blocks or so."

After another few blocks, I notice a familiar elderly monk standing at the corner on Burton Way, bowing at me as we drive by. "Look, Blaine! That monk over there is from the monastery Sebastian saved. Wonder what he's doing here?"

A wave of peace passes over me; seeing him seems to have that effect on me. Blaine doesn't look over in time and misses him. "A monk? Here in L.A.?"

He snuggles back into his seat, tightening his seat belt. "So, when are you going to see Sebastian again?"

"This weekend—"

"Oh god, Eve! Are you okay?! The police and ambulance are on their way. Just don't move. It's going to be okay."

What?

I feel my hair being stroked. "Eve, Eve? Stay with me."

Stay with you?

"Sir, please get out of the way. We need to help your wife."

"She's not my wife; she's my boss. Is she okay? This is horrible. Is she going to be okay?"

He sounds panicked. *Who? Is who going to be okay?*

"Ma'am?"

"Her name is Eve."

Eve? Yes, that's me.

"Eve? Open your eyes. Eve, open your eyes."

Who is that man in a dark blue uniform looking at me?

"Eve, you were in a car accident. You're going to be okay, but I need to know where you have pain."

Where am I?

"Sebastian?"

"Ma'am, I'm going to touch your extremities, and I need you to tell me if they hurt, okay?"

Okay.

"Ahhhhhhhhhhhhh!"

"It looks like she may have a couple of broken femurs. Let's check her arms."

That doesn't hurt.

"Ahhhhhhhhhhhhh!"

"The scrapes on her face look worse than they really are, but she does have a few broken bones. They'll have to check for internal bleeding when she reaches the hospital."

"Eve? For god's sake, Eve, open your damn eyes and look at me!"

I want to, but I can't. Come back later, please . . .

"Eve?"

Yes?

"Eve? It's Peter. Open your beautiful green eyes and look at me."

Peter? Why does it sound like he's crying? Is that Charlie barking?

"Eve?"

I'm too tired, Peter.

"Eve? It's Doctor Marshall. Can you hear me?"

Yes.

"If you can hear me, Eve, open your eyes."

He has such a soothing, gentle voice. I open my heavy eyes to see a fuzzy-looking man with a white coat standing over me, flashing a light into my eyes.

"Welcome back," he says, with a grateful smile. "You're at Cedars-Sinai hospital. You were in a car crash. You're a little banged up, but you're going to be fine."

Everything is blurry. Is that Blaine? Is Peter holding Charlie in his arms? Marla?

"What happened?" I whisper.

My eyes clear to see Blaine push the doctor out of his way in order to hold my hand. He has a tear running down his face.

"We were only a block away from the SLS Hotel. Out of nowhere this guy slammed straight into us at the intersection of San Vicente and La Cienega...yesterday."

Yesterday?

I look up to get a good view of Blaine and see a bandage wrapped around his head. "The guy who hit us...well...it wasn't really his fault. He was having a seizure. It looks like he was badly beaten, but he's going to be okay."

I look down at my body to find my left leg in a cast as well as my right arm. "It hurts a little when I breathe."

Dr. Marshall, who is standing at the end of the bed, flips open his electronic pad. "Well, you have a couple of bruised ribs, which will cause you some pain for a short time."

"How long is a short time, exactly? I have events to organize!"

"That's our Eve," Peter cries, placing Charlie next to me, where he curls up close to my good arm.

"To answer your question," Doctor Marshall says, "six, maybe seven weeks, and then a few additional weeks for physical therapy."

"What about time off for good behavior?"

He chuckles. "Ms. Walker, you are not in prison—you are in a hospital, and your body is going to require time to recover."

Marla removes a one-hundred-dollar bill from her wallet and shoves it down deep into his pants pocket. "Okay, Mr. M.D., there's more where that came from if you can heal her in three weeks or less."

Doctor Marshall hands her back the cash. "I'm sorry, ladies, but this is nonnegotiable. A few more days to a week in here, and you"—he looks back at me—"young lady, will be housebound for another few weeks while you recover."

M playfully sticks her tongue out at him.

It suddenly occurs to me that this accident happened over twenty-four hours ago. So where is Sebastian?

I scan the room to see dozens of flower vases and more being brought in every few minutes. The room looks more like a funeral parlor than a hospital. "They're almost all from Sebastian," Blaine mutters.

"Where is he?"

"Who, honey?" M asks.

"Sebastian. Is he here?"

Marla sits down on the ten inches of bed available next to me. "Blaine left word about the accident with one of Sebastian's assistants. But no one has actually talked to him..."

The next morning I awake to a large-screen television in my room and a note on it that says, "Push play." I feel around till I locate the remote control.

Sebastian fills the frame.

"Hello, my Schatzi, I want you to know how much I care for you and how badly I want to be there with you. But we are closing this media deal, so I need to be here to make certain it happens. As soon as the final papers are signed, I will be by your side to take care of you."

I push the off button, wondering why a media deal is more important than our relationship, and place the remote on the cart next to the bed, only to find Blaine asleep in a chair across the room.

"Blaine? What are you doing here?"

Blaine gets up, stretches, and looks out the window. "Hey, there's a health food store across the way. Would you like me to see if they have a green drink? Cucumbers, parsley, kale, spinach, and green apple, right?"

"That sounds great. You sure know how to cheer someone up."

Not long after, Blaine returns with a green concoction for me and a cappuccino for himself. "Just what the doctor ordered," he says, handing me the large paper cup with a straw.

He pulls a chair alongside the bed, then pulls out a bagel with cream cheese for himself. I watch him, a wave of gratitude hitting me hard.

"So are you ready to get back to work?" I ask, taking a long sip of my drink.

He looks at me, sadness in his eyes. "Well, you heard what the doctor said."

I shrug. "Not my work, *your* work. Due to the change of circumstances, it appears I have plenty of time. Where shall we start?"

A huge grin spreads across Blaine's face. "Are you sure?"

I nod.

He jumps up, grabbing his iPad. "Well...um, why don't you tell me about who you are and how you got into this crazy industry?"

I pause, feeling my face warm. "You know what? I don't even know. I've come to realize it's time for me to figure that out. But how about we start with the one thing I've never told anyone before?"

Blaine's eyes go wide. "You mean the secret to your events? Eve! You have kept this under wraps for so long that it's virtually become your trademark. What is it?"

Taking a moment, I feel the time has come. This is a new beginning, a new start. It feels right. Gazing at him, I smile, "Spicy food and uncultivated dreams. Next question."